Foot Soldier
in the
CIA

James Williams

Printed in the United States of America
Library of Congress Control Number: 2024921427
ISBN: Softcover   979-8-89518-391-5
            e-Book   979-8-89518-392-2
Published by: WP Lighthouse
Publication Date: 10/09/2024

To buy a copy of this book, please contact:
WP Lighthouse
Phone: +1-888-668-2459
support@wplighthouse.com
wplighthouse.com

To Those at the Sharp End

Foreword

This book has been reviewed by the Publication Review Board of the CIA. The operations and procedures described are either fictional or have already been disclosed to the public. All the characters are what are now called "composites" and any resemblance to officers currently or formally employed is unintentional. The dedication, capabilities, and morale of CIA officers are entirely real.

Note: For those not familiar with the many acronyms and abbreviations used by Agency officers, a glossary is provided at the end of the book.

Acknowledgment

Many thanks to Jane Williams and Jackie Abrams who read this book, corrected a myriad of grammatical, punctuation, and miscellaneous errors of all kinds, and suggested changes to make it more readable, but who steadfastly refuse to accept any blame for the writing.

Chapter 1

As they approached the door to the pub, Nate began searching his pockets for something, finally coming to a complete stop as the search intensified. His young companion, Mike, also stopped, wondering why Nate, who had been in a great hurry to leave the office, was now holding up their progress just when they were so close to their objective.

"What's the problem?" Mike asked.

"Thank goodness!" Nate said, "Here it is! Couldn't go in there today without this!"

As Nate spoke, he triumphantly held up a child's clicker on which was painted a bright, especially stupid, caricature of a Bozo clown. Grinning broadly, he clicked it several times. "Now, my young, inexperienced friend," he said, "let's begin your real introduction to the outfit!"

As Nate entered the darkened pub, he and Mike were met with a raucous chorus of voices raised in rough, intimate greetings punctuated by a storm of clicking from other Bozos exactly like the one Nate carried. Advancing a few feet into the pub Nate shouted, "May the brotherhood be reunited!" at which another wave of clicking and a louder cacophony of greeting ensued.

Mike leaned close to Nate so that he could be heard and said, "What does that mean?"

Turning slightly toward Mike, but still smiling at the scene before him, Nate said, "I'll tell you later, and if I forget, don't worry about it; you'll figure it out for yourself before the night's over."

Nate then began moving among his colleagues, shaking hands, exchanging insults, slapping backs, and continually snapping the

1

Bozo toy as all the others were doing. Finally, he held up his hands for quiet. When the last clicking and talking died away, he turned to Mike who had stopped behind him just a few feet inside the door. "This, gentlemen," he said, turning toward the hesitant young man, "is Mike, new on board today, but already come to Charlie's to find out what this business is all about."

The gray-haired man at the head of the table eyed Mike carefully, then looked back at Nate. "It's a good thing you told us, Nate," he said. "I thought he might have been a civilian there for a minute and tonight any civilian is gonna have a rough time in here." As he spoke, he rose slowly from his chair, extending his hand to Mike as he did so.

"Welcome, Mike," he said, "now sit down and have a beer before these old whores get restless. They haven't had a drop for the last thirty seconds and that's about as long as they can stand it."

As the older man shook hands with the rookie the pub burst again into cheering and clicking. Over the racket, the older man said to Mike: "I'm Dave. I'm not retiring; Bill is. I've been gone two years already."

Mike found a beer thrust into his hand even before he found a seat. For a short while, he tried to keep up with the others, letting them fill up his stein every time they filled their own, but he soon saw this was folly. It was obvious there was no way he could match these determined men who drank as enthusiastically as they talked. Finally, Nate who had been slowly working his way around the table a second time, returned once more and soon noticed Mike had slowed his drinking drastically. "I see you slowed down a bit on the booze," he said to the young man.

"Do they do this on a regular basis," Mike asked, "drink like this, I mean?"

"It's something you learn in the outfit," Nate said, "but don't worry, by the time you've put in the years they have, you'll be able to do this all night and fly half way around the world next day."

2

"You mean," Mike said, "they're going stay here for a long time yet?"

"Damn!" Nate said, "you are a virgin! Yes, they got here at 5:30, some before that, and they'll close the pub in the morning somewhere around 2AM—and we'll be here with 'em."

"I don't know," Mike said. "I don't think I can make it. I know I can't drink for that long...."

"Listen!" Nate said. "Listen and learn! Tonight you'll find out more about how things really are than you will by listening to all the dull initiation lectures they're going to give you, or by attending all the official training courses you'll have to take, or by all the documents you'll be forced to read and sign. Think of this night as a chance to skip a grade—maybe several grades—in technical operations school. Just sit back, sip that beer just enough to keep a buzz on, and learn from the pros."

Nate stopped to look closely at the young man to see if he understood what he had said. Since Mike still looked doubtful, he decided to add one more bit of persuasion in an effort to hold the rookie in his seat throughout what would certainly be a long night.

"Mike," he said, "you know you've been assigned to my group for that apprenticeship that all newbies have to have. In the outfit, it's possible to make a big mistake right off the bat, so they don't want you wandering around on your own just yet. You'll get plenty of chances to screw up very early in your career no matter how hard we try to protect you so it would be a real good idea if you put yourself completely under my control—actually those I will assign to look after you—for these first few months, this evening especially. Besides, one thing you need to learn immediately is not to piss off a very high ranking officer who has just this afternoon, officially hired you."

"I think I'll stay after all," Mike said.

"Good boy," Nate said. "Now, the first thing you must understand is the value of the war story. A war story was surely the first verbal communication ever experienced by mankind. It happened sometime between 40,000 and a million years ago. A bunch of cavemen were sitting around the fire after a day of hunting and wenching and one of them tried to tell the others how many mastodons he had killed that day and how many women he had serviced. The others replied to his grunts with the first use of the word, 'bullshit!'. It was the first commentary on the first war story, but the form and the value of the content have not changed since.

"There are a few basic rules to the telling of war stories. A good war story has to have some possibility that some of it could be true; it ought to be plausible enough so that it can be passed on without making the teller look like a total fool. Most important, it has to be a good tale on its own, with the embellishment on just the right parts. The very best war stories also have an element of hard-earned wisdom to be passed on to the audience, sort of like a parable from the Bible. You should also know that women can't tell war stories. They don't have the capacity to take the small kernel of truth and surround it with the perfect amount of exaggeration to stop just short of impossibility. A woman can tell an outright lie, but that's not the same. In every war story, something really did happen; it just gets more impressive in the re-telling. Don't worry about the finer points now, it will become second nature to you in time. It *is* necessary for you to learn right away to recognize a war story. As I said, it will soon be second nature to you, but for now the easiest way to be sure is this: A fairy tale begins: 'Once upon a time.' A war story begins: 'This is no shit.' Got that?"

"Yes, I think so," Mike said.

"Good," Nate said. "Keep it in mind as the night progresses."

As Nate was about to proceed, he was interrupted by another round of loud greetings and frenzied clicking. A woman had just come through the door bearing a clicker of her own. It took almost fifteen minutes for her to run the gauntlet of all the revelers as each one must have a hug or a kiss on the cheek from her and each must say something close to her ear before she could pass on to the next.

Finally she wound up sitting next to Mike at the end of the table, opposite Dave who was obviously the orchestrator of the evening. Mike was introduced to her as the last waves of the bedlam she had caused began to subside into the general noise level of the busy pub. "Hi!" she said. "I'm Betty. You must be Mike. Welcome aboard. Don't listen to anything any of these old farts tells you."

As Mike was about to speak in return, the man on the other side of Betty grabbed her by the arm as the prelude to what seemed an urgent, private conversation. Mike turned back to Nate, shrugging his shoulders as he did so. "Guess we'll talk later," he said.

"Don't worry," Nate said, "Betty's been around as long as Dave, but she's still at work; she didn't make any real money until a few years ago. Up to then, regular women techs rarely ever made GS-14. She'll have to work until she's sixty, plenty of time for you two to talk. By the way, she's the only woman who was authorized a clicker. She was a bench chemist supporting operations in the lab when Dave started back in the year one. They've known each other all their careers. She's seen it all and she saw it at the same time as these others were seeing it. I'll bet she knows at least something on every one of these old whores that would cause instant divorce if she told—for those who are still married, I mean—lots of divorces in the outfit, lots of divorces."

Nate appeared about to continue, but hesitated for a few seconds studying the worn surface of the table top which bore the dents and scrapes of a great many long nights of war stories, or worse. Suddenly, he looked up again with the smile restored to his face. "Well!" he said, "let's get on with your instruction!"

"This party is not for Dave," Nate continued, "although it might seem that way. It's for the man who just came in and is sitting over there on the corner of the table next to Dave—the one who looks a little like Ichabod Crane. He's the one who's retiring: Bill Graham. He did for me more than twenty years ago what I'm beginning to do for you now. He brought me on board, showed me who was important and who wasn't, who could be trusted and who couldn't, explained the way things really work, and kept me from getting myself fired or ruining any operations until I was ready to make my own mistakes. The first advice I can remember from him on that very first day at work was when he said, 'Always remember: You're not only with the Agency now, but you're a Technical Services Officer. Ain't nobody any better than you.' Got that?"

"Yes," Mike said.

"Now," Nate said as he held his glass up to the pitcher for yet another refill, "tonight I'm going to tell you about Bill Graham's career, not all of it of course, just the parts that contain lessons you need to learn, like what can happen to somebody who never pays sufficient attention to covering their ass. Bill didn't tell me that on the first day; I learned it for myself. You'd think a man who lived a life under cover, where deception was absolutely necessary, would understand the value of a bit of ass-covering in his own career, but Bill never did.

"Something happened to Bill on his first job, or maybe it was just a typical thirties crisis, that changed him from the simple, country boy, working man, he was intended to be to a tech officer for a mysterious organization that people either love or hate depending on their gut feelings. It may even have had something to do with the god-awful 1960s. I know you're too young to have had any real connection to that time, but do you know anything at all about it?"

"I'm afraid not," Mike said. "I was too young."

"It's just as well," Nate said.

"I met Bill on my first day down at a place called South Building. It was in the original technical headquarters complex many years ago, but it has belonged to the State Department for quite a while now. However, when I came on board, we were still headquartered there even though most of the rest of our directorate had already moved to Langley."

Nate paused for a moment, smiling as he thought about times long ago. As the smile on his face got even broader, he said, "You know, I remember now. There was a retirement party on my first day too and Bill took me to that party just like I did for you today. Of course, it was at the Governor Shepherd across from State, not here. The Governor Shepherd is gone now too. Don't have a clue as to what's there now, probably some law firm—Washington's got more law firms than Rover has fleas—anyway it was a good spot in those days."

Nate paused to take a long drink as if to put an end to the brief digression in his story. When he resumed, he was firmly back on track.

"I had just arrived at South Building after being officially inducted at headquarters at Langley. That morning South Building was just a stop on the route of the CIA inter-office bus line. All I knew at the time was that I would be working there. The buses were named Bluebirds and they really were blue, but their windows were almost black. We could see out but folks outside couldn't see in. I had just gotten off the bus and was standing in the quadrangle of the three buildings, absolutely terrified. The huge guard on the door of South Building was watching me with an intensity that told me if I made a sudden move, I was a dead man. I had no idea who would meet me, but I fervently wished he would show up. After a few minutes of quiet panic it finally occurred to me that perhaps no one knew I had arrived. I decided I had to talk to the guard even if he did draw down on me…"

Chapter 2

Once Nate had identified himself to the huge black man at the guard station, the man picked up the phone, spoke very briefly to someone, then said, "Wait here." At first Nate stood right in front of the guard, shifting from one foot to the other, feeling that not only the guard, but everyone passing by the station, was eyeing him with suspicion if not hostility. Finally, he moved back away from the guard again into the small quadrangle, pretending to look at the grounds and watching the planes as they roared overhead straining for altitude after taking off from National Airport. After a few more minutes, he heard from behind him a quiet voice saying, "You must be Nate."

"Yes," Nate said, turning to the man behind him, "Nate Forest." The man was taller than Nate, but thinner. He was smiling broadly. "You wouldn't by any chance be named for Nathan Bedford Forrest, would you? I've been wondering about that ever since I first read your bio sheet. On the off chance that it could be true, I asked to be the one to get you started—name's Bill Graham."

"Glad to know you, Bill," Nate said as they shook hands. "My daddy never said officially, and I never asked officially, but I do have brothers named Jeb and Robert. If I had to guess…"

"Got it! Welcome aboard, Nate," Bill said. "I know it's a little early for you to realize it, but you just signed up with an outfit that's almost as good as the Confederate infantry once was. I might as well start to prove it right now. This terrifying black man here is Rufus. He knows everybody in this building on sight and he now knows you too, but if you don't show him your badge every time you go through these doors, you won't get in." Turning to the guard, Bill said, "Rufus, this is Nate, still another Confederate joining up with us."

When Rufus stood up to shake his hand, Nate was astounded at just how big he was. He was not only even taller than Bill, he was built like a football lineman. As they shook hands, his face remained completely stern. "I've got my eye on you damn rebels," he said. "If there gets to be many more of you in this building, I'm going to get the brothers together and let you all know officially that the South rising again is just as much bullshit now as it always was."

"Rufus," Bill said, "you planning on being Santa Claus at the Christmas party again this year?" He turned to Nate as he finished speaking, winking as he did so. "Rufus has been Santa Clause for the last five years. Kids love him. They know he's a pushover and so he never terrifies them, just us. He's only really fearsome if you try to sneak by him or cause any disturbance in his building, then he's awful. Have your badge ready every morning. It will save a *lot* of trouble."

"I promise," Nate said.

"Well, Rufus," Bill said, "I can't stand out here all day talking about history. Nate and I have to get busy holding back the Red Tide and I don't mean the crappy Redskins..."

"Don't be bad-mouthing my Redskins!" Rufus said, "I've killed men for less than that!"

"As I was saying," Bill continued, talking again to Nate, "now we need to get your badge so Rufus can make you show it to him every day from now on, even if you're in a terrible hurry, or your hands are full, or it's four degrees below zero...or especially when the Cowboys have just mauled the Redskins yet again..."

"Bill..." Rufus began.

"It's OK, Rufus," Bill said, "we're going."

"Damn good idea!" Rufus said as they disappeared through the door.

Once they passed the guard station they entered a wide hallway stretching almost the entire length of the building. At either end, double doors terminated the long open space.

"Training's on that end," Bill said. "You'll be spending a lot of your time there for the next few months. Admin's just ahead of us. We'll see a fellow named John who will get you officially signed in. If you wind up thinking something's not quite right with John, it'll be his toupee. I don't know where he got the thing, maybe from some feed and seed catalog, but the problem is he sometimes gets it on a little bit off center. Even that wouldn't be so bad, but the thing has a part in it. When he gets that part crossways on his head, you can't tell for sure which way he's going."

A moment later, Nate was seated at a desk with a sheaf of papers spread out before him requiring that each be read carefully then acknowledged with multiple signatures. Seeing that Nate was clearly bewildered, Bill helpfully explained that he would never see the documents again unless he committed some awful transgression in the future. John bustled around the new recruit, providing his more practical advice on what each sheet contained and what it really meant. Bill asked John to call him when Nate had signed all the papers or had decided not to take the job after all. John promised to do so, adding that Bill's departure would speed the process considerably. In another thirty minutes, Nate was firmly on board.

Bill then led him downstairs to another pair of double doors, but these doors were made of steel with combination locks keeping the area secure. Bill explained the area was vaulted, meaning that behind the doors, classified materials, with certain exceptions, could be left out overnight. He gave Nate the combinations to the locks, mentioning that having the combinations written down in the clear could constitute a security violation. Nate promised to memorize the numbers before leaving that day.

Inside, the same long hall as on the ground floor stretched across the building to end in another set of steel doors at the other end. All along the hall on both sides, doors were open, people were walking from one office to another, and all along the corridor, voices were raised in discussion, rough banter, or greetings to Bill. To Nate, the scene defied all his conceptions of the work environment he had expected. It seemed more like a huge locker room than a series of laboratories. His surprise showed clearly on his face.

Bill smiled as he saw the young man's reaction. "I know it looks a little discombobulated," he said, "but believe me, there's more work done here in a day's time than in any other part of the US Government. Now let's meet the Chief."

Bill turned into the third door on the left, greeting the secretary as he entered. "Hi, Maud," he said. "How're you today. This is Nate. He needs to meet Fred so that he can start work knowing who his leader is."

"Why, Bill?" Maud asked, "the rest of us work every day without paying any attention to leadership."

"It can now be revealed," Bill said, "that Fred has been meaning to talk to you about that. He wants you to quit signing his decrees unless he has read them first. He believes it would make him feel more important. However, it's good that you brought up the chain of command because Nate needs to know that if he doesn't suit you, his ass is grass no matter what the Chief thinks. You got that, Nate?"

"Yes," Nate said. "Glad to know you, Maud."

"Welcome aboard," Maud said, "good luck. Let me, not any of these others, know if you need something or have any questions." Turning from the two officers, Maud yelled at the closed door directly in front of her, "Fred! Nate's here! You need to say hello to him!"

Bill smiled at Nate. "I guess you know now why we don't bother with one of those fancy buzzer systems to allow Fred and Maud to converse," he said.

From inside the closed door, a muffled acknowledgment of Maud's summons could be heard. "Go on in," she said.

Inside the door a middle-aged man sat at the end of a long conference table. The only other office furniture to be seen was a two-drawer file safe against the wall behind the man, an "In" box on his

11

right, a few sheets of paper directly in front of him, and a huge ashtray filled to overflowing at his right hand. A can of Pepsi sat next to the ashtray. Smoke rose from the cigarette he held in his hand to join a blue haze floating above his head. As they walked toward him across the long room, he balanced the cigarette on the edge of the ashtray and moved forward to shake hands with Nate.

"Welcome to the basement," he said. "We're glad you showed up. We've always a little short of help in the summer when so many people rotate out to the field, and the ones returning don't exactly hurry back to their jobs. We'll put you right to work. May even have to put off your first training courses until the fall..." Before he could finish, he lapsed into a fit of coughing terminated only when he took a sip of the Pepsi.

"Damn, Fred," Bill said, "those cigarettes are gonna kill you for sure. I used to raise tobacco so I know it'll kill you. I don't need the Surgeon-General to tell me that."

"You're right," he said, "I gotta stop this. Do you smoke, Nate?"

"No," Nate said.

"Good," Fred said. "Don't start. Do you have any questions right now?"

"No," Nate said, "I don't know enough yet to ask any."

"That's good," Fred said. "Let me know right away if you think of any—that Bill or Maud can't answer. Again, welcome aboard."

Bill led Nate back through the door as Fred dissolved into another coughing spasm. "He's not exactly dynamic," Bill said as they regained the corridor, "but he knows what to do. He'll stand up for you when the promotion panels meet, he'll never give you bad advice, and most important of all, he'll never put you in a quandary in that he won't tell you to be aggressive on a project or operation and then, after a mistake, say to you, 'Why the hell did you do that?'"

"You'll understand this better in time, but basically we are always encouraged to think for ourselves, work on our own, and be aggressive in getting things done. It's all part of the famous 'can do' image all our chiefs try to maintain. All of them encourage us to go ahead if it's at all sensible, but they also realize the result of forging ahead aggressively can be a mistake. Starting today, you will constantly face situations where you don't have all the information you need, but you need to do something. How good you are at getting the job done as soon as possible, but at the same time avoiding mistakes, will mostly determine how well you will do in your career. Our chiefs don't want you to bother asking them for guidance if you know what has to be done. It's only when you are really unsure what to do that you ask their opinion. Of all our people, there are only a very few who will tell you to go ahead in every situation, then disown you when a mistake happens. You will soon learn who those managers are and you will need to be a bit cautious when working for them."

Bill hesitated as they walked up to the only closed door they had yet encountered on the hallway, falling silent as he contemplated something. Finally, he turned from the door to face Nate.

"Before we go in," he said, "you need to know a little about the way we're organized here. In each operational branch, there is an operations chief. He's the most important man in every branch, especially regarding your daily work. He is the first to see the morning cable traffic. He reads it over, decides which cables require action, then assigns the actions to the sections under him. At that point, the section chiefs, who are really just senior technical officers, decide who will actually work on the individual projects. You certainly need to please your section chief, but it's the ops chief who really matters. If he's satisfied, everything is all right; if he's upset, the entire branch is upset. Fred is important certainly, but the man behind this door is the one you really have to worry about on a daily basis. Any questions on that?"

"No," Nate said.

"Then let's go in," Bill said as he turned to knock on the door.

From inside, they heard a voice say, "Come!" As they entered the room, Nate was immediately struck by the precise arrangement of the furniture. Directly in front of the single window, through which only a growth of thick bushes could be seen, sat a heavy wooden desk, shined to perfection. In front of the desk, three chairs sat in a perfectly straight row with the middle chair directly opposite the middle of the desk. On the desk itself, everything from the single, small notepad to the family pictures, was set in a mathematically neat arrangement. Even the stack of cables had been shaken into such exact alignment that they more closely resembled a newly opened ream of copy paper than a series of sheets torn from a teletype machine. On the walls, testimonials and awards of all kinds hung in neat arrangements. The man seated rigidly upright behind the desk did not move as they entered the office or as they took the two chairs on the right side of the precise row. He was a young man, certainly no older than Bill, but his hair had already begun to thin out in a circular pattern from an almost bald spot near the crown of his head. Nate felt sure the steady gaze with which he regarded them was the same as that he applied to the stack of cables on the desk in front of him. "Good morning," he said. "Welcome aboard. I'm Anthony Wilson. You must be Mr. Forest."

"Yes," Nate said, "glad to know you, sir."

"Well," Anthony Wilson said to Bill, "make sure Mr. Forest learns as much as possible as quickly as possible. Let him do as much as he can on his own. I presume you will take care of getting him settled, sign him up for his training courses, and show him the ropes so to speak."

Turning back to Nate, he said, "Mr. Forest, do you know what is required of a technical operations officer?" The question caught Nate off guard, but in a second, he realized it had been merely rhetorical. "It requires everything you have to give," Anthony Wilson continued. "Everyone is not cut out for operations. Some cannot stand the constant pressures. Some cannot make decisions in the time required. Some cannot endure the long and irregular hours or the difficult travel."

Here Anthony Wilson paused for a moment as if to let Nate consider what he had just said. When he had judged the quiet to have lasted long enough, he began once more. "You probably wonder why

14

I did not mention competency," he said, "that is because it is never a problem. Anyone who is chosen for this group has high intelligence and good technical skills. Today, our recruiters only take the very best college graduates. You will, however, note that some of our older technical officers are not college educated, but you will discover that their hands-on skills are superb and their experience is invaluable. Do not expect commendations from me for excellent work. In this branch, excellent work is routine; I expect it every day. Do you have any questions of me at this time?"

"No," Nate said without conviction.

"Good!" Anthony Wilson said as he stood up, signaling that the interview was finished. He reached across the desk to shake hands with Nate, then quickly sat back down. Nate stumbled briefly over his chair as he started to leave, then, without thinking, stopped to realign it carefully before backing out the door in mild confusion.

"The man's impressive don't you think?" Bill said once they were again outside the door which had automatically closed behind them.

"I don't know if he's impressive or frightening," Nate said, "but he certainly seems to know what he's doing."

"Precisely!" Bill said. "If I had a technical operation and it was very important, and it was very difficult, and it had to be done in a very short time, and it had a lot of blow-back potential; he's the man I'd want to run it for me...I just wouldn't invite him to the bar for a drink after it was all over. Now, let's meet a few more folks. I'm not going to introduce you to everyone individually today; you'll work with them all in the next few days anyway. I want you to meet just a few special individuals."

Bill walked on down the hall acknowledging various greetings as he went, but not stopping to talk to any of those calling to him. Near the end of the corridor, he came to the only other closed door, except for Anthony Wilson's, on the entire hall. He knocked softly, hesitated for a second, and then went in. Lab benches ran along both sides of the room, but near the door on the right side was a small alcove containing a desk where an older man sat pouring over a small pile of cables. Behind him stood a young woman dressed in a white lab coat. In her hand, she held a pipette from which she was discharging a clear liquid into a beaker whose contents were gradually changing from colorless to tan as the liquid mixed with that already in the beaker. Bill waited until the woman had finished the transfer, then said, "New recruit, folks. He has already been impressed with the charisma of Fred and the joviality of Mr. Anthony Wilson. Now he needs to see happy workers at work."

Both the woman and the man broke into smiles in acknowledgment of Bill and his friend. "Hi," the woman said as she put down the pipette to shake hands with Nate, "I'm Betty. This is Sam."

Nate suddenly wished Bill had warned him about Betty as well as Anthony Wilson. As Sam stood up to shake hands with him, Nate still held firmly onto Betty's hand. She was tall, blonde, had deep blue eyes, and a smile that seemed to put him immediately at ease. She reminded him so much of Marilyn Monroe that he inadvertently said, "Betty?" as if to confirm he had heard her correctly.

"Yes," she said again as he continued to hold her hand. "Now," she said firmly, "this is Sam."

Nate took Sam's hand in mild embarrassment, "Hi, Sam," he said, still clearly flustered at having just met Betty, "glad to know you."

"Welcome to counter-measures," Sam said, grinning in obvious appreciation of the young man's surprise. "We are the ones who try to figure out what the opposition is doing. All the others down here are doing offensive work—or is it that they're simply offensive. I'm never sure."

"Sam's just an old dinosaur," Bill said. "He's sure the Russkies are picking our pockets, reading our mail, listening to our conversations, and watching our every move. Fred is never sure if Sam's a worthwhile check on our aggressiveness or just a burr under his saddle. What you do need to know is this: After you get your initial training from me, you will next come to Sam for a while. Fred believes every young officer needs to have the crap scared out of him right before he begins to work on his own. Betty's just about half way through her stay with Sam. If/when he finally decides she's ready, she will be the first woman technical operations officer."

"What do you mean 'if'?" Betty said with an exaggerated show of indignation. "You overgrown boys are afraid a woman will do just as well as you and that macho myth will be finished once and for all."

"Whatever you say, Betty," Bill said, giving an obvious wink to Sam. "I'd like to stay and discuss this some more, but Nate and I have to hurry over to the Governor Shepherd so we can get a good seat for Tom's retirement. I need to be at the head table because I have a few war stories to tell on him before we let him go away in peace. You going to let Betty come over, Sam?"

"I'm going to let her decide," Sam said with his most serious voice. "It will be a good test of her dedication to the mission of the office: whether she opts to continue her work keeping Communism from the gate or whether she opts for an afternoon of debauchery."

"You old coot!" Betty said. "When's the last time you ever missed a retirement party—or came back to work after it was over!"

"Well," Bill said, "I guess we'll see you both over there—not that I ever doubted if for a minute. Say good-by, Nate."

"Good-by," Nate said.

They walked around the driveway circling the quadrangle until it passed by the side of Central Building. There they walked up two flights of stairs and came abruptly out onto the parking lot for the complex. It was the highest spot on the hill. Below, to their left, was the Kennedy Center with the Potomac in the middle distance and Rosslyn in the background. Further to the left, Memorial Bridge joined the Lincoln Memorial to the National Cemetery whose green height was crowned with the former Lee Mansion. On the far right, the Watergate complex brought back to Nate fresh memories of the Nixon debacle. Terminating the view on the right was Columbia Plaza which seemed very near after the long views presented by the rest of the panorama.

Bill waited patiently as Nate surveyed his new surroundings from this highest vantage. When he was ready to move on, Bill said, "The view's not bad, is it? Of course, you'll only see it on your way to and from work. In the basement, Mr. Willy (That's what we call Anthony Wilson, behind his back of course.) has the only office with a view."

"You mean those bushes I saw through the window?" Nate asked.

"In the basement," Bill said, "we like to think of that as a vista. Did you notice that Fred's window opens onto the back of the electrical transformers for the building? Fred never gets a break. I'm sure if he ever gets to heaven, it will be closed for the day."

As they walked along the guard rail separating the parking lot from the steep drop down to Virginia Avenue, Bill waved his hand at the apartments in Columbia Plaza across the street from where they stood. "Smile nice," he said.

"What!" Nate said. "Smile for what?"

"You wouldn't want the Russkies living in those apartments to get an ugly picture would you?" Bill said. "When they send your picture back to the Kremlin and out to the rest of the Bloc countries, you want to look your best."

"You mean the Russians have cameras in those apartments right over there?" Nate said, staring across the street into the darkened windows facing him.

"We can't prove it, of course," Bill said. "We can't raid folks over there just because we might suspect something, but why would any intel service not take advantage of an ideal observation post like that?"

"Aren't you worried about being found out?" Nate said. "I can certainly see that we could be photographed from there. Doesn't anybody try to avoid being seen?"

"We call it 'blown,'" Bill said. "Obviously we do use special precautions for folks who just visit the building. That's the idea of the darkened windows in the Bluebirds—the buses. We do what we can to keep our cover intact. But if you *work* here, it's different. It's too hard to hide your face—and the license plate of your car—every day. Look, Nate, over time, cover erodes no matter how good it is, no matter who you are, no matter how careful you are. We always walk the fine line between maintaining the security of good cover and taking the risks necessary to get on with the job. Excellent cover almost always means too little accomplished. Too little cover means serious security problems."

"It all seems a little daunting right now," Nate said.

"Don't worry," Bill said, "everyone soon arrives at their own way of handling cover. You will too. All I'm telling right now is that a lot of people will very soon know who you are. It's for sure the Russians, East Germans, and British will know. That's not really a problem you understand. None of them are going to expose you. It's to their advantage, now that they know you, to let you operate any way you want. They don't care about you. Generally speaking, they don't even care about the case officers who operate in their countries. It's the locals, the agents, their own citizens, they worry about. The only real danger you have of getting blown here is your friends and neighbors. If they blab about you, the local bed-wetters might demonstrate in front of your house or the true radicals might put your name in one of their books. That could really be a problem. Otherwise, don't sweat it. Most of your close friends and family will figure it out in no time but it won't matter. The way you can tell if someone has discovered you is if they don't ask you any questions about your job. The dumb ones will question you constantly, but never figure it out."

"It may take a while to assimilate all of it," Nate said smiling, "but I'm working on it. I may have more questions."

"Good," Bill said, "there's nothing as dangerous as a new officer who doesn't ask questions. That almost always means he's a smart-ass who thinks he knows it all. Those are the ones who can actually put you or the case officer or the agent in danger. Fortunately we have Mr. Willy who is an excellent smart-ass corrector. He loves smart-asses. When he finishes with them they have to go straight from his office to the local ass re-capper before they can even sit down again."

"I'll definitely have a lot of questions," Nate said.

Chapter 3

The next morning, Rufus surveyed Nate's new badge as if he had never seen him before. Finally Nate asked if the picture looked like him. Rufus remained stern as he handed back the badge mentioning that Nate looked out of focus; not in the picture, but in person. Nate confirmed he was not yet finished with a monumental hangover from yesterday's retirement. "Well," Rufus said, "just be glad folks don't retire often."

When Nate showed up at the door of Bill's office downstairs, Bill shook his head in sympathy. "Do you think you'll live?" he said.

"I'm not sure I want to," Nate said. "Don't you feel bad?"

"Not too bad, actually," Bill said, "but I don't know if it's just getting used to it over the years or that I've killed so many brain cells now that any response is damped down."

"I hope we don't have much to do today," Nate said.

"In a way we do; in a way we don't," Bill said. "We just got assigned a simple training job, with no issuance of materials, for the day after tomorrow. We do have to plan what we will do, but we won't have to do too much. By the way, are you able to listen effectively?"

"Yes," Nate said, "I think so."

"Then we'll start slow," Bill said. "I'll talk and you listen. Ask questions at any time."

"OK," Nate said, pulling up a lab stool as Bill closed his door.

"Now," Bill said, "the most basic thing you need to know is that the Office of Technical Service is not a part of the DO, that's the Directorate of Operations, but we support them. Although they aren't the only ones we support, they are the 800 pound gorilla of our existence. The day they don't think they need us is the day we in OTS ops, and just about all the rest of OTS, disappear.

"You won't run any operations or handle any but the simplest ops details, write any intel reports, or even know the true names of any agents. As a matter of fact, if you do ever hear the true name of an agent, put it immediately out of your mind. You won't need it anyway. The CO, the case officer, will run the case, of which you will be a small part. In fact, on any given case, we only receive the cable traffic we absolutely have to have to do our technical job; a DO file on an agent might be several volumes, but we may have only ten pages in our files. Always ask the CO only what you have to know to do your work, but don't hesitate to ask for that. The CO is always going to think his agent is better than he really is so don't worry about the description of the agent's value or his intelligence, but you do need to pin the CO down on basic facts such as how well does the agent speak English."

"If our job is to support the DO, but we work for OTS," Nate said, "doesn't that cause some divided loyalties sometimes?"

"It does indeed," Bill said, "but always remember: no matter how macho our leaders seem to be, the DO is going to do what they want. If you ever get crossways of a high-ranking DO officer, don't look to our folks for help. Of all the chiefs in OTS, there is only one who I am sure will fight for you against the DO hierarchy. You'd never believe it when you see him. He's short, going bald, a little chubby, looks a lot like a monk—even looks like he has a tonsure—but he'll fight a circle-saw for you if you're one of his boys. A lot of our chiefs claim they have brass balls, but he really does. Stay on his good side. There is nothing worse than being called to his office when you don't know what he wants, especially if he is red-faced when you walk in or he seems bigger—I really believe he actually gets bigger when he gets mad. Our Mr. Willie is tough, but compared to this fellow, he's a Sunday-school teacher."

"I guess I ought to meet him soon," Nate said tentatively.

"In due time," Bill said, "but for now, you need to know the basics about dealing with case officers. Working as a technical officer supporting the DO is never easy, but some techs make it much harder than it really is. The one thing about them that you must never forget is that they are the most results-oriented organization you will ever encounter. They live by recruitment of agents and dissems—intel that is worthy of dissemination to various parts of the US Government. You can't help them recruit agents, but you can help them get the info they need for dissems. Most of them would rather be face-to-face with the agent when they solicit him for intel, but that's sometimes very risky for both the CO and the agent. That's where we come in. When the information is transferred by impersonal means, we can be of great help. Our equipment can allow the CO to get his intel and protect his agent and himself at the same time.

"Now here's the three things you need to always keep in mind when you provide technical assistance to the DO: They want the equipment to work the first time and every time; they want it to be easy to operate; they want it *now*. If you have a choice between a simple piece of equipment or a sophisticated one; take the simple solution. If you have a choice of two systems, one of which can be delivered immediately and one that might be slightly better but would be take longer to provide, take the one that's immediately available. But never, ever agree to issue a fieldable prototype to speed up deployment of new equipment. That's just a way the R&D boys have of field testing equipment they haven't finished engineering. When it goes belly up, it's *your* ass, not theirs."

"What about the security of the equipment?" Nate asked. "I assume the sophisticated, hard to operate equipment would be more secure than the simple items."

"Maybe yes, maybe no," Bill said. "Remember, even the most sophisticated equipment used incorrectly can get the agent shot. It's up to you to present to the case officer an honest appraisal of the trade-off between the security of the equipment and its reliability in the hands of the individual agent involved. This is one area where you can legitimately ask the CO for more than just the basic facts about the agent. You must always tell him how inherently secure the equipment is, how hard it is to use, what could happen if it is misused, and the significance of the loss of technology if it is compromised. He, in turn, should be honest with you about the technical abilities of the agent and the difficulty of operating in the local environment. You will be trying to pick the equipment that is most reliable and easy to use while providing the necessary level of security for that particular operation. The CO will be trying to get the most information as quickly as possible from his agent without putting him in danger of detection. You and the case officer, for the rest of your careers in operations, will constantly face the shifting equations of risk versus gain. Neither of you will ever be completely sure if you have done exactly the right thing, but you both have to decide and go forward. Otherwise nothing will ever get gone. How well you both decide, or how lucky you are, will affect both your careers. As Mr. Willy said, some folks are not cut out for ops."

"I believe it," Nate said. "I'm not sure how I would react if an agent I had trained ever got caught or got shot."

"Believe me," Bill said, "it *will* happen to you. You can't be in ops and avoid it. You also need to understand that the technical ops officer really is a special breed. He doesn't have to be a technical genius; guys like that should sit at the bench developing astounding new gadgets to help all of us. He doesn't have to be macho; the macho types have a way of getting the agent shot. He doesn't have to be excellent at tradecraft; follow the case officer's lead in that because he knows the local operational environment ten times better than you ever could.

"The tech does have to be a fellow who can get off the airplane in a foreign country, look over the situation on the ground, and without ever having all the time or information he needs, make a good, common sense decision on what to do to get the CO what he wants. Don't worry about it for now; you'll know soon enough if you're a tech ops officer or not. What you need to remember is that it is not a disgrace if it isn't for you. For example, it would be foolish to take a wonderful scientist who could help the entire intel community, and make him an ops officer. That's a terrible use of an excellent resource. It would be like having Willie Mays play football instead of baseball. I'm sure he could have done it—but what a waste.

"Now, this afternoon we're going to ride the Bluebird out to Headquarters and talk to the CO who's in charge of the local training I mentioned. What we'll be doing is ironing out details such as where the training will be, what aliases of convenience we will use with the agent, what are the meeting arrangements, how long will we have, and can you come along to observe. Obviously, there's a lot of other things to be considered, but you'll learn them as we go along. By the way, Nate, did anyone ever get around to telling what you would actually be doing? I know Fred and Mr. Willy didn't."

"Actually," Nate said, "I really don't know. I assume it involves chemistry since I'm a chemist."

"A good guess," Bill said, "but probably not what you had in mind. If you want to actually do chemistry, you can do that; we have some very good ones you could work with, but that kind of job is in our Developing and Engineering, D&E, branch. In ops, the chemistry you need will be much more basic. You are in the Secret Writing/Photography branch. We're the guys on the very bottom of the totem pole. Audio, the boys who put the microphones in the walls, have most of the budget and almost all the glamour and prestige. They may put in twenty-five bugs for every one that actually gets good intel, but that one—which provides real time intel directly from the mouths of the bad guys—is always sensational. Your photos and secret writing messages may well provide seventy-five percent of the real intel collected, but it's not sexy.

"As an SW tech, you'll be known as a 'lemon squeezer' for one of the first SW systems ever developed, and as a 'Brownie' for the Kodak Brownie camera. We get about three percent of the budget and about that much recognition, but our agents provide more hard intel than all the other parts of OTS combined. Our branch has always been known as an easy going bunch whose members have no swagger at all, but an excellent sense of humor; and except for Mr. Willy, that's just about the truth.

"And finally before we go I want to show you something now in order to avoid having a genuine, highly educated technical officer show amazement at something really simple right in front of the asset, a thing that should never happen to us really cool spy guys. I have noticed that if the asset is new to the business he will always be much more astounded by the destruction of incriminating paper than by the million-dollar SW system he will be using. Observe:"

Bill took a sheet of paper from a pad, and beginning with the short dimension, folded over about one half inch of the edge of the sheet. His next crease was the same size but folded backward from the first one. The sheet quickly took on a fan or accordion shape. When he finished folding the entire sheet it was sufficiently strong to stand by itself. He set it up in the sink and touched a match to the tops of a few of the individual folds just at the apex of the creases. In a couple of seconds the paper began to burn evenly across the entire sheet with no smoke. As Bill had expected Nate watched in fascination as the flame burned evenly down to the base of the sheet and went out with only the tiniest wisp of smoke. Bill flushed the completely burned ash down the sink.

"You're right," Nate said, "I did find that astounding."

"Elementary, my Dear WaOTSn," Bill said. "It's the ancient chimney at work. By lighting the top of the creases the heat brings the air up through the miniature chimneys created by the folds, providing plenty of oxygen so there's no smoke, but by burning from the top down the flame doesn't get out of control as it would if you lit the bottom."

"I'm glad you showed me," Nate said. "Who knows, maybe scientific principles really do really work."

***

"Wait a second," Bill said as he and Nate got off the elevator at Headquarters, "I always have to study the maps in this building. There's something about this layout that confuses me. I suppose the idea was to dazzle the Russkies, but the real effect is to keep me bouncing off the walls like a rat in a maze. OK, got it now; we go left to the end of the corridor, then right."

The two officers arrived at a door secured, like those in South Building, with combination locks. Bill pressed the buzzer at the side of the door as he put his hand on the doorknob. A second later, he pushed in as soon as he heard a click from inside the door. "You gotta be ready to go in when you press the buzzer," he said to Nate, "the DO secretaries won't hold down the release for more than just a second; they're too busy."

Inside, the officers found themselves on a narrow corridor between two desks manned by a young woman on one side and an older woman on the other, both hammering away at IBM typewriters. Bill waited patiently for one of them to decide she was at a convenient stopping place. "Yes?" the older one said finally.

"Is Nancy here?" Bill said.

"Go to the end of the corridor," she said. "Nancy's in the office on the left."

"Thanks," Bill said as the rattling of the IBM began once more. The two officers walked down the narrow internal corridor off which were a number of small, almost claustrophobic cubicles, each of which held two desks. In each office, the walls were filled with maps, line charts showing the organization of the government in the specific country being handled by each case officer, framed commendations that officer had received from higher management, pictures of the principal figures in the governments of each country, favorite cartoons, and all kinds of reminders ranging from elaborate charts of projects underway to simple yellow notes demanding the return of a call or attendance at a meeting. Although the individual items made each wall different even to the casual observer, the desks all looked the same. In every case, cables covered the working area either in stacks, or were scattered in random fashion among the cups holding pens and pencils, the phones, and the ash trays for the smokers.

"I thought it would be more...impressive," Nate said as they passed the crowded, busy offices.

Bill smiled at the young man before answering. "You mean," he said, "that you thought those whose duty it is to gather intelligence for the US Government—intelligence which could literally lead to a change in the course of history—would be housed in the fancy, wood-paneled offices you've always seen in the movies; but it looks more like the working desk at an auto parts place."

"Yes," Nate said, "I guess so."

"Well, Nate," Bill said, "you've already learned something today and we haven't even met your first CO yet. I often wish the American people could see what really goes on in the outfit. Then they'd understand just how much effort they get for the money they spend on us. They don't have any idea about us except the one they see in the movies and TV, and those entertainment folks are so dumb they don't even know the difference between the agent and the case officer; they always call the case officer the 'agent.' The offices they show correspond to the ones on the seventh floor where the most-high leadership sits, and they think every officer is engaged in trying to overthrow the liberal, humanitarian, enlightened leadership of Flyspeckia where everybody would be absolutely equal and unbelievably happy if we'd just let them alone. People do this job, Nate, because they want to do it. If they divided the hours they worked into the money they make, the teenagers at McDonald's would probably have a higher hourly rate. Every year we turn in hundreds of thousands of hours of unused leave. Very few officers even bother to turn in their overtime, and the disrupted family schedules and other inconveniences don't even get mentioned. It's expected; no one thinks it's the least bit unusual...here we are."

"Hi, Nancy," Bill said, "the last time I saw you, you were in NE." Turning back toward Nate he said, "That's Near East division to you, Nate."

"Looking again at Nancy, Bill continued, " I suppose the adventure and romance of AF—Africa Division, Nate—was just too great an attraction to pass up."

"For a woman, every day spent working with agents from a spoiled brat culture was just another wonderful day in paradise," Nancy said, "but the agents in AF really are much easier to deal with than the Arabs in NE. I keep asking when I'm going to get an EUR assignment—European Division," Nancy said, smiling at Nate, "where women have an almost equal chance with the men, but those are reserved for the seniors in the old boy network. Now, who's this new, old boy with you today?"

"Nancy, meet Nate," Bill said. "He's new and innocent, not yet acquainted with bitter, female officers who refuse to understand the god-given superiority of male officers."

"Well, Nate," Nancy said, "if we have any luck at all, maybe you'll see the women around here get their chance during your career—if it lasts thirty-five years. Bill says even OTS is training a female tech. If that happens, I'll know for sure it's the millennium."

As Nancy prepared to speak again Nate raised his hand just as if he had been in high school, then dropped it when it occurred to him that the gesture must look foolish.

"There," Bill said nodding his head toward Nate while looking at Nancy, "there *is* hope, Nancy. This young man already respects you as a female case officer; he has raised his hand to ask you a question instead of just blurting it out like us ordinary techs."

Nancy looked at Bill clearly showing her exasperation with him. "Yes, Nate," she said, "I'll be happy to answer any question put forward in such a *gentlemanly* way." Here she finished looking at Bill and turned toward Nate.

"Spoiled brat?" he asked.

Nancy hesitated for a few seconds before she answered. "It's not the *spoiled brat* you're thinking about," she began. "It's the characteristic of any culture where the women have no real control—where they are mistreated, disregarded, and under-valued on a daily basis. The only way they can have any value or security or protection is through the men. The mothers have no choice but to spoil their sons from the first day and hope the boys will appreciate them later in life. Arab cultures are the worst, but Africa isn't far behind. You still see it to a lesser degree even in some thoroughly modern Asian nations. It's difficult for any woman, no matter who she is or what she represents, to deal with men from such cultures, let alone control them as agents."

"I see," Nate said. "I admit I never thought about it…"

"Well," Bill interrupted, "we won't solve it today. What's up Nancy."

"Sit down, guys," she said. "Here's the deal: AFBEOBAB/1, a mid-rank military officer, is in town visiting some distant members of his family. He was recruited about two months ago in country. The local CO can meet him periodically, but he could get worthwhile intel at any time since he attends some meetings of the general staff. He needs impersonal commo; secret writing will do. What the station wants is for B/1 to be thoroughly trained in the basic procedures, with issuance of materials to be done at a face-to-face in country. I have a meeting set up for tomorrow at the Marriott in Crystal City at 9AM. I've told him to be prepared to stay until at least 4PM. Will that do for you?"

"Absolutely fine," Bill said, "much more time than we'll need even if it goes slow. I'd like to bring Nate along if you don't mind. Do you think it would cause any problems?"

"No problem," Nancy said. "I'll be there in plenty of time to put him at ease regarding you guys, but I don't know how he'll do with the tech part. Give me maybe thirty minutes; plan to arrive around 9:30-9:45."

"Has the guy passed the box?" Bill said.

"Yes," Nancy said, "he's NDI."

"That's 'no deception indicated,'" Bill said to Nate. "It means Mr. Willy won't have my ass for exposing you as a brand new officer to some double who will go straight home and tell everyone about you. "Nancy, how are you known to the fellow?"

"I'm 'Peggy Thompson,'" Nancy said. "Who do you want to be?"

"I'll use 'Patrick Cleburne' as always…," Bill began but was suddenly interrupted by Nate who had been very quite until that moment.

"The Irish general!", Nate said, "a superb fighting man, killed in that insane attack by Hood at Franklin. He's one of my favorites too!"

"Your *are* a Confederate!" Bill said. "Did you know Churchill was born ten years to the day after that battle?"

"Actually, I did know that," Nate said, "Churchill is one of my greatest heroes."

Bill stood up and offered his hand to Nate, "You have definitely signed up with the right outfit," he said. "May the brotherhood be reunited!"

Nate stood to take Bill's hand although it was clear he had no idea what Bill had meant. "It's a phrase one of our officers picked up in an Irish pub one night," Bill explained. "It's probably an IRA code or something, but a small group in our office, who truly appreciate Irish pubs, have been using it as a special greeting ever since. I've never been in an Irish bar myself, you understand, but I've been told a fellow can have a drink there and listen to some really fine Irish rebel tunes. I can see you are definitely brotherhood material."

As they continued the handshake Bill reached across to grab Nate by the shoulder. Suddenly they remembered Nancy and, still holding hands, looked again at her. She sat completely still staring at them in incomprehension. Finally she slowly shook her head. "Why don't you two finish this off by grabbing the tails on your raccoon hats like Ralph and Ed did in *The Honeymooners*?" she said.

"Nancy," Bill said, "do you remember *The Honeymooners*?"

"No,…" she said, "somebody told me about it just like somebody told you about what happens in Irish pubs—now, who would you like to be, Nate?"

Nate considered the problem for a moment, but for some reason, couldn't decide. He became embarrassed, even a bit flustered, then finally blurted out, "Bob!...Bob...Lee."

"That'll fool 'em!" Bill said, smiling broadly. Then taking Nate gently by the shoulder once more, he said, "Don't worry, Nate. I know your mamma raised you to always tell the truth, but after a few years, you'll be able to lie with the best of us. Actually, the agent knows you're not using your Christian name, as we call it. He won't be using his either. All you have to remember is Bob, Peggy, and Patrick. Think you can do that?"

Nate took a deep breath, then began to smile. "I believe so," he said.

Nate said nothing more as Bill and Nancy spent another half hour in settling all the parameters of the training. As he listened, he began to see just how many mundane details could cause trouble in what both Bill and Nancy had agreed would be a very simple clandestine activity.

Finally, when both Bill and Nancy were satisfied, the two officers took their leave. As they waited for the Bluebird at the outdoors bus stop near the front of the building, it seemed impossible to Nate that the sedate, businesslike building set in the middle of a park, could be the headquarters of a worldwide spy network. "This seems almost unreal," he said. "I still can't believe I'm here, at work, about to engage in a spy case, and that it will be controlled from a building that could house the local court, or the Chamber of Commerce, or the Agricultural Extension office."

"You're about to engage in a clandestine operation, not a spy case," Bill corrected. "That other description is for the TV folks. Yes, I know what you mean about how the early days with the outfit feel to you. It does seem surreal, but what's great about this job is you'll still get that same feeling twenty years from now. There'll always be something new, something you haven't done before, some place you never thought you'd see, someone you never thought you'd meet. It will never be like working in a factory where in two weeks you know all you will ever need to know about the job and the only changes come when the engineers have made some small variation to whatever gizmo you crank out for eight hours every day. There's nothing like this job, Nate, nothing."

Chapter 4

When Bill and Nate arrived at the training site next day, they found a little black man, introduced as "Mohammed," who was both anxious to please and anxious about his own safety. After the introductions, Nancy sat down with him to reassure him as much as possible. Finally, she declared that Bill was the head of the entire chemical research lab while Nate was said to be in charge of the special branch handling secret writing. At these revelations, the man rose to shake the hands of both officers again as he told them how flattered he was that they had come to work with him. To Nate's surprise, Bill took the compliment in stride, assuring the man in turn that only Mohammed's potential for the collection and reporting of significant intelligence had caused him to briefly leave his important scientific duties. With that, the training began.

Bill first explained what he intended to do, impressing Mohammed with the technical sophistication of the systems he would soon see and stressing especially the very high security inherent in their proper use. Bill then went through the entire process himself, requesting only that Mohammed watch the process carefully, and ask any questions as he thought of them. As Nate watched the training, he was fascinated by the absolutely clear, simple way Bill explained things. Although several steps were involved, Bill's explanation seemed to make the reasons for each step completely sensible and the sequence of the individual steps absolutely inevitable; he was certain he could have prepared a message himself after Bill's initial demonstration. For this reason, he was mystified when Mohammed made one mistake after another when he was asked to do the work himself.

Despite the abysmal performance in Mohammed's first trial, Bill did not seem worried in the least. At the end his concern was not to drill Mohammed on the mistakes he had made, but to praise him for doing so well in his first time through the complicated process. Mohammed, who had seemed very distressed, began to calm down, especially when Bill turned to Nancy saying that since it was going so well, there was plenty of time for a break. Nancy, who seemed just as confident, immediately agreed. She called room service to order a fresh pot of coffee. The entire group engaged in small talk until the coffee arrived, when Nancy suggested Mohammed wait in the bathroom until the bellboy had gone.

Throughout this whole performance, Nate had been almost speechless both from his surprise at the way the training was going and from the apparent unconcern shown by Nancy and Bill despite the discouraging results. Now he thought it necessary to show that he too was a part of the operation. "Bill," he began, but immediately realized his mistake, then forgot what he intended to say. Mohammed stared in surprise at Nate, then turned the same look on Bill. Bill smiled at Mohammed as he said, "Bill, or rather William, is my middle name. I prefer it to my first name, Patrick, so around the office everyone calls me Bill."

Mohammed smiled, "Yes," he said, "I understand. It is like a... nickname."

"Exactly," Bill said. "Are you ready to get back to the training?"

As Mohammed took up his materials again, Bill gave Nate a quick look to let him know everything was all right. To Nate's great surprise, Mohammed went through the entire procedure with almost no prompting from Bill. Where he had been totally quiet as he applied the utmost concentration to his work in his first practice, now he laughed and talked throughout the various steps. After two more flawless practices, Bill declared that Mohammed should train him next time. The small man's face split into an enormous wide grin, he bowed his head slightly to Bill, and took Bill's hand in both his own as Bill congratulated him. In a tactful way, Bill suggested one more brief training session tomorrow just to make sure the procedures, especially those dedicated to security, had become second nature to Mohammed. He also explained that an overnight rest would allow Mohammed to thoroughly consider all he had learned and that some questions might occur to him that had not yet been addressed. These could be answered in the next short session. Mohammed eagerly agreed.

As Bill prepared to conclude the session by showing Mohammed the fan-fold/burn method of destroying his practice message, he winked at Nate. Mohammed watched the paper burn with the amazement Bill had predicted. He was so fascinated he turned to Bill after the paper had gone out, but couldn't speak. Having seen this reaction before, Bill anticipated his question. "No," he said, "it isn't special paper; any paper will work. And, Mohammed, do not, do not, show this to anybody else."

"I promise," he said. "May I burn a sheet?"

"Sure," Bill said.

Mohammed carefully folded a sheet of paper, lit the tops of a few creases, and in obvious pleasure, watched it burn.

"Now, remember," Bill said, "you do this only to sheets that have something sensitive on them...OK, Mohammed."

"Yes," Mohammed said, "but I will look forward to it."

"No doubt," Bill said with another wink at Nate.

A few minutes later, the two technical officers were heading back to South Building in Bill's car.

"I can tell by your silence that you learned something today," Bill said to Nate, "but you don't know yet exactly what it was."

"Frankly," Nate said, "I'm astounded. I don't know what I expected, but this wasn't it."

Bill laughed, "Let me guess," he said, "you thought the agent would look like Peter Lorre, skulking all over the place, suspicious of everyone, smoking a cigarette in a six-inch long holder or you thought he would be a wild-eyed radical with a bandanna tied around his head and eyes burning like Che' Guevara."

"Something like that," Nate admitted.

"Real agents aren't like that," Bill said. "Most of them are ordinary people who think they can make some extra money or get their children into American universities if they help us out with a little inside information on the local officials or the Russkies stationed at the local embassy. The real ones tend to be awed by the outfit just on general principles, but when we're represented by old, gray-headed, tall, scientists like me, the effect is even better. In cultures other than ours, age is still valued. In the Far East, for example, if you use a 22-year-old whiz kid or a woman to train an elderly Oriental man, you might as well slap him in the face. I know we can't officially say that because our women are becoming more militant, but it's the truth. You'll find the outfit has a superb reputation all around the world, either because they are afraid of us or because they love us. In either case, they think we can do anything—and we *can* do one hell of a lot if we're allowed to."

"Will Mohammed be a good agent?" Nate asked.

"Well," Bill said, "at least he's for real. Now it's all up to the case officer on the ground in country and how he handles the operation. If you mean will he provide useful intel, that will depend on what the CO thinks is worth reporting. He might really find out some significant policy decision and report it to us or he might just find out that the Prime Minister is taking bribes from the opposition or that he's a homosexual. Any of that could be useful."

Bill then paused as if wondering whether to continue. Nate remained quiet not knowing what else needed to be said, but sensing that Bill was not finished. Finally, Bill sighed, then began once more. "But...," he said, "it could also be that Mohammed is only a mark in the column. You must understand that case officers, regardless of what you may hear, live by recruitments and dissems, especially recruitments. If they don't recruit, they don't get promoted. The average CO will recruit any agent who might possibly, hopefully, maybe, perhaps provide something useful at some time in the future. You will find yourself, as you get more experience, wondering what could agent 'X' possibly contribute. Don't think about it; just do your job. If it makes you feel better, tell yourself that the CO expects agent 'X' to report on something that is either so important or so esoteric you wouldn't understand it. If you let yourself start to worry about the worth of the agent, you'll drive yourself nuts. I once trained an agent in secret writing under a scenario that I thought could not possibly work but I didn't worry about it because I thought the agent would have nothing to report anyway. About six months later I passed back by that station and did the routine check to see if the COs needed any technical help with any on-going ops. I found out the agent had written eight times resulting in eleven dissems; most of the dissems got high grades. You must always assume the CO knows what he's doing.

"Coming back to Mohammed, we know already that he is not expected to do great work. First, the CO who will handle him did not fly back here to supervise the training. If Mohammed had been red hot, that CO would have been here a week ahead to make sure everything went off just right and he would have sat at my side watching everything I did with an eagle eye. Secondly, they let Nancy handle the case. Don't get me wrong; she's a fine officer, but she's a woman. If they expected Mohammed to be wonderful, they would not have risked having him react badly to a woman case officer. Nate, all this doesn't mean that Mohammed will be useless, just that he isn't expected to provide us the keys to the kingdom."

"How bad was the name thing I messed up?" Nate asked.

"Not a problem," Bill said, "Mohammed was totally brand new or he wouldn't even have appeared to notice it, and he took my explanation at face value; it satisfied him completely. If he had been experienced, he would not even have made a comment because he would have been completely used to all the aliases. He wouldn't have even tried to remember our names at all."

"So it didn't hurt?" Nate said.

"If you don't ever make a mistake any bigger than that, "Bill said, "you're destined to sit in the big chair one of these days. Now let's stop off at the Lonestar while we're in the general area; there's no use in hurrying back to the office. With Fred and Mr. Willy on the job, what could possibly go wrong."

Chapter 5

During Nate's narrative of his first agent training with Bill, Mike had come to a modest equilibrium with his intake of spirits, but now he began to feel the need to establish the other half of the drinking cycle and relieve himself. "Mr. Forest," he said, "I have to go to the john."

"It's funny," Nate said, "that you can sit for hours drinking beer and not have to go, but when you finally go that first time, it's every five minutes thereafter."

When Mike returned, he found Nate in serious conversation with Betty. As he sat down, Nate decided, or had forgotten, that she had already met Mike and introduced him again. Betty smiled and said, "Hi, Mike. Have you heard enough war stories yet?"

Mike started to answer, but Nate interrupted. "I was just telling him about Bill's career and how he got me started right, just like I intend to start him off right. That's not exactly a war story."

"But it's close," Betty said.

"Betty," Nate said, "you can back me up in this. Wasn't it you who told me just the other day how much Bill helped you when you were at NORTECH?—NORTECH is an overseas technical support base, Mike. Was that a war story?"

"No," Betty said, allowing a thoughtful look to settle on her face for the first time that evening. She turned to look directly at Mike. "Nate's right," she said. "I was the first female tech to make it to an overseas posting. I was about a year into my tech training when Nate came on board although I had been at work for a long time even then; the opportunity to be a female tech didn't show its ugly head for years after I signed on. When I arrived in NORTECH, Bill had gotten Nate up and running at OTS headquarters and had been sent to NORTECH about a year before I arrived. Nate came over PCS after I had been there about six months."

"That means Permanent Change of Station," Nate interrupted.

"If I had thought I had it made," Betty said, "I quickly found out differently. Before I left here, I thought if I knew the systems very well and had become a good trainer I would have the toughest part behind me, but that was foolish. It wasn't the technical aspect of the tour that caused me trouble, it was the way the men treated me. They told me at great length how to do the simplest things and if I showed them I knew something they were either insulted or astonished. But the toughest thing was that no one wanted to go TDY with me."

"That means Temporary Duty for a Year," Nate interrupted again, "but we use it to denote any short trip."

"Nobody wanted to travel with you?" Mike asked in obvious amazement. "I'd have thought it would be just the opposite!"

Betty smiled before answering. "I know what you're thinking," she said, "but the reasons were a little more complicated. Most of the men were married and some of their wives tended to be a bit concerned if their husbands went off with me for a long swing through Africa or even a short trip somewhere in Europe. Funny thing was, I agreed with them. There's something about traveling around outside the social restrictions of home that makes some married men a menace to society, but I got that straightened out fairly fast. The wives relaxed, and soon I was accepted into their company just as if I had been a married woman myself.

"Still, if it hadn't been for Bill, the first few months would have been very rough. Later when Nate showed up, things got better still. He, Bill, and I became sort of the Three Musketeers in NORTECH. I know it's a blot on their machismo to say this, but I could trust both of them."

"Jesus!" Nate said, "now Mike will never respect me! You could have talked all night without using the word 'trust'. Every man hates to be trusted by a woman; it's disgusting."

41

"Well, I should point out," Betty continued, ignoring Nate, "that by the time Nate arrived, Bill had already showed me most of the things I badly needed to know. Nate just didn't make things any worse. Bill wasn't trying to save my soul or enhance my career or be a big brother; he was just trying to be a friend."

"Listen, Mike," Nate interrupted yet again, "before Betty gets completely emotional, let me tell you about my first long TDY with Bill. Once you see how these things work, what she is saying will make more sense to you—give you a more accurate picture."

Betty smiled again at Mike. "It never changes," she said. "After all these years, even if they mean well, even after sensitivity training; men believe a woman needs help with everything—a man's help!"

"It's just God's way," Nate said.

"Right," Betty said.

"Anyway," Nate continued, "they say you don't know a man until you work with him and believe me that's even more true when you've been on TDY together, especially on an African swing...but I need to begin when I first arrived at NORTECH."

"I'll come back in an hour or two," Betty said as she stood up, "when Nate begins at the beginning, time has no meaning."

***

The 747 floated gently down through a soft, late spring snowfall. As it slowly settled, the sound of the engines was muffled, almost quiet, giving Nate a moment of eerie silence to consider the three years ahead. He decided the delightful arrival was a good omen for the beginning of his tour at NORTECH, that the very last snow of the spring had waited just to make his arrival as lovely as possible. He had not been able to sleep on the flight, but on this early morning, the usual sluggishness he normally experienced after a sleepless night was banished by the adrenaline of his eager anticipation for the days ahead.

With his black passport speeding up the normal European efficiency, he was at the baggage claim in moments. As he stared at the circling bags, he heard a familiar voice from behind. "May the brotherhood be reunited," it said.

Nate turned to see Bill's smiling face and his hand already outstretched in greeting. As Nate shook his friend's hand, he said in surprise, "Bill, good to see you again! I didn't expect you to be here, especially so early in the morning! I thought I might see a driver who would hold up a sign with 'hey you' on it or something, but not someone from the office."

"Don't worry," Bill said, "this will be the last time you'll be met during the whole tour. Enjoy it. Now let's whiz through customs so we can get a cheap breakfast on the compound. I've had some coffee but it wore off long ago. After that, I'll take you to your temporary quarters, then to the office. As soon as the jet lag hits you, you're excused for the rest of today. Tomorrow, and for the next three years, it's business as usual. By the way, we leave for Africa on Monday."

"Do you think I'll be ready by then?" Nate laughed.

"No doubt about it," Bill said. "Now that you're overseas, ain't nothing you can't do and right away at that. Once you get overseas it's nothing but adventure and romance."

Nate wandered through NORTECH with Bill for most of the morning. Immediately after his official greeting from Dave, Bill took Nate to the laboratory where the first person he met was Betty. After that happy reunion, the two men continued their progression through the building with Nate meeting officers in other branches he had never seen before and renewing his acquaintance with those he had known at headquarters. Finally, Bill left Nate with the personnel staff, just as he had on Nate's first day of work at South Building, so that the essential administrative work could be done and he could meet the chief and deputy of the entire American facility. By the time the two men met with Betty for lunch, Nate had been issued his credentials, had had his preliminary security briefing, had been suitably welcomed by the branch chiefs of NORTECH, and had been scheduled for the appointments he would have to keep outside the office.

"Are you all certified now?" Betty asked.

"Everything but a tag in the ear," Nate said.

"What?" Betty said.

"It's a country expression," Bill explained. "Don't worry about it."

"Yes," Nate said, "I'm all done here, but I still have some checking in to do with the local State Department folks. I presume that won't be a problem."

"It won't if you take someone from personnel with you as you check in," Betty said. "Otherwise you'll find yourself trying to answer some questions you don't understand. That's not good, especially when you're just starting your tour."

"If personnel goes along, won't that blow the cover?" Nate asked.

Bill sighed and shook his head, "Nate," he said, "you have to understand that just about everybody who has any official contact with you already knows what you do, or they will find it out very soon. It's just like home: only the dummies won't know. As a matter of fact, when you meet the outsiders in the next few days, be sure to get their names. That way when you need some help or some verification in the future, you can call them up personally and get it done pronto. I'm sure our personnel officers will make that very clear, but if they don't—remember it anyway."

"Listen to the man," Betty said.

"I always do," Nate laughed.

By the time the trio had finished lunch, it was obvious that Nate was beginning to fade. Bill accompanied him to personnel for a last summation of what had been done and what still needed doing, then took him back to his quarters. "Get some rest if you can," Bill said. "Do you want me to come by for you at supper, or do you want to sleep through?"

Nate fought the increasing dullness of the jet lag to consider for a moment, then decided he would sleep through if possible. Bill gave him his phone number with instructions to call if he decided to go to dinner or if he needed anything. "Otherwise," Bill said, "see you tomorrow around eight."

***

The next morning Nate walked from his apartment to the squat, brick building surrounded by a high wire fence, guarded by elite Marine guards, and containing all the capabilities of NORTECH. Once the guard had closely examined Nate's new ID card, he asked if Nate knew where to go inside the compound. As Nate assured him he did, the guard handed over the card, giving him a final stare as if to fix him forever in memory. It reminded him of the way Rufus guarded South Building.

When he walked into the SW branch, the first one he saw was Bill who sat in the hideous, green, overstuffed armchair outside Dave's office. The now famous chair had been known for many years as "The Truth Chair." It had been left by mistake in the building when it had first become the property of the US Government. The first workers in the technical shop had saved it from destruction because their chief at the time was a very intellectual man who was completely out of his element as the leader of a group of very skilled, but earthy, technicians, therefore automatically becoming a butt for endless practical jokes. As they anticipated, he hated the chair on sight, but endured its presence so as not to irritate his men who, with straight faces, declared they loved it. When their chief finally figured out that the chair was just another joke on him, he banished it to the trash, but the chief of SW at the time, had saved it yet again.

He placed the chair just outside his office next to the small table where the daily reading boards were kept. By long tradition, the incoming cables were first read by the branch chief, or whoever might be acting for him, then the cables were sorted into "admin", "general read", and "action." At NORTECH, the action board was a brilliant red; every officer looked over its contents at least twice, and generally many more times, during each day. As they read, they sat in the chair;

as they waited to see the chief, they sat in the chair; as they talked to the secretary, they sat in the chair. The chief soon named it the "The Truth Chair." No one who sat in it was allowed to bullshit the chief or pretend he hadn't seen all the actions pending.

As soon as Nate entered, Bill got up from the ugly chair to shake hands once again. In his hand was one of the guest coffee cups on which a belligerent frog sat high on his haunches above the legend, "I'm so happy here, I could just shit."

"Coffee," he said.

Nate followed him to the lab which was already busy with officers mixing chemicals. "You'll need to bring in your own cup as soon as you get unpacked," Bill said. "Until then, you can use one of these guest cups like this one. I've left mine somewhere in the building, but I couldn't find it this morning before the no-coffee shakes hit me. I thought I could better stand a guest cup than to go to pieces right in front of my colleagues."

Nate surveyed the cups hanging on the wooden peg board above the sink amid the chemical beakers and flasks. He chose one on which a Green Beret figure was shouting, "Kill 'em all! Let God sort 'em out!"

"Good choice," Bill said. "Our guest cups are a source of pride in the office, along with the Truth Chair. As long as it isn't positively obscene, anything goes."

As Nate finished doctoring his coffee, Bill asked how he had spent the night. When Nate assured him that he had gotten some sleep, but had awakened quite early, Bill nodded his head. "That's about as good as can be expected," he said. "Can you listen carefully now?"

"Yes," Nate said as he followed Bill back to his desk just outside the front office. Once both officers had settled down, Bill began to speak in the way Nate now recognized as the introduction to an important transfer of information.

"Now that you're overseas," Bill said, "things have changed again, not in the general support to the Directorate of Operations, but in some of the particulars. At home, the desk officers tended to be more cautious in their judgments. If they had a question, they could bump it up to the higher management; we could do the same. Now their higher authority is always just down the hall in the Chief of Station's office. Our higher authority is us. Once we show up at a given station, there is no avoiding the issue by passing on the responsibility, no waiting for a committee to meet, no searching of the files or reference to the technical expert in the lab at home. We make our decisions by ourselves on the spot. If we are right, nothing will be said. If we are wrong, the chiefs at home will take a week while they sit around that big mahogany table in the big conference room, drinking coffee and munching doughnuts while they decide what to do about our errors. We decide in five minutes under great pressure, in plain view of the case officer, with too little information, with too little time, but with the hope that the final outcome will be good. At home they have all the time they want, no pressure at all, and the great advantage of hindsight. So don't worry about getting some ragging from home. As long as they don't haul you back to Washington or fire you, it's OK. If you're sensitive to a little criticism or general carping, it will be a long tour. Take your cue from Dave: if he isn't upset, you need not be.

"Now a word about the Chiefs of Station you'll meet here at the sharp end: they are the closest thing to God that you will ever meet on this earth. The ambassador generally thinks he runs his country, but it's as likely to be the COS. One thing is for sure, the ambassador knows only whatever the COS tells him no matter what he does to keep tabs on us. Most ambassadors are content to just let us alone as long as there are no flaps or international embarrassments. It's easier than trying to pry information out of the COS who has been superbly trained in deception and subterfuge.

"The COS has the power to send his officers back home on the day of their arrival if he wants to. He can also put a visiting tech on the next plane back to NORTECH with instructions to never set foot in his country again. That's the ultimate disaster for a tech. For that, the chiefs back home call a special meeting at that big mahogany table and the shit flows from there all the way to your own personal cubbyhole right here in NORTECH. Don't ever get on the wrong side a COS. Most of them are excellent men—one saved my career during my first tour—but they have such awesome power that you can't risk finding out how they will react after you've screwed up. Got all that?"

"Yes," Nate said. "What happened on your first tour?"

"It's classified," Bill said with a smile. "One day, I'll tell you. For now you need to worry about you. By the way, there's a saying in the field you might not have heard yet. If something goes well, it's 'clandestine', if it goes badly, it's 'candlestein'. Just try to stay on the clandestine side.

"Now for the particulars of our TDY: we will begin with development and printing of an unknown film in Bamako, a requirement we got just this morning. It could be tricky; the film is loose in a can. God knows what it is or, more interestingly, how long it is. After that we have an SW training, a routine visit to a station we haven't checked lately, some re-training for a DO secretary who's running a station darkroom, and establishment of an observation post on a local Cuban compound if possible. Of course, at every stop we'll bring the station's technical inventory up to date. It ought to be a good first foray into the life of the overseas tech officer. Do you have any Lomotil or anything like that?"

"No," Nate said.

"How about tetracycline?" Bill asked.

"No," Nate said.

"Painkillers?" Bill asked.

"Only aspirin," Nate said.

"That's OK for now, Bill said. "If we need special medicine we can use mine. We can also buy more on the way."

"How? Nate asked. "Isn't all that stuff prescription medicine?".

"Damn right," Bill said, "but the chickenshit State doctors won't give it to us unless we show up at their office, and not even then unless we are clearly at death's door, so they force us to buy it on the local market. I know it's a gamble, but when your guts are in absolute rebellion and you have to take the only flight that leaves for the next six days, you take the Lomotil and you fly anyway.

"Don't get me started on State doctors. If you're really sick on TDY, try to get to a British doctor. They know the difference between tennis elbow and leprosy; sometimes our guys don't. The nurses are a different story. These women, provided they don't pay any attention to the doctors, will pull you through. If there are any real saints on this earth, it's nurses, not just in the State Department, but anywhere. Enough! I promised not to get started on this. Are we ready?"

"Yes, now that you've scared me to death about my health," Nate said, "I'm even more eager."

"Listen, Nate," Bill said, "all the good old boys know that a shot of Jim Beam can defeat anything from gout to malaria. You'll be OK, I promise."

Three days later they were on what Bill usually called "The Great Silver Bird" winging its way into Africa.

***

"Have you ever heard of the WAWA theory?" Bill said as the DC-10 descended into the airport at Abidjan.

"No," Nate said, "should I have heard of it?"

"No," Bill said, "but for the rest of this tour, you will need to pay it the same heed as Murphy's Law. It stands for 'West Africa Wins Again'. I don't know who thought it up, but he was right. Take Abidjan for instance: the city itself, which you won't see this trip, seems quite modern—even has an ice rink—but this airport is one of the worst you'll ever encounter. When we get our bags, the locals will almost jerk them out of your hand. If you're not met by someone from the embassy, you'll be ripped off for sure by the cabbie, and customs will be a nightmare. And that's just Abidjan. I once got off the plane at a

49

stopover in Dakar. When I tried to get back on, I literally had to fight through the line even though I had a transit pass, and when I did get back to my seat, a fist-fight broke out between the steward and a passenger in the seat next to me. I could go on for hours on the perils of WAWA, but why bother. You'll be able to start your own scrapbook in about fifteen minutes."

"But we're only transiting Abidjan," Nate said. "how much of a problem could we have?"

Bill stared at Nate in silence, finally shaking his head at the young man's ignorance. "There's one more thing you need to understand about WAWA," he said. "You never, never risk jinxing yourself. As a baseball man, you know you're not supposed to talk about a no-hitter while it's in progress. It's the same with WAWA: *never* say that things are going well; it's an invitation to disaster. It may now already be too late to save us at this stop."

Despite Bill's caution, the line at immigration seemed to move fairly efficiently. Nate began to kid Bill about the dire problems he had supposed, but Bill remained grim, warning Nate several times that they were not yet safe in the transit lounge. When Bill handed his passport to the tall, dignified immigration officer, he looked it over carefully, then asked where was the visa for the Ivory Coast. Bill explained they were not planning to enter the country; they only intended to be in Abidjan long enough to catch the Air Ivoire flight to Bamako. The official next asked to see Bill's onward reservations. After Bill handed over his ticket, the officer studied it carefully, then asked him to step aside and wait for a moment. He kept both the ticket and the passport. Bill protested briefly, but had no choice. Nate suffered the same fate, despite arguing that his black passport meant that he deserved special treatment.

When Nate finally gave up, he walked over to Bill who was sitting quietly on a crate just outside the immigration booths. "Have any luck?" Bill asked his fuming friend. "You know, of course, that the dip passport only officially helps you in the country of your diplomatic posting. It *might* help, I admit, if the local officials are willing to be intimidated, but if they aren't, your ass is grass. Right now they've got our tickets and our passports. We're fastened."

"Damn!" Nate said. "We're just going about fifty feet. I can see the domestic terminal from here. What are we going to do, call the embassy?"

"We could do that," Bill said, "but first let's see what happens."

As Bill finished speaking, the last of the line passed through immigration freeing up the official who immediately came over to the two hot, disgruntled travelers. "Collect your baggage, please," he said.

The two officers followed him into the baggage area where their bags were the only ones left. "Wait here," he said.

"This is a good sign," Bill said. "If the bags were gone, it really would be the beginning of a nightmare."

"But we're still stuck," Nate said, "and the connecting flight is due in about an hour."

"Now it's my turn to be hopeful," Bill said. "First, the flight will be late, it always is. Second, you have to realize these guys know that we can call the embassy as you said, but then they don't get anything out of it. They aren't interested in causing us to miss our flight or in getting into any trouble with our embassy or their bosses. They just want a little something for their trouble."

As Bill spoke, he indicated an animated discussion amid a gathering of four officials at the other end of the baggage claim. "They're deciding our fate right now," he said.

A moment later, one of the officials collected their passports and tickets from the officer who had initially confiscated them. "It's been decided," Bill said. "Today, our guy loses out—better luck tomorrow. We'll know in a moment what's required."

The oldest of the participants in the conference just concluded, who now had their passports and their tickets, walked slowly back to them. "There seems to be a bit of irregular," he said in heavily accented English.

Nate immediately began to explain the situation, but Bill reached up to touch Nate's shoulder from his sitting position to let him know he should cease. Turning to look at Bill, he said, "What!"

Bill smiled at him, then stood to face the serious official. Looking closely at the name tag, Bill said very slowly and clearly: "Mr... Guillame, we are very sorry we do not have the correct visa for your country. We did not know we would need it to go from one terminal to the other. Perhaps there is some way we could resolve this problem between us without getting anyone else involved."

Immediately, Guillame began to grin. "Perhaps something can be done," he said.

"Should we all have a beer while we talk?" Bill asked. "I would like to buy if you do not mind."

"Yes!" Guillame said. "Let us go."

The three men walked over to the bar at the corner of the main terminal where Guillame ordered three of the large local beers. In the halting conversation which ensued, the weather, the economy, and life in the civil service were discussed. It seemed to Nate that they carefully avoided discussing the only thing that really mattered: whether they would make the Air Ivoire flight or not. Eventually the hot African afternoon, coupled with the now empty tarmac, seemed to stop time entirely. The terminal grew quiet as the baggage grabbers, the local police, the few transit passengers, and even the dogs either slept or fell into suspended animation with eyes open but brains shut down. The quieter it got, the more agitated Nate became although he fought the impulse, telling himself to be cool and to avoid showing his concern. However, when he looked out through the shimmering heat at an Air Ivoire flight now drifting onto the runway, he felt he must say something to get the desultory conversation back on track. "Do you think that might be our flight?" he said as calmly as he could manage.

"Yes!" Guillame said happily, "and it is not very late."

"Then," Bill said to Guillame, "we must get ready to leave. As he spoke he pulled a twenty-dollar bill out of his wallet and placed it carefully on the bar. "Mr. Guillame," he said, "I do not have any Francs with me. If you would buy the beers for all of us, I would be very grateful. I know it will be a lot of trouble for you, but you could change the American dollars at the bank later on. If there happens to be any money left over, I would be most happy if you kept it for the trouble we have caused you today."

Guillame smiled hugely once again. "It is a good way to handle the situation," he said. "Let us go into the other terminal."

A half hour later, Guillame personally escorted the smiling Bill and the astounded Nate from the first class lounge onto the Air Ivoire flight while the rest of the passengers waited in the terminal under the restraint of the three other officers who had not been chosen to engage in bribery on this day. Once Guillame had seen to the storage of their hand-carry luggage, and had seated them in the first two seats in the airplane, he shook hands warmly with the two officers, wishing them God speed and announcing his anticipation of their return. Then, throwing them a final salute, he stepped out the door. A second later, a mass of overheated, jostling, shouting passengers poured in through the same door, transforming the interior of the plane from a scene of serenity to one of chaos. When the tumult had finally settled down, Nate turned to Bill with consternation still clearly showing on his face. "Why didn't you give him *fifty* dollars so we could have been the *only* passengers!"

"No need to overdo it," Bill laughed. "The trick in bribery is to look ahead. Next time we may need something that's really illegal, but with luck we can get it without going much above the twenty-dollar basic bribery floor. Besides, we might have been able to get the same thing for ten dollars. I may actually have over-bribed our friend."

"The idea of bribery for very ordinary things just doesn't sit well with me, Nate said. "Things shouldn't be that way."

"You're absolutely right," Bill agreed, "but you'll find that the third world, especially, moves on the basis of who you know, who you can bribe, and how big a bribe you can afford. It ain't pretty, but we won't change it in our lifetimes. Just think of it as a contribution to the local economy or a humanitarian act like the missionaries might perform—only worth a lot more to the natives, of course. How does it feel to be a contributor to third-world relief?"

"Right now it feels like my jaws are uncomfortably tight," Nate said.

"They'll loosen up soon," Bill said.

Chapter 6

In contrast to his initial joviality at Abidjan immigration, Nate was grim as he and Bill joined the line at Bamako. This time, however, Bill seemed quite relaxed.

"Why aren't you worried?" Nate said. "This place really looks like the third world. If they don't cooperate, it may take all the rest of our cash to get us through."

"Here it's no problem," Bill said. "First, the Malians don't have the same general attitude that the Ivorians have. Second, we're not transiting this time, we're arriving. And the COS over here is an excellent man who always looks after his visitors; I'm sure we'll see an expediter soon."

As if Bill's last comment had summoned him, a black man worked his way through the crowd to approach the two officers. On his chest was a black, plastic nameplate emblazoned on the left end with a small American flag. "Mr. Graham, Mr. Forest?" he said as he walked up to them.

"Yes, sir!" Bill said. "We are very glad to see you."

The man smiled in return, asked for their passports, led them to a quiet corner forming an eddy in the swirling mass of arrivals, and disappeared again into the brilliantly colored flow. In fifteen minutes he was back. In another five minutes, they were on the way to the hotel.

"I guess the film's not urgent," Bill said, "or we would be headed to the embassy instead of the hotel. Of course, the COS here is one of the really decent ones who knows that we've likely had a hard trip and need a little rest before we start work. He'll give us as much courtesy as he can, that's for sure."

Bill's monologue was interrupted as his attention was diverted to the milling humanity just outside the window of the embassy van. He was always fascinated at the way the embassy drivers managed to extract their vehicles from the enveloping mass without injuring anyone. Situations which would completely immobilize an American driver were never a problem for the locals who simply moved slowly ahead never running over anyone but never coming to a complete stop. Once the van had nosed its way through the last of the vendors, bag grabbers, cab drivers, family members, and assorted animals, he continued his thoughts on the man who ran the station. "Bob's a good man, an old Africa hand. He really likes the country and the people and he's willing to labor for their best interests. He really believes the Russkies would make them worse off than they are now."

"I'm not sure anyone could make this any worse," Nate said as he stared out the window of the van, now gaining speed as it moved onto the highway leading away from the airport.

"Just wait," Bill said, "In Khartoum I once drove out to a CO's house over a stretch where people were living in bundles of twigs patched with cardboard. This also isn't as bad as Ouagadougou where there's an enormous, permanent trash dump on the corner about a block from the embassy where the huge buzzards don't even bother to move as you pass by, or as bad as Dar es Salaam where they're almost back to the stone age on account of the socialist government, or in Accra where it's hard to find even a box of matches on the economy. At least it's pretty here in a rough way. You have to admit the French did a good thing when they planted these trees along the road. Notice how everything looks golden in the low sun. If you consider the light and the smell of the wood smoke and the colorful clothes and the ancient trees, it's almost like a travel poster."

"Whatever you say," Nate said.

***

The next morning, the two officers took a cab to the embassy. Now, unlike the previous late afternoon, the heat was just getting a grip on the land instead of just letting go. The golden glow of yesterday's late afternoon was replaced with the glaring, almost white, reflection of the high African sun from the desert soil. By the time the two arrived at the embassy, they were hot, sweating, and dirty.

Bill handed their passports to the Marine guard and asked for the office secretary. The young man first asked them to sit down across from him on a bench facing his station, then made the requested call. As they began to cool down in the air conditioned lobby, Nate's spirits began to rise once more. He had wondered if the embassy would be as basic, as sparse as the country itself. Now he fully experienced for the first time the way Americans lived and worked in even the most harsh field environments. For the rest of his career, whenever he found himself surprised at the way Americans doggedly maintained their creature comforts no matter how desperate the country in which they served, he always thought back to that first morning in the cool lobby of the embassy in Bamako while the rest of the country burned outside.

In a few moments, the station secretary appeared to escort them upstairs to see the COS. When they passed through the second secured door, they found themselves in the middle of the office which was simply a large room divided artificially by two desks set away from the walls on opposite sides and a part metal, part glass petition hiding a cubbyhole at the far end of the room. Standing at the coffee pot was a big man dressed in short-sleeve shirt and casual slacks. As they walked in he turned from pouring the coffee, broke into a smile and extended his hand to Bill. "Bill!" he said, "good to see you again! How's everything in that damned freezing Europe where they never have a summer."

"Everything's fine, Bob," Bill replied. "It's balmy in NORTECH now—almost forty degrees on the average—springtime. This is Nate. It's his first TDY. They tried to get him to go to Sweden for his first trip, but he said he missed his native Southern heat so I told him to come on to Africa with me. Now that he's here, he knows he made the right decision."

"Bill's still prefers bullshit to reality, I see," Bob said as he shook hands with Nate. "Are you still in shock or have you decided it's all a dream?"

By now Nate was use to the constant joking that pervaded the entire outfit, but it still took a moment to appreciate the big, obviously happy man standing before him in casual clothes, drinking steaming coffee on this blistering day, in a tiny station in a county most folks could not find on the map, and clearly enjoying himself. When he had overcome his fleeting confusion, he too broke into a grin. "As Bill always says, it's only adventure and romance in the field. I'm just glad I'm finally out here."

Bob pumped Nate's hand for another few seconds as he continued grinning at the young officer. "You'll do," he said. "Get yourselves some coffee and come on in."

Once the two officers had settled down in the cramped space behind the separating panel, Bob produced a thoroughly taped, metal film can which had, at one time long ago, contained microfilm. As he handed the can to Bill, he shook it carelessly. The contents rustled. "This is the film," he said. "God knows what kind of shape it's in. I got it from my asset in the local police force. They confiscated it on a raid on the office of a local 'usual suspect' who has now disappeared. They didn't want to develop it since they didn't know what it was."

"Do you have any idea what the film is?" Bill asked.

"No," Bob said, "except that it's certainly black and white. It's probably nothing, may even be blank, but I'd like to do it for them just as a favor."

"OK," Bill said, "we'll get rolling on it. To be on the safe side, we'll make new developing solutions first. That'll probably take most of the morning. We'll let the chemicals cool over lunch and develop the film in the early afternoon. We should have the prints on your desk before close of business today."

"Fine," Bob said, "good luck."

***

After they had made up the new solutions, Bill opened the small tool kit that ever OTS tech carried with him on every TDY and took out the one item always sure to be found: a roll of duct tape.

"Now what?" Nate asked.

"Now we sit quietly in the dark for twenty minutes so our eyes can adjust," Bill said as he reached for the light switch. "It's always a good idea to check out a darkroom like this to see if it's really a darkroom or a twilight room. There's nothing as charming as realizing half way through loading the film that you can see what you're doing. If you don't have time to sit a while to check out an unfamiliar darkroom before you have to begin developing, I recommend you load the film in a changing bag. In this case, it will be even more important to be light tight because we may decide to develop the film in a bucket or tray if it won't fit on a Nikor reel. By the way, it's no use asking a COS about his darkroom. To him the whole thing is an infinitesimal detail; he'll always say it's fine. However, when you show him fogged film, it won't be fine. We'll just sit here in the dark for a few minutes as our eyes adjust, putting pieces of this tape over anything that glows and telling war stories. It'll be part insurance, part entertainment. You want to tell the first whopper, or should I?"

"I still don't have many war stories," Nate said. "How about a serious question?"

"Oh, God," Bill said, "go ahead."

"Why do we have a station here? What could possibly happen in this country that would harm the US of A.? If this country fell through into China, I don't see why it would matter—except in a humanitarian way."

"That's a good question, Nate," Bill said, "but I do have an answer because I once asked Bob, who always tells the truth unless a lie is actually required. He told me we are here because the Russkies are here and the Russkies are here because we are here. Otherwise, you're right, none of this makes any sense. You have to remember that dull, desperate, third-world countries are wonderful places to meet Russians. They don't live like we do even if they do live a lot better than the locals. We've got good, cheap booze available; good, cheap cigarettes; first class beef; air conditioning; good transportation; first run movies—all kinds of things. Our COs can meet a lot of Russians (and other Commies) just by offering them a chance to see a decent movie or come to a decent dinner in a decent, air-conditioned house. As far as the local government is concerned, we generally try to buy the president of the country so we don't need a lot of agents reporting on the local scene. That frees up all the case officers' time so they can troll for Russians.

"Hey, over there near the ceiling—see that glow? Since you're younger and closer to it, you wouldn't want to fumble your way over there and tape it up would you?"

Nate's cautious progress toward the weak yellow glow was punctuated by assorted stumblings followed by mumbled curses. Finally he managed to locate the light leak. A moment later, the area had been darkened again after the accurate application of a piece of tape. "Got it!" he said. "Damned if I remember so many things being in the way while the light was on."

"Murphy's Law of Darkroom Locomotion clearly states that any object grows in size when the lights are off, and is free to move from its original position to one of maximum hindrance," Bill said helpfully.

"Yes," Nate said, "I just tested it."

Although Bill had suggested war stories, Nate found the dark more conducive to serious discussion. When he had managed to relocate his seat, he began the conversation again on that note. "How did you sign on?" he said. "The better I know you, the less you seem like the espionage type."

"I don't know if that's a compliment or not, but you're right," Bill answered. "I sometimes can't believe it myself. Part of it was incredible luck: I'm the only one I know who just wrote the outfit a letter. Everyone else was recruited. Part of it is that I had just had what we used to call a mid-life crisis. I'd had an experience where something very bad had happened for no reason. It was so bad that I wanted to do the most opposite thing I could think of. That's about it. How about you?"

"The usual," Nate said. "I was first interviewed on campus, then contacted clandestinely. I was fascinated from the first. Beyond that, I never thought about it...I guess you don't want to talk about that life-changing occurrence, do you?"

"That's the best way," Bill said, ignoring Nate's question, "don't waste time thinking about it. Just enjoy it. See any other light leaks?"

"No," Nate said.

"OK," Bill said, "let's see first if this film will fit on a Nikor reel."

Both men were silent as Bill un-taped the can. Nate next heard the click as Bill snapped the end of the film onto the inner spiral of the stainless steel reel. For the next several seconds, the slight hiss of the film being wound onto the reel was the only sound, then total silence returned to the darkroom. "Here," Bill said as he held the film toward Nate.

As soon as Nate managed to find the film, he knew why Bill's voice had not sounded happy: a few inches of the film spilled out of the reel. "Decision time," Bill said. "Should we cut it and develop it on two Nikors or spaghetti it in a tray?"

"If you don't mind," Nate said, "I think I'll defer to the senior tech in this case."

Bill laughed. "A wise decision," he said. "In this case, it probably would be safe to cut it, but then we just took half an hour to make sure we have total darkness so that we can develop the film in the open without fogging it. I think I'll soup it in a tray. For you youngsters, the advantage is that the film stays whole. The disadvantage is that the extra handling could lead to damage."

"There's one other thing," Nate said, "since we don't know what the film is, how long should it be developed?"

"This is where we earn our keep," Bill said. "I'm going to revert to the advice of the best photo tech I ever knew. He always said to develop any unknown black-and-white film in full strength D-76 for eight minutes at 68 degrees, and you'll get images. That supposes, of course, that the film has been more or less properly exposed."

"And if it hasn't?" Nate asked.

"Then," Bill said, "it depends on the COS. If he's decent, like Bob, he won't be happy but he'll understand. If he's a bastard, he'll chew our butts to ribbons and maybe send out a cable to the regional base and headquarters. Now, are we ready to start?"

"No," Nate said.

***

Bob studied the finished prints intently while the two officers sat in silence. Finally, he pitched them back on the desk without comment as he stood up to move once more to the coffee pot. After he had filled his cup he returned to his desk but did not sit down. "That certainly is our compound," he said. "What else can you tell me?"

"Well," Bill said, "the film was a long load; we developed it in a tray. As for the equipment, the total lens length was probably about 500mm, but not of good quality. Notice the spherical aberrations—the fuzziness—showing up at the edges of the image. Nikon, or any other excellent manufacturer would be shamed by it. I would guess it's a cheap 200mm with a 2X or maybe even a 3X tele-converter. The film is British."

"So it's not the Russians," Bob said, "At least not the equipment and the film."

"Right," Bill said, "Nate and I will visit the local photo shops to see what we can find on sale here, to see if that kind of equipment might be locally available. Did you, by any chance, give your local friends any cameras?"

"Yes," Bob said hesitantly, "I did issue some old Spotmatics about a year ago, but it was just a friendly gift with no strings attached. They came with only 50mm lenses."

"OK," Bill said, "just checking. Nate and I will head out and let you know something soonest."

***

"Well, what's the verdict?" Bob said asked as the two officers returned from their foray.

"We got lucky," Bill began, "the first photo shop we tried, Ahmed's Photo, just a few blocks from here, had bulk film and he was selling hand-loaded film in canisters at a cheap price. He also had a collection of odds and ends of equipment, including some cheap lenses and tele-converters. We didn't question him about anything, just looked over his stuff like any American trying to get a wonderful deal off a third-world shopkeeper, then asked for something we knew he wouldn't have. We're not saying your man ever visited this fellow or bought anything from him. All it means is that at least one local place *could* have provided some hand-loaded film, a cheap 200mm lens, and a way to convert it into a longer length; it didn't have to come from outside the country."

"OK," Bob said thoughtfully, "I appreciate it. What's your schedule?"

"Unless you need us for something else," Bill said, "we'll walk over to State travel to make sure our tickets are still good, then we'll get with your secretary and go over your technical inventory to make sure it's OK. Whatever time we have after that today we'll spend in straightening up your darkroom. After that, we'll head back to the hotel and hit the road early tomorrow."

"Good enough," Bob said as he stood to shake their hands. "You guys are welcome any time. Thanks for your help. Say hello to Dave for me. Tell him he still owes me a pot of Texas chili the next time I pass through NORTECH."

"We'll do it," Bill said. "See you next time."

As the two officers walked toward the State travel section, Nate asked, "What does Bob intend to do now that he knows someone took pictures of the compound? I thought he might react with a little more concern."

"Oh, he's concerned," Bill said. "It could be anything. That local 'usual suspect,' might really have been checking out the compound for some reason, but he has now 'disappeared' and can't be questioned—verrrry in-deresting—or Bob's own asset could be preparing to diddle him in some way. He's thinking now about how to determine what's really going on and what he can do to make it work for him somehow. Here's where those peculiar case officer skills come into play. He's good and he's seen it all. He'll be fine."

"Why didn't you at least offer to discuss it with him?" Nate asked.

"Well," Bill said, "he knows the local situation better even than the local police, he has instant communication to headquarters and their experts if he wants their advice or research, and given the benign operational situation here he has the freedom of action to figure it out. And for your personal notebook: You must never say to a case officer that you think his asset is bad.

"First, the CO knows the case and the agent much better than you do. Second, saying something like that is the ultimate interference in his business. It may be obvious that the agent is bad. He may be so bad he stinks, but you never even bring it up unless you're dealing with a good man like Bob. Even then you wait for his lead before you say anything. You have to remember that the training of a tech officer and a case officer are entirely different. We're trained to think in the classic scientific way: to base our actions on the facts, apply cold hard reason to the situation, accept what we see at face value. They're trained to deal with ambiguity, to explore every possible nuance, to look beyond the obvious to the possibilities of a case. That's the basic, never-ending conflict between the thinking of the case officer and the tech. We're both right, but the CO has the hammer. No matter what, the operational call is always his. If you want to get sent home in a hurry, just interfere with his operational handling of a case and you're history."

"Do you think they're smarter than we are?" Nate asked.

"Of course not," Bill said. "In college they majored in things that science majors took only if they flunked out of the hard sciences. In fact, we are the only ones in the outfit who aren't awed by case officers because we know we're basically more intelligent than they are—but the intelligence is of a different kind. What you're reacting to is their enormous confidence, or arrogance in some cases. That's the result of their training. Suppose your job was to meet people you didn't really like, befriend them to gain their confidence, then talk them into committing treason against their country with no security for their personal safety except your operational expertise. That takes the nerve of a riverboat gambler. Nobody comes in off the street with that kind of confidence. They get that in their initial training at the Farm. A lot don't make it through. By the time they do get through, they have to think they can do anything, that they're a special breed—and it's absolutely true. I wouldn't—couldn't—do their job in a million years.

"Yes, we're as smart as they are, often smarter in practical things, but they have a special talent. That's what you must remember when some wet-behind-the-ears-CO proposes something so dumb technically it would make Gomer Pyle look like a genius. You can't get upset. Just pretend to consider it carefully and gently talk him out of it.

"I know your personality well enough already to see it will be hard for you to suffer much foolishness, but you have to do it...Right? ...Nate?"

"Right," Nate said without enthusiasm.

Bill clapped Nate on the shoulder as he smiled broadly. "Don't worry, Nate," he said, "before long, you'll be just as comfortable wading through the bullshit as the rest of us."

Chapter 7

"Most techs stay at the Hilton or at the New Stanley while they're in Nairobi," Bill said, "but we'll put up at the Serena. It's a little bit out of the city on a low hill. It's a great view, there's a small park for the runners amongst us, and the Lufthansa stewardesses stay there. They are beautiful women, but I'm terrified of them. You should do all right though, your personality is a lot more forceful."

"Now what does that mean?" Nate asked. "Am I supposed to insult them to get their attention or something?"

"No, no, nothing like that," Bill said. "It's just that when one of them tells you to start having a good time *now*, you'll be able to do it without momentarily turning to stone and looking like a complete fool."

"I see," Nate said. "Now how is the station here?"

"Real good, real good—the COS is a character," Bill said. "He's a great officer who happens to love Kenya. He wears khaki shorts to work, complete with those high, British bobby socks. He talks about seeing 'elephant' or 'giraffe' the way white hunters do, without adding the 's' like us civilians. If there's ever a need for an emergency exfiltration, he intends to do it overland in a Land Rover instead of in the air. When he talks, it sounds like the gravel crunching under the tires of the big, green Chevrolet stake truck when it backs up to the local hog-butchering shed. As a country boy I know you understand how that sounds.

"They don't know it, but he's the best friend the Kenyans have, he may be more on their side than even the Brits. As for us, he always treats us right. He listens to what we say, makes allowances as best he can if we screw up, and sends a kudos cable if we do anything right. His officers and the techs would all do anything for him.

"Nairobi itself is always a treat. The people are decent, they work hard, they try to do the right thing, everything's inexpensive, the climate is wonderful, there's a real African game park just outside town, the food is terrific. The only thing is that crime is on the increase. It's not gratuitous crime. It's basically stealing to live because there's just too many people no matter how carefully you try to divide the country's resources. Moi has done his best to get the population under control, but it's a losing battle. There's just too many people now and the population is so young that there's going to be a lot more no matter what.

"If our Congress could see first hand what overpopulation can do, they'd stop all the AID projects except for family planning. A good program to reduce the population of a country like this would be worth more that a dozen, billion-kilowatt hydro dams or those really useless sports stadiums the Chinese are so hot to give away...Sorry, it's just that as a scientist, I get very impatient with leadership that won't even discuss the single most disastrous force in any poor county. Kenya really is God's country and to see it become a basket case is difficult...oh, well, what's the use thinking about it."

After Bill's serious comment, both men were silent for the remainder of the cab ride to the Serena. When Bill stepped out of the taxi, the busboys immediately swarmed him, calling him by name and welcoming him back to the hotel. Nate was clearly amazed at the reception, but said nothing until they had finished checking in. As they followed the room boy to their rooms, he finally decided to ask Bill about the reception they had received. "That was quite a welcome," he said.

"Yes," Bill said, "obviously it's because I've tipped them well in the past, but they also sense when someone likes them and their country and they appreciate that. In West Africa, you could kiss their ass and they wouldn't give you any credit for it."

Bill smiled broadly as the room boy opened the door to his room which was beautifully furnished, bright, and directly overlooked the pool. "For now," he said to Nate, "you'll be on the non-pool side, but if you act right with them, you'll wind up eventually on this side of the corridor."

"I'll bet all the stewardesses stay on this side too," Nate said as the boy dithered around the room making small, unnecessary adjustments to the brochures on the desk, the towels in the bathroom, and the position of the drapes.

"No way!" Bill said. "All over the world, the Americans get the best treatment because we tip better, not because we're better looking. We appreciate someone helping out because we've never had servants, we never send food back to the chef, we're more patient if something goes wrong, and we're trusting to a fault. I'll never forget once when the Thais got all pissed off at us for something and decided their real friends were the German and Japanese tourists. They put 'Willkommen' signs all over everything in Bangkok. I went back three months later and they were so determined to make it up to the Americans they would even give you the girls at a reduced rate. It was almost embarrassing. Here the stewardesses are magnificently handsome, but they don't tip like we do so they're on your side of the hall. I tell you once again, Nate, for us Americans it's only adventure and romance at the sharp end."

"Right," Nate said.

***

After the mandatory introductions for Nate and the happy re-acquaintances for Bill among the office staff, the two officers were ushered into the chief's office. Even before they got completely into the room, the big man behind the desk said, "Where's my cigars?"

Bill smiled as he drew two large boxes of expensive cigars from a paper bag, "You didn't really think we'd forget your cigars did you, Clint?"

"You never know," the big man rasped, damned techs come to Nairobi and all they can think about is trying to see some topless women at the Hilton pool or going out to the local game park or trying to eat one of everything at the Carnivore. If it wasn't for the cigars, I doubt I'd ever let you people come here."

Both men grinned as they shook hands while Bill handed over the cigars. "This is Nate," Bill said. "It's his first trip to Africa so I had to include Nairobi. Thought he might as well see the best first—and learn about the cigars."

Nate stepped forward to shake hands with Clint who looked him over intently as had Bob in Bamako and so many of the other case officers he had met. As he had become used to the initial close inspection, he had begun to appreciate the special training given to these men. It was obvious the good ones were expert at swiftly reading people whether they were potential agents or OTS technicians whose character had yet to be decided. "Howdy," he said, "glad to be here. Bill already told me about Nairobi, that it was the best place in Africa."

"Did he tell you I was the best COS?" Clint growled.

"Yes sir," Nate said, "and the best hunter."

Clint then looked at Bill, shook his head in mock disgust, then said, "Sit down. Let's talk."

No one spoke until Clint lit one of the Cigars and groaned in ecstasy as the smoke began to fill the room. "Ever read that poem by Kipling called *The Betrothed*"? he asked. "Damn good poem—lot of truth to it, but I can't even recite it anymore. The damn women think it's sexist. They think I'm a male chauvinist pig, as they like to call it nowadays. If they only knew how proud that makes me...Anyway, you boys got it easy this time. I need four case officers trained so they know which end of the camera to point at the target, but they don't need to know anything about processing the film; our lab assistant can do that. However, I would like you to give her a little advanced training or maybe give her a good review of the basics. Sometimes her prints look a little...foggy. Of course, it may not be her fault; she says not, but if the COs get trained and she gets retrained, it's gonna be OK—right?"

"Right, Clint," Bill said. "we'll see to it."

"Good, if there's anything you need while you're here, just let me know. How much for the cigars?"

"For you, Clint, there's never a charge," Bill said. "Dave told us he intends to keep you firmly in his debt so that you can buy him the best dinner in Europe on your next visit to NORTECH."

Clint snorted, "That damn Dave ought to buy *me* a dinner for the way I've put up with his shitty technical help these last two years. You tell him we'll settle up when I come up there in November for the Chief's Conference."

"Will do," Bill said as he stood up. "Who are the COs you want trained?"

"Ask Brenda," Clint said, "she knows a hell of a lot more about this station than I do—could probably run it if I'd let her."

Once again outside the door, the two officers grinned at each other. "This ought to be fun," Nate said.

"Tell you what," Bill said, "why don't you work with the lab assistant and I'll do the COs."

"OK," Nate said, "is there any special reason for doing it that way? Seems it would be harder to train four COs than check out the lab assistant."

"I think," Bill said, "that it would be well for you to work with Adele because training a station secretary to do technical things is something you will do over and over again in your career. It's only a really huge station that can devote a full-time position to day-to-day technical matters. The overworked secretary dealing with yet another duty is a standard position in the outfit. I think you will find Adele to be very smart, but that's part of the problem. She is the classic example of the secretary who wants to be a case officer, and sees no reason why not. She tends to race through her routine work so she can be available to assist in any aspect of operations. You may find it hard to get and keep her complete attention if there's anything at all going on in ops which she believes she could handle or assist. Of course, I'm sure you'll

70

have no problem."

"You mean that my more forceful personality might be of use in this case like with the Lufthansa stewardesses." Nate said. "Thanks a lot."

"Don't mention it, Nate," Bill said, smiling. "I'm constantly looking to provide you with the widest possible field experience."

***

At the end of the day, the two officers sat on the verandah of the Serena Hotel sipping *Tusker* beer and looking back toward the city as the Kenyatta tower began to reflect the orange light of the lowering sun. Bill was first to break the silence. "I really like the Brits," he said, "but they have left this country with that awful British tradition of warm beer. On a day like this, in a country like this, in a good hotel like this, we're sitting here in an otherwise perfect situation, sipping warm beer. It's no wonder they lost their empire. I'll bet the real reason for all the insurrections and freedom movements in the '60's was the built-up frustration at their damn hot beer. Talking about little irritations, how did the day go with Adele? Did you need your forceful personality or not?"

Nate exhaled slowly and thoughtfully before he spoke. "One thing is for sure," he said. "she definitely is very smart and has her own ideas about things. But I did find out why some of the prints aren't first rate; they're just muddy. She's opening the enlarger lens to full aperture, blasting the paper, then developing for only a few seconds—thinks it will save time. She estimates she's saving maybe 20-30 seconds per print."

Nate paused to see if Bill was going to react to his discovery, but he continued to stare off toward the city skyline in silence. "I know it seems logical to us that the small saving in time, if there really is one, would be completely offset by the better quality of the prints if she developed longer," he said, "but the only way I could get her to change her procedure was to point out that if she developed longer to increase the contrast, she could simply Xerox the prints containing only text instead of having to make multiple prints. Since doc copy seems to be her main assignment, it really would save a lot of time. She finally bought that. Maybe the problem is fixed."

"Did I hear a 'maybe' in there?" Bill asked with a huge grin on his face. "Didn't you use your stronger personality to drive the point home?"

"Yes," Nate said, "I surely did, but Adele also has a strong personality and ideas which are not easily altered. I now know why I got her while you took the case officers."

"Nothing," Bill said, "beats on-the-job training. You'll thank me for this later or you could just thank me now and get it over with."

"I'll wait," Nate said.

"A reasonable decision," Bill continued, "because just this afternoon, while you and Adele were in the dark, or at least one of you was in the dark, Clint suddenly informed me that he had changed his mind. He now thinks it would be good if the case officers learned a little about darkroom work just as a backup in case Adele should be out for some reason. I told him it had been our experience that it was better to train another secretary as the backup because the COs don't usually like it, they don't normally have time so for it so they never get really good at it, and finally I gently suggested that it really wasn't their job. I suggested we train Brenda as a backup instead of the CO's. He thought it over, but decided he wanted the COs to do it anyway. Turns out he thinks it would be a good exercise in that it would give Adele some experience in training as well as increase her own competence."

"Ouch!" Nate said. "First, I already know Adele isn't about to let *anyone* into that darkroom; she regards it as her personal property. Second, I can't imagine what misinformation she might pass on the these poor guys if she does train them. Any chance Clint might reconsider?"

"Nate," Bill said, "one of the primary things you have to learn in the field is to accurately estimate just how much discussion you can safely have with the COS if there's a difference of opinion, realizing of course that you must never openly disagree with him. I can't do any more. You'll have to do the best you can."

"Waiter!" Nate yelled, "I'll have another beer. Please make sure it's as hot as the last one."

***

As they headed for Clint's office, neither technician felt talkative. Although they had received no indication that anything was wrong, Bill was concerned, saying that a surprise summons from the COS always meant something unusual had happened which invariably meant either that a new requirement had come up or that something was not going right with the current TDY. Bill had admitted that on rare occasions he had been called in to receive a personal invitation to a dinner or a reception, but he knew this station was a bit too big for that. It was generally only in the smaller stations that the COS ever invited techs to anything much beyond a working lunch or a drink after work. To confirm Bill's suspicions, the two met billowing cigar smoke as soon as they opened the door. "Sit down," Clint said to them through the haze.

They waited while Clint took one last hit from the current cigar. "Thank God for a good, nasty, satisfying vice," he said as he stubbed out the butt in the ash tray made from an elephant's foot, "otherwise life would be like eating one huge bran muffin. How's the darkroom training?"

"Fine," Nate said, " Adele seems completely capable of doing the job and we've figured out what's been the problem with the prints."

"You think she can train the COs alright?" Clint said. "I mean can she get them to where they could develop a roll of film and make prints if they had to?"

"Yes, certainly," Nate said, "she thoroughly understands all the processes."

"You think she needs any special equipment beyond what she has now?" Clint asked.

"No," Nate said, now clearly beginning to wonder what the questioning was all about, "you have a very good, completely furnished darkroom."

"What about these Paterson reels," Clint said making a dismissing motion with his hands. "Any reason why we have to have 'em?"

Nate looked at Bill before answering, but it was clear that Bill had no more idea what was wrong than did he. "No, Clint," Nate said, "there's plenty of regular stainless steel Nikor reels in the darkroom. I mentioned the Patersons to Adele because they're a lot easier to load for someone who is either new to darkroom work or someone who might have trouble with the Nikors. They make it very easy to stay away from purple hearts even for folks who aren't experienced technicians. For the complete newcomers, there's even a way to start threading the film onto the reel in the light. They're almost foolproof. They're new on the market. I thought Adele might find it easier to train the CO's in loading the film if she let them use the Patersons. I offered to send some down here at no charge..."

Nate did not actually finish his comments, but simply ran out of steam as he began to see what the problem might be. He looked again at Bill, but there was no indication that Bill had yet thought of anything. Nate decided to take a guess: "Does Adele not want the Patersons?" he asked.

As Clint fumbled around in his desk drawer for a new package of cigars, he said without looking back at Nate, "You know, sometimes a little sensitivity develops in some folks who aren't totally confident in their skills. I've noticed that sometimes it turns out better if the management shows confidence in such an employee even if they aren't absolutely sure of the person's capability right at the moment—gives the employee confidence, keeps their morale high, encourages them to do more, keeps them out of the COS's office. You think Adele can use those stainless steel reels pretty good herself, maybe good enough to train the COs on them if she took the time and they were motivated to learn?"

"Yes, surely," Nate stammered, "I never thought Adele couldn't use the reels or that she couldn't train others how to use them. I just thought it would be easier for the COs, since they don't usually keep in practice..."

"I understand," Clint said, "but maybe for right now you should put off sending the extra reels. I'll be sure to send a note to Dave up in NORTECH if I see we need them."

Bill could see that Nate was getting ready to either defend himself or tell Clint more than he wanted to hear about Adele. Before Nate could speak, he said, "Well, Clint, I guess that about does it unless you need us for something else. We're scheduled to leave late tonight. As usual it's been a great visit—can't wait for the next one. Any messages for Dave or anyone else at NORTECH?"

"Nah," Clint said, standing to offer his hand as he spoke, "just tell him I'll see him at the Chiefs' Conference."

"Will do," Bill said as he shook Clint's hand.

"Nice to meet you, young fellah," Clint said as he shook Nate's hand, "good luck in your career. Don't let the old whores ruin your morality."

For only a fraction of a second as he shook hands, Nate hesitated, making Bill hold his breath ever so slightly, then he said, "Very good to meet you, sir. I hope I'll get a lot more trips to your station."

"I'm sure you will," Clint said with a huge parting grin on his face.

Even before the door to Clint's office had completely shut, Nate started to explain what had happened in the darkroom, but Bill forbade him to continue. They had tied up all the administrative loose ends of the TDY, checked the station technical inventory, said good-bye to all their friends, had lunch, returned to the hotel to pack up for the trip, and were sitting again on the verandah of the hotel before Bill would let Nate talk about his adventure with Adele.

"Can we talk about this thing now?" Nate asked.

"Yes," Bill said, "now is the time. There was no sense in talking about it before and there's no use in talking about it now as far as an explanation goes because I think I know exactly what happened. The only reason to talk about it is to make it one more in the long series of what we now call learning experiences, which used to be called the school of hard knocks."

"All I did," Nate said, "was suggest the simpler reels as a way to speed up the learning process. It seems crazy to me not to take advantage of doing something the easy way if it's available. She didn't want to do it because she thought it was unprofessional to use the new technology, that it would be good for the COs to struggle a little with the Nikors, that it would make them more appreciative of her efforts. We argued a tiny bit."

"Then you probably told her it was the results that mattered," Bill continued, "and that the COs would be more likely to want to do the work if they had some initial success instead of a string of purple hearts showing how klutzy they were."

"Yes," Nate said with mild surprise sounding in his voice, "almost word for word."

Bill laughed quietly as he took another sip of the warm beer. "I thought something like that might happen he said. Adele will never change until she either becomes a case officer or one of them kills her. I know, from other drink-after-work occasions with Clint's COs, that what concerns them is not Adele's technical work, but her judgment, or as we country boys would say, her common sense. They are concerned she could pose a real threat if they unleashed her in operations so they are determined it will not happen. As for you and your little dust-up with her, don't worry. Clint already knows the situation."

"Then why," Nate said, "does he put up with it?"

"First," Bill began," Clint is now an important COS in charge of an important station, but remember he was a case officer before. He still knows how to evaluate people, knows exactly what kind of person Adele is, and knows how to control her—most of the time. He knows what a problem she is to deal with, but she does for him one of those essential, dull jobs that has to be done. She's a pain in the ass, but she's *his* pain in the ass.

"To a large degree, each field station takes the personality of the COS whether it's a big station or a three-person outpost, but there are other people at any station who have no important rank but who have enormous influence on daily life. Right off the top of my head, I can name the support chief as the most influential. He can affect where you live while you're at a given station, how soon you get a housing problem remedied, how easy it is to get anything done either in your home or in the local community. In some countries, he can even affect how well or badly you eat when the food has to be imported. Other than the COS, he's going to have the most significant effect on your existence, more even than the ambassador or the president of the country, but you'll almost never see his name officially mentioned. The chief's secretary is another very important person. If she is a platinum bitch, everything will be harder for you. You'll have a tougher time seeing the COS, getting your cable traffic out, making contact when you're out of the embassy, simply getting in and out of the office, and an awful lot of other things.

"Most of the time, these people are excellent. But that reflects the care with which they are chosen. I know several COSs who will pick their support chief before they pick their deputy or any of their case officers if they have the chance. It's these people who make the station run on a daily basis. Do you remember how Clint said that folks like Adele keep others out of his office? Although the COS has total power over all his people and doesn't hesitate to use it when necessary, he would rather upset almost anyone other than those few who can keep his days free from worry over little things. He wants to collect intelligence, not deal with somebody's housing problem or somebody's hurt feelings. That's where Adele comes in.

"She works hard, quickly, and diligently. With her on the job, he never has to listen to a CO complaining that it's been two weeks since he submitted his hot operational film for development. She also orders all technical materials and supplies, hands out batteries for tape recorders and other equipment, keeps up his inventory, photographs all station parties and other gatherings, sees to the maintenance of his copiers, and God knows what else. He would much prefer to pacify her since she affects him every day, than to be totally fair to a tech who visits for a few days every three to six months. Remember this, Nate: the COS will *always* side with the one who keeps him happy on a daily basis, and so would you if you were in his position. Does that help?"

Nate hesitated before answering. "Yes," he said finally, "I see what you mean."

"Nate," Bill said with a little exasperation in his voice, "there was no contest. You never had a chance. But look at it this way: although Adele may aggravate visiting techs worse than a bad case of chiggers, she will never be in charge of anything but a darkroom or a storeroom. She will never become a case officer.

"Let's head out to the airport. I don't think I can handle another hot beer."

"That's it!" Nate said. "Adele is like hot beer: aggravating as hell, but essential if there' s nothing better available."

"Let's go," Bill said. "I can see you're ready. It's on to Mifuna, City of Light."

Chapter 8

"This COS is another decent fellow," Bill said to Nate as they sat at dinner the evening before their arrival at the embassy, "but he's never failed to propose some kind of operation that is technically outlandish. He's only a free thinker though; he's not malicious. Just don't laugh when you hear the proposals."

"Until I get Adele out of my head," Nate said, "I don't think I'm going to be too jovial about anything."

"Aaah, forget it!" Bill said. "There's going to be dozens of times when you're going to be implicated in a screw-up not of your own making, or be assigned the complete blame for it. Just remember, the COS knows what really happened in every case. If he doesn't send a cable home, you're fine."

"Still...," Nate began, but stopped without finishing the thought. "You're right, Bill. Let's have another round. I'm starting to forget that hot beer in Nairobi already."

***

"Good morning!" John said, "welcome to Mifuna. Good to see you again, Bill. How's things at NORTECH?"

"We're busy as a tomcat at a mouse convention," Bill said, "but just as happy. Dave sends his regards and wants you to save a night for dinner with him during the Chief's Conference. This is Nate, new on board."

"Welcome, Nate," John said enthusiastically, then turned back to Bill. "By all means, Bill, tell Dave he's got a date, but that I have to know if he'll respect me in the morning."

"Dave says his middle name is Respect," Bill said.

"His middle name," John said, "is Raising Hell. I've never had even a reasonable night out with him. We somehow always wind up at some nefarious spot known only to him and the most questionable locals. Now sit down and let me tell you about some fun technical problems that have come up just in time for your visit."

As the two officers took seats, Nate glanced at Bill who winked in return.

As usual John Grun was blazing with enthusiasm. As he spoke he first sat on his chair, then got up to lean on his desk. After a few more seconds he began to walk around the room constantly fiddling with things while making jabbing and swirling hand motions to accompany his narrative. The swift motions coupled with his short statue made Nate think of the office-boy character in old TV sit-coms.

"I know you're here basically just to give us our periodic technical check-up," John began, "but something new and really interesting has just happened. Here's the deal: There's a local group here that intends to cause trouble for our friend, President Bouaki. We've got an asset close to them so we know what's brewing, but our man isn't in their inner circle. He knows only one of them for a certainty and this one is certainly too dumb to be a leader, otherwise he wouldn't have blabbed to our asset. Through him we know they intend to meet on Sunday at the weekly soccer matches. What we need is to get ID photos of the plotters. What do you think?"

Both officers were silent for a moment. Bill glanced at Nate, but it was obvious Nate was not going to say anything; he was learning quickly. "Will your asset be at the match, John? If he is, can he support carrying a camera to get some snapshots?"

"No," John said, "not a chance. He has never owned a camera and if he showed up with one, even a cheap, snapshot model might cause suspicion."

"Right," Bill said, "just checking. Will he be there at all? Is there some way you can corral these guys for us so that we know who our targets will be and where they will be?"

"I can't risk it, Bill," John said. "I'm afraid if he shows up it might cause a problem for him, especially if something bad eventually happens to some of the plotters. We won't know who's who at the matches. We just know they will be there. His friend will certainly be in attendance, but I haven't met him and we don't have a photo of him."

"That's a tough one," Bill said. "If we don't know who to photograph, I don't see how we can be of much help."

"Photograph them all!" John said. "When we find his friend in the photos, those with him will be the right group. I'm sure my asset will know at least half the people at the matches so he'll surely identify the people in the photos with his friend; Mifuna City is a small town, really."

"All?" Bill said, glancing quickly at Nate whose face showed surprise even though he was clearly trying to maintain his professional aplomb, "How many do you think will be there?"

"Oh, I don't know," John said. "It's not like the World Cup—maybe a hundred, maybe a few more. One good thing is that if they intend to sit around and plot, they can't be players, they'll be gathered up into a group. They'll be young men not children. No women will be involved. All that narrows it down, right?"

"Yes," Bill said, "I suppose it does. Is there any way you can get us to a choke point, like a ticket gate or a walkway, or anything else that forces everyone to pass the same point?"

John laughed, "It's just an open field, guys. Anybody can come from anywhere. Besides, if they're the least bit smart they'll drift in at different times and from different directions."

"Any white folks ever attend these matches?" Bill asked.

"Not likely," John said, "maybe a couple of Peace Corps volunteers, but that's about it. It's a local Sunday afternoon tradition. People just go there to have a little fun, talk a little, drink some beer; you know what it's like, Bill."

"Right," Bill said," can you get us some cover at least; maybe a van or a house nearby or maybe there's a picnic area or at least some shade trees we might sit under? With the equipment we have with us, we'd have to be no farther than 100 feet away to have any chance at getting ID quality photos."

John sat back in his chair, forming his fingers into a ridge of triangles as he considered. Finally, he touched the triangle of his two index fingers to his lips for an instant, then shook his head. "No," he said, "there's nothing."

"About all that leaves us," Bill said, "is for us to show up at the match and pretend to be taking pictures of the action. Is that operationally feasible?"

"No," John said, "a couple of white men, openly taking pictures on the very day of a clandestine meeting, when white people almost never show up, would be a dead giveaway. What can you do other than that?"

Bill again glanced at Nate before answering. "The only thing I can think of, John, is a walk-through. It would be hit-and-miss of the highest order. We'd have to conceal our cameras in some way too, or else we might draw too much attention. Do you happen to have any concealment devices for cameras here at the station by any chance?"

John considered for a moment before answering. "I do think we have a bag of some sort. As I recall, it was pouched down here for an op that never went down. It was here when I showed up. I think I saw it in the storeroom about a year ago."

"Let us take a look for it then," Bill said, "and if it won't be a problem, we'd also like to see the soccer field so we know better what we're up against on Sunday. Do you think we can visit it without causing any problems?"

"Tell you what," John said, "I don't want you to case the area the way I'm sure you'd like. I don't want to chance having two white men looking the place over just before a meeting; word might get back. I can have Jim Harrigan, one of our COs drive you around the area, but

I don't want you on the ground over there. Would that help?"

"Yes, of course," Bill said, "whatever we learn, it will be helpful."

"Do you know Jim?" John said. "He's been here longer than I have; thought you might have met before."

"Yes, I know him," Bill said. "He'll be a great help. If we can, let's go this afternoon."

***

"I don't envy you guys on this one," Jim said as he drove toward the soccer field. "John is really reaching this time."

"Tell me about it," Bill said. "All we have to do is photograph everybody at the match in one walk-through while not arousing any suspicion among men who are plotting against the government—and that's after we fabricate some CDs for the cameras. Do you have any ideas that might help, Jim?"

"Your only possible cover is pretending to be Peace Corps volunteers," Jim said. "Their compound is just over the road at the border of the field so it's conceivable they might wander through and take a minute to watch the games. I can give you a couple of my kids' backpacks and a couple of floppy hats like they wear, but that's about it. It might disguise Nate since he looks young, but you, Bill, look older than dirt so I suggest you pretend to be Nate's father on a visit if you talk to anybody. It might get you through the field once, but don't try to sit in the stands or stop for more than a minute."

"Thanks, Jim," Bill said, "you always had a way of putting the best face on a problem."

"Don't mention it," Jim said with a huge grin. "Just helping out whenever I can. Here we are."

Jim slowed the car as they passed the field on the main road. Today only a few ragged boys were kicking around a ball which might have once been a soccer ball, but was now so worn that it was completely gray, the color of the grassless playing field. Perpendicular to the main road a rack of rickety stands stood a few yards from the field. Even from the road, it was obvious their upper rows were damaged and partly missing. Only the lowest row seemed intact enough to support the weight of any onlookers. The field and the stands were in the middle of a large open area which was strewn with trash of all kinds, but completely bereft of any sort of cover.

"Damn!" Bill said. "There's no way to hide, no way to blend in, no quick escape if anything goes wrong! We'll stand out like two turds in a punchbowl!"

Jim laughed. "Bill," he said, "you've got to stop mincing words. Tell it like it is why don't you."

For a moment there was complete silence in the car, then they all burst out into laughter. They were still laughing when they passed Jim's favorite local bar where they stopped for a couple of beers. "Well, Jim," Bill said finally, "what do you think?"

"Even with my disguises," Jim said, "even if you manage to hide the cameras, even if the action in the match is at fever pitch when you cross, you still might get accosted. Since you're white folks, I doubt they'd take a chance on shooting you though."

"Thanks," Bill said, "I certainly feel better now."

They began to laugh once more, but the laughter now died quickly as they began to accept the situation presented them and to try to find some way to get the job done. "Is there any reason why Peace Corps volunteers, or any other white folks, would walk through that field other than just wandering around?" Bill asked. "Is there anything on the other side that anyone might want to visit: a store, an office, a theater, a church..."

"Let's go look," Jim said.

On the back side of the field away from the main road, the streets became narrow, only partially paved, very twisty, and entirely local. As Jim eased the car through the clutter, the unabashed stares of the locals clearly told them it was not the usual thing for strangers to be in the area. "It doesn't look good," Jim said as they surveyed the surroundings. "Wait!" he said suddenly, "look at this!"

As Jim spoke a dingy, open air bar came into view on their left. It opened onto the narrow, dusty street on one side and onto the scraggly soccer field on the other. "With any luck you might be able to watch the field from there while you have a beer," Jim said. "You might be able to wait there until you see a group form up somewhere before you make your pass."

No one spoke until they had driven past the bar. Jim had just begun to speculate on its operational possibilities when they encountered increased crowding along the sides of the road leading to an area where a good many pedestrians were milling around in the road itself. "Market," Jim said, "that's good. Gives you a possible reason to be on the opposite side of the bar; a lot of Peace Corps people buy on the local economy. You could conceivably be in this area to buy something here, then stop off for a beer at the bar on the way back to the compound. It's not good, but it might work. Now let's get out of here before we draw any more attention than we have already."

Back at the embassy the officers separated, but not before they had agreed to meet at the end of the work day to plan for the operation. Bill and Nate went to the station storeroom/darkroom to look over all the technical material that had accumulated there since the last OTS officer had taken the time to send back to NORTECH what was not needed and worth salvaging. As they plowed through the items, Bill vacillated between being irritated that so many things had been allowed to lie useless in the small station, and hopeful that among the haphazard collection there might be something they could use. "Disguise materials," he mumbled as he searched, "Uher tape recorder, 500mm cat lens—we have got to send that thing back—half a signaling system, old miniature tape recorder, Robot Star camera, lamp CD, bookend CD, two-way radio base station, old photo chemicals, out of date film... Here it is, Nate!"

From the pile, Bill had extracted a black bag. He pulled it open so that Nate could look inside. "Yep!" Nate said, "sure enough!"

The two officers took the bag out of the dim light of the darkroom into the brilliance of the fluorescent lighting of the office. After a few seconds, Bill said, "Damn!" as he handed the bag to Nate.

As Nate took the bag from him, he immediately saw the problem: "It's a woman's bag," he said.

"Yes," Bill said, "but that's OK. The problem is, it was built to take the Robot, not one of our FS-1s. At least now we know. In the next few hours, we've got to cobble up two concealments for our cameras instead of one. Let's head out to the local shops."

✻✻✻

Early the next day, Jim found the two officers hard at work in the storeroom. Scattered around them were bits of Styrofoam, pieces of leather, assorted small tools, a tube of glue, black markers and many items he could not identify. Nate had glued a Styrofoam construction to the side of an old cardboard box. In the bright light of a gooseneck lamp, Bill was completely intent in very carefully cutting away tiny pieces of leather from a small man's purse of obvious local manufacture. After surveying the scene for a few seconds, he said, "How's it going?"

"Actually," Bill said, "we won't know until tomorrow about whether the CDs will fool anybody, but I wanted to ask you what you thought of our operational plan: We conceal one camera in the cardboard box under something, maybe fruit, that we could have bought at the market. The other one will be in this fag bag we bought from a local shop. One camera shoots through the gap in the box where the panels almost meet. The other one shoots from the bag through this medallion; it's actually one half of a pair of earrings."

Jim looked closely at both of the unfinished CDs, but finally shook his head in indecision. "I can't tell about the CDs right now guys, but the operational reasoning is sound. If you show up at the bar carrying something that looks like it came from the market, that makes sense. You stop for a few beers after your shopping, then head back toward the Peace Corps compound. How much more do you have to do here?"

"A lot," Bill said. "First, we've got to finish the CDs, then determine the light loss we'll have when the cameras shoot through the reduced openings. If it's too severe, we may have to redo the CDs or try something else—if there's time. Then we test our equipment, put fresh batteries in the FS-1s, load the film, decide on the camera settings; then go out to shop for something to put in the box. It'll be a very long day and we'll need to start early again tomorrow."

"Good luck!" Jim said. "Let's do a little more planning right now. First, I'll make sure the Marine guard knows you may be here late. Let him lock up when you leave. I'll meet you here tomorrow at maybe 11 A.M. You get your gear together, we drive to my house to talk over the final details, I outfit you with the best Peace Corps props I can come up with, and we have lunch there. What do you think?"

"At least for now," Bill said, "it sounds fine. Can you make sure the Marine guard will let us in early tomorrow?"

"Yes," Jim said. "I'll start making the arrangements right now. See you tomorrow. Good luck today."

As Jim closed the door behind him, Bill turned to Nate who was mumbling to himself as he tried to fit the Konica FS-1 into the Styrofoam saddle he had glued to the side of the box. "Well, Nate," he said, "what do you think?"

Nate stopped talking to the resisting camera for a moment as he looked back at Bill. "I think it's about time we got to the adventure and romance part," he said.

***

"OK," Jim said as the three officers moved from the dining room to the small, private room he used as his den, "let's go over it to make sure we know exactly what should happen. I'll drop you off just past the market so that you can approach the bar from the right direction. You go in, sit down where you can easily see the soccer field, order a beer and wait. You might have to wait for a good while; nothing is going to start on time in Africa, especially not a cabal. There's no sense in moving until a group forms up somewhere on the field and stays together for a few minutes. If you think you see something suspicious then make your walk-by. Don't try to loiter around the group unless you can stop for a minute to look at some particularly good action on the field. If anyone, repeat, anyone, takes notice of you, move out quickly. If you don't get the plotters, we're no worse off, but if you alert them or raise the station's profile in this, John will have a cow. Remember, he knows the chances of success are not great; he's just trying to take advantage of a situation. Starting about 2:30, I'll be waiting for you out of sight near the Peace Corps compound. If you haven't seen anything by 4:00, abort the operation. You can't possibly stay in the bar any longer than that. As a matter of fact, if I were them, I would station my counter surveillance at the bar, so be careful even while you're there."

"Jim," Bill said, "what do you think our chances are—off the record, of course."

"There's always a chance," Jim began, "that a long shot will work; you might be completely successful. However, my best guess is that you'll get pictures of some folks, but they might not be the ones we want. First, you have to pick the right group by guesswork. Second, our asset's friend has to be with them to give any credibility to the information. Third, they may not show up at all. John isn't totally sure of the quality of his asset just yet; he thinks it's possible the man might have tried to impress him by passing on gossip as opposed to fact."

"So John isn't completely sure of the asset," Bill said, "but he can't lose. No matter what happens, he gets another piece of information about the reliability of his man."

"Right," Jim said, "you're always checking the asset at every opportunity throughout the life of the operation. Besides, any CO who believes all of anything any asset ever tells him is a complete idiot. It's almost one o'clock. Let's saddle up."

The two officers checked their equipment as they began final preparations for the op. Both checked their shutter speed settings, the sharp focus distance, that the film was firmly attached to the take-up sprockets, that the button on the shutter release cable was easy to locate by feel, and that the film rewind knob would not be bound by the CD. Bill had decided to carry the man's purse, reasoning that only someone his age would allow himself to be seen carrying a fag bag. Nate would use the cardboard box CD. He now placed a shallow layer of bananas over the Styrofoam, which he had blackened with a magic marker, then both officers shot two frames each with the cameras mounted in the CD's to make sure the film transport was clear and that any light-fogged area on the film leader had been advanced onto the take-up sprocket. In the quiet of Jim's den, the zipping sound of the motor drive of the FS-1s sounded loud enough to make him very uneasy, but Bill assured him it would not be noticeable outside, especially during a loud soccer match. When the two officers had donned their backpacks, floppy hats and sunglasses, they were ready.

***

As the two officers sat in the dilapidated bar at a table offering a good view of the field, they both began to feel the power of the African heat. Nate mentioned that the cool beer was a good idea whether or not they actually took any pictures. Even in the heat, a group of small boys were racing through a never-ending match which apparently had no rules for play or designated teams for sorting out the players.

"I don't see how they can play so hard in this heat," Bill said. "I don't think I could move that fast today even if our targets draw down on us...but they won't," he added quickly. "Jim says they won't have many guns available even if they eventually try to overthrow the government. I know of one coup in West Africa where thirty-two men almost took over the country."

"I suppose, though," Nate said, "that the thirty-two *did* have guns. As the old farmer said about trains, it only takes one to kill you. I figure it's the same with guns."

Bill laughed. "Yes," he said, "that's true, but today, I don't think we're in any danger. If they had guns, I doubt they'd bring them to a soccer field where anyone, including one of the very few local policemen, might see them."

Nate started to answer, but stopped without speaking as he nodded toward the field, "The grownups just started to arrive," he said.

Over the next hour, a mixture of young men, older men, and a few women drifted onto the field, taking seats either on the first row of the rickety stands or on the borders of the dusty playing field, but no suspicious group formed up. After another half hour, the officers were beginning to wonder if there would even be anything for them to photograph. They had stayed longer in the bar than they had expected already although they were still within the window for action that Jim had specified. In addition, Nate now claimed he had noticed a difference in the behavior of the bartender; he was sure the man had begun to watch them. After a few more minutes, Bill agreed with him. They decided they would move off in ten minutes whether they saw anything worth shooting or not.

Ten minutes later, as they stepped from the shaded heat of the bar into the blasting heat of the field, they noticed two men heading in the direction of two other men who had been standing for some time just beyond the end of the ragged bleachers. "Damn!" Bill said as they walked toward the field, "if this is the beginning of a meeting, we're going to either miss it altogether or hit it just as they collect! After waiting the whole afternoon, the timing couldn't be worse! Damn!"

"Hold on a minute, pardner," Nate said, "I'll buy us a minute or two."

As he spoke, Nate handed the banana-box CD to Bill. Not having any idea what Nate had in mind, Bill automatically took the box. Nate smiled at him, then turned back toward the bar. "Nate...!" Bill said as urgently as possible without raising his voice as Nate walked away.

Bill stood transfixed as Nate went first to the table where they had sat. There he took off his sunglasses, pretending to look for something.

After completing his examination of the area around the table, he went back to the street entrance of the bar as if he were going to backtrack even farther but stopped there as if to ponder the situation. Instead, he turned back to the bar and walked over to the bartender. "Oh, shit!" Bill said very quietly.

After a moment's discussion with the bartender, he returned again to Bill who had not moved an inch since the reckless pantomime had begun. "What did you ask him?" Bill said with some consternation.

"I just asked him if he had noticed whether there had been a folded map in the banana box when we showed up. I told him I had just realized I had lost it somewhere. He didn't know, of course, so I asked him if he had one I could buy—fooled him completely."

"We'll know that when we get safely across this soccer field," Bill said, "now that I've stood here like a statue in front of God and everybody until *nobody* could have failed to notice me...us!"

"Well then," Nate said, grinning broadly, "we'll just have to be extra cool when we walk by our men."

"Right!" Bill said as he handed back the box. "Let's do it before they stop the game to get an even better look at us."

As they moved out toward the border of the field nearest the stands, it seemed to Bill that he was watching the scene from a distance. He had found that throughout his career it had always seemed this way whenever he felt the tingles of possible danger. "Let's fire one more test frame just to make us feel better," he said.

Both officers pressed the shutter release button once. Bill heard his own camera advance the film with a muffled whine, but he heard nothing from Nate's CD. "Did you fire?" he said.

"Yes," Nate said. "Did you?"

"Sure enough," Bill said, "looks like we're OK. When we get close, don't try anything fancy, just hold the hammer down. Let's hope they hold still; we can't chase them."

The two officers only glanced quickly at the small group of men as they approached, making a great display of their attention to the game, looking out at the field, pointing at it with their free hands, talking about the action, hoping that while they could not help being noticed, they might at least not appear suspicious.

When they were within twenty feet of the small group, each officer found the slight roundness of the shutter release button and held it down. Neither looked at the targets as they passed by. Although the passage took only seconds, to the officers it seemed to proceed in slow motion. Once they were clear of the playing field, it then seemed to take only a couple of minutes until they found themselves at the edge of the main highway opposite the driveway into the Peace Corps compound. Here, where there was a logical reason to pause, they finally looked back at the field. Nothing seemed amiss: the match continued, the spectators watched as before, the small target group still stood together, nobody seemed to be looking their way. "Looks like we didn't upset anybody at least," Bill said. "Unfortunately, that could mean there was nobody there to be upset."

They crossed the unpaved driveway toward the Peace Corps compound. As they reached the rough side street passing beside it, they turned right. In only a few seconds, Jim pulled up to them. "How'd it go?" he said.

"The good news is the locals didn't seem to notice us," Bill said. "The bad news is that it could mean there was nothing going on to make them pay any attention to us. We'll know when John sees the prints."

***

"Damn!" Bill said as he reviewed the prints, "I didn't get one single, usable shot! Thank God, you got enough good ones to ID at least three of the group."

"Ho hum," Nate said in exaggerated indifference, "just another successful mobile surveillance. I've always wondered why you old farts always make it out to be so hard."

"It's because this is the most difficult photo surveillance there is," Bill said in exasperation. "You've got to keep the shutter speed high to keep away from blurred images. You've got to get within 20-25 feet for a 50mm lens or the grain of the film won't allow resolution of the faces. You've got to hope the target won't be wearing sunglasses or that he won't look away from the camera just when you take the picture. You've got to aim accurately without looking through the viewfinder. If you put a four-man team on the street and one of them gets one ID quality photo, it's a great success. If..."

Bill stopped talking and looked up from the prints to see the smile on Nate's face. "Dammit!" he said, "you know all this. You're just trying to aggravate me...and doing a damn good job of it!"

Nate slapped Bill on the shoulder as his grin reached its greatest expanse. "It's just that you old farts try too hard and worry too much, and the more you struggle, the worse it gets."

Bill stared at Nate for several seconds before shaking his head and looking back at the prints, "I'll try to remember that," he said.

A half hour later, they delivered the prints to John who left immediately to show them to his agent. A couple of hours later, he was back. "My man doesn't know any of them," he said. "Looks like we washed out on this one."

"Sorry, John," Bill said, "it was the best we could do under the circumstances."

"Don't worry," John said, "it was a long shot anyhow, but we've got another chance."

"Another photo surveillance?" Bill asked.

"No," John said, "something better. My asset says he's going out to meet with his contact tonight to have a few drinks. He's sure the contact will talk about the coup. He's going to pick up his contact in his car and believes he can get the conversation to take place there. He says we can bug his car if we want to. We ought to get the goods this time if there's anything to any of this."

"By the way," John said to Jim who had been sitting in on the meeting, "he claims his contact is close to Juba."

"Damn!" Jim said, "the deputy of Internal Security, maybe there's something here after all."

"Right!" John continued as he turned his attention back to the technical officers. "Now, can you two bug an automobile with the stuff we have on hand?"

For a moment neither officer spoke then Bill said, "I don't think so, John. We can't use a Uher, it's too big..."

"What about that funny little tape recorder," John asked, "the one that's not commercial. It's very flat at least and it's got some kind of a remote start, doesn't it?"

Again Bill hesitated, "It might be possible," he said finally, "if it works..."

"Great!" John said, "be ready at 7:00 tonight. We'll meet the agent just before he meets with his friend. Do you think an hour will be time enough for you to bug the car?"

Bill glanced at Nate before answering. "Well," he said, "with what we have to work with, we should have time to succeed or fail in an hour...if the recorder works, that is. It must have been in that storeroom for quite a while..."

"I know it will be fine," John said. "OTS never lets a COS down."

"Right," Bill said.

***

"I found it," Nate said. "For a while there, I thought it was a lost cause. But I don't see the remote or the mike, just the recorder."

The officers resumed their plundering through the miscellaneous equipment in the packed storeroom. Finally they managed to locate all the parts for the miniature recorder and four rolls of audio tape. "Now let's see if it works," Bill said.

When Bill pushed the "play" button, nothing happened. "Batteries?" he said mainly to himself. A moment later, both officers were convinced the batteries were the likely cause for failure. One of them, in particular, was so old it had a small, crescent-shaped rust stain on the bottom. "Let's head to the commo shop," Bill said. "The commo man will help us. They always do."

"Can we just buy some on the economy?" Nate asked. "I'm sure commo needs all the good batteries they have."

"You're right on both counts," Bill agreed, "but you can bet the commo batteries have been in the refrigerator since they were shipped so they're going to be better than any we can get locally. It's also true that the commo man will need them himself, but commo always helps out no matter what. For your rookie notebook: always remember that the commo man will always help you whether it's to give you the last of his good batteries, or to meet you at some god-forsaken airport while all the COs are at home sound asleep, or to look after your cover when some State Department dork starts asking stupid questions in the cafeteria, or to make sure you've got a place to go for a little entertainment when you've been left on your own in a country where the only electric lights are at the embassy and the local whorehouse, or to send your desperate plea for advice to the nearest regional base in back-channel traffic and not say anything about it to the COS. Of all the folks you'll ever meet in your career, the commo people will always be the most professional, the most dedicated, the most helpful... and generally the least appreciated by the station."

On their way to the commo shop, Bill continued to regale Nate with stories of the many times he had been saved by the assistance of commo officers. By the time they arrived at the door of the commo vault, he was sure Bill had spoken so highly of these officers that he had certainly jinxed himself this time. To his great surprise, however, it only took Bill five minutes to get a supply of brand new batteries from the commo man who had never seen Bill before, having arrived at the station after Bill's last visit. By the time they returned to the darkroom to work on the recorder, he was as convinced of the helpfulness of the commo officers as was Bill.

As usual, the instruction manual for the proprietary recorder had been lost, forcing the two officers to test each control both for its purpose and functionality. Since the small recorder did not have a speaker, the recorded tapes had to be transferred to a Uher recorder for playback, making the testing even more inefficient. They had just finished testing the recorder and were loading it with tape when John showed up at the door suggesting they head out for dinner on the way to the meeting with the agent. Bill said they would need a few more minutes, but that John should go on to dinner; they would meet him at the front of the embassy at 6:30.

After John's departure, the two officers sat silent in the quiet darkroom for a few minutes as both considered the task ahead. "OK," Bill said finally, "let's put our heads together and try to think this thing out as best we can. First, the one thing I know for sure from the audio boys is that you never bug a car if you can help it. There's too much interfering racket: the engine, the road noise, anything that rubs over the mike or muffles it in any way. It's a bitch. If the agent doesn't stop the car at just the right moment, we're dead—and that's if we do everything right."

"How are we going to hide the thing is what bothers me," Nate said. "The remote has to be close to the driver so he can turn on the recorder, the mike has to be as close to the passenger as possible, but both the mike and the remote are hard wired to the recorder. It's going to be like trying to keep an ear to the ground and straddle the fence at the same time—like politicians."

Bill looked up from the recorder to stare once more at Nate in consternation. "Nate," he said, "sometimes I think you're one of the most practical men I know. Other times, I think you just beamed in. We're facing that classical situation where an op is either going to be clandestine or candlestine in about thirty minutes. It's likely the very best we can hope for is that we do the right technical thing, convince

John of it, and get out of town before he changes his mind. Do you think you could get serious for the next little while?"

"Easy, pardner!" Nate said. "I *am* serious. This thing is going to be a mess. The way I see it, we can't count on finding any way to hide the recorder in the car. I vote we take along the fag bag, put the recorder in that if we have to and maybe just have the agent put it on the seat between the two of them. It's risky, but it might be our only option."

"Yes," Bill said, nodding his head, "that's good thinking. If we can't find a concealment in the car, we've at least got some sort of fall-back solution. We don't even know what kind of car the agent has and we've only got an hour at most no matter what. It stands to reason we aren't going to modify anything. We'll either discover some natural hiding place or just go with the fag bag. Now, what materials will we need?"

"The small tool kit, always," Nate said, "and a flashlight—and the one thing no tech ever leaves home without..."

"Duct tape!" both officers said together.

"Right," Bill said. "Anything else?"

"A roll of toilet paper?" Nate suggested.

***

"Now this guy's a good one," John said as he drove through the twilight toward the meeting place. "He's fearless, smart, and needs money really bad. If you fellows can come up with anything that isn't obviously suicidal, he'll go along with it. Here we are."

John turned the car off the main road onto an unpaved track that became increasingly sandy as they headed toward the beach. After a few minutes of driving, a pair of headlights appeared behind them and followed them closely as they proceeded toward the water. "That's him," John said. "Unlike most Africans, he's never late, always uses good common sense, and watches out for his own ass—makes it a lot easier on the CO."

John drove until the increasingly sandy road dead-ended at a dense clump of scrub with three large palm trees stretching tall above. "Easy place to describe for a meeting," John explained.

The officers got out of their car as the agent got out of his. After a few moments spent in greeting, introductions, and small talk, John announced that he and the agent were going to take up positions on a small rise from which they could see a ways down the road they had just traversed. John warned the two technical officers to be ready to bug out immediately if he came back and told them to do so. They assured him their work on the automobile would not take long, nor involve noticeable disturbance to the interior of the agent's car. Both he and the agent nodded their approval. "Let's go," John said.

"Wait," the agent said, "I need to make sure I'm ready." As he spoke, he drew a large caliber gun from his belt. It had been completely hidden by the typical loose shirt designed to be worn outside the pants so it surprised the officers. He opened the door of the car so that he could use the dome light to see what he was doing. As he checked the huge weapon in the weak, yellow light, making sure each chamber contained a bullet and that the safety was on, the two officers stared in immobile silence. When he was satisfied, he nodded to John and the two men headed off up the road. The hissing sound of their footsteps in the sand sounded very loud as they walked away. Only after the sound had completely faded did the two officers turn their attention to the agent's car.

"I thought none of these locals were supposed to have guns!" Nate said. "Did you see that size of that thing! If he shoots somebody with it, they've got real trouble! It won't be a trip to the hospital; it'll be to the morgue!"

"OK, Nate, OK!" Bill said. "I guess Jim was just making a general statement when he said there weren't many guns around. Besides it's only one gun and it's on our side. What was it anyway, a .45?"

"It must have been at least a .46 as big as it was," Nate said. "By the way did you notice those pearl handles on that thing—a real pimp protector if I've ever seen one."

Bill stared at Nate for several seconds without speaking. "Nate..." he began, then shook his head. "Let's stop wasting time and look at this car."

"Right, pardner," Nate said, "it's a Mercedes. I never would have guessed that."

"It's only the really good cars that can stand a long life in Africa," Bill said. "If the car is more than a few years old you can bet it's either German or Japanese. Let's look it over."

Bill opened the driver's side door while Nate opened the other door. Neither spoke as they searched the old Mercedes for some likely hiding place for their small recorder. Finally, Bill looked over at Nate who was still poking around under the dash. "I don't see a damned thing," he said, "looks like the fag bag or nothing."

For a minute Nate did not answer. "Hold on!" he said finally. "Look here, this isn't the original carpet by a long shot. Looks like it's from the local carpet rip-off shop. It isn't even glued down."

As Nate spoke, he pulled back the entire piece of carpet covering the firewall on the passenger side. "How about just taping the recorder high up here, under the dash, and then taping the carpet down over it?"

"If we can place the mike and the remote," Bill said, "it looks like it might work."

Nate was now on his back under the dash looking up into the maze of wiring to which local mechanics had added, over the years, their own unique solutions to electrical malfunctions. "No problem," he said, "there's no way anyone will notice one more wire in all this mess. There's also a good place to mount the mike: here on this cross-brace behind the ashtray. Nobody can see it and it will be completely open to the air if the agent doesn't shut up the ashtray. I can tape the remote activate right next to it. All he'll have to do is reach near the ashtray to start recording."

"Do it!" Bill said, handing the duct tape to Nate.

When the two officers showed their work to John and the agent, both seemed highly pleased. After a very brief instruction in the use of the recorder, the agent said he was ready to go. Bill admonished him that he must try to get his contact to talk in the car, but with the engine off, explaining the difficulty of recording amid noises from the engine and the road. He clearly understood the problem, but was not certain he could engineer the conversation as completely as they demanded. He would do his best. Once again, just before the agent drove away, they all shook hands. "Good luck," John said almost to himself as the old Mercedes labored away through the soft sand.

Chapter 9

John waited for the last sound from the defective muffler to die away, then turned to the two techs. "Well," he said. "Now it's up to God. Let's have a beer while we wait. It could be a while."

He opened the trunk of his car where he had stashed a large cooler filled to overflowing with beer now wonderfully cold from the several hours it had been covered in ice. "Let's head for the beach," he said. "Nate, grab one of the handles and help me carry this thing."

After struggling though the loose sand, the trio emerged from the palm scrub onto an empty pristine beach made silvery by the brilliant African moon. "Stop here," John said as they stepped onto the edge of the beach. "We need to wait where we can be sure to hear our man, or anyone else, who decides to visit tonight."

For a few moments no one spoke as they looked at the lovely panorama before them. The sound of the waves breaking on the unmarked sand was barely audible. The moonlight was so brilliant that distinct shadows radiated from even the smallest projection above the flat sand.

"To look at this," John said, "you'd never think about the awful poverty; or the brutal, corrupt governments; or the illiteracy; or the ancient, virulent diseases; or the hopelessness that starts just beyond the palm trees behind us. You'd think everything was just fine. You'd think this was an ad for a credit card or the beginning of a romantic comedy or the start of someone's honeymoon. Africa! It's the land of extremes. The greatest beauty, the ugliest poverty; the kindest people, the most brutal governments; the greatest natural wealth, the worst inefficiency in its use; the birthplace of mankind, the last place to join the 20th century. It has snowcapped mountains at the equator, the world's greatest desert and the world's greatest jungle. It has whole towns carved out of solid rock and huts made of mud and straw. It has the world's longest river and several of the world's greatest rivers. It is bordered by two oceans, and one sea where Western civilization started and one sea parted by God himself to help out his captured people. But one of the greatest problems for the average person is trying to get a decent drink of water.

It was ruled by some of the most powerful kings, but it's greatest legacy is the slaves it provided for the rest of the world. Like every white man who has lived here for a while, I love and hate it, but it gets to you over time. You are sure the problems are too great for any human to solve, but you don't want to give up... Sorry, guys, I guess it's that kind of talk on moonlit nights that gives us the word 'lunacy'. Let's talk about something else."

As usual when admonished to talk, everyone immediately fell silent. Finally, Bill spoke into the quiet, a question sure to bring discussion from every officer of every kind in the Agency. "Well, John, what's your next assignment?"

"Afghanistan or near by," John said. "I love Africa but for a career move, it's Afghanistan for the near future. The Russians have screwed up big time there. Looks like they didn't learn a thing from our Vietnam. When they fail miserably I want to be among the COSs who caused it. I want to be called to the seventh floor and get a medal at one of those exclusive dinners in the executive dining room. I want young COs to kiss my ass because they admire me instead of the usual fear that I'll ruin their careers if they don't. I want people to say, 'There goes John, the bad-ass COS who ruined the Russkies.' Afghanistan will do that for me. It's odd that the Brits and the Russkies have fought over the same area for so long and now it's still the Russkies, but we've replaced the Brits. I can't wait. Thank God Jimmie Carter looked so weak the Russians thought they could get away with anything. He didn't mean it, but he suckered them into a mess they can't clean up."

"You mean," Bill said, "the Russians won't be able to defeat the guerrillas or at least force them into the hills so they can't do any harm?"

"The Russians might well damage the guerrillas," John said, "if the guerrillas only had their wits and a few Enfield rifles to fight with, but imagine what that same bunch could do with a little training and 21st century weapons provided by you-know-who. Imagine the terrible Hind helicopters if all they turned out to be was big fat targets for Stinger missiles. Imagine a Russian patrol rounding a bend in the road and finding a triangle of Claymore mines in their way. Imagine if the rebels had excellent radio communications instead of sending notes by runners. And best of all, imagine that everything was generic with no way to trace it back to the US. How do you think the Russians would feel about their project then?"

"Can we do all that and get away with it?" Bill said.

"Hell, Bill," John said, "you know damn well we can do just about anything if the politicians in Washington will give us their blessing, or just get out of the way. Besides, it won't take all that much—just a few senior chiefs who know what they're doing: me, Milt, Frank, Fred—maybe a few others—is all that's needed. The Russians' asses are already ours; they just don't know it yet. Now, let's talk about women, or some other less exciting thing, or else I might have an orgasm right here."

Since the beer had already begun to have an effect, the talk did slide easily onto less and less critical topics as the bright night wore on. Their revelry was finally interrupted by the distant but clear sound of a bad muffler. "He's back." John said. "As soon as he pulls up, you boys take the gear out of his car."

While John and the agent conversed quietly, Bill and Nate quickly removed the recorder from the old Mercedes, both operations taking less than two minutes. The agent left immediately, the three officers following after John had decided enough time had elapsed between their separate goings.

Back at the embassy, the two technical officers put the tapes from the miniature recorder onto the Uher to begin the playback. As the first buzzing escaped the Uher speaker, Bill began to lose hope. He could hear voices, but the distant rumble of the bad muffler, the sharper dissonant rattles of the loose wiring near the microphone, and the hissing of the tires obscured them almost completely. He looked at John apologetically, but John was engrossed in his listening. Finally, Bill said, "John, can you understand this?"

"Parts of it at least," John said.

"I can't hear a thing," Bill said.

"You're not used to the accent or the local language," John said. "This won't be easy, but we might get something."

After a few more minutes, John looked up at the two very weary officers. "Look," he said, "there's no use in you two staying around here listening to this. Go back to the hotel, get some rest, come in late tomorrow. We'll know by then. There's always a driver on duty at the Marine guard post; he'll take you. See you tomorrow."

The two rode back to the hotel in complete, tired silence. As they started to enter their rooms, Nate finally said, "Bill, any hope?"

"Not likely," Bill said, "but John is satisfied at what we did even if it doesn't work. Listen, for once let's not worry about getting there on time. It's about 3:00 now. Let's plan to meet about 9:00 for breakfast. There shouldn't be any real hurry. Whether it worked or not, about all we have to do tomorrow is see what else John wants, if anything, and send out our wrap-up cable. OK?"

"Right," Nate said, "see you tomorrow."

***

Next morning the two officers trudged into the station just after 10AM expecting the worst. When they were met by John's quiet, almost grave secretary they felt their worst estimation to have been confirmed. The secretary told them to report directly to John. As soon as they were seated John pressed the "play" lever on the Uher recorder.

Although the sound was scratchy and hissing, the other noises from the automobile were absent. A deep voice began speaking while the other voice, which they recognized as that of the agent, offered short grunts or brief sentence fragments of encouragement. Both officers listened to the recording for a few seconds without understanding either the significance or most of the words. John shut the recorder off, looked at them without comment and sat down behind his desk opening a drawer as he sat. When he placed a bottle of bourbon on the desk top, they looked at each other in even greater consternation.

"I have to say," he said as he broke out some paper cups, "I've never seen anything go any better. Not only did our contact name the conspirators, he spelled out their names and he did it on our tape, a tape that will guarantee us unlimited access to President Bouaki. When he hears this, he may adopt me as an extra son, although I think he already had about twenty at last count. I'll probably be promoted. If there's any justice you boys might get one too, at least that's what my cable will recommend."

As John handed each officer a half cup of bourbon his face broke into a huge grin. "Cheers!" he said to the flabbergasted techs, "now let's go to the ambassador's conference room. I borrowed it for the occasion—told him we moved vespers up from Friday this week."

The two followed him to the conference room where there was a full celebration in progress, including, when they entered, a round of applause. The two, who had not yet said a word, were even less able to speak until the applause died down and Jim edged close to them. "There's nothing better than the feeling I always get from the perfect execution of a well-planned op," he said. "What about you?"

Bill hesitated for only another few seconds then began to laugh. So did Nate. As the two officers touched their paper cups to Jim's, he too started to laugh. It was only when John began to think the laughter was for more than good fortune that they were able to stop. In a subsequent quiet moment in the midst of the party, Bill moved over to Nate who touched cups with him yet again. "I think I'm getting a little drunk,"

Nate said.

"Don't worry," Bill said, "this time it's OK. I only hope John sobers up a little before the goes to see Bouaki. We wouldn't want this intelligence coup to be diminished by a shit-faced COS. Yep, our first great coup. As I think about this, I remember the words of Fred Haney: 'What would you rather be than lucky.' I am also reminded of the words of countless generations of our Southern ancestors: 'Even a blind hog finds an acorn every once in a while.'"

"Amen!" Nate said.

Chapter 10

"And that was just part of one TDY," Nate said to the completely attentive Mike, "but it'll give you some idea of what can happen. We actually got a kudos from the Director himself; I've still got a copy in my office."

"You might as well claim you can't wait to see it," Betty said to Mike, "he's going to force it on you anyway real soon."

"Did I get promoted right after that or not?" Nate said to Betty.

"Yes," Betty said, "and you kept getting promoted; God knows why."

"My modesty, probably," Nate said.

"And did Bill get promoted?" Mike asked.

Betty gave a small grunt, but said nothing. Nate glanced at her in apparent annoyance. "Sometimes," he said, "Betty has a way of expressing herself in unladylike gestures and mannerisms, which tendency has likely been a factor keeping her out of the higher ranks."

Betty started to speak, but decided to remain silent. When Nate was sure she would remain quiet he turned his attention back to Mike. "Bill had a way of canceling out a good performance by immediately doing something so blatantly foolish that it couldn't be ignored. He had a way of going along just fine for most of a tour, keeping his immediate superiors pleased and the higher ranks totally ignorant of his existence, but then inevitably one morning he would get up with brain paralysis. Couple that with the fact that he never gained any expertise in making a mess and getting away with it and you can imagine what happened.

"At the end of that op, he was just as golden as I was, but within

107

a month he managed to leave out a classified folder at another field station, which was found by the Marine guard. He and the case officer had both understood the office would be manned until they returned after work—had even made a point of telling the duty officer when they would be back—but the duty officer forgot. It was a hell of a stink; the COS demanded a warning be placed in Bill's permanent file. If Dave hadn't gone to see the COS in person, Bill might even have been fired. Of course, the only thing Bill really regretted was that a secretary, who was working overtime for the COS on another project, was the last one out so she had to take half the violation."

"It was ugly," Betty said.

At that they all fell silent for a moment amid the increasingly boisterous pub. Mike waited for the talk to begin once more, but only silence ensued. "Well," he said, what happened after that tour?"

"I did well," Nate said, "I got a lateral to another field station and got my first management position as a branch chief. Bill came home and wound up in counter-measures again with Sam. I should point out that Sam had the official job of getting rookies started on their careers without letting them commit a series of security violations, and the unofficial job of providing a low-profile, safe haven for experienced officers who had fallen out of grace for whatever reason. At least Bill missed the office's move over to the headquarters building. According to those who had to participate, it was a nightmare. But, as it turned out, that was about the only good thing that happened in Bill's career for a long time. He is still grateful to Sam for saving him that time when he got back to headquarters. I have heard him, on several occasions, describe how easy Sam made his return.

***

"Welcome home," Sam said as Bill came into the lab.

"Actually," Bill said, "this doesn't feel much like home. It feels like... headquarters. But it's good to be back. I see you're at the very end of the hall once more."

"Yes," Sam said, "this location sets counter-measures apart from the offensive ops going on in every other lab, or maybe it just shuts out the offensive ops youngsters who are each certain they will eventually run the entire outfit. And it's a tradition, which is enough in itself. I suppose it's good to be here, so convenient to the DO. All they have to do is walk over, or more likely, have us walk over to them, to get something done. But I believe I do detect the beginning of a loss of that special camaraderie we had at South Building. Even though we were in three buildings there, we seemed closer than here where we're distributed among just two floors. Fortunately, I was able to get the least accessible of all the offices. It's suits counter-measures to be off in the corner and away from the limelight.

"I requested you again. I'm tired of shepherding inherently cocky newbies through their early months. I told the leaders I wanted someone who could work, not more infants who required work. Are you ready?"

Bill had already been told that Sam really had requested him, but he also knew Sam would have done almost anything to save him the indignity of having to actually look for a job, "I reckon," he said. "And Sam,...thanks."

"Alright," Sam said with a very slight nod of his head in acknowledgment. "Other than your normal duties, I want you to take on a special watch-dog assignment. It's covered in dingle-berries and still in it's infancy, but I can't kill it—yet. Apparently it will have to fail spectacularly of its own weakness for that to happen. If you can, I hope you can make it either go away or at least keep it from being considered a viable ops system."

"What happened?" Bill asked, "Did Warner Barret have another epiphany?"

"No," Sam said, "not by himself, Warner has allies this time: Plato Dinwiddie and the military.

"The problem is that these guys are brilliant, absolutely brilliant, and have done some absolutely fantastic things. Take secret writing system 555A, everybody's favorite: it's easy to prepare, easy to develop, almost indestructible, secure to all censorship, and will work on anything from German bond to grocery bags. How many dissems and how much invaluable information have been transmitted by it. That one system earned Warner his salary for the next twenty years, and he deserves it. It's worth enduring a dozen duds for one like that—but he and his group sometimes can't tell the difference. Unfortunately, that's where we always have to step in. If we can keep it down to having them hate us only periodically, we're doing a perfect job...I think they're going to hate you on this one.

"They've got a new project and it's another one of those developed-in-the-isolation-of-the-lab-without-prior-ops-input classics. Worse still, someone, probably Plato, went over to the military and talked them into expressing an interest in it. I hate to be so unenthusiastic before they even get the thing out of research, but lately they've haven't been able to hit the ground with their hats as far as practicality is concerned. As usual anything developed by Warner and his group involves first-rate science, but the last three projects have all been almost useless for real-world ops and I can't get them to die. The things are like vampires: I keep shooting them in the head, but I can't ever seem to get the wooden stake through the heart.

"Warner is going to brief the prototype to the DO division chiefs and the military in a couple of days. Your first assignment will be to attend that meeting and see what you can do, if anything."

"Is it really worth worrying about?" Bill said, "or is it totally foolish?"

"Well," Sam said, "it's the usual situation in which the thing has no great value to us, but someone can always come up with a scenario in which it is the only thing that will work. It reminds me of the time I was an instructor in the service. No matter what I said or proposed or explained, there was always some buck private who could envision some cockeyed situation in which whatever I had just said, could not possibly work. That's why we officers didn't have to explain or persuade; in the end we just had to order. Sometimes I long for those simple years."

"So what is it basically?" Bill asked.

"In a nutshell, it's a glorified microdot produced with today's technology," Sam said, "but while the materials, equipment, and science used are state-of-the-art, the basic idea is the same as the Germans used in WW two-eye. The attraction is obviously the gee-whiz of the thing. They use a laser—ta-da!—to imprint the message onto a plastic thing such as a credit card, or really any plastic or suitably impervious item, and the item is passed to the agent by contact or dead-drop. But get this: it takes a microscope to read it out reliably. Now, I ask you, if you have to pass something to an agent who has a microscope why not either send him the old tried and tested WW-two-eye microdot, or better still, forget the microscope and use the much more secure SW letter, neither of which requires any personal contact or any dead-drops?"

"I give up," Bill said. "Why not?"

"Because," Sam said, "those things are old hat. And those operational geniuses also pointed out that they can send a great deal more data this new way."

"I thought," Bill said, "that the idea was for the agent to send *us* the great deal of data and we would only send him instructions, questions, requirements, and maybe warnings."

"That's ops thinking, you fool!" Sam said. "We don't want that kind of realistic negativism at visionary strategy meetings! But they do have one other use which seems reasonable in a way: they also intend eventually to put the messages on mail to the agent. Can you think of anything wrong with that?"

"Not at first glance," Bill admitted.

"Well," Sam said, "let me ask you again after I tell you that in this case, we are back to the traditional short messages you just mentioned.

Now how does it look?"

"Hmmmm," Bill said, "let's see: for a short message why not use SW as we do now. The agent will need a developer, probably a pill, but that's much easier to account for than a microscope. And if concealment is a concern, there is no contest; the microscope, or whatever kind of reader is used, loses hands-down compared to the pill."

"And...," Sam said.

"Preparation of an SW message is infinitely easier for us, or any tech shop, and even some stations can do it. All those high-tech messages need a laser."

"And...," Sam said.

Bill hesitated and thought hard for a moment in silence, then smiled broadly at Sam: "The laser message is completely overt if anyone looks at it through sufficient magnification since it depends only on little teenie letters that can't be seen with the naked eye. The SW message is secure even if they take it to a lab; the old way is infinitely more secure if the message gets real censorship!"

"Well done, my son," Sam said. "I see you have retained at least some of my early instruction in counter-measures. Good show!"

***

When Bill walked into the conference room he saw, on the Technical Directorate side of the table, all the familiar faces he expected and one face that startled him: Adele. He immediately went over to sit next to her. "Adele," he said, "the last time I saw you was in Nairobi. How are you doing?"

"Fine," she said. "You?"

"OK," Bill said. "Why are you here?"

"This outfit has finally decided to let people other than techs see what they can do in tech ops," she said, then paused for a few seconds, "even if they don't have a scientific background and even if they aren't men. It was clear while I was in Nairobi that no matter how good I was in the lab or how much operational experience I got, they were never going to let me become a case officer. Clint let me shop my file all over. When Dr. Barret read it and saw that I had excellent lab skills and great operational experience he called me for an interview and hired me on the spot. I've been doing a lot of testing and diagnostic work helping him get the kinks out of some new systems and I'm also his liaison to ops sections in the Agency and the military, including OTS. So, here I am."

As Bill searched for something to say to cover his surprise, Warner Barret came in and sat down on the other side of Adele. Leaning forward to see around her, he said to Bill, "I hear you two knew each other overseas."

"Yes," Bill said, "in Nairobi. Adele ran the tech shop there. We met several times during my tour in NORTECH. I didn't know until just now that Adele was interested in working in OTS."

"That's typical of ops types," Warner said, "you boys never know anything about the office or its policies. Headquarters is always just a time-out until you can get overseas again. Right now, there's a new office directive to bring this organization into the twentieth century which I'm sure you've never heard about. OTS is going to join the rest of the world in giving every capable person a chance to do whatever they can. Adele is just one of the first group of people with a non-technical background to be given such a chance in OTS."

After pausing for a second or two, Warner continued, "I heard you might not be going back out for a while, and now that you've fetched up in counter-measures, I believe it. How is it, winding up in Sam's shop again. Didn't you start out there?"

"Sam's always a good man to work for," Bill said. "He never loses his enthusiasm for finding all the problems with new systems and pointing them out. And he still hasn't lost his sense of humor. Right now I need that about as much as anything."

"I can believe that," Warner said.

For a moment, no one spoke, but Bill found the silence so uncomfortable he had to say something. In desperation, he thought it would be wise to at least turn the conversation away from himself. "Is Adele a tech in your lab now?" he asked.

"She's a hell of a lot more than that," Warner said in the lecturing way he always adopted when he tried to explain a fundamental scientific principle to ops officers. "She's my ops advisor. From now on, when you and your buddies pull the no-ops-experience routine on me, I'll have someone with real operational savvy to talk back for the office."

Now Bill was truly speechless. At first, he tried to tell himself that he had not heard correctly or had misinterpreted Warner's words, but it proved hopeless. Over the years he had come to understand Warner well enough to know that in the world inside Warner's head, Adele's opinion would mean as much as his or any other ops officer. As he struggled to hide his astonishment the military contingent walked in and Warner called the meeting to order. For once Bill was glad a staff meeting had begun.

***

"Sam," Bill said even before he had closed the door, "you've really tied a knot in my shorts this time. Do you know who is supposedly going to advise Warner on ops matters?"

"I heard it was a woman from the field," Sam said. "I heard she was mighty knowledgeable on ops and knew all about running a tech shop too."

For a moment, Sam sat expressionless as Bill stared at him. Finally, he began trying to hold back a grin. "You old whore!" Bill said. "You do know who's involved."

"Well," Sam said, "your friend and colleague, Nate, has told some war stories on this young lady to various folks over time so she was not unknown to us when Warner made his decision. Rumor Control and I have lunch about once a week and he sometimes tests the rumors on me. I heard about it from him, but at first, I advised him against floating it—thought it was too outrageous and no one would believe it..."

"It's true all right," Bill interrupted, "as big as life and twice as ugly. But why, how, did it happen?

"It's not exactly Warner's fault," Sam said. "Pull up a chair and listen to some office politics for once. This time, we're all going to be affected, especially dinosaurs like us."

Bill put down his briefcase, walked over to the sink, took down one of Sam's chemical beakers, and half filled it with water. As he began to drink it down, Sam said, "You should be careful with that."

"I'm not worried," Bill said. "I know you've got the cleanest beakers in the building."

"It's not that," Sam said. "It's the tap water. If one of those idiots turns the wrong tap over at the treatment plant, we could all be dead of plague by morning."

Without answering, Bill took one more drink from the beaker and carried it with him as he pulled his chair closer to Sam's. "OK," he said, "what's the problem?"

"It's not supposed to be a problem," Sam said. "It's supposed to make the outfit stronger and smarter and more efficient—and more diverse, understanding, creative, fair, empowered, self-fulfilling—and a lot more buzz words I can't recall right now. In fact, what you just said about this being a problem would have been considered a real no-no. The basic idea is for us dinosaurs to become more 'sensitive'—I put that word in quotes. If you had made that last remark at a sensitivity session, they might have been forced to send you to remedial sensitivity. In fact, you're a prime candidate for that no matter what happens."

"Didn't the Chinese do that kind of thing during the Cultural Revolution?" Bill asked. "Wouldn't that make it Communistic or something?"

"No, no," Sam said, "you've got it mixed up with 'struggle sessions' where the Chinese officials persuaded the reluctant intellectuals, or anyone else who was confused, to get their mind right or head for the countryside and hard labor. Those 'struggle sessions' were childish compared to the sensitivity sessions you're going to have to attend."

"Wait," Bill said, "it sounds like this is something extra on top of the usual 'Blue Skies' thinking from Warner. Am I to understand that what I heard from him about 'opportunity' at the meeting was not just a brain child of his but something mandated at the division level."

"Division, hell!" Sam said. "It comes from Capitol Hill itself. Our heavy hitters were summoned to the seventh floor at headquarters about three months ago and told that we *would* catch up with the soft agencies in the new social thinking as it applies to the workplace. Some of our old dinosaurs have been beet-red ever since. They don't have a clue what to do, but they know they've got to do something. Right now, even if our Director himself pinches the lowest secretary on the ass, he could lose his job. And that's just the tip of the sensitivity iceberg. In reality, if a man was so foolish as to really pinch something, he might be shot.

"There's a lot more. Warner is just on board a lot sooner than the others. He may not know an operation from a sno-cone, but no one ever accused him of not understanding office politics. The leaders didn't mandate his upward mobility move for Adele, he did it on his own, and he got an official attaboy for it."

Seeing that Bill was still not completely comprehending the situation, Sam continued. "You have to remember, Warner is totally Design and Engineering. That's why he was hired away from Restoration Research. Neither Warner nor anyone else in his shop has had fifteen minutes of ops familiarization or training. They really do need someone in ops to guide them, but none of you ops types wants to work there so Warner has settled on Adele. As he sees it she gives him operational bonifides and the extra bonus of showing he is 'getting with the program,' which has become a watchword in the last few months.

"There's also a thing called 'multi-cultural diversity' headed our way. I'm not sure if it's part of sensitivity or the other way around and I don't know if these things are going to hit us simultaneously or separately, but they are related. We'll just have to see how it goes.

"And finally, we are in for a new management system called TQM or Total Quality Management. It has done wonders for the Japanese and we *will* try it; it has been so decreed. I do believe it was just a coincidence that the new management system has arrived at the same time as sensitivity. I can't imagine anyone would plan it this way."

Bill sat perfectly still and stared at Sam. "My God, Sam," he said finally, "this reminds me of one of those science fiction novels where the guy goes out for a hamburger and when he gets back, it's the year 2150."

"Don't shoot me," Sam said, "I'm just the piano player."

"OK," Bill said after a brief, silent walk around the lab, "let's put all that behind us and talk about the project. They've encrypted it as 'CYNOSURE' and officially offered it to the military as well as to the DO. I'm sure it's going to be accepted. Adele told them our chemical tests do not detect it. That makes it an 'A' system."

"Oh, God!" Sam said. "I suppose you pointed out that our test battery is directed against high level, *chemical* SW systems."

"Of course," Bill said, "but by then they were transported on the wings of cutting-edge science, and somehow they didn't get the idea that little bitty letters are actually completely overt if you happen to look at them through proper magnification. One case officer, after looking at the exemplars, with the naked eye only of course, opined the Russkies would never detect it in a thousand years—I believe it was a thousand."

"Then we've lost this round," Sam said, "but you can bet your ass we're gonna hear from this thing again one of these days, and God knows what the context will be."

Chapter 11

Suddenly Nate was interrupted in his narrative by an earnest, urgent, and noisy discussion about how many pitchers of beer would be needed in the immediate future at their end of the table and what brand it would be. Once it had been decided that three pitchers of Sam Adams would suffice, he turned again to Mike. "Where was I?" he asked

"You were overseas," Mike said, "and Bill had come back to work with Sam."

"Yes," Nate said, "yes, you're right. Yes…you're doing better controlling the beer than I am tonight…but this is a very special night…OK..

"For a while there, for more than a year really, while I was overseas, Bill and I communicated by letter or by an occasional phone call. When I got back I was made a section chief in SW so I was very busy. Bill and I did see each other just about every day in passing, but it wasn't like before while he was training me or while we were overseas together. For us to have a long, general conversation required making an actual arrangement, something like a night at an Irish bar or a lunch in the cafeteria. We almost never had a long talk at work. Sam always kept his door shut and knocking was required to get in. Also Sam didn't want a lot of discussion about his projects; there were no staff meetings in counter-measures. That was partly because his section was always working on at least a few truly sensitive cases and partly because Sam always maintained an atmosphere of discretion about everything; he considered it essential to the nature of his work. For instance, we were aware of the concept of CYNOSURE, but how it was progressing and what Sam was doing about it was never a topic of discussion.

"However, those new guidelines on things such as opportunities for women, non-technical personnel, and minorities and the imposition of TQM, Total Quality Management, methods to our daily tasks did, indeed, merit a lot of discussion—and argument. All of the new ideas and innovations percolated around the outfit for months with some officers 'getting with the program' and others hoping the whole thing would go away if they did as little as was absolutely necessary to show compliance. But then in just one morning all was made plain, at least for those of us who could see the way ahead. I remember clearly to this day, and this night despite the beer, when those of us destined to move up heard the facts and took appropriate action.

"Bill and I hadn't had a decent conversation for weeks so we decided to walk over together to get the word from on high."

***

Bill and Nate walked slowly along the wide corridor near the front of the headquarters building, talking intently as they progressed. All hands had been summoned to the Bubble, as the Agency auditorium was known, for a message from the Office Director himself. It was already being called "Trouble in the Bubble," and no one was allowed to miss it except for the most junior secretary in each branch who had to man all the phones. It was known that the newly mandated procedures regarding personnel and attitude in the work place would be the topic of the address, but no one knew why an all hands meeting was merited, especially one called by the Director.

"Has SW initiated any of the new ideas yet?" Bill asked.

"Well," Nate said, "just last week we had a staff meeting conducted according to TQM guidelines, but I'm not sure exactly how it all came out. It seemed to me that we didn't accomplish anything, but our process-keeper, or whatever they call it, claimed the process was perfect. Maybe we just don't have the hang of it; it works wonders for the Japanese. Does Sam use it in his office?"

"Is this a real question?" Bill said. "Do you really think Sam is going to start something new at this stage in his career? When they gave him the daily sheets to fill out, he shredded them all the same day. But the best part was when Phil Looper came down and gave him the official TQM notebook with all the various binders and sections and colored tabs and stickers and God knows what. He listened patiently while Phil explained just how to fill out every single little block, and then, as soon as Phil went out the door, he put the notebook under that beaker of sulfuric acid and dichromate cleaning solution he always keeps handy for his beakers. Then he turned to me and said we should always protect the countertops from chemical spills. There's already a six-inch circle dissolved out of the middle of it. Sam knows no one is going to mess with him. He knows more about counter-measures than God."

"As for the sensitivity and multi-cultural thing," Nate said, "I haven't seen any evidence of it yet. Betty is doing fine in her career but she got her assignment to ops because she had convinced everyone she deserved it. She got her well-deserved break before we ever heard of multi-sensitivity. I don't know if it will effect her at all.

"I wonder if this isn't too much at once. I know our leaders mean well, and since the decree has come down from on high, they don't have any choice anyway, but TQM, sensitivity, and multi-cultural diversity are a lot to dump all at once on a bunch of dinosaurs who are still trying to understand the concept of female techs.

"Well, anyway, today we're all gonna find out something. When Frank calls an 'all-hands' for the Bubble, it's serious. I wonder...hey RC! Hey! Wait a minute!"

At Nate's repeated hails, a rotund man, impeccably dressed, even down to a handkerchief in his breast pocket, and sporting a fine mane of white hair, hesitated in his quick, purposeful walk and looked in their direction. "What!" he said, "I can't fool with you two right now; gotta get a front row seat so I can read Frank's body language and see how really bad he's hurting."

"This won't take a minute, RC," Nate said, "and we need your expertise in the worst way, especially Bill."

The man hesitated, then walked briskly over to them. "Make it quick," he said, "and I'm only doing this for Bill. You young fast-trackers don't need my help."

Fitzroy McGann, or Rumor Control as he had been known for years, had been a newspaper reporter in his early career and had been recruited by a friend at a time when the recommendation of the right friend was all that was needed to join the Agency. Over time, he had become an expert "Flaps and Seals" man and was now regularly teaching that esoteric skill to certain of the new officers who seemed to have a knack for it. His technical ability to clandestinely open letters and pouches, even those sealed with wax or special tampering detectors, was legendary. His facility for accurate snooping and rumor management was almost as legendary and had raised him to the pinnacle of the famous office grapevine.

If someone heard a rumor and brought it to him, he would validate it if he already had reason to believe it or knew it to be true. If he had not heard it, he would seek out not only the facts concerning it, but trace it to the unlucky originator who had started it without his knowledge and assent. He had reached the point where only rookies and other fools dared float a rumor without first checking with him. He felt no compunction about starting a retaliation rumor against any upstart who launched a rumor without his approval and he had an unerring way of finding something the subject was sensitive about and starting a rumor bringing that sensitivity to light. No one wanted to be the subject of a retaliation rumor from RC. One young officer who had bragged about defying RC, was still trying to recover from the powerful rumor that his early brush with ballet had changed his "personality."

Looking at Bill, he said, "Bill, I haven't heard anything about you except that you're in exile right now and flying below the radar. I recommend you stay there. If I hear anything credible, either way, I'll let you know soonest."

"Thanks, RC," Nate said, "but that wasn't why I called you over."

"Then what," RC said, "I just told you I'm on a mission."

"What caused the 'all hands'?" Nate asked, "I'm sure you know, or you at least know more than anyone else."

RC smiled at the left-handed compliment and decided he could take a minute or two for an explanation after all.

"I don't think I have to tell you how sensitive Tom Broadston is," he began. "Well, he tried that famous line of his 'Lie down I want to talk to you,' on a new secretary a couple of weeks ago. She didn't say much if anything to him, probably because she could envision his hopeless dinosaur brain, but she did go up to speak with Frank later that day. Evidently, Frank tried the old way of smoothing things over by noting that Tom was un-trainable, didn't mean anything by the remark, etc. Maybe if he had stopped there, it might have been OK. Apparently he then asked the young woman if she might not be making too big a thing out of it and may even have said something about it being a bad day for her. Next day, he gets a summons from the IG director herself and gets his ass chewed to ribbons. Word has it that he's already called Tom everything but Jesus Christ and now it's our turn. If anyone causes another incident so severe that someone shows up in Frank's office, he's a goner, believe me. So be nice to the ladies. Listen...I gotta go!"

"Thanks, RC," Nate said, "you never disappoint."

"That's what the ladies always say too," RC said as he hastened back into the crowd.

"Well," Nate said, "I guess it's time us dinosaurs started looking for the comet. Let's go."

***

"What do you think?" Bill asked as they filed out with the rest of the unusually quiet crowd.

"I think," Nate said, "that when someone of Frank's stature begins his lecture with 'I was reviewed by the IG staff and I got an "F,"' it would be a wise idea for the rest of us to listen up. I didn't need to sit where RC sat to see Frank's body language. He was entirely serious and thoroughly pissed off. I believe he's mostly mad at himself for mistaking how serious top management was about the new reality, but now he's got to make sure we all get the message. It's too late for him, of course, but what else is he going to do."

"What do you mean it's too late?" Bill said.

"At that level," Nate said, "an officer should anticipate what's about to descend on him. If he doesn't like it, he can choose to register a protest, or even quit if he just can't tolerate it, and he might still recover and salvage a career in some other office, but when he's surprised, that's deadly. No matter what he does now, his career has topped out. I would expect to see him land either in some exalted staff position or bail out of OTS in the next few months."

Bill stared at Nate for a few seconds and remained silent until they again reached the point of separation on the way back to their offices. "Nate," Bill said, "when did you get so knowledgeable about office politics and high-level decision making, and all that?"

"Why," Nate said, "I just took your advice. Remember a long time ago when you said anyone in any bureaucracy could see which path was likely to lead to the top if they looked carefully for it, but that some just didn't want to acknowledge it, or just didn't care, or were content to do a job they liked and didn't worry about advancing? Well, I believed you. As for our current delicate situation, now is the time, even before Frank implements any of his proposals, for a smart individual to 'get with the program.'

"It's painfully clear that up to now Frank didn't really take any of this warm fuzziness very seriously. After all, just because some arrested development case from the 60s has finally found a strong enough policy-making position on Capitol Hill to unleash his mushy ideas on other parts of the government, doesn't mean the real world has changed. It isn't going to be any easier for a female case officer to recruit or control Arab agents, or that TQM is going to work any better in providing the next miracle microphone for the audio boys, or that Tom Broadston will be truly concerned about female sensitivities. Frank knows that and probably thought his superiors would protect him from having to actually translate any of those 60s ideas into action. But as of today, he's got to go forward with something. The tricky part for us will be to show some success at our real jobs while paying lip service to whatever his new policies will be. For at least the next little while we are going to have to pretend the new guidelines, whatever they turn out to be, are just what we needed to empower us and make us whole and cause us to wet our pants in an ecstasy of sensitivity and multi-cultural diversity. Now would be an excellent time to be overseas. In fact, I intend to begin trying to get myself a rotation to somewhere as of this very day."

***

In the bar, as Nate finished his monologue on how he had decided upon the first great maneuver in his career, he noted Mike seemed to be losing interest slightly either from the effects of the beer or because he had moved the discussion to non-operational matters. He decided the young man needed to be brought up short to make sure he understood the importance of politics, even in the Agency.

"Mike, listen, Mike!" Nate said, "Are you listening? This may seem dull to you, but this is the kind of thing that can make or break your career these days. I know you'd rather hear about sexy ops and miracle technology, but unless you recruit the Soviet president or invent the first cloaking device, politics will get you selected or rejected quicker than anything. I do believe the agency is as immune to politics as any bureaucracy in our government, but we're infected. We're just not as sick as most."

"Yes," Mike said, "I hear you, but it seems the thoughts are taking a little longer to get from my ears to my brain. I slacked off the booze long ago but I can't seem to get fully recovered."

"Not a problem," Nate said. "Now you're at the stage where this stuff is registering but can't be fully evaluated. It will be like a cow's cud: you'll be able to bring it up during the excitement of the next staff meeting and fully appreciate it then."

"I don't think the comparison to a cow's cud is a good idea right now," Mike said.

"That could be," Nate admitted, "sorry. Tell you what: why don't you just concentrate on your unlimited future for a minute. That will calm your stomach for sure."

"God, Nate!" Betty said, "Now I'm getting queasy."

Mike raised his hands as if surrender. "It's OK," he said. "I'm fine now. I just had a momentary weakness—probably the last disturbance from the gut bomb I had for lunch. Please go on. I know there's another lesson coming."

"You're absolutely right," Nate said, "and although what I have said in the past is golden, this will be even more important."

"Please," Betty interrupted, "now I'm really in danger of barfing."

"Just as an aside," Nate continued, "always remember that women will try to make fun of your most important thoughts and plans. That's to keep all men uncertain and prevent our reaching our full potential. It takes a good man indeed to pretend to listen, but in reality, dismiss whatever they say..."

"Nate!" Betty said, this time with a slight edge to her voice.

"OK, OK," Nate said, "I'm back on track. Now, Mike, listen up. It was during that conversation after the 'Trouble in the Bubble', that I moved beyond Bill. By the time I got back to the office, I knew his career was over and that I was going to advance. He couldn't take his own advice: identify the path upward and take it. The situation was too radical for him and many other dinosaurs. You can see a great number of them right around you now. In fact, just about every face you see here, with the exception of us of course, will be gone or shuffled off to a corner by the time you get your first promotion. They just couldn't believe what was, to me, completely clear: a transition was coming and to ride it out, it was necessary to change or do a damn good impression

125

of it. The dinosaurs could not imagine any bureaucratic ideology ever getting in the way of operations or that 'sensitivity' would ever be preferred over aggressiveness. They heard what Frank said, but just like you a moment ago, what they heard stayed in their ears, not in their brains."

"Nate," Betty interrupted, "don't you think that's a little harsh, especially when you're laying it on someone who's just stepped in the door. These are all good men who did their best every day of their careers and believed in everything they did..."

"Yes, Betty, Yes!" Nate said. "That's exactly the point. It is a tragedy. All I'm trying to do is let Mike know what can happen even though everyone means well. Far be it from me to be literate, but as Hazlitt once said, 'We as often repent the good we do as the ill.' There is no doubt that women, as you certainly know, didn't use to get a fair shake and had to endure considerable harassment, even if it wasn't meant that way, and we never even thought about minorities. And when the change came, these guys were just simply caught in the headlights."

"Wait," Mike said, "you said these guys were very smart. Didn't they wise up, even over time?"

"Yes," Nate said, "of course they did, but it was an intellectual change; most never felt it in their gut. They were used to the way the Agency had been fairly well shielded from any outside interference, sometimes even from the President. The idea that a Congressional committee, or a White House staffer, or some study commissioned in one of the soft agencies could ever have any effect, never sank in. I will cite the classic example which is funny in a way and tragic in a way. My example is on the working level but I'm sure the same kind of thing happened all the way to top management. It involves a man you will probably never meet and that's a pity. He was a master instructor a few years ago and would certainly be here tonight if he didn't live now in Florida. He was our instructor in all types of electronic gear. If you were dumb as a post in electronics and had trouble with 'on' and 'off' knobs, he could show you how to set up a signaling system if you attended a week of his classes. He was not only an excellent instructor but his classes were fun. He had a great sense of humor and you were finished with the class before you realized you had learned a hell of a lot without knowing it. He was, though, a real dinosaur. That, and the fact that his facility was off in the boonies as opposed to being at HQ, caused him to be fairly well out of touch with any political changes. Still, he was no fool and did his best to keep with the program. That's what's so funny..."

"Yes," Betty said with a forceful interruption, "but taking his class was not as much fun for a woman, unless she understood the situation quite well. I was the first woman tech to go through one of his high-level electronic COVCOM classes. The first day, I wore normally tight jeans and a sweater top. Next day I wore the baggiest things I could find and was covered from neck to ankle..."

"What Betty is trying to say," Nate interrupted in turn, "is that, like the rest of us, he appreciated a spectacular woman..."

"And," Betty interrupted once more, "in those days the separation between appreciation and what is now called sexual harassment was razor thin."

"Anyway," Nate said, "he had a great, off-beat sense of humor. For instance he had the legendary 'Butt-Crack Hall of Fame.' In the days when he had been a regular tech who could fly eighteen hours on some emergency and then work for another twenty-four hours straight without stopping, he put in a lot of installations—bugs, to you, Mike. And he was also an excellent photographer so he always took pictures of the installation for the file. Invariably during all that work, someone would be repainting a baseboard or bending over a conduit or something and their butt-crack would appear. Just as invariably, he photographed that moment. By the time he became a full-time instructor, he had a marvelous collection mounted on a wall of the storage closet in his office. He had on his wall, the butt-cracks or four former group chiefs, at least a half-dozen division chiefs, and dozens of branch chiefs and regular techs. You only got to see it if he both liked you and thought you were a good tech. You could even be removed from the wall if you screwed up through carelessness or improper preparation. Betty was the first, and for a long while, the only woman to see it. It was one of her finest moments…"

"Mike," Betty said, "I admit it was almost endearing the way he showed it to me, much as if he was showing a priceless heirloom or a Congressional Medal of Honor, but I do not, repeat not, rank this among my finest moments." After a brief pause for effect, she continued, "I just wanted make that clear."

"OK," Nate said, "moving on… He also had a picture he had doctored, of himself and Hitler. He had removed Goebbels or somebody and inserted his own head. He was sort of leaning in toward Hitler as if he was whispering in Hitler's ear as Hitler spoke from a podium. The bubble coming out of Hitler's mouth always said: 'The National-Socialist Party will save Germany!' He changed the words in the bubble coming out of his own mouth from time to time. I remember seeing it one time when he was saying: 'Adolph, let's go get some women.' Another time he was saying: 'Let's invade Poland!' That picture was not in the storage room; it was always on top of the file cabinet. Everybody always got a kick out of it."

"As you can see," Betty said, "this was about the same as standing on the golf course during a thunder storm holding your putter towards the heavens—given the new sensitivity. I think you can see what's coming."

"Will you let me tell this, please!" Nate said.

"By all means," Betty said, "go ahead."

"Bill and I were the first two who found out about the incident," Nate Began, "and that was by a remarkably fortunate accident. It happened in the cafeteria a few months after the 'Trouble in the Bubble.' Bill and I were sitting near the burrito bar in the cafeteria having one of our periodic meetings. I was telling Bill that, as I had promised, I had just gotten involved in extra training in preparation for an overseas assignment."

Chapter 12

"I don't see how you got another overseas assignment," Bill said, "when you just had a tour about a year and a half ago."

"As Kenny Rogers would say," Nate replied, "'If you're gonna play the game, boy, you gotta learn to play it right.' One reason it was easy is that most of the good ol' boys now at my grade level who are aiming for the sky, want to stay here at HQ so they can watch each other and be ready to step into any good position that might open up. What they don't yet understand is that for the next couple of years at least, this is going to be a minefield. They can't see why I'm willing to take a deputy chief job, as thankless as that is, and lose time on the way up. But I'm betting my reputation will be spotless when I come back, while a lot of them will have their ox in the ditch for years after the new regime gets through with them. At the appropriate moment, I will just return like MacArthur and save a division or group and jump right over them."

Bill shook his head. "You have amazed me from the first day I met you," he said, "and it's always a different kind of amazement. I'm sure this is going to work out just as you say, but right now I'm baffled."

"You see," Nate said, "it's working already—not that I'm trying to confuse you—I know you don't care about this sort of thing, but just think how the others are either confused or figure I'm making a bad move."

"Well," Bill said, "I wish you luck."

"I won't need it," Nate said. "Now, how are you doing?"

"Fine," Bill said, "working with Sam is always a treat. It's wonderful to watch him cut right to the essential elements of any project, especially when a case officer or hotshot rookie is just getting started in some overblown explanation."

"And how about CYNOSURE?" Nate asked.

Bill hesitated then took a long breath before answering. "To use Sam's procedure and get to the bottom line: Adele and Warner completely skunked me on it. I wrote up my opinion in what I thought was a crystal-clear summation and sent it Warner who simply ignored it. As a result, I was left to defend my position verbally at the meetings. As you know, when it comes to verbal argument, I can undermine my own position in just one sentence. They simply asked questions about my write-up and by the time I finished explaining my explanation, I sounded as smart as Ramsey Clark usually does. If the audience had any questions about what a wonderful thing CYNOSURE was, I put all their little anxieties to rest."

"What does Sam think about it?" Nate asked.

"As usual," Bill said, "Sam thinks that once someone has been adequately warned, especially in writing, the job of the warner has been done. After that, it's up to the warnee. If they still screw up, it's their ass.

"I don't know if you've heard, but the Soviet Europe Division took it as a proprietary so nobody else can use it and we'll never know if, or who, ever gets an operational issuance. And to make matters worse they wanted Warner to handle the issuance and maybe even the training, although the training is just looking through some sort of magnifier. When Mr. Willie heard about it, he blew up like a tromped-on toad frog and washed his hands of the whole thing. Unless SE specifically asks SW ops to get involved, it's Warner and Adele on their own. Hell, it may work fine if they take the time do it right and put the message in a book or magazine. Then it will really be unlikely someone could find it, and I'm sure Adele will do a fine job preparing the messages. She has always been good at the 'hands on' part of her work.

"And one more thing I will have to give her: if you find yourself arguing with her in front of others, she will already have the best defensive position. She's damn clever that way—ought to be a lawyer or a politician—or is there a difference..."

Bill's voice had trailed off as he began to stare over Nate's shoulder toward the end of the burrito bar. "What?" Nate said, turning around.

At the cash register stood Roland Freeman dressed in the finest suit in which they had ever seen him. Not only was it a conservative pin-stripe and appeared to be new, but he was wearing a matching vest. The spectacle of the clothes would have been enough to draw their attention, but his obvious agitation was such that even others who certainly did not know him were beginning to take notice. His face was as red as that of any of his Scottish ancestors in a desperate battle with the English. He walked away from the register without his change, had to be called back, and had to have the change thrust at him before he responded. Then he jammed it into his pocket and moved away as if in a daze.

"Holy shit!" Nate muttered. "Roland! Roland! Dammit, *Roland*!"

Roland walked right up to the table, looked at them as if he had never seen them before, then finally said, "What?"

"Would you like to sit down and join us, Roland?" Nate asked, "or would you rather have a heart attack standing up?"

Without speaking, Roland sat down at their table. Bill looked at his tray which contained two cans of diet Coke and four desserts. He looked up at Nate, then they both looked at Roland.

"What the hell's the matter with you?" Nate said. "I've never seen you like this. Did something happen to Amy or the kids...what's wrong?"

Roland opened one of the cans of Coke and swallowed about half its contents. He sat the can down slowly and precisely in the small indentation in the tray intended for cans or cups and finally looked up at them. "I just almost got fired," he began, then fell silent again.

Nate and Bill looked at each other but neither had anything useful to say in their surprise so they waited for Roland. He remained mute. Finally Nate decided something had to be said, perhaps something to lighten the atmosphere. "Did you grab a woman on the ass or something?" he said.

Roland visibly flinched. "No, dammit, no!" he said. "I tried to be as nice as possible."

Both Nate and Bill realized Nate had actually come close to hitting on the problem, whatever it was. "We don't know anything," Nate said. "I was just making a joke..."

"I tried my best!" Roland said. "I'm not crazy, I got the message. I read the headquarters bulletins. I understand multi-diversional culturosity and I'm doing what I can."

"Multi-cultural diversity," Nate corrected. "What happened? Why don't you start at the beginning so us country boys can understand."

"OK," Roland began after a long hesitation, "Adele Spenlow finally showed up in my basic COVCOM class, and I thought everything was going well. She tried hard. She learned about as much as could be expected from someone who had no technical background whatsoever. I gave her the best possible eval—said she was a good student, but needed more training before being allowed to actively participate in COVCOM ops. It was the best I could do and be halfway truthful, I swear."

He picked up the Coke and drained the rest of it. Setting the now empty can down as precisely as before. He opened the second can and started on it.

"I was so concerned I called her into the office to make sure she understood the situation and that I was not displeased and that she just needed more time. I wasn't more than a minute into the thing before I could see I had screwed up. I'm not sure what she expected, but what I was saying was not what she wanted to hear. Maybe if I had just had the guts to stick to it or just shut up, that would have been unsatisfactory but not awful. You know, it's when you try to really please somebody that you really foul up."

The Coke finally caught up with him and he belched a few times while they waited patiently. "Damn, that feels better," he said."

"So what happened," Nate said, "did she get on your case?"

"No, no, not then," Roland said. "I didn't know anything until today. You know the fourteens are going to be announced in the next few days, but the lucky ones normally get word ahead of time. I got a phone call in person from Frank and he told me to come right down so I figured I was gonna be one of 'em. I put on this new suit just in case they were planning to make pictures in his office..."

"Wait, wait a minute," Nate said, "did you think Frank himself would call you just because you made fourteen and would have you in *his* office to take pictures?"

"Kind of dumb, huh!" Roland said.

"'Dumb' does it too much justice," Nate said. "You should have suspected something. You've been in the boonies too long. When the supreme leader, in person, calls anyone on your level it's always trouble."

"Anyway," Roland said, "the secretary sends me right on in as soon as I show up..." Roland thought for a few seconds then said, "That should have been a hint right there. Frank sits me down in a big red leather chair and wants to know if I want something to drink. I'm thinking: promotion, merit raise, something, but he immediately mentioned the Adele class. He did ask me at first how she had done, but when he asked me about that conversation after the class I knew I was in trouble, but I told him as honestly as I could. I thought he was going to bust. He said how could I have showed her the Butt-Crack Hall of Fame..."

"Whoa! pardner!" Nate interrupted. "You didn't show her that did you? I thought you only showed that to veteran, accomplished techs, and only then when you personally liked 'em."

"You didn't show me that hall until my third class with you!" Bill said. "But you showed it to Adele after that first class where she didn't even do well! What kind of bullshit was that!"

"I'm sorry, Bill," Roland said, now obviously embarrassed for his friend. "I liked you right off, but you were slow to catch onto the signaling—even the STU III..."

"OK, OK,!" Bill said. "So why exactly did you do it?"

"Like I said," Roland began again, "I could tell I was dying in the conversation so I remembered what all the briefs from HQ had said abut being sensitive and nice to women and minorities and decided to do her the great honor of showing her the Hall. I even said I hoped to have a picture of her ass up there one day. What greater compliment could I have paid her?"

As Roland looked at them for an answer, Bill and Nate looked at each other. After a pause for perhaps five seconds, both burst into laughter. Bill began to tear up after the first paroxysm and actually lost his breath for a moment. He quickly turned a blotchy red in the face while Nate turned a solid red. For a good five minutes they couldn't speak. By the time they got themselves under shaky control, almost everyone in the cafeteria was staring or glancing in their direction.

"Dammit! Roland said, "you bastards didn't just about get fired. It's not so funny if Frank is locked on your ass like a bull alligator in heat."

Immediately they were off again on another laughing jag. When Nate actually began to feel weak from the effort, he finally tapered off. "You know, Roland," he said, "I've seen a lot of instances where somebody stepped on their crank, but it's rare that somebody just lays the thing out on the floor and does a fandango on it...anyway, what happens now?"

"If you mean what's going to happen with my future work," Roland said, "I don't know. But right now, as soon as I get back to the office, I have to pack up all the butt-crack pictures and pouch them to Frank. He doesn't even trust me to shred them myself; he wants to do it." He paused for a moment and then added in a voice weighted with sad resignation: "He wants the Hitler picture too."

"I clean forgot about that," Bill said, "but I can see how that would have been trouble sooner or later in today's social climate."

Nate put his hand on Roland's arm and said, "Just for the sake of completeness, what were you saying in the picture this time?"

Roland winced. "Blondes have more fun," he said.

As exhausted as they were from their former bouts of laughter, that set them off again. When they were so tired they could not even squeak, Roland spoke again. "Now that I look at all this, it is funny—in a way. But what should I do now—or is there anything to be done?"

"Look, Roland," Nate said, "I'm making every effort to get overseas ASAP. In a way, you're already overseas. If you don't do anything else to rile Frank, he's going to forget this in short order because he has real problems to deal with. If you think your chewing was bad, think what he had to endure in the IG's office."

"Nate's right," Bill said, "I've been keeping a low profile for over a year and a half now—for different reasons, of course—but the effect is the same. For the next few months, maybe a year or so, the best thing anyone can do is lay low. Frank knows you're the best instructor he's got. He can't do without you. You better believe he wants today to be the start and end of this thing. My guess is the next time you see him somewhere it's going to seem like nothing ever happened."

"I hope you're right," Roland said. He started to speak but held up. He tried once more but stopped again. "There is one more thing," he said finally. "There's a picture of Frank's butt-crack in there too. I pointed it out specially because he's the only office director in the whole Hall. Do you think Adele mentioned that to him too?"

"I have no doubt," Nate said. He started to laugh, but was too exhausted. "Hell," he said, "I can't laugh at this any more right now. I'll save that one for later."

"Well," Roland said, "I got a long drive ahead and it'll take me right up to the end of the day, maybe longer, to get that stuff in the pouch for tomorrow."

"You didn't eat anything, Roland," Nate noted as Roland stood up to leave, "except for the Cokes."

Roland looked at his tray, apparently for the first time. "All desserts," he said in surprise. "You boys want an extra dessert?"

"Sure," Nate said, "and Roland—keep it between the ditches."

"Will do," Roland said and headed out.

"Well," Nate said, "I'll take the chocolate pie and the banana pudding. You can have the Jello and the fruit cup."

"Why do I always get the damn Jello and the fruit cup?" Bill said.

Chapter 13

"So what happened next?" Mike asked.

"Well," Nate said, "a lot happens in the outfit every day. But if you're asking specifically about the characters in this story: Roland had no more trouble with upper management and finally did make fourteen. Frank, as I predicted, wound up in staff positions, got pissed at the whole thing, and is now a very high-powered consultant. You see him on TV from time to time when there's some story about the outfit. Me, I went overseas, came back untouched by any screw-ups, and progressed rapidly in my career."

As he finished the last sentence, he glanced over at Betty who was looking away. "I'm not saying anything," she said without turning back toward the table.

"As I was saying," Nate continued, "Bill stayed with Sam for almost another year, then accepted a thankless assignment in a small tech shop in Latin America. As before, he did competent work and supervised one op that should have gotten him a promotion, but it didn't. Bill has an amazing way of screwing up just before he returns to HQ each time so that higher management can't possibly forget it when they hand out the next assignments.

"The op came up because the COS had had his eye on a young Russian whose career was going nowhere and who was drinking a little too much and showing a mediocre attitude. The COS befriended him at lectures, parties, holiday celebrations, and anywhere he could meet him without raising his profile too much. Then he found out the Russian had been handed the job of running a mid-level government minister who was doing something, probably just a little reporting on the higher government personnel, for the KGB. The COS thought if he caught the Russian red-handed—no pun intended—during a payoff, especially if he could criticize the Russian's tradecraft, he thought the fellow might roll. His sources had found the payoff venue was a resort hotel on the edge of the city where the better people went to relax and the grandees could meet their mistresses in pleasant surroundings. It belonged to the minister's brother. The COS asked Bill if he could photograph or video the meeting.

Bill cased the hotel and discovered each room had a digital clock which projected big, easy-to-read, glow-in-the-dark numbers through a large smoked-glass face plate. Bill got the make and model number and found he could buy the same clock locally. It was as if God had reached down from above."

"Why?" Mike interrupted.

"Oh, yeah, sorry," Nate said. "Our boys in the lab can make anything from the ground up, but if they can start with something already in existence, and that thing is suited to the purpose intended, they can do the impossible faster than the Marines. Think about the clock: It already had a power source which could be adapted to run extra electronic equipment, it had a natural concealment in that smoked-glass face plate, and digital clockworks are small so the large case was almost empty, and the hotel had a load of these things so another one wouldn't draw attention. And to top it all, the clock was supposed to be on the night stand right by the bed; it had a natural view of most of the room.

"Bill proposed the clock be fitted with a video camera. He didn't have any expertise in that, nor did I, but I was the Latin America branch chief in SW at the time and I supervised the modification of the clocks after Bill pouched them home. The boys in the lab had the video working in a couple of days, but there wasn't room for the camera and a recorder inside the case which meant the signal would have to be sent from the camera to a recorder located somewhere outside the room. Since we couldn't be sure which room would be used, we decided we would have to modify a vehicle to receive the signal and to conceal us and the recorder while taping the meeting.

"I organized a team which included the concealment guys and an expert auto body man from the lab, a video expert, a couple of very experienced audio techs, and a couple of bang-and-burn guys for surveillance and security—if we needed it. In less than three weeks, we had the modified clocks on site, the audio boys had modified a station vehicle to receive the output, and we were all down there just kicked back drinking beer waiting for the next meeting. When things are going your way, it really is fun. The meeting went down four days after we arrived. It went so well, I still tear up when I think about it..."

"I'm about to tear up now," Betty said. "Why don't you tell Mike what really made the whole thing happen."

"In time, Betty, in time!" Nate said.

Turning from Betty back to Mike, Nate leaned closer to the young man. "The Russian brought in the briefcase with the money and opened it on the bed directly in front of the clock! You could see the agent and the Russian and the money just like in the movies! It was beautiful!"

"And now," Betty said, "you need to hear the 'rest of the story', as Paul Harvey would say."

"Betty," Nate said with exasperation, "are you telling this or am I. Mike needs to hear the whole thing to get the very best appreciation for our wonderful technical folks."

"Mike needs," Betty said, "to know how the clock was put in the right room at the right time and how it was recovered after the op was over."

"I was coming to that," Nate said. "The HQ desk sent down a young Latina transplant CO who hadn't been on board long, but who had moxie or grit or whatever you want to call it. She got a job as a maid at the hotel and had been working there for a little more than a week before we showed up. We gave her the clock and once she knew which room the minister would be in, she switched it for the real one, activated the video camera, and replaced the real clock again after the op was over."

"That's it! That's best you can do?" Betty said to Nate, then turned to Mike. "Look, Mike, this young woman could have been shot if things had gone wrong and all the lab techs did would have been of no use whatever. Through it all they were back at the station or out in the van with the recorder or sitting in the lobby drinking beer."

"Now, wait, Betty!" Nate said, "Don't forget I also brought along the bang-and-burn boys who would have kicked some ass if it had been needed. But when things go well, nobody's panties get in a twist, nobody gets excited, and the locals don't know anything at all has happened. What we did was clandestine. What Betty's talking about is candlestein."

"I see, I think," Mike said.

"I wish you could have heard the COS tell about the pitch," Nate continued. "He does a hell of job with the story; it gets better all the time. He invites the usual suspects over to his villa for one of those elaborate diplomatic drink-offs and takes the Russian aside for a buddy drink in the study. As soon as they get started the COS turns on the VCR and there's the Russian in glorious black and white making the pay-off. The Russian never turns a hair, watches the whole thing, gets another drink, and turns to the COS and says, 'So what do you want?' It was wonderful! I understand the fellow rose quite high in their ranks and got quite a few coups—with our help—and was one of the best we ever recruited.

"Everybody got well off it: The COS got a promotion and a very good next assignment, the lab techs and the audio guys got an achievement bonus, Bill got a write-up from the COS that would have guaranteed anyone but Bill a promotion, and I was promoted at the next panel a bit earlier than some others who were eligible. Of course, I would have been promoted anyway. Right, Betty?"

"Yes, of course," Betty said, "as usual just your day-to-day performance kept them constantly dazzled."

For a moment they all fell silent as each contemplated the conversation just completed. Finally, Mike asked the inevitable question.

"So why didn't Bill get the promotion?" he asked.

Nate gave a small sigh and hesitated before the began. "I suppose you'd have to say Bill was the living embodiment of 'Murphy's Law'. He really does manage to not only have things go wrong, but to have them go wrong at the absolute worst moment. About a week before he was set to rotate back home—not too long after the op—he was developing some doc copy film of some really good intel. The station had been after these docs for some time and when they finally got a chance to photograph them, they were ecstatic. They managed to get four full rolls of film and handed them over to Bill for developing. Bill had just loaded all four reels for a four-roll Nikor developing tank when he knocked another tank off the counter. The darkroom had an audio switch—maybe you know what I mean. You could turn the lights on and off by squeezing a little air bulb that gave off a high-pitched squeak. Bill never used the thing and had never given it a thought during his entire tour.

"When that stainless steel Nikor fell, it didn't hit the rubber mat. It fell onto the steel leg of the stool he was sitting on. That noise was loud enough and had enough of the right frequency to activate the switch. All the lights came on. It was what we at the old Nikon school call 'available light photography'. He lost all four rolls.

"To this day Bill couldn't tell you why he didn't put the rolls in the tank as he loaded them instead of leaving them out on the counter and he said he didn't remember the other tank being there at all. Even then, if the tank had landed on the rubber mat, the sound would have been deadened. It was fate. By the time he got home, no one in management even wanted to admit they knew him. He wound up in one of our warehouses testing supplies. If you're ever caught out in a meteor shower with him, run like hell."

"Did he ever recover from that disaster?" Mike asked.

"Now this gets really strange," Nate said. "Bill would have recovered from that sooner or later, when he was sufficiently needed somewhere, just like all the rest who screw up. But about a year after he started at the warehouse, a really big problem reared its ugly head, and this was the kind you don't recover from.

"Given Bill's penchant for being out of the loop, the first thing I thought of after I heard about it was did Bill himself know anything. I decided to find out so I headed off to the warehouse."

Chapter 14

"Nate!" Bill said, "How have you been? It seems like we haven't talked since Hector was a pup. What possible reason could you have for coming to the warehouse unless, of course, you missed me."

"I guess that's about right," Nate said, "I just don't get down this way very often. You know how it is in the heady atmosphere of higher management. I just got out of a staff meeting at HQ where Phil Looper told us about his trip to the efficiency conference—that's not the real name of it, but that's what it amounted to. Anyway, Phil said the info was so good, it almost set his hair on fire."

Here Nate paused to give Bill a chance to make the obvious joke. "I guess that would be a pretty small blaze on that almost bald head of his," Bill said.

Both men had a good laugh before Nate continued. "Then Phil turned to the board and wrote down the principal principles of the whole thing and misspelled innovation. I just couldn't get my mind right after that, and it's close to 4 o'clock anyway, and I live out this way too. So how's the work—anything interesting happening?"

"I can't imagine anything interesting happening here unless it was bad," Bill said, "maybe some bad supplies or something. Otherwise it's not too exciting."

"I guess," Nate said as he got up from his chair and began looking around at the various tests in progress and occasionally touching something without speaking.

"I just remembered," Bill said, "it had slipped my mind over the last few years since we haven't worked closely together: As I recall, whenever you started aimless wandering, it always meant you had something on your mind and most of the time it wasn't good. However, since I'm already on warehouse patrol, it can't be anything bad for me. Is there some problem you've got that we might want to talk over?"

"Nah," Nate said, "I just heard from RC that you made a training tape down here a few weeks ago and I wondered what happened to it. Maybe we could use a copy for our library. That's getting to be a big thing now—giving the rookies a tape of a training session before the actual class begins."

"Yeah," Bill said, "I did do a tape now that you mention it, but you can't get this one; it was for SE."

"What did they want a tape for?" Nate said. Bill stared back without speaking.

"Right," Nate said, "they never say what they intend to do—about anything. Have you heard anything about it since?"

"Not a word," Bill said, "and I don't expect to."

After that, the conversation drifted to old times and wondering about how old friends were doing. Eventually, they had talked up all the safe topics and Nate rose to leave. "Well," he said, "I'm outta here. Keep it between the ditches."

"I need to see Sam," Nate thought as he walked out the door.

⁎

As Nate walked down the wide, modern hallways on his way to the Counter-Intelligence section, he recalled the way Sam's shop had once been at the very end of the dim basement corridor in South Building. It had seemed the proper place for a section devoted to mistrusting virtually everyone and everything until they had been tested and vetted. It had always seemed the quiet isolation at the dead end of the hallway was the best place for careful, uninterrupted consideration followed by unofficial meetings at which solid suspicion would be revealed to those who might be directly involved or affected in some less obvious way. It was hard for him to imagine how such a serious, circumspect office could retain its focus among the bright, utilitarian corridors and offices of the new headquarters building, even if Sam was still in residence.

At South Building all the doors had always stood open except for Anthony Wilson's and those offices occasionally doing work for SE— and the door to Sam's lab. Now the new, brightly painted doors were all always shut, but no one ever hesitated to just go through any door not blocked by a cipher lock; it was the new headquarters way. Still, when Nate reached Sam's door, he instinctively reached up to knock, then hesitated. "Damn!" he thought, "it's the new era and I'm three levels up in management, but I'm still afraid to just barge in on him." He moved his hand down to the doorknob without knocking, but opened the door very slowly in spite of himself. About half way down the room, Sam sat at his desk looking at a file positioned between his arms so that they almost surrounded it, just as Nate always remembered. Now his hair had gone completely gray, but when he turned to see his visitor, he still lowered his head and looked over his glasses with the same intensity as on that first day.

"Well," Sam said as Nate approached, "I haven't seen you except at 'all-hands' meetings for a long while. Pull up a stool."

Nate took a stool from the lab bench and moved it close to Sam. Once again Sam looked over his glasses at Nate and then took them off and put them carefully on the desk. "It's not a social visit then," he said.

"Not entirely," Nate said. "It would certainly be that if I had the time, but it seems now all I do is go from one meeting to another and no two are ever near the same place."

"One of the thrills of higher management," Sam said. "OK what can I do for you."

"Bill recently made a training tape for SE," Nate said. "Have you heard anything about it?"

"A training tape...for SE?" Sam said. "Training for what?"

"Basic secret writing procedures," Nate said.

Sam sat silent looking at Nate, then got up and headed for the sink. "Want some coffee?" he said.

"No thanks," Nate said.

Sam carefully poured the coffee, doctored it with great care, and thoroughly rinsed the spoon before carefully turning it out onto a new paper towel. "Where'd you hear this?" he asked.

"RC told me," Nate said, "in a friendly, confidential way. As usual, RC was right; I checked it out with Bill."

"What did Bill think about it?" Sam asked.

"Nothing," Nate said. "He accepted it as something SE wanted and after years of dealing with them on an occasional basis, he just did it and forgot about it."

Sam smiled. "Bill never could get the concept of underhandedness or sneakiness or skullduggery," he said. "He understood it all intellectually, but he never had the gut instincts of a CI expert—or a division chief such as yourself. What do *you* think it means?"

"That's why I'm here now," Nate said. "As one distrustful tech to another, I just want to find out for sure if it really is just an SE wild hair or if it has something to do specifically with Bill."

"You know," Sam said, "that if there was anything significant about it and SE had asked my help or advice on it and I had some knowledge of it, I couldn't pass it on without their approval."

"Yes," Nate said, "I do know that, but if there wasn't anything to it, you could certainly say that, could you not? And if there wasn't anything to it, you would certainly tell me not to waste my time in pursuing it any farther, I reckon."

"Yes," Sam said, "I suppose I would, given the circumstances you mentioned. And I know that if you did keep looking into it, I would never be mentioned as having said anything to encourage you in any way."

"Never in a million years," Nate said.

"You want some coffee?" Sam asked.

***

146

"I can't believe it," Bill said as Nate again entered the lab, "two visits in two months. We've got to stop spending so much time together—or that's what my sweetie recently told me."

"Women don't ever appreciate nothin'," Nate said as they shook hands. "Did you tell her you worked for you-know-who to try to win her over?"

"No," Bill said, "she's already Agency."

"Always a bad move," Nate said. "I hope she doesn't work in this building."

"No way," Bill said. "Being lust crazed doesn't make you plumb crazy, as we say down home. Is it the social situation that brings you back this way so soon?"

"Not entirely," Nate said, "but we are social animals subject to all the busy destructive urges we've had for the last three million years and I'll bet the first real conversation the cave men had was over some hot woman.

"But I do have a question for you. Did you have another poly recently?"

"Yes," Bill said, "as I'm sure you already know or you wouldn't have asked, but it was the usual, routine check. What about it?"

"Do you remember when you had your last routine exam prior to the most recent one?" Nate asked.

"I dunno exactly," Bill said, "but I'm sure it was on the usual schedule?"

"Would you believe less than half the normal interval between routine exams," Nate said.

"If you say so, I would," Bill said. "Maybe they had some downtime or lost track and moved me up...I see that's the wrong answer."

"'Fraid so," Nate said. "At least I think so, and so does Sam."

"Sam!" Bill said. "How's he doing? I haven't seen him since Michael Jackson was black!"

"I'll pretend I didn't hear that," Nate said, "or I'd have to turn you in for remedial sensitivity. Anyway, there's something wrong in SE and you seem to be involved."

"Oh, God!" Bill said, "is there a contract out on me?"

"I'm serious," Nate said. "I wouldn't know about if it hadn't involved SW ops and if Sam hadn't given me some info that he shouldn't have."

"Jesus!" Bill said, "I've only worked with them at odd intervals over my career. I don't think I've ever done enough to create a good screw-up. Can you say what it is, or what you think—or Sam— thinks it is?"

"Some of it," Nate said, "but there's a lot of it Sam doesn't know. And of course if anyone in SE finds out about this conversation, I'm dead meat."

"Don't worry," Bill said, "I probably won't want to hear about it anyway and it will be easy to pretend I haven't heard anything. It's been that way all through my career; when I hear something, it's not news, it's history."

"You're probably right that it will get out sooner or later and that it will be history by then," Nate said, "but right now, something is in the wind. Let me mention some crypts to you; see if they ring any bells."

As Nate mentioned each agent crypt, Bill took a few seconds to try and remember if it sounded at all familiar but none registered.

"Not a one," he said, "but you know that doesn't mean anything. I never paid any attention to the crypts used when I worked with SE because they always double or triple-encrypted everything. I knew the crypts I heard were made up just for the time I was involved and that for sure they weren't the real ones. I do remember that almost all of my work with SE was in about a two year period when we were occasionally shorthanded in SW ops—can't remember the reasons why—and I had to fill in for those Mr. Willy had specifically designated to work with SE. But I just got the spill-overs: preparing a message now and then; developing a few messages; three, maybe five, trainings. All the trainings were just the basic techniques. I don't remember issuing any supplies or even giving any of the assets the usual second session. Didn't think of it as anything but headquarters hand-holding from my standpoint. I figured the second session was probably handled by our guys overseas or maybe the SE tech referents. What's the matter, some bad agents?"

"Looks like it," Nate said. "FYI, those I mentioned were thought to be excellent producers for several years. They seemed to have exactly what SE was looking for and one at least rose quite high in the Russian hierarchy. All the cases went well with no apparent suspicion from the KGB and their reports were technically very good as well as providing great intel. SE was pridefully satisfied with all of them and some of the COs involved advanced significantly based on the cases. So this is very, very sensitive."

Bill sat in silence for a minute or so staring at the periodic chart over the sink and mumbling slightly to himself. "Excellent intel, no trouble reporting, no CI concerns from the Russkies..."

"Mind if I have some coffee?" Nate asked.

"Nah," Bill said, "help yourself, but be careful; by this time of day, it might change your personality."

"I'll just sip it at first," Nate said, "like I would some of that bust-head that's just come out of a still where I haven't personally seen what's in the fermentation tank."

As Nate puttered with the coffee Bill stared at the chart. Nate saw he hadn't changed: It took Bill a long time to digest new information. He fooled with the coffee until he decided Bill had had time to think it through.

"They were probably bad from the git-go," Bill said. "You know SE always had the greatest tendency to talk themselves into being true believers. Most of their assets were so hard to vet they had to go with just their gut most of the time. I know most of us techs thought most SE cases were bad."

"Let two great minds—three, including Sam's—be reunited,"

Nate said. "But for now, 'bad agents' is not an option. Right now the assumption is that they were as pure as the driven snow, at least to begin. We have to approach it that way until something concrete says otherwise."

"So why is the technical aspect involved?" Bill said.

"This is nothing but a guess," Nate said, "but suppose these assets were pure to begin and suppose they were blown either by their send or receive SW systems. Maybe an SW message was somehow detected. You know any good intel service wants to identify an agent and then turn them. Just shooting the guy or throwing him in prison means failure of a sort. No service is going to do that until everything to get them to cooperate has failed."

"So right now they're trying to find out if I screwed up the training or the messages," Bill said. "That was the reason for the tape."

"Right," Nate said. "They showed it to Sam to see if a CI expert could find anything wrong, but as you might expect, the technique was flawless."

"It damn well should be!" Bill said. "I've been doing this for almost twenty years...so what happens now?"

"You wait as if you know nothing," Nate said, "unless you remember something Sam and I should know. If we hear anything, I'll be in touch. We have to let the investigation play out. Now that they've seen the training tape and your poly has been done, I doubt you will hear anything else. I would guess that pretty soon they will have to eliminate you as a problem."

***

For almost three months, no one came up with any new information on the case, not even RC, and Nate was beginning to believe it had all been some sort of huge mistake when he got a very brief, very firm request from Sam to come to his lab. Nate headed for Sam's lab as soon as he hung up the phone. He knew from past experience that Sam hated to waste time and if he wanted to talk personally, it meant he needed not to simply pass on information, but that something needed face-to-face discussion.

"I guess you've got some news," Nate said in greeting.

"Yes," Sam said, "and I don't like it. The more you know about something, the simpler it should get, but this thing involving Bill is getting stranger. Do you know how the SE boys first noticed a problem with Bill's cases?"

"No," Nate said, "I assumed it was part of a routine check or that something raised a red flag."

"Right on the first guess," Sam said. "Being a true professional, and constantly vetting his agent, the CO for SEBORIS initiated a routine check of the agent's handwriting to look for signs of stress. So he submitted one of the first SW messages received and the last one. He didn't expect the normal level of detail from the graphologist since the messages were in cyrillic; just wanted to see if the stress level had changed, as it might if the asset was feeling threatened or more than usually concerned. Well, you can imagine what happened when our graphology tech returned the messages and said she couldn't tell anything because the messages had been written by two different people! Once the CO emptied his pants, the re-vetting began, not just for that asset, but for every one in the entire division. It took a while, which has only complicated things more.

"Right now, the bottom line is that at least five bad SE assets have Bill as a common factor. They were either trained by him and/ or received SW messages prepared by him. Two were replaced by someone, probably a KGB tech, during the reporting period of the op, suggesting that at least those two were righteous to begin. The others may have been too, and may have been simply turned by the Russians and continued writing under KGB instructions. Of course, I believe it's possible all the assets could have been bad from the start, but SE refuses to buy that. They are convinced at least some were initially genuine—they believe all—and got blown during the op— we're talking a few years here.

"They think maybe a send or receive message was detected, the assets were watched for a while, then the KGB moved in. Maybe some of them turned when confronted, and maybe some, for whatever reason, were thrown in jail, or worse. We just don't know. But the crucial thing is: So far, of the assets that have been re-vetted, five who are known to be bad involve Bill in some way. Yes, of course, at least one other tech was involved in each operation, but only Bill is common to all five."

"Hell, Sam," Nate said, "you know how SE hates to have one of its big accounts turn bad, and the way they can talk themselves into things. I'll bet at least half of all their assets are bad..."

"Yes," Sam said, "that's probably right, but they surely did admit, in this case, that five significant reporters were bad and that must have hurt like the devil."

"What about Bill then?" Nate asked.

"So far," Sam said, "he's still the only common element in multiple cases, but the damage assessment is far from over."

"Damn!" Nate said, "he has to be the unluckiest bastard who ever lived."

"But keep in mind," Sam said, "SE has not mentioned him since the initial investigation. I'm not sure they still think it has anything to do with him, but they can't find anything else, or at least they haven't told me any different. My guess is our window is closed until they sort it all out. I also guess Bill won't hear another word unless something else breaks bad for him. Of course, he needs to be told where he stands by someone, just as a courtesy."

"And the initials of that someone are 'Nate Forest', I suppose," Nate said. "OK, Sam, I'm on my way to give Bill the bad news."

Chapter 15

As Bill and Nate sat near the burrito bar in the cafeteria it occurred to both of them just how long it had been since they had last met there and Bill again mentioned the day Roland had almost had the heart attack in front of them. Once they had laughed yet again at that, Bill decided he might as well begin to turn the conversation to what he assumed was its real purpose. "You know," he said, "I'll bet more real ops talk and planning has been done right here at this burrito bar than in all the sterile conference rooms in headquarters."

"No doubt," Nate agreed. "They use the sterile rooms for talk about money and promotion. That ops stuff can be done anywhere."

"You remember Dave's old Truth Chair," Bill continued. You couldn't sit in it unless you told the whole, unvarnished, truth. Most importantly, if you had bad news for Dave and told it to him while sitting in the Truth Chair, he would take no action other than to try to fix the screw-up you had just revealed. I've never been Catholic, but it must have been like their confession. I always thought the main thing that kept Catholicism going was the psychological benefit of being forgiven and allowed to start over. Anyway, as long as you held to the rules, you might be in Dave's doghouse for while, but you got another chance. On the other hand, if he caught you hiding something or found out about your disaster from someone else, he descended on you as only an old-time chief could.

"I always planned, if I ever got to that level, to get myself a Truth Chair for my office. You think anyone would sit in it nowadays?"

"Bill" Nate said, "if you had one of those things nowadays, it would be like it was radioactive; nobody, nobody would get near it. However, there's a couple of people I'd like to see squirming in that chair for a few minutes."

"Would you pardon 'em?" Bill asked.

"Today," Nate said, "even a division chief dare not do anything but send the screw-ups to remedial training, and if you upset them emotionally, they have to get counseled, not fired."

"Then right now," Bill said, "this burrito bar is the closest thing to a Truth Chair, don't you think?"

"I reckon," Nate said. "If somebody had something important to say, I suppose this would be as good a venue as any. Do you think I have something important to say today? After all, I couldn't help but notice your subtle parable on the Truth Chair."

"Well," Bill said, "I figure if I get personally invited to meet at the burrito bar, which has sort of been 'our place' over the later years, instead of your office, I think it means the meeting is official for me, off the record for you—a bad omen for sure."

"Nah," Nate said, "just an up-date. Sam and I have found out a little more about the problem in SE. It looks like at least two of the assets I told you about were good after all, at least initially. One of our graphologists found out that one of them had been replaced by another writer and things progressed from there. A full-scale damage assessment is still going on and probably will for a while yet."

Bill sat in silence as he thought it over. Nate sat quiet giving him time to think. "I guess the essential question is how did the good ones get blown," Bill said finally.

"That's what Sam has been involved with," Nate agreed, "and from our personal standpoint, it's the most important factor."

"In a way," Bill said, "it would be best, even for us, if I did something. That way, at least the integrity and security of our systems would not be in question. If I didn't do anything, it could be the systems, the tradecraft, their security procedures...a lot of unpleasant things."

"Yes," Nate said, "it's unfortunate no matter how it finally turns out."

"Do we know what happened to the known good ones who are no longer writing?" Bill asked.

"We don't know anything yet," Nate said, "or at least we haven't been able to find it out from SE. I put RC on it but it's very delicate; even he's having trouble."

"I don't suppose it matters," Bill said. "What's done is done. We know for sure it's either prison or execution for the good ones who disappeared..."

Nate had realized this moment was sure to come up in the conversation and he had thought of a dozen things to say to make it less painful, but now he realized Bill would not appreciate any of his euphemisms. It was better just to let the truth alone. It was the way Bill had always preferred it.

"I remember the philosophy you believed in during your career," Nate said, "was always: 'I can stand bad news, but don't bullshit me'. I know you haven't changed. I thought you ought to know as much as I do. I'll be in touch the minute I hear anything new, good or bad."

"I appreciate it," Bill said, "but there's really no hurry."

Both officers knew the process involving any complete re-assessment of the assets of any operational section would, indeed, be very long. They departed the cafeteria with Nate determined to find the whole truth and Bill resigned to endure uncertainty for as long as was required. At least he now knew the full scope of the problem.

***

Given the long interval expected before any definitive news of the security breach could be obtained and the fact that he knew he might never hear anything more, Bill had no expectation the next meeting with Nate would be any time soon. Therefore, when Nate again showed up at his lab, Bill was truly surprised.

"Let me guess," Bill said as Nate walked in, "I've been promoted

155

and you're here to let me know about the surprise party because you know how I hate surprises."

"Not really," Nate said, "I don't have any news of any kind. This is purely social."

"I wish we had beer," Bill said. "Do you remember when vespers was wet and held every Friday?"

"Yep," Nate said, "now vespers is closer to actual vespers."

"It's really better now, you know," Bill said, "putting all those semi-drunks on the road just at the end of rush-hour was always risky. Of course, most of them wound up at Charley's Place or Murphy's anyway. They didn't go all the way home. Have you noticed how we talk so much about the good old days now instead of the future?"

"Well," Nate said, "it's either the good old days that are safely past or the uncertain times ahead; it makes sense to me."

"Actually," Bill said, "I have been thinking about the future. I think I'm going to hang it up fairly soon now that we've got a window of early-outs coming up."

"But the problem is," Nate said, "that most of the early- outs have in thirty-plus years and you only have just over twenty. Can you afford it?"

"Yes," Bill said, "I think I can, and I know I can if I hightail it back down home. Down there, I'd be making more than the sheriff just to get up in the morning, and he's risking his life for his salary."

"What about the Irish bars and the Birchmere and bagpipes in Old Town and all that?" Nate asked.

"I'd adjust." Bill said.

"Don't you like the work any more?" Nate asked. "I know testing supplies doesn't make your heart race, but this won't last forever."

"Actually, when I'm boiling ethanol, sometimes my heart does race," Bill said, "but I do like this work, simple as it is. And just like the last twenty years, the people I work with are first rate.

"Do you remember the time we had that discussion about how they paid us twenty thousand when we were doing sixty thousand worth of work, but at the moment of that conversation we didn't feel we were quite earning our total keep? As I remember, we were just carping because we hadn't been overseas or TDY recently, but now I really am getting that backing-up-to-take-the-paycheck feeling. I don't like it."

"Bill," Nate said in obvious exasperation, "there is no reason to think you will stay here. It's only a matter of time before you're needed in ops again."

"Now we come to it," Bill said, "that's not right. I've had RC doing a little work for me lately too, and what he found out is not pretty. I sent him to check unofficially about possibly getting overseas again. We both know that's the only place I was ever better than mediocre. When I get back to headquarters my IQ drops twenty points and I lose the last molecule of confidence."

Here Nate held up his hand, but Bill did not want to be interrupted. "Hold on," he said, "let me finish this. RC checked with all the potential base chiefs and not one was interested in having me show up. Unless someone dies, I'm stuck at HQ even if I don't stay right here."

Although Bill had not mentioned it Nate knew uncertainty over the trouble in SE was a large factor in Bills grounding and until it was cleared up nothing was going to change. He decided to bring the painful issue forward once more.

"Well," Nate said, "the thing in SE is dormant. I haven't heard anything..."

"Whoa!" Bill said, "did you hear me say anything about SE? There's another reason no one needs me in ops right now, and the reason for that is sitting right on this desk." Here Bill indicated the Wang workstation. "Do you see what it says on the TV there?" he asked.

"Monitor," Nate corrected. "Yes. It says 'entry suspended.'"

"That's what it says most of the time," Bill said. "There's something about these things that just makes me feel like my mental shorts are too tight. Do you know I've been sent to three classes already—our management is doing its damnedest to help me out—and I was deep into the third class before I found out that those symbols on the thing where 'on' and 'off' should be are a '1' and a '0'? When we let the computer nerds take 'on' and 'off' away from us, we should have arisen *en mass* and beat hell out of every geek we could find. Now the game is over. They control our lives and we are helpless.

"In the first class I attended, the young fellow began with: 'This is a computer,' and I swear the next sentence out of his mouth sounded like: 'If you auto-exec bat your mouse files, the skuzzy drive will overload and your machine will go critical.' In that class, I got a grade of: 'passed, but needs extra instruction.' In the next class, I got: 'should re-take the course.' In the last class, I got: 'attended all sessions.' Even here, the so-called experts can't fix anything, probably because of all their training. But our eighteen-year-old secretary can hit a few keys, think a few seconds, hit a few more keys, and the damned thing straightens right out. We don't call the experts anymore; they're almost as complete dinosaurs as we are. Now we call for Mandy."

"Bill...," Nate began, but hesitated before continuing, "all right, let's say computers are a pain for us dinosaurs, but I've done OK on the things. And I know you can too if you hang in there. Anyone who can balance a redox equation or put in a darkroom with a Swiss army knife has to be useful even if he isn't a computer whiz."

"But think about it this way, Nate," Bill said, "even though right now, we are mainly passing disks, the obvious future is to send the intel over the phone lines at the speed of light. That's where the crunch will come. I would never, never be sure after I finished a training, that the agent understood things well enough so that he could not fail to encrypt his information before sending it. I know that just one keystroke can change everything. I would always wonder if his reports ever went out in the clear."

"But, Bill," Nate said, "our own computer nerds will make the systems foolproof. The agent won't be able to foul up...Anyway, don't pull the plug too soon, OK?"

"I promise I will proceed with caution," Bill said, "just like granddaddy when he saw the radiator hooked up to the still; he didn't take a drink until he was sure the last of the anti-freeze was gone."

Chapter 16

In the bar, the peak of noise, hilarity, and boisterousness had passed. Those who had only come by for a drink after work were long absent, those who had significant errands to run early next day had departed, and those few did not drink had gone with them. Those left would be staying right up to closing time. The conversations had quieted and those participating had moved closer to each other and had begun to talk face to face or in small groups. Next to the walls in sheltered booths and at the bar, men tried to talk women into coming home with them and the women tried to determine if the men were worth the risk. The three tables of Agency people had been condensed to one large group at one table, and here too, the conversations had become quieter, smaller, and more serious.

"Did Bill ever reconsider retirement," Mike asked, "or did he come to this point tonight just as he said he would?"

"Bill has a funny way of doing things," Nate said, "in that once he decides something after thinking it over carefully, he rarely changes no matter what happens. I don't mean he's stubborn or unreasonable or can't change his mind, he just sort of stops considering alternatives unless they are forced on him. From the time I had that conversation where he said he was going early, he never faltered."

"Was it computers that made him quit—in your opinion?" Mike asked.

"Yes," Nate said, "it was, but it was tied in with the wondering about those blown agents. I believe, repeat, believe that bothered him and that he just did not want to take the chance of putting someone else in danger by training in computer-based systems he didn't really understand. Even he admits now that he doesn't really have trouble using computers to do ordinary things in the office and at home."

"Did you ever find out what happened?" Mike asked.

"Yes," Nate said, "but the answer didn't come quickly and, once again, it was Sam who made the breakthrough. It began when Sam got a call from Plato Dinwiddie our tech referent in SE."

***

As Sam entered Plato Dinwiddie's cubicle, he was astounded at the heaps of folders lying on the tops of file cabinets, near the hot plate, and even on the floor. He had never seen any file left unattended anywhere in SE at any time. The casualness of it all raised his counter-measures antennae and he convinced himself that no matter how many files were out or how they were scattered, at the end of the day, they would all wind up in some file cabinet or in the vault. Yes, he told himself, they would have to be put in the vault even if it took a good while to gather all of them up.

Plato sat at the desk in his small cubicle surrounded by more stacks of files, some of which had fallen over. "Hi, Sam," he said, "thanks for coming over so fast. It's good to see you."

"Yes," Sam said, pushing some encroaching files out of the way as he sat down, "good to see you too. I didn't see much of you after you took the referent job over here. You sort of dropped off the OTS radar after that."

"Oh, I was in your area a lot actually," Plato said, "but I didn't see you much in person which was good, really—I mean we only came to see you if we had some trouble with the technical aspects of a case and even then not if the young Turks could solve it..."

"So what is it now that I can help with?" Sam interrupted.

"Look around," Plato said with a note of desperation in his voice as he indicated the files. "Have you ever seen anything like this?"

"No, can't say I have," Sam said, "at least not in SE."

"Right," Plato said, "do you remember how it was when we worked and waited for any useful scrap of information, how we even had the Russian newspapers completely translated, how we scrutinized every overt source from every Bloc country to try to add something to our intel reports.

"Now we've got a flood, not a trickle. As I understand it, an East German officer drove into the embassy in Berlin a couple of weeks ago with a pickup truck full of files. For years we struggled for a decent report and now we've literally got truckloads of intel. We recently sent a group of case officers out to the Bloc with notebook computers. They just show up, put out the word, and let the Commies come in. It's almost like a job interview to see who can tell the most.

"All these files have been pulled for review because all these assets are terminated. But now that can mean anything from having been shot, to defecting, to being retired because they were no longer needed, to having been moved to the US and given new identities. In a way it's a nightmare even though we won the Cold War. I never thought when the Wall came down it would ever lead to this."

"Well, Plato," Sam said, "don't give up. Maybe we can start the war again with any luck. I can't believe all the Russians are our blood-brothers overnight. I'm sure we can still piss each other off enough for some useful spying to continue. Besides, if we can't generate something like that, the old SE case officers will all commit suicide. They need the Russians to make their lives complete."

"Sam," Plato said, "you shouldn't joke about this. Some of them really do seem lost."

"Hell, Plato," Sam said, "I wasn't joking. I know exactly what you mean. I'll bet they find some kind of crisis to deal with as soon as they recover from the shock. Now what is it you want me do exactly?"

"SE wants a summary of the technical operations for every file in this office. They want to know what worked, what didn't, how our systems were detected if they were, what technical censorship methods were used against us—everything useful regarding the technical

162

aspects of every individual case."

"Well, Plato," Sam said, "it looks like about five years of work just in that pile that fell over near the window, not to mention the ones behind your chair and under your desk and on top of the file cabinets..."

"Please, Sam!" Plato said.

"OK," Sam said, "I'll put as much time in as I possibly can, but you must remember that in a few months, I'm out the door."

"We can bring you back on a green badge," Plato said. "You retire on Friday; on Monday you get the greenie."

"Yes," Sam said, "no doubt. But you know, Plato, some of us call that the Green Badge of Shame. It's like some folks can't quit. It's like they're addicted..."

"Dammit, Sam!" Plato said. "Quit gigging me and help out—please!"

***

"Nate?" the voice on the phone said.

"Yes," Nate answered, "...Sam?"

"Come see me when you get a chance," Sam said and hung up.

"Dammit!" Nate thought. "Sam still doesn't trust even the secure lines in the building."

Nate thought about calling Sam back immediately to say he could not possible talk to him for a couple of days due to the press of business, but he knew Sam would understand that already. If the meeting had been urgent, Sam would certainly have said so. It was very late on the second day after the call before he entered Sam's lab again.

"I know it's been a few days, Sam," Nate began, "but I just could not get free until now. Sorry it's almost quitting time."

"No problem," Sam said, "I guess I can stay over a few minutes today. I'll just pretend it's like the early years in my career when I put in thousands of overtime hours for free and enjoyed every minute."

"Am I going to enjoy this?" Nate asked.

"Parts of it you will enjoy," Sam said, "parts, maybe not. I think I finally know what happened to Bill."

"Amen!" Nate said. "Let's hear it."

"You remember," Sam began, "that some time ago when SE seemed to lose interest in Bill, we figured he was in the clear but couldn't prove it."

"Right," Nate said, "even though they never said anything, that didn't mean much. Once they were satisfied, that was it. They didn't have to say anything and, as usual, none of us would have been cleared to hear it anyway."

"And we still wouldn't have the story, or what I think is the story," Sam said, "except that Plato Dinwiddie is almost literally covered up in terminated files that SE wants examined from the technical aspect. And those files are complete. Everything's there. I never before in my life saw any complete SE file until now. The best we ever got was the few pages devoted to the technical training and equipment. Now Plato is giving out the whole folder to whoever is willing to help. Of course, since Plato was so desperate for assistance, he didn't give a damn which files I took to investigate, just so I took some. I chose carefully."

"No doubt," Nate said.

"Now for those assets that probably kept Bill awake some nights," Sam continued. "There were apparently three good assets—initially good, that is, who were recruited overseas in various hell-holes where even the most dedicated Russian craved friendship with our COs who had steaks, air conditioning, good-quality booze, first-run movies... And they did what they were asked as they moved around and up. One had reported for several years and was in a position where his stuff was extremely valuable when he was blown. The other two were still lesser lights when they were detected but they were starting to give really good intel. The other two were providing what we thought was very good stuff but we now believe they were bad from the start, probably

KGB officers writing from the very beginning.

"They all had high-level receiving and sending SW systems and I'm sure they were not chemically detected. These systems are so good, our own best labs can't detect them. That was why SE figured it must either be the asset's preparation technique, or ours—that is, Bill's—that gave the game away. Although we knew our work was perfect, SE didn't, at least for a while. I couldn't figure it out either, but I was sure our techs, not just Bill, but any who ever worked on any of the cases, never made even the slightest mistake. I also saw the training reports and the test messages the assets themselves had prepared before they began writing for real. I examined them myself and could not find any flaw in their technique; they had been very well trained as we would expect. Still, SE couldn't find anything other than detection of the messages to account for the assets' being blown."

"Then what?" Nate said.

"I got to thinking about that Chinese asset from long ago," Sam said, "the one who was receiving microdots and who got arrested and confessed when they showed him one of his own dots."

"I remember that," Nate said, "and I remember how Gordon Charles felt about it when he heard the asset was in prison. He never worked on another microdot case. As I recall, Gordon was burying the dots in the glue seam of the envelopes. To have even a chance to detect the dot, the censors had to take the entire envelope apart. He was also the best I've ever seen at burying the damn things...I hated microdot cases."

"Right," Sam said, "and you remember how he tested the envelopes over and over to see if maybe a seam had let go, or if the glue he used could have been somehow differentiated from the factory glue, and all the other things he tried. I worked with him for a good two months on it and we couldn't find a thing. Then we reported to East Asia Division and they thought about terminating all microdot cases. In fact, an EA case officer was working with Gordon and me to write up the All Stations and Bases cable on the thing when we found out what had actually happened. Do you recall what it really was?"

"Yes," Nate said, "I surely do: the refrigerator."

"Give the man a kewpie doll!" Sam said. "When the asset showed up with that bottom-of-the-line refrigerator, it wasn't two days until he was reported by the village headman. The censors took every letter he got over the next few weeks and soaked all of them in water until one day a dot floated out. He confessed at the next struggle session.

"In the initial damage assessment for Bill's cases, the part I got to see, concerned itself with the technical details only, and since I hadn't been able to find anything wrong with any of that, I began to think there must be a 'refrigerator'. When Plato handed over the complete files I began looking for it."

"And did you find it?" Nate asked.

"I believe so," Sam said, "but I can't prove it. I ran across references to one other agent in three of the files—those of the righteous assets— but he was then, and might still be, a long-time, absolutely trustworthy, very valuable asset. I put Plato on the case, but he couldn't actually see that file because it's still active and that means the 'refrigerator' asset is either still viable or very sensitive for some other reason. Plato did say the asset reported, among other things, on potential targets, either individuals who might be susceptible to recruitment or might have specific information we were looking for. He must either be high up with a good overview of their operations, or at least able to see personnel records if he's spotting for us. But—and this you will find interesting—Plato did find out that the asset is receiving CYNOSURE. After I heard that, I did some checking back in SW and found out that Warner Barret himself is running the technical part of the case."

Nate stared at Sam for several seconds. "What the hell was Warner doing running this thing by himself?" he asked. "I know CYNOSURE was his baby and that he and Adele pushed it past Bill, but to actually let him run the case...Did Tony Wilson agree to it?"

"No," Sam said, "and he was unhappy about it in the way only Mr.

Willie can be unhappy about things. But he was asked by SE to bow out a long time ago. Warner apparently sold SE on the idea that he, who had invented CYNOSURE, would be best at handling it and, as always, the fewer folks who knew anything, the better. You know how Mr. Willie can wash his hands of something if it doesn't suit him. He made no effort to monitor the case or assist Warner and Adele, who was Warner's personal assistant at the time. Of course, I'm sure that's exactly how Warner and SE wanted it."

"Damn!" Nate said, "I had forgotten Adele. OK, Sam, so what are you thinking?"

"I'm thinking," Sam said, "that Bill did a shitty job of explaining the dangers of CYNOSURE to SE and that Warner convinced them it really was an 'A' system. Plato said the 'refrigerator' asset had been receiving regular dots. We all know what a pain in the ass that is, and I'll bet the asset was probably complaining about how difficult it was to read them, as they all do. My guess is Warner's presentation got them thinking about CYNOSURE, and since it was an on-going case, it was easy to simply substitute it for dots. The agent required no actual retraining other than being shown where the message would be. I would guess he read it out with a microscope, maybe a child's microscope—if he has kids. And finally, I'll bet the asset loved it. I know I would have, compared to dots. But I'm betting that's where he bought the refrigerator.

"It's certain Warner changed the carrier—it had been a regular letter—to something suitable for CYNOSURE and that the Russkies, who trust no one and constantly scrutinize everyone, noticed the change and gave it their routine counter-measures once-over. And remember: at the time, their whole CI/security force was still intact and superb. I'll bet they read the little bitty letters completely unbeknownst to the asset and started searching for anyone he might have mentioned or had knowledge of who could have been of any interest to us, given our requirements. Knowing the requirements we laid on him also made it easy to put forward dangles in just the right places which he could not fail to notice and then recommend to us. Of course, we recruited them and began running the cases."

"Strong words, Sam," Nate said, "and scary, and inflammatory. Can you prove it?"

"No," Sam said, "remember, the 'refrigerator' file is still active for some reason and even Plato could only get the bare bones technical data. While I'm now sure Bill is in the clear there is no way we can officially exonerate him at this stage. Knowing his luck, I think he was just in the wrong place at the wrong time—five times in fact. The only thing to do, in my estimation, is for someone to talk to Warner about the 'refrigerator' asset. I'm sure he will have no idea about the operational details, but he certainly knows the technical details and what's going on with CYNOSURE. I tried but he wouldn't talk to me about it. He wouldn't even admit he was involved. I would guess it might take a higher power to get the info."

"And I guess that means me," Nate said.

"Who else do you know," Sam said, "who can run a bluff, is powerful enough to demand the info, and cares enough about Bill to be concerned about what happens to him. Good luck, my friend. You can tell me all about it at my retirement party."

Chapter 17

"So," Mike said, "did you get the straight story when you talked to Warner? What did Bill say when you told him? When..."

"Whoa, Pardner!" Nate said, "let's go back to question number one. I thought, repeat, thought I had enough pull to get the story, but I was wrong. Of course, whenever I encounter anything like that now, I have no trouble with it."

"That means, Mike," Betty interrupted, "that he has now reached the 'his-ass-weighs-a-ton' status...I offer that just in case you, being completely new, might not have understood it from the context—and the accumulative effect of the beer tonight."

"Thank you, Betty," Nate said. "Now, as I was saying, since I could not get a definitive answer from Warner, I didn't say anything to Bill. He's the kind of fellow who likes to know rather than believe, and I knew my speculation, good as it was, wouldn't have made a difference."

"So Bill had to go on not knowing," Mike said, staring for a moment at the table. "What about his work and his career?" he said, looking back up at Nate. "How was that affected?"

"Two separate questions," Nate said, "very separate. Bill's work went on as before. That's the way of professionals. But his career was well and truly off the track. Everyone in OTS knew he was a competent ops officer, but there was no way the upper reaches of management were going to send him out as the chief of anything, and with his experience and seniority, only chiefs positions would have been appropriate. That meant he was permanently grounded, or headquarters-based, if you will. However his experience and expertise were too useful to ignore, so he wound up on umpteen study groups, promotion panels, training seminars, etc.; and especially in assistance to overseas liaison.

"Liaison is a strange animal. If a COS has a good relation with local liaison—and it can be an intelligence group or the police or the military or maybe parts of all of them—he can really operate. We cooperate with first-world services such as MI-5, and we give assistance to the lesser liaison services, especially in the third world. The trick is to get good cooperation but not to give away anything worthwhile in the process. It's a ticklish job and requires the experience of a seasoned tech, but once a tech is known to liaison his ability to operate under cover is compromised, at least to some degree, and he is then not as useful for important unilateral operations. The job usually falls to senior techs who have been declared to a few liaison services or who have had other exposures during their careers, or who, like Bill, might be under a cloud for some reason. Whatever the complication, they cannot function as first-line, un-compromised techs. All the while he was at the warehouse Bill's single, most important job was liaison training and operations. You might as well begin to get some appreciation for liaison ops tonight even though you won't be involved with them for many years yet.

"A good example is one op that Bill handled while I was Chief at NORTECH on my second tour out there, and to top it off, it's a good war story."

"Wait," Betty said, "are you actually starting another war story at this time of night. Didn't Tom, in photo training, ever give you that famous maxim of his: 'Never start another elephant at five o'clock?'"

"I do recall that, Betty," Nate said, "but I never figured out what he meant."

"That's clear," Betty said as she stood up. "Mike, good to meet you. I hate to abandon you to Nate and I hope he won't cause you to resign before the night is over. See you at work if you do survive. Good night all."

"'Nite, Betty," Nate said, "y'all drive careful, ya hear."

"Good night, Betty," Mike said. "It's been a pleasure."

"Don't keep him here all night," Betty said as she bent down to give Nate a peck on the cheek.

Nate smiled at her and she turned to go. Both men watched her as she headed for the door. "Fine woman," Nate said, "but not much stamina."

Mike turned back to Nate and stared at him in silence.

"Not enough stamina for drinking all night," Nate explained, "or maybe she's just too smart. Now about that story: It began when I met Bill at the airport."

***

Bill stared groggily at the bags slowly bumping along on the carousel. He thought how many times he had stood just as now, half awake, half asleep, after yet another overnight flight without sleeping. He wondered how, after more than two million air miles, he still could not sleep on airplanes. The best he had ever done was an occasional few minutes of fretful dozing at the nadir of exhaustion and too much alcohol. Through the mental fog, he seemed to hear a familiar voice with a familiar greeting: "May the brotherhood be reunited!"

To make sure he hadn't just imagined it, he turned toward the sound to find Nate with hand already outstretched and a big grin on his face. After a few seconds of recovery he took Nate's hand and pumped it heartily. "I never thought a base chief ever met an ordinary tech," he said.

"Well," Nate said, "you once met me here long ago. I just thought I might return the favor.

"Now that I know you're here and you know I'm here, I'll go get the car and meet you at 'arrivals'. You ought to be just about there by the time I drive up, given the usual split-second timing for which our outfit is so justifiably famous."

"I have no doubt," Bill said as Nate disappeared into the crowd.

As the two old friends drove back toward NORTECH, they talked over old times and old friends as they had done so many times in the past, but now, except for the instance when Nate had tried to help Bill with the trouble in SE, the two had not seen each other except on unusual occasions such as retirement parties or chance meetings in the course of work. In none of those situations had they ever had long to talk, always because Nate was needed somewhere immediately. Both now looked forward to the few days Bill would spend in NORTECH making final preparations for his liaison training.

"Let's follow the ancient drill," Nate said. "Let's drop off your bags at the motel, then we'll go to the office and you can stay until you feel ready to crash. I promise nothing significant will be said today and we'll start fresh tomorrow, but right now, even before that, I think we ought to get some cheap, taxpayer-subsidized breakfast."

"And some cheap, taxpayer-subsidized coffee," Bill said. "Can you believe that some of our young officers drink that boutique tea or bottled water, and after work that white wine. It's a good thing the Russkies went down when they did. I don't think this bunch could have dealt with them. It took techs and case officers stoked up on coffee and doughnuts and booze to finally whip their ass."

"I think Reagan and Afghanistan and Star Wars helped too," Nate said. "Of course the lion's share of the glory did go to the OTS techs, as I recall."

"I don't think all the techs got in on the glory," Bill said, "but we knew it in our hearts. That was enough."

"Right," Nate said as they entered the cafeteria. "Looks like we're among the very first customers today. I should warn you, the price has gone up to $3.50 for all you can eat."

"If the taxpayers only knew," Bill said.

By the time the two sat down at their table, the cafeteria began to be more active. The first people to show up were always those who were TDY to one of the many agencies or commands headquartered at the American enclave. A couple of Nate's TDYers stopped by to speak to him and so did a couple of the older ones happy to see Bill again. Next came the single men and women who were housed in the area, but who chose not to cook. Among these was a young man whose studious appearance was enhanced by a pair of black-framed glasses with very thick lenses. Nate called to him as he was about to sit at another table, and asked him to join them. As the young man sat down, he leaned toward Bill and raised his head to bring the lower part of his glasses to bear, making Bill feel he was being memorized as well as introduced.

Bill had already been told by Nate that this young man would be very important to him in the next few weeks. Bill knew from long experience that he was not handy in shop skills of any kind. Whenever his liaison trainings included any construction, he always requested an officer from the shop to accompany him. Since virtually every third-world training involved either the installation of a darkroom or the modification of an existing one, he almost always had a skilled shop officer as a partner for the job. When the training extended to the fabrication of basic concealments for cameras, an officer with shop skills was especially important. Officers from the shop loved to get a decent, interesting TDY as a break from their usual work and any base chief, who could spare a man, was always happy to have his shop personnel get genuine, on-the-ground experience in operations and in the skills of traveling and living in a foreign environment.

"This is Kirby Corson," Nate said to Bill, "the man who will be with you on the training. You would have met him today anyhow so now is as good a time as any. You two would have met eventually at HQ, but I know from Kirby that you haven't met officially."

"Glad to know you, Kirby," Bill said. "I do know something about you, of course, even though this is our first face-to-face. I've heard some very good things about you, except from Nate."

The young man's mouth fell open and he stared at Nate. "He's just kidding," Nate said. "He does that because of the long years people have made fun of him and now he tries it on everybody else. I personally recommended him for remedial sensitivity, but he evaded it somehow."

Immediately Kirby's face broke into a grin so huge it brought to Bill's mind the grin of the Cheshire Cat. "Anyway," Bill said, "after this trip you'll be so experienced and famous your career will become mercurial."

"He read 'mercurial' in one of his comic books," Nate said. "They use it a lot in the *Action Comics* series."

Now Kirby fastened the same honest, baffled stare at Bill. "He's kidding," Bill said then paused for a few seconds. "Actually it comes from *Gilligan's Island*. I have the official, memorial collection with extra footage and interviews."

All three men sat silent for a few more seconds until Bill and then Nate began to suppress a laugh. "OK," Kirby said, "I get it. You're just jerking around the new kid."

"By the time you get back from this TDY," Nate said to Kirby, "you'll be just as cynical as we are and all your sensitivity training will be for naught."

"I can't wait!" Kirby said.

***

The next morning as Bill entered Nate's office, the first thing he noticed was the ancient Truth Chair. It was only a little worse off for all the years of steady wear, providing living proof of the strength of Naugahide. "I see you still have the Chief's greatest friend right at hand," Bill said in greeting.

"Damn right," Nate said, "and if the celestial daddy-rabbits on the 7th floor don't shoot me down, I'm taking it with me when I head back home.

"Let's talk this thing over. You need a little info on the situation on the ground in Mifuna and on Kirby. But first I have to ask, did you ever think, so many years ago, that we'd still be dealing with Mifuna and that Bouaki would still be in charge. Talk about poetic justice or

174

small world or *deja vu* or whatever!"

"I never thought Mifuna would last out that year," Bill said, "not with the mess that country was in at the time. The old man must have done quite a job."

"He has indeed," Nate said. "Ever since we worked our miracle so long ago, he's done his dead-level best for his country and his people. How rare is that in Africa! After we saved him (or made it possible for him to save himself), he has cooperated entirely with every COS.

"The current COS, a young fellow named Baxter, new to both of us, passed through here a couple of months ago and brought me up to date on the situation down there. Right now Bouaki needs something besides financial and managerial advice and foreign aid. He's old and tired and the buzzards are circling. Of all those kids of his, the only one who deserves to live is his first-born son, Kubo, the only child he had with his chief wife. The problem is that the boy is the bookworm not the soldier, and in Africa you'd better be a soldier or have a trusted one right at hand.

"Bouaki's no fool. He intends Kubo to take over and he's sent the boy to the states, Yale or Brown or Columbia or somewhere, for his education, but in Africa education never has stood up well against the man with the gun. We don't know how many of his other sons would love to take over the country but there's only one, fellow named Kwame, who both wants to do it and has the nerve and guts to pull it off. We can't really do anything except make sure Kubo has a thoroughly trained, up to date internal security force when he takes over; that's where you and Kirby help out. Kubo will have to outmaneuver or outwit Kwame himself."

"How about this Kwame?" Bill interrupted. "Is he such a disaster?"

"Let's put it this way," Nate said, "he's either in bed with a rival tribal leader who calls himself 'Martin Luther Lumumba', or at least admires him. That should give you some idea of his mental processes. I suppose Lumumba chose his title to let folks know that if they favor

175

peace or war he's their champion.

"I know. I laughed about it at first myself, and it's true that in America Lumumba would be ridiculous, sort of like our right-wing militias playing soldier in the woods and swamps of outer Boondockia, but in Africa he's potentially a genuine threat to the country. Right now he's simply an anti-Bouaki agitator, but Baxter says he is truly a bad actor and that he has somehow convinced Kwame that together they can overthrow Bouaki and rule jointly, or some other nonsense arrangement; Baxter hasn't found out the details yet. But whatever Kwame thinks, he has his head in the lion's mouth. As soon as he disposes of Kubo and takes over, Lumumba is probably going to assassinate him. Mind, we don't care what happens to Kwame, but the old man has done his best for Mifuna and we want to help him out and keep Lumumba confined to the distant bush if we can.

"You remember before when we were in Mifuna we were just trying to scoop up dissatisfied Russkies; now we're actually trying to help a decent old man save his country. For once there's no ambiguity; even the most leftist, tree-fornicating professor, inciting the most leftist students in the most leftist college couldn't fault us this time."

"Hold on padnuh!" Bill said. "Don't tell me we're getting ready to do a thing so good even the *Post* would approve; I might have to stop using it for emergency toilet paper."

"If you were any kind of red-blooded American," Nate said, "you'd be using it for toilet paper full time. And it would be environmentally correct; one of their Sunday editions would last you at least six months—save a good part of an entire tree.

"By the way, did you think we'd ever survive it?"

"What," Bill said, "the slanted reporting in the *Post*?"

"No, No," Nate said, "not just that but the whole thing: the sensitivity and political correctness and warm fuzzies and TQM and official equality of all kinds and all the rest. It's amazing it happened the way it did. If it had happened any sooner, it would have ruined

OTS completely."

"Now hold on a minute," Bill said. "I thought the thing did almost ruin OTS. I swear, there for a while staff meetings and sensitivity and TQM and God knows what else took precedence over operations. The DO had to notice. And it's been very hard on all of us dinosaurs. All the old farts my age or older are either retired, getting ready to retire, or have been kicked upstairs or out of OTS. Some went to the IG office, some to the new CI center, some to staff positions, but very few are still working at the sharp end. The ops chiefs are all mid-career folks; those who came through the whirlwind without too much damage. I know you personally did well, but how do you figure it all worked out so well for the rest of OTS?"

"First," Nate began, "I didn't say it worked out perfectly. Right now some divisions in the DO are back to the old practice of maintaining their own small tech shops, so we did lose some business, but it could have been disastrous. Those of us in charge overseas at the time saw what was happening and just took over, running our parts of the world until HQ could get back on track. We knew what to do anyway, we just quit asking for permission before we took action. Our management at HQ was so preoccupied they hardly ever noticed. That kept the DO field stations and bases happy even if the DO desks at headquarters did wonder sometimes what the hell OTS was doing. Keep in mind too, that the DO was not immune. They had their own dust-up with the fuzzy thinkers. It took them a while to settle down again, the same as OTS.

"The damned ironic thing, though, is that it was your old friend, 'entry suspended' that saved SW. For instance do you know how many ops prints OTS's photo lab averaged per year in the early and mid-80s?"

"I don't know," Bill said, "maybe twenty-five thousand?"

"Almost seventy thousand," Nate said. "Got any idea how many they did three years ago: not quite six thousand."

"It changed that much in just the last few years?" Bill said, "I know I haven't kept up with ops since I've been down at the warehouse, but that really is surprising."

"Once the DO grabbed onto the computer with both hands," Nate said, "the technical requirements changed more in a year than they had in the previous twenty. Why make prints from film and pouch them home? Put the info on a disk and send hundreds of pages back at the speed of light. Why break into someone's office when our hackers can break into his computer? Why spend time building concealments to hide documents? Just hide them on a disk, the way our young geniuses can, and don't use any concealments at all. Why try to sneak around with proprietary signaling devices when slightly modified commercial pagers work perfectly. Why use some suspicious hand held radio when a modified portable phone will do the job. Of course, that's all very much in the future in Africa where you're going, but it will get there much sooner than you think.

"We don't need a battalion of experienced audio techs for electronic COVCOM now and we don't need five experienced techs in the photo lab. I could cite a dozen other examples, but the point is: The needs of the DO were changing just as the technical dinosaurs were being removed from the action. OTS was very lucky in the timing. And you'll have to admit, even the ancients in OTS, who got the message and became computer literate, actually did fairly well in the upheaval.

"You remember our conversation outside the Bubble back when dinosaurs roamed the earth? I told you then what was coming and that I was going to beat it. That was a long time ago and now, I dare say, when I go back, I'm not going to face the trouble Dave did when he returned from NORTECH and they didn't really have an appropriate job for him."

"I'm sure you're right," Bill said, "you haven't made a career mistake yet. But I'm still going to have to think a little bit about this before I completely agree. Maybe it's true we survived technically because of the computer, but the experience of actually running tech ops is almost gone now. In this business, I can't believe experience, history, tradition, don't still mean something.

"And I have a little story to tell you, especially since you just pointed out how you managers of the future are taking all the changes in stride. Let me note first that I know you have been chosen as the base chief who will be responsible for finally unleashing Adele as a full-fledged, field-capable OTS ops tech on an unsuspecting world. I..."

"Wait right there!" Nate said. "You're behind the times as usual. Dave and I have discussed this at length face-to-face and in back-channel traffic, and he knows I'm prepared to give up a slot rather than take her."

Bill waited a few seconds to see if Nate had more to say. When he saw this was not the case, he continued. "You know Dave is on staff now, not ops, so he has to carry out the wishes of those above him like he hasn't had to for at least the last twenty years. He certainly doesn't like it, but he was one of those who got the shaft during all the changes and he has no choice. If you continue to refuse, he's going to get a lot of flak. If he's ever going to get back into ops management, he's got to show he can handle regional base chiefs. By the way, as you might suspect, I got all that from RC who actually understands these things."

"Once again," Nate began, "my compliments to RC; he knows his politics. But Dave is near the end and no matter what I do, his situation won't get much better. I know that's harsh, but that's the way it is. He only *thinks* he still has a life in ops."

"Maybe for the first time," Bill said, "I know something you don't—two things, in fact. First, I have worked with, or confronted, Adele several times in the past, and you need to understand that she never argues unless she has a perfect defense. Whenever she and Warner were pushing CYNOSURE and I was trying to kill it and I was loaded for bear—that is, being entirely right and able to destroy them on some aspect of the project—she immediately conceded the point. It was frustrating as hell to be ready to crush them and then have the item passed over as a simple, no-brainer that never even caused a ripple in the discussions. However, when I was arguing something extemporaneously or she was contesting me in any way, she always had some info I didn't have, or an ally I didn't know about, or had conjured up some circumstance in which whatever I was arguing could not possible work, or already knew about a success or failure that I didn't know about—and I always got nailed.

"She immediately conceded my unassailable points as painfully obvious and undermined me on everything else. Either way, I looked like a collie who had finally caught a car—or had been hit by one."

"Bill," Nate said, "with all due respect, you are abysmal at verbal argument of any kind. If you write a position paper, you're fine, but otherwise, you're dead. You know it's true. I'm sure you were not the toughest opponent Adele ever took on."

"Yes," Bill said, "you're right, but we both know she is very smart; I wasn't the only one she beat up. You saw what happened to Roland, for instance. She not only sent him to the wood shed, but got an official commendation for bringing his famous Hall to the attention of higher management."

"Are you saying those in higher management, who have spent decades in the outfit, didn't know about Roland's Hall and his other special enterprises?" Nate interrupted.

"Of course they knew about it," Bill said, "but in the current atmosphere, if they had admitted prior knowledge they would have been before a Congressional committee begging for forgiveness.

"And one more thing: Adele's reputation is much better in the last few years. She was clever enough to understand the future was in computers, as you said, and while she was with Warner she learned a lot about them. After all Warner was one of the few people on this earth who can understand a computer user manual. She never really worried about the traditional photo and SW and WW two-eye electronic COVCOM. She's still not in the same class on computers as our newest techs, but she's now way ahead of us ancients. You need to know that now she officially represents 'experience', in Dave's very words."

"Bullshit!" Nate said. "There's no way Dave ever said that! It's impossible! Who did he say it to?"

Bill smiled a huge knowing grin and remained silent until he had enjoyed the moment sufficiently. "For once," he began, "I'm going to give you a piece of news that could affect your career that you never anticipated. It's that second thing I know about that you don't."

Here Bill paused again until Nate finally gave in and said, "Well, dammit, what it is!"

"I have to tell it as a story," Bill began, "and it's not a war story. If you want, I'll even be happy to move to the Truth Chair before I start."

"No," Nate said, "I know it will be gospel if it comes from you. Go ahead."

"Just a couple of nights ago," Bill began, "I was invited out to Dave's house for dinner. Now, keep in mind that although we've been friends since Hector was a pup, I would have to go all the way back to Governor Shepherd days to find a time when Dave and I just sat down as regular techs and talked things over. I figured I'd been invited along with maybe twenty/thirty more folks for some award celebration or something. When I got there it was just Dave and Arlene, even the dog was out in yard. As soon as I hit the door, Dave handed me a beer even before we shook hands. We had country ham for supper. Now how many times do you think Arlene let him have that, with his high blood pressure. They even had peppermint ice cream for dessert. I felt like the Queen for a day. But after the supper and the Drambuie, Dave turned serious on me and Arlene left us alone. Frankly, at that point, I started to panic—thought I was going to have to go sooner than I had planned—but then he said he just wanted to talk about this TDY. David Henderson wants to talk to me about a TDY to train third-world liaison—no way!

"It wasn't more than two or three sentences before he brought up

181

Adele and the way you're giving him grief over her. Seeing as how we've been best buddies since day one of your career, he thought maybe he might have better luck if I carried to you, in person and off the record, his absolute fondest wish that you'd just take Adele and live with it. Since I have known you so long, I told him it was not going to happen. He launched into a description of how hard Adele worked and how she was willing to put in non-paid overtime and how she kept herself up to date and how she could do all the other things we all do routinely. When he finished, I offered the opinion that he had just described every tech ops officer.

"That's when he made the remark about her experience. I said I doubted it. He got a little red, which is unusual for Dave, but I thought I was on a roll so I mentioned we had our own home-grown OTS female techs who were at least as good technically as Adele, had put in just as much time in training as she had, were completely superior to her in judgment, and had not yet had a chance at an overseas base either. I mentioned specifically Jackie, Sandy, and Elinore. He agreed that all of them were better than Adele.

"At that point I thought I was rounding third while the right fielder was still trying to pick up the ball, but he just shook his head and said it didn't matter. Then he went to the Bible on me, and you and I well know that when Dave goes there, it's serious. He quoted part of Matthew 5:45. '... for he maketh his sun to rise on the evil and on the good, and sendeth rain on the just and on the unjust.' After the quotation he said the sun was now going to shine on Adele, no matter what.

"He did not, repeat, not say it officially. In fact, he specifically said he was not saying it officially, which means that's exactly what he did mean to say: If you don't take Adele, she's going to take the outfit to court for discrimination, and it's going to be your fault. Note, I did not say that officially."

Nate got up and began to prowl the office. He fooled with his "In" basket, he looked out the window, he sat for a moment on the corner of his desk, and then took his chair again.

"I never thought I'd see this day," he said. Then with a weak smile, he said, "I'll handle it. Let's talk about something else."

After a moment of mutual reflection, Bill began once more. "RC says you're due for a Group Chief's job, but he won't say which one. Does he know?"

"Yes," Nate said. "As usual, he's figured it out, but I won't confirm it for him. I plan to inform him just a few days before it's announced so that he can have one last major coup before he hangs it up."

"Don't tell me," Bill said. "I've been more than twenty years never knowing anything ahead of time, other than Dave's warning of course, and I don't want to start now. Besides, for all the warnings RC has given me over the years, I'd have to tell him just in partial pay-back.

"Why don't you tell me a little about Kirby instead. I do need to know that."

"Fair enough," Nate said, "and there are some things you really do need to know. First, he's green as a gourd, but smart as a whip. He believes everything anyone in management tells him, falls in love with every girl he dates more than once, and thinks you are a living legend."

"What!" Bill said, "Did you tell him that or are you just trying to aggravate me?"

"I did tell him," Nate said. "and that I was a living legend too. After I finished the war story version of Mifuna, he was so in awe I had to go back over some of it and tone it down a little—he looked like we did the first time uncle Beau took us to a whorehouse. The point is, he's going to reverence, and probably try to imitate, everything you do or say."

"Wonderful," Bill said, "I get to take an innocent and show him how not to pursue a career. Is he really cut out for this line of work?"

"Well," Nate said, "you don't think I'd let a promising ops officer be exposed to a liaison service at the ripe old age of twenty-two do you? He's a fine boy and will be a national resource by the time he's thirty, but just not in ops. You want to talk to him today or wait until tomorrow?"

"Do you mean," Bill said, "talk to him about what we are actually going to do, or try to dispel the bullshit you've laid on him?"

"Talk about the training, of course," Nate said. "There's no use talking about your exploits in Mifuna. I've already told him how you're the most modest man I know so if you talk it down, it's just going to confirm what I've already said."

"Jesus!" Bill said.

Chapter 18

As Bill approached Kirby on the shop floor, the young man was intently measuring a piece of metal on the drill press. After he had drilled the required holes and looked up, Bill asked, "Is this a good time to talk?"

"Sure," Kirby said, "this little job can wait. I guess you want to talk about the trip?"

"Right," Bill said, "let's go to the conference room. I noticed it was free."

Both officers got a cup of coffee on the way. Bill began the conversation by noting that now all the cups were very plain with no slogans or titles or exhortations on them. It was immediately obvious that Kirby had no idea what Bill meant by mentioning it. To him, it had never occurred that insensitive coffee cups had ever hung on the rack. Bill made a mental note to begin at the beginning.

"First," Bill said, "do you have any questions?"

"Will we be able to drink the water?" Kirby asked.

"Well...," Bill began, "yes, Kirby, we'll be staying at a good hotel. No matter how desperate the surrounding country, there will always be a hotel suitable for tourists—and anyone who isn't used to the local food and water and has enough cash can avoid them."

"We will get to see the local sights and learn a little about the culture though?" Kirby asked.

Alarm bells began to go off in Bill's head and he decided to put to rest any ideas of "going native."

"Kirby," he began, "you have to always remember we are working, not just visiting, and that we are always needed somewhere else as soon as we finish. If we get sick—and we might no matter how careful we are—it will mean extra work and worry for the station and for NORTECH; for instance, someone else will have to deal with that thing you were just working on if you get delayed on TDY or have to recover from some illness before you can finish it.

"Let me tell you about a young case officer who showed up at the embassy cafeteria at breakfast one morning in Jakarta. We were both TDY so we ate together. He was gung-ho to experience Indonesia, including sampling the local cuisine. I offered the caution that he should only eat at the Hilton or the Intercon or at restaurants recommended to him by the embassy folks. He said I was the typical American who lived in a culture but never experienced it and furthermore his stomach was iron; he could eat anything. I said 'Go with God.' Two days later they had to medevac the idiot all the way to the military hospital in Japan.

"FYI, Kirby, if you do find yourself in a questionable country and there's no Hilton and no one to advise you, pick a Chinese restaurant. They always cut the food up into small pieces and the wok cooks it thoroughly. The tea is made from boiled water. If you eat their food and drink either their tea or bottled beer—out of the bottle—not the glass, you will likely be safe. Remember the tech mantra: 'One beer, no glass, please.' Never ever eat a salad at any place that is either not a first-class hotel or certified by the local station personnel."

"I get it," Kirby said.

"Now," Bill began, "let's go over the basics. We'll be training an elite group chosen from the best of the army. Our bang-and-burn guys will be there at the same time training the same group in special operations such as hostage rescue and interdiction. We will have the students some of the time and bang-and-burn will have them some of the time, but they'll be divided into two groups so there shouldn't be a problem with scheduling.

"We will begin with the absolute basics of photography. You have to keep in mind that these young fellows may be very intelligent but many of them will never have held a 35mm camera. We'll go from basic photo all the way to mobile surveillance, that's where the CDs will come in and that's where you take over. We'll have to make CDs from locally available stuff with very simple tools. You must *not* use anything that can't be purchased at the most basic hardware store. Have you pouched anything yet?"

"Yes," Kirby said, "some things, but nothing more complicated than a power drill."

"Good!" Bill said. "Perfect! We'll buy whatever else we need when we get there.

"I've had logistics pouch twenty K-1000s and twenty FS-1s already. We'll teach them basic photo on the K-1000, the finest 35mm training tool ever invented, and introduce the FS-1s when we begin using the CDs. We'll finish up with long lenses and a little bit on doc copy. Of course, we'll have to teach them basic black and white processing at the same time. I'm always amazed at how much they can do after only one month's training, especially when you consider how much we hit them with and almost every bit of it entirely new to them.

"Since it's liaison, you'll have to be careful what you say or promise. Let me do most of the talking until you see how it goes. We will concentrate only on 35mm photography. When we get to the CDs and they have to conceal a full-sized camera, they are sure to ask about small cameras. We can admit to the Minox and the Tessina, otherwise we'd look like idiots, but processing Minox film is a bitch and printing either negative is a problem. We talk down both systems if it comes up. We also discourage any color processing. Trying to do color processing in a third world country where even the power can be a problem is a nightmare. Avoid it all costs. And by the way, always talk down color processing at stations and bases too. A lot of young case officers have taken their film to K-Mart or the local photo shop and got prints in one hour so they wonder why not process color at their station. What they don't think about is the $75,000 dollars of automated processing equipment, maintained by Kodak, that's actually doing the work. Color processing by hand, other than as a hobby, is like loading sand with a splinter.

"In your area of special expertise, you can't show them any proprietary concealment device techniques or equipment, such as hidden hinges, etc. If we see we have to go beyond basics, we bump the request up to NORTECH.

"I've seen the room they have set aside for us on a previous TDY. It's rugged but it will do. When I left, it had no water. My guess is it still won't have water when we get there although I left detailed instructions about that—and a sink, and a refrigerator, and other things. The training facility is out in the boonies about a forty-five minute drive from the hotel. It was once a barracks for the regular army but now it's set aside for Mifuna's special forces units of all kinds. Right now that means the ones we'll be training since they will be the first special forces in the history of the country."

Bill paused to take several long sips of coffee as he reviewed the basic preparations in his mind. He decided to make sure their travel arrangements had been completed and were satisfactory.

"Central Processing made my reservations for a departure day after tomorrow. I assume NORTECH logistics has you on the same flights."

"Yes," Kirby said, "I'll be ready. What do I need to take other than money, clothes, and passport?"

"Those are the absolute basics," Bill agreed, "but don't take too much money. We can take advances from station logistics if we need it. Carry your wallet in your front pocket, and if someone bumps into you, don't shove back or get pissed. Immediately grab your wallet through your pants and hold on like a possum eating persimmons; the pickpocket's hand will probably be in your pocket by then. Once he thinks you might grab him, he'll break off the attempt and disappear into the crowd."

Kirby stared at Bill as if he had never heard of pickpockets. "It's the third world, Kirby," Bill said. "These folks have nothing and you have everything. What you have in your pocket would last them six months. Just be a little cautious; you'll be fine.

"Oh! I forgot one thing you really need to know. Once we hit the ground in Mifuna, you are officially declared to liaison. Since we'll be there for a good while we will certainly see other TDY'ers and meet all the station personnel; I believe it's only a five/six-man station anyway. But when we're not in the station, we cannot contact or be seen with any TDY'er or station officer not declared to liaison. I'm sure the chief will brief us on who's kosher and who's not, but if you're not sure, don't acknowledge anyone you know outside the station. Got that?"

"Got it," Kirby said.

"Well," Bill said, "let's stop for now. If either of us thinks of anything else we have a day to straighten it out."

***

That night Bill and Nate had dinner and re-visited some of their favorite local bars of years gone by. As they moved deeper into the night, the talk became more honest as the liquor reduced some of their long-practiced reticence about personal matters.

"You still going to hang it up early?" Nate asked.

"Yes," Bill said, "I am. It's been a great ride as they say, but times have changed, maybe for the better, but I'm not sure. I'm only sure they have changed and I'm not as comfortable as I was, even when I'm doing traditional work like this training. The young folks treat me with great respect, but it's the same way they would treat an old historical piece of furniture with great respect. I'm used to being chewed with gusto by management for every mistake and made fun of at every opportunity by the rest of the techs. This being nice makes me very uneasy."

"Yes," Nate agreed, "I know what you mean. You have no idea how many excellent opportunities to have a little fun with folks that I've passed up in the last few years. The way everyone's so serious and sensitive now makes it even harder to resist—what perfect targets. You remember how we used to dummy up cables that supposedly canceled a tour or sent a tech to New Delhi instead of Paris. If we tried that now, the sensitivity police would have a cow."

"Remember when Gordon and RC used to do the deaf news?" Bill asked. "That performance was a good as anything *Laugh-in* ever did. Or the time Betty made those tiny prints of Phil Looper so that his head was all distorted and came to a peak at the top, and then put a zillion of them everywhere: the water fountain, the bulletin board, the john—I hope she didn't personally put 'em in there—and especially that one large one she stuck on the cover of that process notebook of his just before he went in to lecture that training class—the good old days. Did Phil ever find out who did it?"

"Nah," Nate said, "Phil is still looking for the perpetrator even today. He just never could imagine a woman would do such a thing, which shows that down deep he's no more in sync with the new age than any other dinosaur."

"I presume he suspects you," Bill said, "because in the past, that would have been a very good guess. How you managed to fool our new higher management into believing you accepted the new thinking, is beyond me."

"Well," Nate said, "we are supposed to be skilled in trickery and deceit, are we not. I mean that's what spying is all about, after all.

"Listen, Bill, if you do hang it up early, what's the next move? Are you going back home?"

"Absolutely," Bill said, "but not immediately. Us country boys always need to sit a spell to make sure before we do anything big. First, I won't have very much money coming in—might have to get a job and any job around D.C. pays more than one down home. Of course, it costs forty percent less to live down there...It's complicated. I'll just have to see how it goes. "I don't suppose you've heard anything more about that problem in SE where we're still waiting to confirm Sam's theory of what happened."

"No," Nate said, "but here in the field is a much better place to find out something, provided an SE officer familiar with it ever passes through. Who knows what might be divulged after a half dozen Pilsener Urquells that would never be mentioned in that buttoned-down atmosphere at HQ. If I do hear anything, I'll let you know wherever you are. Is this thing still causing you heartburn?"

"Nah," Bill said, "I'd just like to tie up loose ends before I go—put it to rest once and for all, you know. Let's knock it off for tonight. Kirby and I have to talk some more tomorrow and then we ride the great silver bird in the early evening."

Nate did not want to stop the evening. He only saw Bill now, especially in unhurried circumstances, on rare occasions. But the mood had changed. He knew that more liquor now would not make them happier, but more somber and reflective, something he wanted to avoid on this night at all costs. "Whatever you say," he said.

Chapter 19

Kirby had begun the long flight to Mifuna with an eager air of adventure, but three stops en route, including a harrowing change of airlines in Abidjan, and almost fifteen hours of traveling had left him exhausted and a little disoriented. Bill had warned him they would be late, but this trip had shown him a new kind of lateness. On his late flights in the states there had always been some reason given for the delays, the ground staff were obviously always aware of the situation, and there would eventually be updates. On this flight, they had lost time at each stop, especially the change in airlines, but no one seemed to notice. No reasons were given for the delays, no one hurried in any way, no one seemed concerned about connections, and no passengers besieged the ticket counters demanding updates.

Bill tried to explain that in Africa, delays were routine, only on-time flights caused a problem. The worst situation, he explained was to begin a flight on an African airline and have to connect with a carrier like Lufthansa or Swissair. For that he recommended factoring in a lay-over of several hours. Going the other way, he advised Kirby that a scheduled ten-minute lay-over from a European carrier to an African one would always be more than adequate. Kirby listened but couldn't relax and was sure the next connecting flight would leave before they arrived. Bill finally gave up and let him walk off his nervousness by pacing constantly over every foot of every transit lounge on the way.

When they did arrive, the expediter met them and they were allowed to sit quietly in the waiting lounge while he fought his way through the controlled chaos at immigration and customs. Since the day was already so late, he took them directly to the hotel. From there, Bill called his contact number and advised that they had arrived more or less as expected and would show up at the embassy next morning.

He then went by to collect the still nervous Kirby and took him down to the bar. As they settled into the comfortable chairs in the lobby, the waiter immediately came over to see what they wanted. "I'll have a cold draft beer," Bill said. "Please make sure it's cold. What for you, Kirby? They've got just about anything you want."

Kirby too ordered a beer, then leaned over to speak quietly to Bill. "Do you think it's a good idea to call me 'Kirby' in front of the waiter?" he asked.

Bill stared at him for a few seconds before he thought of anything to say, then began to smile. "Well, Kirby," he began, "we're registered here in true name and we have already been declared to liaison in true name. It won't matter if the waiter finds out our names."

"Is that wise?" Kirby asked. "I hadn't thought much about it until I had all that time to worry on the flight down."

"I thought all you were worrying about was being late," Bill said. "Yes, sometimes we do use aliases when we travel, especially the bang-and-burn guys, but they work with folks who engage in violence and they may well interact with some others who either don't like us or who would like to expose our association with a local government. Nate thought, this time, it wasn't worth arranging alias docs for us. Mifuna is very friendly to the US and there's not much danger from any bad guys inside or outside the country. You have to remember that traveling and working in alias is a huge pain, and you run the constant risk of exposure either by accident or design. Then the trouble really starts. I have only rarely traveled in alias and I never wanted to."

"Is it really that hard?" Kirby asked. "I understand the COs do it all the time."

"That's true Kirby," Bill said, "but they have been trained from day one in how to do it convincingly and they have thoroughly vetted and backstopped cover. All we would ever have on a job such as this would be an alias tourist passport, throw-away pocket-litter IDs, and maybe a backstopped telephone number. If anyone really wants to know, they can blow that kind of cover in a heartbeat."

"It might be better than nothing," Kirby said.

"OK, Kirby," Bill said, "let's say you've got an alias tourist passport and the immigration officer asks what you're doing in Mifuna."

"I'm here on vacation," Kirby said.

"First, Kirby," Bill said, "very few folks come to Mifuna on vacation, especially from the states. What are you planning to see?"

"The local game parks?" Kirby offered.

"There aren't any," Bill said. "Try again."

"Well, maybe I'm here to visit my...brother who lives here, Kirby said."

"Where does your brother live, what is his name, and what does he do?" Bill asked.

"It's none of your business," Kirby said. "Why does it matter where he lives or what he does."

"Oops! Wrong answer!" Bill said. "This is not America and I'm a double-rectified Mifunan immigration officer and that is *not* a diplomatic passport. Looks like we're gonna have to go to the office to talk things over—and let me hold your wallet for you while we talk.

"I'm always amazed at how easily the COs can function in alias. It's more than training; it's an art, or maybe a gift. For folks like you and me, Kirby, we'd better just try to maintain the classic 'low profile' and let the real spies do the clever things."

"Maybe you're right," Kirby said. "Let's go to dinner and then hit the sack. I don't know why but I'm not only mentally tired, I'm physically beat."

"It could be those ten miles you walked in the transit lounges on the way here," Bill said.

***

The next morning Kirby had his first experience at getting into

Agency territory at an embassy. The Marine guard had examined their docs very carefully, making Kirby nervous again, but when Bill asked for the station secretary by name, it was obvious he understood. In a few more minutes they were in the ritual meeting with the COS who looked, to Bill, as if he were no older than Kirby. He introduced himself as Mark Baxter, but Bill noticed the name 'Marcellus' on one of his framed awards. Bill also noticed the Roman numeral IV following the name. He decided Mark was either descended from old line Agency predecessors or was doing this kind of work for the sheer love of it. Before the interview was over, he knew he had been right on both counts.

Since the young man was completely unknown to him, and from a different generation, he decided to refrain from any references to the good old days, or to take any liberties of familiarity in the discussion. The young COS began the meeting by welcoming the two of them and saying he was glad they had come. He was, he said, looking forward to improving the already good relations between the station and President Bouaki. He thought the liaison training would strengthen the country both through the extra security the special forces would bring and by closer ties to the Agency. He told them their contact would be a station officer named Oliver Clark. They should work with officer Clark and he would serve as the link between them and himself. He understood that Bill already knew Clark and had worked with him at other stations around the world. Bill said he had done so and the meeting was over. It had lasted only about five minutes.

"Does he know you saved Mifuna?" Kirby asked as they followed the secretary down the hall to Clark's office.

"Kirby," Bill said, "please remind me to sit down with you real soon and go through the difference between a war story and a fairy tale."

The secretary showed them to Oliver Clark's door. As soon as Clark saw Bill he extended his hand. "Welcome once again to Mifuna, Pearl of Africa," he said. "It's been a while this time hasn't it, Bill?"

"I reckon so, Ollie," Bill said, "how have you been?"

"No complaints," Ollie said. "Helen and I live like royalty here, Mark's a decent boss, and soon all three kids will be out of college, and that's out of college without much debt. I think it all worked out well."

"Sounds good to me," Bill said. "You think this might be your last tour?"

"Yes," Ollie said, "I think Helen would like to stay permanently in our beach cottage once we get home. It'll be very close to thirty years for me when I get back and that's enough. There's no use in pretending to stay around for my 'high three' since I've been at my 'high three' for the last ten."

"I know what you mean," Bill said. "There is always a time, or several times, when a fellow can really move up, but you've got to be ready, willing, and maybe a little lucky right at that moment. If you miss it, the opportunity can be a long time coming around again."

"You remember Hong Kong?" Ollie said, "when we met for the first time and I was the deputy? I thought I had it made then, and I did almost, but then the Schlesinger shuffle hit us and I wound up on the bottom of the deck. That was when Jack was forced to resign on account of the thing with his secretary and they called Bad Bob down from Seoul to straighten us out. Did you know Jack retired in Hong Kong?"

"I did, Ollie," Bill said. "Did I ever tell you about running into the secretary—can't recall the name right now—a year later—or maybe more—in the Wanchi market where she was selling mushrooms. I found out Jack had bought a mushroom farm over in Kowloon somewhere and he was doing pretty well."

"Damn!" Ollie said, "I never heard that. By then, of course, I was in exile at the Farm—damn! I hope he did well. He always did really like Hong Kong."

Both men fell silent as they mulled over old friends and old memories. Suddenly, they remembered Kirby who was staring at them with that astounded gaze Bill had now grown used to. "Kirby...," he began, then stopped and looked at Ollie.

"Ollie," he said, "This is Kirby Corson. He's new to the outfit and Nate wants him to get a little field experience. He's already a shop expert but he hasn't had many TDYs yet. He'll be the one doing the hard work. I'll do most of the talking and get the all the glory, or share it with you, as in the past."

Ollie snorted, "Right, Bill, the glory of the past! We shared it all right! Now maybe we'd better talk this thing over as if we were serious."

They both looked at Kirby. "We *are* serious, Kirby," Bill said.

"I understand," Kirby said.

"Ooooh K," Ollie said, "here's the deal. Today I'll take you over to meet Benjamin—I think you know him already, Bill," here Bill nodded his assent. "and he'll take you out to the training site. I'm sure it will need something, or maybe a lot. Whenever you need an advance, or special transportation, or to send a cable, or anything else, work through me. Mark wants weekly progress reports, but he won't be seeing you unless something unusual happens. Just come to the station and use my terminal to do your typing. He expects you will be busy all day, every weekday, so the reporting will almost certainly have to be done Saturday morning, but we're all always here so it's no problem. I'm also your emergency contact. I'll give you a set of numbers where I can be reached twenty-four hours a day. I'm declared so there's no reason to worry about contacting me. Only Mark, of the rest of the officers at the station, is officially known so there can be no contact away from this area unless it's cleared with Mark beforehand. If I need to contact you when you're out at the site, I'll work through Benjamin. He will always have a way to get to you while you're out in the boonies.

"And now I'll answer the questions you won't ask but need to know. Mark's a good guy; he's just very young. Even though this is Africa, to be a full-fledged COS at his age should tell you something. His father was a director in one of the divisions in DA so he's old-line Agency and Ivy League to boot. He truly believes that if he can somehow save

197

Mifuna, it will be some sort of beacon for all the other African nations that are floating around on the fringes of democracy without a clue as to their home port…I know, Bill, but that's how he thinks. In fact, what I just said was a direct quote from him—given a little degradation due to my memory failure over time. He's smart, tireless, ambitious, and believe it or not, a pretty good listener if you've actually got something to say. Otherwise, don't bother him."

"We get the picture," Bill said. "I'd much rather have it that way. If the COS is in on every session or wants daily progress updates, it gets to be tiresome and aggravating right away."

"You ready to meet Benjamin?" Ollie asked.

Chapter 20

As Ollie drove through Mifuna City, he and Bill felt free to ignore Kirby and talk over old times. As their conversation became more and more arcane to him, Kirby began to pay more attention to the surroundings. It seemed to him as if he were looking at a film which had been randomly spliced together from very different movies. Adjacent to a 21st century high-rise surrounded by a high wall topped with decorative tiles, stood tin shacks bordered with bare, gray earth and beyond that with tall scraggly weeds the same color as the earth.

On the same corner where a local businessman waited on the traffic, clutching his leather briefcase and perspiring heavily in his dark blue suit, stood a small, emaciated boy selling individual cigarettes. Waiting outside what appeared to a quite fashionable store sat a beggar with twisted legs and a nub of skin for a left hand. They passed a gas station with modern pumps and a decent-looking public phone, but just behind the booth stood a maribou stork picking over garbage dumped just outside the building.

He could see the heat shimmering off the concrete but the air-conditioned embassy van kept it at a comfortable distance. Sitting in the cool isolation, Kirby felt a little guilty, like most westerners when they first see Africa up close.

His reverie was disturbed when Ollie turned through a gap between two sections of a rusty fence and stopped in front of a building that must have been impressive during colonial times, but which now showed only a remnant of its past glory. The sturdy stonework had loosened in places and the ugly gashes and chips had not been repaired. In fact, Kirby could see some of the broken pieces still lying scattered beneath the location from which they had fallen. Several of the windows had individual panes covered with tape, cardboard, or ugly plywood. A thin, local dog slept at the very edge of the short terrace which formed the bridge from the last of the stone steps to two old, massive, intricately carved doors. One door was shut, but the other stood partly open. The contrast with the bright African sun made the shaded interior beyond the door seen even darker.

When Kirby stepped outside his protection, the heat hit like a physical force. For a moment, it seemed he actually had to struggle against it to move away from the car. In seconds, he was sweating in rivulets. Bill and Ollie were not doing any better, but still deep in conversation, they didn't seem to notice. He trailed them as they headed for the dark behind the door. When they were half way up the steps a small, very black man appeared out of the deeper darkness inside the doorway. He walked very rapidly to meet them before they had crossed the terrace.

"Mr. Bill!" he said, "Good to see you again finally!"

As they shook hands Bill grabbed the man by the left shoulder in a the rough, awkward way men do when more than a handshake is called for, but no kind of embrace is appropriate. "Benjamin!" he said, "it is really good to see you too. You look as young as before and more prosperous. You must have done well since the last time I saw you."

As they talked they never let go of their handshake. It was only when Bill introduced Kirby that Benjamin came to him with the same hearty and lasting grip. Kirby said he was glad to be there, but Benjamin still held his hand. Kirby next said he was glad to finally meet Benjamin, but Benjamin just gripped his hand more tightly. He next said he was glad to be in Africa, glad to be in Mifuna City, and glad to be assigned to the training before Benjamin finally let go. "Let us go in from the heat," he said finally to Kirby's great relief.

Inside, the reduction of the heat was only relative as they walked into the steaming main corridor. The locals stared at them in the frank way of unsophisticated folks all over the world, making Kirby slightly nervous once more. He focused his attention on the building which had been very stoutly constructed, suggesting those responsible had intended to stay for a very long time. Given the obvious strength of the building despite its age, he thought perhaps they had; but given the unattended damage to the facade, he thought they had also been gone a long time.

Unlike the outside, damage inside was almost totally due to intended changes such as the addition of electrical wiring and changes to the width of doorways. Even though some effort at repair had been made here, the quality of the repair work was far below that of the original builders. Kirby's sense of order was jarred by the way rough plywood doors hung surrounded by door frames rich with ancient carvings, and finely crafted cornices and shelves and window seats were pitted with nail holes or carelessly painted or shattered by hard usage. The wobbling overhead fans had to be suspended on very long rods reaching down from the very high ceilings which had been necessary to dissipate the brutal heat before electricity came. Kirby thought of Chinese Gordon and Cecil Rhodes and Speke and Burton as they labored up the long staircase leading to the offices on the second floor.

When Benjamin let them into his office, Kirby's eyes immediately rested on an ancient room air-conditioner sitting precariously on the window sill directly behind Benjamin's desk. It was making a noise composed of part squeak, part wheeze, part rattle, and part sigh. It was surrounded by stained plywood cut roughly to fill the gaps between it and the window sill, but still leaving plenty of crevices open to the outside. It did have one wonderful attribute: it was working; the room was not cool, but not oppressively hot. Benjamin sat behind his desk while they ranged themselves in front. "Can I get you something to drink?" he asked.

To Kirby's surprise, both Bill and Ollie accepted so he decided to take the risk too. Benjamin stepped outside the door for a moment and then returned to his chair. "Mr. Bill," he said, "when will you want to go out to the site?"

"If you can take the time," Bill said, "I'd like to go today. I just want to see how the darkroom is coming along and what the water situation is and basic things like that. If necessary, we can start classroom training before the darkroom is finished, but probably not more than a day or two before; it's better to get to 'hands-on' as soon as possible. How soon can you have the students ready for us when we give the word?"

"They are on site now," he said, "some of your officers are already here training them in military skills. Whenever you are ready, they can be ready. We plan to take groups of them from the other training while you are here and return them again after you are finished. I believe the other training is more general and covers many things."

Here Benjamin turned to Ollie who agreed the bang-and-burn training took much longer since it involved the equivalent of basic training followed by training in specific military skills and finally the specialized training for emergency situations.

There was a soft knock on the door to which Benjamin said, "Come." A young man brought in a platter on which there were four Cokes, still capped. There were also four paper cups, but Bill and Ollie drank out of the bottle. Kirby followed their example.

"I will be here whenever you need anything," Benjamin began once more, "I will also visit the camp at least once per day. Do you need a car?"

"I believe we will just rent one locally," Bill said. "That way we won't be inconveniencing anyone here or at the embassy and we will have it immediately available whenever we need it. I'll see to that this afternoon or evening."

They spent a few more minutes deciding details such as the length of the training day, transportation of supplies, contact telephones numbers, and provision for meals on site. Finally, everyone sat silent trying to think of something that had been left out, each knowing that at least several things should have been mentioned but could not be brought to mind at the moment. When all had agreed they would mention other things as they came up and the Cokes were drained, Benjamin suggested they head out.

Downstairs once more in the heat, Ollie quickly said good-bye and drove off in the air-conditioned van. Benjamin and Bill headed for a late-seventies vintage Toyota with Kirby again trailing behind. The car was painted white, but like almost everything else in this dry season, it was the color of the dust. Bill and Benjamin got in the front seat leaving Kirby to fight his way into the rear behind Bill. He immediately shifted to the other side where the short Benjamin had pulled his seat forward, but even with the extra space his knees were still very high and very close to his chest.

By that time he had noticed two things: the car was not air-conditioned and covering the dash and encircling the entire windshield was a border of brilliant orange knit-work. At intervals of about four inches along the entire border edging the windshield and on the bottom of the covering of the dash, hung fluffy orange dingle-balls about the size of golf balls. The slightest disturbance set them in motion. As Benjamin bumped toward the gap in the fence, they engaged in a frenetic bout of jangling, jumping, and crashing into each other. Once Benjamin took the street they continued their mystifying motions as they responded to the rough road and his swift driving. The only time they all seemed to go in the same direction, even for an instant, was when Benjamin made hard, sweeping turns. Otherwise, even individuals located side-by-side gyrated with complete independence. Kirby was still staring at them when Bill turned around to speak to him. Seeing Kirby's fascination with the colorful commotion, he smiled broadly and said, "You got anything like this in your car at home, Kirby?"

"No," Kirby said.

"This is Benjamin's car," Bill continued, "but the fringe was a gift from the people in the office. They like him as a person and as a manager. This was for a promotion—was it, Benjamin?"

"Yes," Benjamin said, "I like orange."

"I see," Kirby said.

Bill smiled again. "Kirby," he said, "I'm sure the other living legend, your boss, Nate, has told you, but I just want to reiterate: Life in the field is nothing but adventure and romance."

Kirby had thought he was growing used to left-hand drive until Benjamin took to the streets where he drove with great determination and invention. If an intersection were blocked, he took the sidewalk. Whenever a pothole of enormous proportions appeared in his lane, he took the other one. At the British round-abouts no one stopped for anything. Whether the traffic was a donkey-cart, a bicycle, a small van carrying people hanging onto the sides and roof, or one of the enormous old Bedford trucks, everyone stayed in motion and no one seemed to be focused on the traffic. Benjamin and Bill certainly were not. Their shouted conversation was steady even during the times when Kirby literally held his breath as Benjamin ran completely off the pavement or headed directly for one of the huge, ugly trucks, just getting back on his side of the road in time to avoid disaster.

Once they cleared the town, the road turned to dust and Benjamin speeded up. Now he was guided only by the line of least delay. He drove on the smoothest, least damaged part of the road no matter where that happened to be. Kirby was sure that on the other side of one of the low hills Benjamin was taking at such reckless velocity, they would encounter a herd of cattle or a donkey-cart or one of those fearsome old trucks head-on. The dust roiled all around them and to his dismay, Kirby noticed it coming through some holes in the floorboard. He happened to glance at this white shirt and noticed it had already begun changing to the grayish color of the dust. At least, he thought to himself, he was no longer so concerned about the heat.

After a bit more than a half-hour of remarkable and memorable progress, Benjamin turned off onto another, even less maintained dirt track leading into a grove of trees. After they passed through the first fringe of the trees, they emerged into a clearing in which there were three block buildings, one of which was a burned-out hulk. Benjamin

204

stopped near the end of the best-looking building. Once they were clear of the car, Kirby slapped his shirt and a small dust cloud puffed out. He looked up to see Bill's large grin and decided to let it go; after all, there was certainly no reason to worry about it now while the return trip still lay ahead.

"This is it," Bill said unnecessarily. "Now let's see how much has been done since last time."

Benjamin led the way in. The outside door led into a corridor extending the length of the building. He walked down about halfway to the end and opened a door on the right-hand side. As they stepped in, he said, "This is the classroom. You can start here and do all the lectures here. We will also use this as a workshop when it is time to make things."

The inside of the room was as rough as the outside. Bare cinder blocks rose from a poured concrete floor to a galvanized roof supported by wooden beams. Twelve school-desks sat bunched up on one side of the large open space. There was a large room air-conditioner mounted through an opening in one wall. "I will have them turn the air-conditioner on about one-half hour before you are to lecture," Benjamin said. "We cannot keep it on all the time. I have a desk for you and a moveable slate board. I will have them moved in here tomorrow."

"Good," Bill said, "look's fine. You will stay for the first part of the first lecture?"

"Yes," Benjamin said, "and whenever you need me."

They went on down the hallway to the last room in the building. Against the far wall was a large stainless steel sink with a spigot poised over each end. The pipes had been put through the wall very recently; in the sink, cinder block chips and dust lay undisturbed.

"I see you got the sink installed," Bill said. Is the water on yet?"

"Yes," Benjamin said, "all we have to do is turn the tap on the outside and water will come."

Near the sink was an electrical conduit terminating in a power sled holding eight receptacles. Another such construction was mounted on the wall about ten feet farther on. In the middle of the room were two rough plywood tables each about four by six feet. Mounted high on the wall opposite the sink was another large air-conditioner.

"This looks good," Bill said, "let's think for a minute about the rest of the stuff. How about the refrigerator? Did you and Ollie get that yet?"

"Yes," Benjamin said, "Mr. Ollie says he has it at the embassy and said he would send it out whenever you want."

"OK," Bill said, "looks like we're almost ready. I'll make some arrangements with Ollie tomorrow morning and send the supplies out by embassy van. I'd like you to be here if you can. We should be here by, say, noon. If that timing isn't right, I'll call you at your office. You have any questions, Kirby?"

"No," Kirby said.

"You ready to ride back into town then?" Bill asked.

"No," Kirby said.

Chapter 21

After the harrowing, dusty trip back to town, Kirby was only too anxious to clean up and relax for a while. After showering, he lay down across the bed for a few minutes but woke over an hour later just as the sun began to sink behind the near-by hills. He tried to call Bill's room, but got no answer. He had already learned that the first logical place to look for officers of Bill's age when they were on TDY was the closest bar. When he walked in, he expected to see Bill already at the bar but Bill was absent. Still confident he was in the right place, he took a seat and ordered a beer. Within minutes his judgment was vindicated as Bill walked in from the lobby.

As if he were arriving at a planned rendezvous, Bill ordered a beer and announced he had been to rent a car for the duration of the TDY. Since the rental would be for weeks instead of days, and since he had shown a diplomatic passport, and since he was a white man, he thought he had gotten a pretty good deal.

"Can I drive some while we're here?" Kirby asked.

"Absolutely," Bill said, "it's a good chance for you to learn left-hand drive while you're here where the road runs just about wherever you want it to. It's damn hard to get off the airplane and suddenly switch over in England or Japan or South Africa where everybody expects you to obey traffic rules."

"What happens tomorrow?" Kirby asked.

"Not much, in a way," Bill said, "but quite a lot in another way. If we get things well situated tomorrow, we can save days over the duration of the training. For instance, we need to get some idea of the timing for the trip out (we will not drive as fast as Benjamin), meet the students, meet the honcho for the bang-and-burn group, turn on the water, check the darkroom for light leaks, cool the place down, install the refrigeratior, put the equipment under lock and key...a hundred little things like that. Each one doesn't seem like much, but each one we don't take into account will represent delays or aggravation sooner or later."

"What should I do?" Kirby asked.

"Tomorrow will be a lot of fetch and carry," Bill said. "Just jump in whenever you see something that needs doing. Once I begin to teach—I doubt there's any real chance we'll get that far tomorrow—I will need you to roam the classroom constantly to see how the students are doing. If you see someone has not understood, you must stop me and we'll go over it again and again and again if necessary. As soon as someone asks a question, we'll be home free. After that, they'll ask questions when they don't understand, but until someone is willing to be the first to admit he doesn't understand something, we'll be guessing at what they've learned. Be very patient at first; the learning curve will be slow. Then, all of a sudden it will click and we'll be on our way.

"We also have Benjamin when we need him. He was the very first liaison officer I met here years ago. He's now not only the government contact for liaison training of all kinds, but he runs their HQ darkroom, and he participates in just about every operation they run. If they're looking for some evil-doer at the airport, Benjamin will be there to coordinate the affair. If some higher-up dedicates a monument, Benjamin will see to security and make sure the whole thing is properly photographed. If a rumor surfaces that there's unrest up-country or some local chief or strong-man has become too big for his britches, Benjamin goes out to get everything back to normal. (My guess is it was Benjamin who first surfaced the problem with Lumumba.). If he sees there's some kind of dire shortage—and that can range from film for the HQ darkroom to food for the enlisted men in the army—he lets the rulers know about it and then tries to take care of it.

"If we had folks like him in the same relative positions all over our government, we'd be a lot better off. Of course, in our system, he would only be allowed to do just one thing and would have to coordinate every single action with every other little potentate and then be sure he didn't hurt anyone's feelings or embarrass anybody or offend anyone's sensibilities, and since he's a member of the largest tribe, he'd have to have at least one representative of some smaller tribe on his staff... Well, let's just say Benjamin is our salvation here on the local scene and leave it at that.

"You ready for supper?"

"It's either that or settle in here for the night," Kirby said.

"It's better to settle in for the night at a bar on Saturday night," Bill said. "Tomorrow's a work day."

"Is the car air-conditioned?" Kirby asked.

"No," Bill said, "that's one reason why I got such a good deal."

"Damn!" Kirby said.

***

As soon as they cleared the city on the trip out, Bill let Kirby drive. At first, he was tentative, but by the time he turned off the main road into the compound, he was enjoying himself immensely and had almost forgotten he was driving on the left.

"Good job, Kirby," Bill said as he pulled up to the main building. "You seem to have a knack for it. I've seen folks that absolutely refused to drive on the left."

"I used to do a little drag-racing before I grew up," Kirby said, "and also a little foolish driving on the regular roads, until a buddy of mine killed an innocent family in a head-on collision. After that, whenever I went fast it brought back that memory so I only go fast on rare occasions now. Looks like we're the first ones here."

"Yep," Bill said, "looks like. We might as well settle down. It might be a while."

As the time dragged on, Kirby began to pace as he had in the airports during the lay-overs, he threw rocks at a tree he picked out at the edge of the clearing, he circled each building on a careful inspection tour, he fiddled with the radio, studied the maps Bill had brought along, and finally returned to pacing. Meanwhile Bill sat quietly in the front seat of the small car with his long legs out the door.

"Kirby," Bill said finally, "if you're gonna do well in working with third-world liaison or in traveling in the third world, you'll have to learn to go into 'slug mode', sort of like frogs in the winter, where your metabolism drops to almost nothing and your brain becomes like snow on a TV screen. Otherwise this work will really age you. I'm a living example. I'm really only twenty-seven years old, but I conducted myself like you're doing right now for just my first overseas tour. That's all it took. Once the aging sets in there's no recovery."

Kirby stopped his pacing and directed at Bill the now familiar owl-like stare. Before Kirby had decided what to say, Benjamin's car arrived at the buildings followed immediately by a billowing dust cloud that gradually drifted over toward their car. Benjamin bounced out of the car in obvious good spirits and complete ignorance of being more than an hour late. "Good morning," he said.

"Good morning," Bill said in return, but Kirby remained silent.

"And good morning to you, Mr. Kirby," Benjamin said.

Kirby finally managed a weak, "Good morning," but Benjamin failed to notice his unenthusiastic attitude.

"Let us go in," Benjamin said.

Benjamin unlocked the door and they headed first to the classroom, then the darkroom. The first order of business was to get the air conditioners going. Next came a trip to a room at the end of the building they had not seen before. There they found a very rudimentary set-up that might have been called an employee lounge. A metal table took up the center of the room whose walls were covered on three sides by rough plywood cabinets. A small sink topped by one spigot had been inserted into the top of one set of lower cabinets. A two-burner hot-plate sat beside the sink and on one of the burners was a large kettle. "We need to start the water for tea," Benjamin said.

Kirby looked at Bill who shrugged and said, "The Brits were here first. What can I say."

Benjamin happily held the kettle under the spigot and cranked the tap but nothing happened. His face fell. "The water does not come," he said with dismay.

"Now I'm interested," Bill said. "Benjamin, if we've got a water problem, we're in a mess."

"Mr. Bill," Benjamin began, "it is probably nothing. Maybe the water is cut off outside. Sometimes we do that so that no one can use it when we are not here."

They tried the main valve outside the building, but the results remained the same. Benjamin began tracing the water line back toward the pump house checking every possible cut-off valve, but finding them all open. "Could it be the pump?" Benjamin said almost in a panic. "If it is, it may take for long to fix it."

Benjamin hurried to the pump house and opened the door, but it was obvious he knew nothing about the machinery inside. Neither did Bill. As they stood there looking at the pump as if somehow a solution would appear if they just stared hard enough, Kirby moved past them to kneel and inspect the pump at close range. After a few minutes, he turned to them and said. "I don't think it's the pump. Where's the breaker box?"

At first Benjamin did not understand what was meant, but finally he asked, "The electric?"

"Yes," Kirby said.

Benjamin led him to a small room in the other usable building where there was in one corner, a rectangular piece of plywood holding a number of large ceramic nodules. From behind the board, a bundle of wires rose to the ceiling. From there, some few wires branched off, obviously to electrify the room. The others continued onward out of sight. A heavy cable entered the building from the other direction and disappeared behind the board. "Power in from there," Kirby said, "power out from there. This is it."

"Are these fuses?" Bill said in amazement.

"Yes!" Benjamin said, "fuses. I remember!"

"I never saw anything like this," Bill said. "These things look like more like the old insulators than fuses. How would you replace them—and how do you find which one is bad?"

"I never saw anything like this either," Kirby said, "but I see how it works. It looks simple really. See this wire here between the two ceramic tips; that has to be the fuse. And look here, I see only one wire burnt out."

"But what kind of wire is that?" Bill said, "and can we find some of it somewhere?"

"Hmmmm," Kirby said, "wait here. I'll be back in a minute."

Bill and Benjamin resumed staring at the homemade fuse box for perhaps five minutes until Kirby returned. In one hand he held a spool of wire and in the other his small tool kit. "Generic wire," he said.

He cut off a length of wire with his wire-cutters and reached for the broken connection. "Wait!" Bill said, "how can you be sure the electricity is off."

"I've turned the pump off at the pump," Kirby explained, "and if you know what you're doing you can work while the main power is on."

"Oh," Bill said.

Kirby connected the wire across the gap and went back outside with Bill and Benjamin trailing after. At the pump house, he threw the switch and the pump began to murmur.

"Mr. Kirby, you have done it!" Benjamin said as his face split into his huge grin and he began pumping Kirby's hand for all he was worth, almost dancing in jubilation. "Now water will come!"

Benjamin was no happier than Bill, but Bill simply offered his hand to Kirby once Benjamin had finally let go. He didn't say a word for few seconds, then said very quietly, "Welcome to life in the field, Kirby."

Bill could see Kirby was very proud of his accomplishment despite his effort not to smile, and it was as if he had suddenly been set free. Before the day was over he had located and repaired a rattle in one of the air-conditioners, rewired and reinstalled a power sled so that a single step-down transformer controlled all receptacles eliminating any chance of the 220-volt line voltage ruining any 110-volt equipment, found and stopped two leaks in the plumbing system, light-proofed the darkroom, installed and stocked the refrigerator with the items needing cooling, repaired one door-lock, and adjusted the carburetor in Benjamin's car.

Kirby sweated rivulets but made no mention of it. He no longer shook his head at the poor construction and installations he saw all around, but regarded them merely as things he was going to fix before he left for home. He began to scribble notes of all sorts to himself as he thought his way through the challenges. Bill could not even get him to stop working long enough to eat the sandwiches they had brought along for lunch from the hotel. Only when Bill reminded him about his previous concern for local hygiene, and that it would be wise to at least wash his hands before eating, did he finally slow him down momentarily. But he was now so busy he only compromised by first holding the sandwiches by the wrapper, and then abandoned even that precaution when it came to wolfing down the chips and the chocolate muffin dessert. Bill made a mental note to discuss Kirby with Nate once more; it looked as if Nate might have been too quick in his judgment. It seemed to Bill that he might be witnessing the emergence of a genuine ops officer.

***

As they settled down for an after-work beer at the bar in the hotel, Bill could see Kirby was still enjoying his triumphs earlier in the day. "I think, Kirby," Bill said, "that you had a very good time today. I know you did some fine work."

Kirby smiled in spite of himself. "It was a good day," he said. "I enjoyed it thoroughly. I can't wait for tomorrow...Is it like this a lot—I mean, the sense of getting things done—things you hadn't thought about before?"

Bill took a long draught of his beer. "What you witnessed today, Kirby, was the single, most important thing that makes this one of the best jobs in the world. That sense of accomplishing beyond what you thought you could is the number one best thing that can happen to a man—other than good health, of course. Now I don't mean that anything you did today was in any way beyond your capabilities, but you didn't know any of it was coming, you had to think on your feet and take action using just your wits and whatever you could immediately lay hands on. The sense that you can handle things no matter what, no matter where, no matter when, is addictive. I worked for twelve years in industry and never had one moment where I had that same satisfaction.

"Now, you'll have some days when everything goes four ways from the middle and you feel like you're trying to break rocks with a rubber hammer, but that just makes days like this all the sweeter. And the great thing is that every day in ops, repeat every day, not just every TDY, offers the same possibilities. Of course, you will certainly find you're twenty IQ points smarter in the field than at headquarters, but it's still a great job even there.

"When you repair a camera installation in the field; or an agent does good, secure work after your training; or you suddenly realize a better way to do something and you're free to try it immediately; or you meet an old friend in Hong Kong that you last saw in Lagos—there's nothing like it. And then, to top it all off, at the end of the day you manage to get a really cold beer in a country formerly ruled by the hot-beer Brits...it can bring tears of joy to your eyes."

Kirby laughed and said, "Nate never told me about that. He did say it was the best job in the world, and he did say job satisfaction was great, but he put a lot of emphasis on advancement, and benefits, and prestige, and service to the country."

"Nate has been in management too long," Bill said, "and it's started to affect his mind. He has come very far and intends to go much farther, and for that you need to sound a little more like the potentates who show up on the D.C. political talk shows. They sound better to the rarefied intellect of the audience than someone telling only the practical truth. Of course, when no one's looking that audience is probably switching back and forth between the talking and the NFL pre-game or the Wide World of Wrestling. Now Nate is sounding much better to our most-high leaders and when he gets back home he will be what we used to call a 'mover and shaker'.

"But don't kid yourself; once an ops officer, always an ops officer. When Nate is in the field, he still shows a personality higher management has never seen—and which he doesn't want them to see. Remember, the higher the management, the more likely they are now to have not been ops officers or perhaps not even Agency people at all. Of course I'll never have to worry about that, and you won't have to worry about it for a while yet."

At that, the two fell silent for a while as they stared contentedly at the sunset. Finally, Kirby turned to Bill and asked, "What's the third best thing that can happen to a man—after good health and accomplishing beyond his capabilities?"

"Figuring out something that has puzzled you for a long time," Bill said. "And the next best thing is going to supper before you've had too many beers to care about eating and you wake up next morning and the whole world is out of focus."

"Then we'd better go," Kirby said.

Chapter 22

Kirby, with the fierce energy of youth, arrived at the training site next day in the highest of spirits. Bill, who had never been a morning person and was suffering from a slight hangover, was not so enthusiastic. Just as he got out of the car, the trailing dust cloud Kirby had raised, settled over them and it occurred to Bill that Kirby was now driving almost as fast as Benjamin despite his previous intellectual rejection of high speed. He decided it would be wise to caution Kirby about it, but did not feel up to it at the moment.

Benjamin had trustingly given them the keys so they headed immediately for the "lounge" where Bill produced a jar of instant coffee and immediately began boiling water. To his surprise, Kirby opted for the tea.

"You know, Kirby," Bill began, "we need not go native just because we like it here."

"I drink tea sometimes at home," Kirby said, "so I thought I might try it here. Of course at home it was always iced tea."

"This will be different," Bill said, "and do not, repeat, do not use the local milk unless you personally see it come out of a carton."

"Milk—in tea?" Kirby said. "I didn't think people really did drink it that way."

"It's a British thing," Bill said. "If you heat the milk too much it forms a gross skim; if you don't heat it enough, the tea is lukewarm. Drinking all that lukewarm tea may explain the Brit tolerance for lukewarm beer."

Before Bill could expound farther on one of his favorite topics, Benjamin arrived in his usual high spirits. After a few minutes of boilerplate discussion about classroom parameters and scheduling and the students and their abilities, he asked Bill if he should stay until the class actually began. Bill said it would be a great favor if he did so.

At the appointed time, they headed to the classroom where, a few minutes later, the students arrived along with the local military liaison officers and the bang-and-burn team leader, Ross Beaulieu. After Bill and Ross had talked briefly—mostly about a joint TDY to Bangkok many years ago—Ross formally handed the students over to Bill and departed.

Bill began talking about photography in the broadest general terms. He next began asking questions of the students regarding their experience, finding that none had any real familiarity with photography, and then moved the conversation into just about anything anyone wanted to discuss. Kirby thought Bill was only establishing rapport with the students and he joined in whenever he felt inclined, but after more than an hour of this, Kirby began to wonder when they would get started. Bill called a break during which Kirby asked when something useful would finally be said, but Bill told him to be patient and have some more tea. Kirby declined and raided Bill's supply of instant coffee.

After the break, Bill handed out the cameras and let the students talk among themselves as they admired the handsome new equipment. At first, they handled the cameras awkwardly, as if they were small atomic bombs. Bill let the informal talking and admiring proceed until the great novelty of the cameras had declined, then again began talking about photography in general terms. By now, Kirby was beginning to fidget and to constantly roam the classroom. Finally Benjamin interrupted Bill suggesting they take another break. As the last student filed out once more, Kirby moved close to Bill and Benjamin and asked, "Are we ever going to get started? We've wasted almost two hours and nothing has been accomplished. You haven't even officially said, 'This is a camera.'"

"Youth, impatient youth," Bill sighed. "Will they never learn, Benjamin?"

Benjamin smiled again and said, "Mr. Kirby, Mr. Bill and I learned long ago that the students cannot soon understand very well. They must be allowed to listen for a while before they are understanding the technical things."

Kirby stared wide-eyed again at Bill and Benjamin in turn. "They speak English," he said.

"Kirby," Bill said, "haven't you ever heard the old saying that America and England are two countries divided by a common language. These students speak Colonial British English, but the Brits didn't stay here as long or rule as thoroughly as they did in Kenya. The use of English is largely confined to the upper classes and the military; they just aren't as used to it as some former British colonies.

"In my very first training here years ago, Benjamin and I found out there's more to understanding than knowing the meaning of individual words. There's syntax, cadence, accent, nuance and God knows what else. And remember, we're not going to be talking about the weather, but technical things requiring some words the students have never heard and a lot of words they haven't heard often. After a lot of experience Benjamin and I have learned it saves confusion later on if they understand right from the git-go. While I talk, Benjamin watches and evaluates. When he's certain they are all following me OK, he calls a break and then the training actually starts. Are they ready now, Benjamin?"

"Yes, Mr. Bill," Benjamin said, "they are ready. I will be going. Call if you need me."

"Will do," Bill said. "Thanks, Benjamin. We'll be in touch at least once every day."

After Benjamin had shaken hands with them once more and departed, Bill turned to Kirby. "Now, Kirby," he said, "it's time for us to win friends for the US of A and save Mifuna once more. Do you want another shot of tea before we begin?"

"No," Kirby said.

***

Once Bill actually began the training, Kirby settled into being as helpful as possible. If a student was having a tough time with something, Kirby worked with him to straighten it out. If Kirby thought a concept was only partially understood, he would ask a question himself that he thought the students should have asked. When the hands-on use of the cameras began, he seemed to be everywhere at once in the classroom while Bill lectured at the blackboard. Soon thereafter, one of the students asked a question. Bill winked at Kirby to let him know they were off and running.

By the first afternoon, the students were ready to be sent out to take a series of photographs without using the light meters in their cameras. For this exercise, both Bill and Kirby went with them, but by the end of the first week they were handling the various exercises on their own. Once darkroom work began, the students were broken up into groups so that only three would be in the darkroom at one time. By using changing bags to load the reels, it was possible for one group to develop film, while the another group made prints, and still another group was sent out on specific shooting exercises.

Given the very low technical knowledge of the students Kirby had witnessed on the first day, he was amazed at how far they had come by the end of the first week. Bill used the first Friday to smooth out the few logistical problems that had cropped up in the training and to make sure everyone was at, or near, the same level of expertise. It was also necessary to make the first report to Mark so Bill shortened the day both for the students and the instructors. As Kirby drove back to Mifuna City at his usual break-neck pace, Bill was satisfied and Kirby was elated at the progress they were making and at how much he was enjoying the work.

"This has really been fun so far," Kirby said, "I never would have believed it on the day we arrived. I thought this was going to be a long, ugly TDY and that I was going to die of heat stroke before we even got started. Like you said, every day is different and there's always some new problem to solve, everything from finding some way to get over a technical concept to repairing the one bad burner on the hot plate in the lounge. Even the weather is better; it isn't nearly so hot as when we arrived."

"Kirby," Bill said, "it's just as hot now as when we got here; you just aren't paying it as much attention. If you think it's especially cool right now it's because you're driving at nearly the speed of light and the wind blast is so high I get wind burns on my elbow every time I stick it out the window. The gale would cool off a blacksmith shop."

Kirby laughed and slowed the car down for a few seconds, but as he began to speak, he inadvertently speeded up again. Bill decided to let him go. He was now so confident of Kirby's driving skill that he was sure the young man could handle any sudden highway problem or that they would hit so hard they would die instantly. "What do we tell Baxter," Kirby asked.

"Exactly what all COSs want to hear from traveling techs," Bill said, "that everything's absolutely fine, cooperation from the locals is excellent, and that he need not take any time away from doing his job to help us out. Unless he asks when we intend to leave, we'll know he's satisfied. Ollie will have kept him up to date and he will have checked with Benjamin's superiors too so he already knows how it's going. Our report will just be a formality."

***

As Bill and Kirby filed into Mark's office, he was bustling around behind the desk either looking for something or getting some papers in order. It was obvious he was not concerned about what they had to report. As they sat down he rested his palms on the desk but continued to stand. Bill thought, "This meeting isn't going to take even five minutes."

"I heard the training is going fine," Mark began. "Do you need anything or do you need to communicate with NORTECH, or is there anything interesting to report?"

"No," Bill said, "we're good. Right now, I can't think of anything we need or anything that's unusual in any way."

"Good," Mark said. "I do have a little extra job for you. I believe you can work it in without disrupting the training."

"Fine," Bill said, "we'll do our best."

"Just today," Mark began, "the embassy held a little celebration for President Bouaki—just a luncheon where he could meet some new people in the State Department—and a chance for us to invite some local people, and a few foreign diplomatic officers that we might not be able to contact conveniently otherwise. My secretary took some pictures and it would be a nice gesture to get them developed and have some enlargements made. Can you do that, maybe this weekend in your spare time?"

"Sure," Bill said, "no problem. It isn't, by any chance, color film is it?"

"Yes," Mark said, "I'll show it to you in just a minute, but I can't find it just now..."

As Mark rummaged through his desk, Bill shot a glance at Kirby who looked as if he were about ready to say something. Kirby noticed him and Bill shook his head to let him know not to speak.

"Finally!" Mark said. "For a minute I thought I'd lost it. Here it is."

"Kodacolor," Bill said. He hesitated for a moment, then said, "Mark, we don't normally do color at small stations like this; it's hard to process without a pretty well equipped darkroom and even then it takes a good while to do it by hand. I'm sorry to say, we haven't checked your darkroom yet, although we certainly intended to do it before we left, but I don't recall the station had any color capability when I was here last. Of course I admit that was a long, long time ago."

"Oh, we're all set," Mark said. "I got some training from one of your techs back at headquarters just before I came out and she sent all the supplies. They've only been here a few months."

"I hesitate to ask," Bill said, "but since this is regular color film, why not just get it developed locally? As I recall there is one local photography studio that has a color processing machine for snapshots. Since their equipment is automated and checked by Kodak or Fuji or whoever has the local concession, their work would probably be just as good as ours in this case and maybe faster."

"I did consider that," Mark said, "and if you weren't here, I would take that chance, but I wanted to present some enlargements to Bouaki, and it would be great to be able to say we made them ourselves just for him. There is also one security consideration: we have a new NOC officer in country and although we wanted him there to meet the local potentates, and business leaders, and certain members of the foreign diplomatic community we're interested in, I'd just as soon not have to say to headquarters that his photo showed up in locally developed prints which were then passed to the local government. One great advantage of having you do the printing is that you can cut him out if he does show up in any of the pictures."

"I understand," Bill said. "I assume you want a proof sheet then?"

"Yes," Mark said, "I'll show you which prints to enlarge and point out the NOC officer—if he shows up in any of them—and I'll also show you which frames need not be printed. That should save time."

"Can the proof be black and white?" Bill asked.

"Yes," Mark said, "I don't see why not. Will that help you out?"

"It will," Bill said. "Developing color film and printing negatives requires several different solutions which are perishable and have to be held at constant temperature to give predictable results. If we can get the film developed tonight, we can give you a black and white proof sheet early tomorrow. If we had to give you a color proof, we'd have to make solutions for print developing tonight as well as making the solutions to develop the film, bring all of them to constant temperature, fiddle with the color filters to give decent color—I haven't worked with color in a while so I'll be rusty at adjusting the filtration—and then give you the proof. You might be gone for the weekend before I got the job done. If possible, Kirby and I will finish this project sometime during the weekend so we can keep the training on schedule. If you can let us know what you need by noon tomorrow, maybe we can be finished by Monday morning. Can you arrange with the Marine guard for us to be here at any time during the weekend?"

"Sure," Mark said, "I'll take care of it right now."

As they headed for the darkroom, Kirby asked, "Didn't you tell me not to get color processing started at small stations and that no tech in his right mind would encourage it?"

"I did for a fact, Kirby," Bill said, "and for your notebook, let me repeat: it's a mistake. I'll bet Mark, being young and eager and on the cutting edge, insisted the tech who gave him the routine technical familiarization at HQ, set him up with color. The customer—the case officer that is—is always right. Still, I'd like to know who let this get started. An experienced photo tech would have made up some kind of horror story about possible sterilization from the color chemicals or something, to talk him out of it."

"Jesus!" Bill said as the entered the darkroom, "this darkroom hasn't been used for a long time. Let's just check first to see if Mark really does have all the stuff we need for color work."

After a search through every cabinet and drawer, Bill finally stopped Kirby who was still dragging items out from the far recesses under the sink, and said, "You can hold up, Kirby, I just found the drums and the rotor. The good news is: I believe, repeat believe, Mark does have everything. The bad news is that I believe Mark does appear to have everything. We're duty bound to give it our best shot. I'm afraid I'm going to have to ask you to do some grunt work. This is going to be one of those times when we've got rocks to break and rubber hammers to do it with."

"It's OK, Bill," Kirby said, "I've had enough adventure and romance for one week anyway."

"First we need to clean up before we can even start," Bill said. "You set up a constant temperature bath. Use the stirrer-hot plate and the largest, deepest developing tray you can find and try to get the water to steady-out at one hundred degrees. I'm going to begin washing beakers so that I can start making solutions. When you finish with the bath, wash up the Ektamatic and charge it with activator and fixer; we'll need that for the black and white proof print. By that time maybe the water bath will be somewhere near the right temperature. Once we get the solutions in the bath, we'll break for supper and let the solutions come to the same temperature as the bath. After that, God willing, I'll develop the film and make the proof. I we can get it to Mark tomorrow early, he can decide what he wants and with luck we can be finished just in time to hand him the prints on Monday on our way out to the training site."

"Piece of cake," Kirby said.

***

Kirby gradually lost his enthusiasm as the long afternoon ground on. It seemed he had washed every beaker and graduated cylinder in the darkroom at least twice while Bill made up the solutions, only to find that Bill intended to use the metal Nikor tanks to hold the individual developing solutions in the water bath. Bill explained the metal would allow faster equilibration between the surrounding liquid and the solutions, and the film could then be dipped and dunked from tank to tank instead of holding the film in one tank and pouring each solution into it. Kirby understood the reasoning but starting to wash all the Nikor tanks just when he had finished the glassware was dispiriting.

When they got back from dinner, the bath was still holding steady but even with the metal tanks, the solutions had to be stirred and allowed to sit for a while longer before they came to the same temperature as the surrounding water. While Kirby worked at adjusting the temperature of the solutions, Bill marked the darkroom timer with glow-in-the-dark tape according to the intervals for the various steps in the developing sequence, cleaned up the enlarger, and cut the paper to the correct size. Finally, they were ready.

"You know, Kirby," Bill said, "if the secretary didn't do a good job with the camera, the negatives are going to be even harder to print—or maybe she didn't get any photos at all—just kidding."

When Bill turned off the lights, Kirby said, "Do you mind if I pray?"

***

"Thank God for the Canon AF35!" Bill said as he unrolled the still-wet negatives. "Look at that even, correct exposure! It's gonna make printing a lot easier. I must be living right. As Lefty Gomez once said: 'Clean livin'—and a fast outfield—makes a man a twenty-game winner.'

"FYI, Kirby, we tested the AF a few years back and sent a bunch of them out to the smaller field stations just for times like this when a secretary, or anyone else who wasn't familiar with photography, had to take pictures on short notice. Of course, we did intend them to use black and white film if it had to be developed at the station.

"The camera's not perfect; the auto-focus will sometimes decide on the wrong thing, but for an inexperienced shooter, you can't beat it. Of course, there's still some purists who make fun of any automatic camera, but those are the folks who would never even drive by a K-Mart on the highway and if they ever had to work under 'field conditions' they'd dissolve in a puff of smoke.

"Now let's get these negatives dried and make that proof."

"Bill," Kirby said, "who was Lefty Gomez?"

Chapter 23

Despite the quality of the negatives, the printing proved to be a long, tiresome process. Mark had chosen twenty-two exposures for printing, leaving out those that were of no interest or were poorly composed or contained no information. Of the twenty-two, he chose only five for eight-by-ten enlargements.

The processing began slowly as Bill's color expertise was rusty, as he had predicted. Once his judgment sharpened again, the work went more smoothly, but it still took several minutes for each print. Kirby handled the actual developing and washing as Bill moved from negative to negative on the enlarger, changing the color filtration and re-framing slightly for each one. At one point, Bill turned from the enlarger to find Kirby staring at the rotating drum as if he were in a trance. "Kirby," he said, "you still with us?"

"Yeah, Bill," he said, "I'm fine. Do people really do this as a hobby?"

"They probably do it once," Bill said. "After that, the only reason would be that they've got some porn pictures they can't send to the one-hour magic developer machine."

"If I ever ask you, in a moment of temporary insanity, to train me in the finer details of this process," Kirby said, "don't do it."

Bill laughed. "Don't worry," he said, "every regional base has its own color processor, and according to Nate, it won't be long before there will be some way of doing it by computer. You'll be able to tell your grand-kids that you once developed film by hand, and they'll say, 'What's film?'"

They worked throughout the afternoon and early evening. At one point, Bill thought about stopping the work and picking it up again on Sunday, but the thought of washing up and starting over seemed just too awful. He said to Kirby, "If you don't mind, Kirby, let's finish it today and take tomorrow off. I warn you it might be tomorrow before we leave here today."

"You're the man, Bill," Kirby said, "you've done fine so far. If you think that's best, let's go for it."

***

Finally the last print was fixed and dried. They were so tired, they did not speak even once as they washed up the glassware and the tanks and the trays and the drums. Bill's shoulders felt knotted from the tense work and his brain was fogged by the hours of unbroken concentration. Kirby seemed physically fine, but it was clear he was desperately tired too; his talking and his spirits had gradually diminished as the day had worn on. It was only as Kirby carefully put the prints into the various envelops to keep them separated as they thought Mark would want that he suddenly came to life again.

"You know, this is damn good work," he said. "Look at these things. The color is sharp and true, the contrast is just right, and you framed every negative to make it look as good as possible. Mark will be ecstatic when he sees this on Monday."

"I hope so," Bill said, "but you have to remember, he doesn't know anything about how hard this kind of processing is and this was not an essential project for him. All this means in his world is a little more consideration and access to the higher reaches of Bouaki's government. If we had failed, or if we hadn't been here, he would have found some other way to get the same result. In their own way, COs are just as resourceful as we are; it just happens to be geared to people, not technical things."

"I think he should turn handsprings when he sees the work," Kirby said.

"You might be right," Bill said, " but I doubt it. He will appreciate it, but that's all. And Kirby...whatever he says, just smile and say, 'our pleasure.'"

"I promise," Kirby said.

***

Kirby was silent as he had promised when they handed over the prints to Mark who had come to the office very early, but not to receive their work. He glanced at the prints, said, "Good job," and put them in his desk. It was obvious he was concerned about something else so Bill made their exit as quickly and uneventfully as possible. Kirby had remained totally quiet as promised.

They had been rocketing out toward the training site for perhaps fifteen minutes when Kirby finally broke his silence. "I remember what you said," he began, "but just getting any prints, even family snapshots, from the drug store would have caused me to react more than he did."

"Yes, you're right," Bill said, "but after you've worked with COs for many years, you learn when to leave them alone. They have the same power of concentration as our pure scientists on those days when they seem to have just beamed in from the planet Zircon. He's preoccupied right now, and he didn't want to be bothered. It's something big and he hasn't decided how to handle it—just like us when we stared at the pump before you fixed it. Lucky for us, it must be totally operational, not technical or we would be doing whatever he wanted right now, regardless of how the training was thrown off schedule.

"Could you slow down just a little. I've been thinking about one of our students and I want to ask you to do him a favor, but at this speed, I feel like that fellow in *2001* when he hit the Jovian atmosphere and I can't really concentrate."

As Kirby slowed down to breakneck speed, Bill continued. "It's Alfred," he said. "I don't know if he's really with us, or if he's attached to this planet, for that matter. Sometimes he does fine and I think he understood what he just did, and other times I feel like God sent him the right answer just to keep us off guard. He needs constant intense help until we definitely decide what to do, and I know you've already spent more time with him than..."

228

"Not Alfred!" Kirby said. "I think I'd rather make some more color prints. I've been on him constantly and the training just isn't sinking in. How do you think he got selected given the way the others are leaving him behind?"

"Just hang with him a little more, Kirby," Bill said, "and maybe he'll really understand or we'll at least be sure before we wash him out. I want to avoid embarrassing him if possible. Today will be the first exercise where we assume they know basic photography and have to use if for some specific purpose without our detailed instructions on what to do. We should know very soon now if we're going to have to flunk him and I'd be most grateful if you gave him your most intense attention."

"If I agree to this, can I go faster?" Kirby asked.

"Yes," Bill answered, "if that's possible."

***

The day's lesson was on ID photography. Bill began by explaining the simple calculation involving millimeters of focal length needed per foot of distance to the target to insure an ID quality print could be made from the image on the negative. As he explained the great advantage of long focal length lenses: allowing the shooter to be at greater distance from the target and still get ID quality photos, Kirby could see Alfred was perplexed. When Bill ran the students through theoretical operational situations asking them what length lenses would be required for different distances to the target, he could see Alfred was lost. When Bill dismissed the group who would be shooting first, Kirby stayed with Alfred, giving him special instruction before letting him go. Then he joined Bill who was with those working in the darkroom.

Kirby was sure he had been able to get Alfred to understand what was wanted so Bill complimented him on his effort and said he would buy him a beer after work.

It was the next day that Kirby learned an important lesson in training where English was not the native language of the students. When they turned in their prints to Bill for his critique they had all done a fairly good job of photographing each other at different distances using all their lenses. When Alfred brought up his prints, Kirby saw Bill look carefully at the first few, then begin to shuffle through the rest. He looked up at Kirby who was then stationed at the back of the room and smiled. Kirby quickly moved to the desk and said, "What?" Bill spread the prints out for him so that they could study them all. When he looked up at Bill with his trademark stare, Bill could not help smiling again. Spread out over the desk were about a dozen photos, all of the small goat herd resident at the training site. Some photos were what could be called group shots and some were close-ups. In some the goats even seemed to be posing.

"Well, Alfred," Bill said, "I would have to admit I could identify every one of those goats at every distance from twenty-five feet to two-hundred feet. How about you, Kirby?"

Kirby stood staring at the photos in silence. "I guess," Bill said, "that Mr. Kirby can do the same. Kirby…right…Kirby?"

Since Kirby still did not answer, Bill continued, "I know we didn't actually stress it too much, Alfred, but we hoped you would take pictures of people for the exercise…but I can see you've got the idea, right, Kirby?"

"Right," Kirby said finally.

"Why don't we take our morning tea a little early today," Bill said, "so Kirby and I can look over all the photos and maybe pick out some especially good ones—or bad ones—for examples."

As the last student filed out, Bill couldn't hold back any longer. He laughed until tears filled his eyes and finally Kirby began to laugh too. The more he thought about it, the more humorous it seemed. "Dammit!" Kirby said finally, "he really did get the idea, you know."

That set Bill off again on another laughing bout. When he was again under control he said, "It's what a professor might call the danger of literal translation, but us old ops whores just call it the 'Oriental Question', and it'll bite you in the ass throughout your career. In the Orient, if you ask a question like, 'Can I go to the bank today?' and the person is not very familiar with English, the answer will always be 'Yes'. First, they're good, kind folks and they don't want to give you any bad news and, literally, you certainly can go to the bank today—or any day. It may not be open, but you can go as many times as you like. I must have used the words 'target' and 'shooter' fifty times in my lecture. I'll bet Alfred associated that with hunting animals, not shooting his friends—despite the fact we thought we had made it absolutely clear."

"I suppose then," Kirby said, "that this is just one more entry in my ops notebook."

"Right," Bill said, "put it on the first page since it starts with 'A'—for Alfred. Now, are we calmed down enough to let the students see us again?"

"Probably not," Kirby said.

***

A week later, they stopped laughing at Alfred. Bill had arranged early on with Ross to let the students photograph parts of the military training he and his men were providing to the new special forces unit. In most of their assignments there were at least a few photos of whatever training exercise was then in progress or snapshots of their friends in the elite unit. When Ross told Bill they would be beginning demolition training, he decided to send all the students down to take photos using the two-hundred millimeter lenses and the tele-converters. His instruction emphasized the now familiar idea that long lens photography could allow the shooter to get close-up photos without being physically close to the target.

The prints from all the other students were similar, showing explosions at a distance, but not from Alfred's prints. Bill immediately asked to see the negatives. In many of Alfred's prints, there were only blurred images of smoke and debris. Only Alfred could say which side was up on the prints. When Bill examined the negatives, he said quietly, "Damn."

As he handed the negatives to Kirby for his inspection, he said to Alfred, "How close were you when you took these?"

"I was at two-hundred feet; I step off first to be sure," Alfred said. "I remember the arithmetic: two millimeters of lens...bigness for foot of distance to target. With the...multiplier to make the bigness really four-hundreds, I must be two-hundred." At this Alfred smiled hugely, certain he had mastered the mathematics and understood the scientific principle involved.

Bill looked at Kirby who was clearly speechless. "Alfred," Bill said, "we use that formula as a rough guideline for surveillance photography to be sure we get an ID quality photograph of people. You should use it only for that. In this case, the idea was to get good photographs of something dangerous from a safe distance. From these prints, it looks like you were in the middle of the explosions."

"I was nearly so," Alfred said. "It knock my hat off once. But the numbers was right, was they not?"

"Yes, Alfred," Bill said, "the numbers was right."

That afternoon, Bill and Kirby met with Benjamin to discuss Alfred. Benjamin was immediately ill at ease and Bill realized there was something more to the story. As Benjamin came up with one platitude after another suggesting Alfred would soon begin to get the idea, Bill became concerned. "Is Alfred a special case?" he asked.

After a long hesitation, Benjamin finally admitted, "Yes, he is, in a way. His father is a very important man in president Bouaki's cabinet. Alfred is the youngest son. He has had...difficulty in...manhood. He was not chosen as the other students. His father put him into the army to make him grow up fast, but he has not done well. It was thought he might do better if he was to be in our special unit..."

"Well," Bill said, "we're not here to dispute the government and we both like Alfred personally so we certainly don't mind keeping him safe and passing him along, but *you* will have to keep him safe after we leave. And also, Benjamin, the group he will be in will be sent on the most difficult, dangerous missions. If just one man is not capable it will put all of them at risk. Do you want to talk to Ross about him? Maybe Ross has a different view or maybe he does well in the things Ross is training him to do. Maybe it's just photography or our method of training that causes him trouble."

"No," Benjamin said, "no, Mr. Bill. I have also talked to Mr. Ross and he suggested Alfred could stay with the special unit only if he was good at photo. He did not do well in using dangerous things. I will see to it."

***

At the beginning of the first class in the last week of training, Alfred came to Bill and Kirby and asked them to talk privately. Bill gave the students an operational problem to consider and walked with Alfred and Kirby down to the lounge. Alfred was obviously excited and happy.

"I have been promote!" he said. "I am sorry I will not finish, but I have to go now to the new work. The job is good. I get paid too well."

"Congratulations!" Bill said. "We're happy for you Alfred. We hate to lose you, but I know you must go."

After Kirby had added his congratulations, Bill announced that he was giving Alfred his own K-1000 kit because he surely knew how to use it. Bill did suggest he use it only to take snapshots of his friends and family however. This pleased Alfred greatly and after warm handshakes, he prepared to leave. As he turned toward the door, Bill said, "Alfred," wait a second. You didn't tell us what the new job is."

"I am to be Mr. Benjamin's assistant," he said. "I will have much to do, but Mr. Benjamin has not said what it is yet. He will be letting me know soon."

After silence had thoroughly enveloped the lounge once more after Alfred's bustling departure, Kirby said very quietly, "Benjamin is a saint."

Chapter 24

Benjamin had just dismissed the students after giving them their ornate certificates of achievement signed by the Chief of Courses himself. In fact, Bill had gotten Ollie to sign them using the name George Washington, rendered nearly unreadable by spectacular swirls in the signature. The cameras were handed over, the supplies were stored under lock and key, and Kirby had been able to show the students how to construct simple concealment devices from locally available materials during the last week. Also he had somehow managed to complete all his extra projects at the training site. Of course the write-up of the training would take a day at least but they were through at the training site itself. They anticipated a long, happy dinner with Benjamin at the best restaurant in town and after that a completely free weekend.

Bill intended to do the wrap-up cable on Monday while Kirby catalogued the local stores where he had bought the items used to construct the concealment devices. Once Kirby had finished that listing, he intended to canvass as many more stores as possible to see what other kinds of materials and equipment were available locally. Having that information on file could really help other techs as they planned their trips to Mifuna City. Bill was feeling that satisfaction of a good job done under hard conditions and he could see Kirby was almost regretting the idea of finishing up now that the time had come.

Just as they were getting into the car, Benjamin came running toward them. Bill already knew they were meeting later for dinner so he wondered at Benjamin's hurry. "What's wrong, Benjamin?" he said.

"Mr. Bill," Benjamin said, "I just got a call from Mr. Oliver. He want you to come to the embassy immediately now."

"Did he say anything else?" Bill asked.

"No," Benjamin said, "just come now."

"Damn," Bill said, "look, Benjamin, we'll have to have the dinner another time, but I'll let you know."

"I understand," Benjamin said.

As they roared back toward Mifuna City, Bill sat in complete silence, for once not paying any attention to Kirby's driving. Finally Kirby said, "Bill, why didn't you just say we would contact Benjamin about the dinner, not call it off without knowing what's up. Maybe Mark just wants a quick comment on the training now that everything's done."

"Not in this world," Bill said. "When a COS wants you to come quick, he's not interested in a comment he could get tomorrow or Monday or next week. It's something new and it's happening now or it's gonna happen very soon—and we're gonna be involved."

***

They found Mark, Ollie, Ross, and two other case officers already in Mark's office when they arrived. Like Mark, the other case officers were very young and Bill had never seen either of them before. Bill had learned to dread situations like this even when he knew what was about to happen, but to encounter staff officers gathered together with planning already underway while he remained uninformed, really made his heart race.

"Come in," Mark said, "let me bring you up to date. About two weeks ago we recruited Kwame's house-boy merely to keep an eye on him—Kwame is one of Bouaki's sons and a trouble-maker. We finished vetting the house-boy just a couple of days ago, at least to the point where we are ready to take a chance. Today at a meeting with Vince," here Mark nodded toward one of the young case officers who acknowledged the gesture by nodding slightly in return, "we found out Kwame may have some very important documents in the safe at his villa. The house-boy says a well-dressed man, who had a driver, came to visit Kwame late last night. They talked for a long time and went over a sheaf of documents. He was in and out of the room serving coffee and liquor several times so he saw the papers. Kwame told him the man was a business colleague and they were talking about a business deal, but he happened to see Kwame put the papers in his safe. Maybe it was nothing, or maybe it really was important, maybe some outside assistance Kwame has secured for his personal ambitions. Either way, we want to photograph those documents.

"Even as we speak, we're getting approvals for a surreptitious entry all the way up the line. For you guys: NORTECH has already approved the entry. Your HQ has not said yes, but I'm sure they will. As luck would have it, one of the fellows who's been temporarily assigned to Ross's training is a good locks man and he thinks he can open the safe with no problem. What we need to know from you is what you need for the op."

Bill thought a moment before answering. "Well," he began, "we need to know about how many docs there will be and the type of docs, by that I mean will it be just print or pictures or maps or blueprints or anything unusual."

"All the house-boy saw were just plain sheets of paper," Mark said, "but we're obviously going to photograph anything that's in that safe no matter what it is. Can you do that with what we have here."

"Yes," Bill said, "of course. You have an attaché copy kit; we found it in the darkroom, and you have Pan-X film; we found that too. That's our best system for unknown docs especially if the number happens to be large. It's compact, reliable, swift, and looks like a regular briefcase. We'll take the station Polaroid and our personal cameras in too."

"So, as far as you know, you're ready?" Mark asked.

"As far as equipment goes," Bill said, "but we do need to know a little more about the target. I assume all the details of that kind will come out as we talk."

"Yes, probably," Mark said. "I assume you mean what the house is like and how it's protected, etc."

"Right," Bill said.

"OK," Mark said, "let's get to that. It's fairly isolated because it's in the best section of the city up on Karga hill. Also it's surrounded by the usual ten-foot-high wall with shards of glass embedded in concrete at the top. The house-boy says there's only one guard who sleeps like a rock after he locks the gate each night. He and the house-boy will be the only ones on site after dark and we've provided the house-boy with a rare bottle of good liquor. When we go in the guard will be so deep in la-la land a volcano probably couldn't wake him and he'll stay that way.

"Every Saturday night without fail, Kwame goes to the Palm restaurant, has a few in the bar, has an elaborate meal, has a few more in the bar to see if there's any action, and chalks the whole thing up to the government. As soon as his car hits the road tomorrow the house-boy will show the guard the booze and within a few minutes he ought to be comatose.

"Ross's guys will be security. Two of his men will follow Kwame and two more will rent a van and drive you, Bill, and you, Kirby, and the locks expert to the area near the house as soon as Kwame leaves. They'll park where you can see the gate. When the house-boy re-opens the gate, you three will go in. If the guard has to be distracted during the night, Ross's boys will see to it."

Here Mark turned to Ross and said, "You can't kill him, Ross, OK?"

"Understood," Ross said. "FYI, Bill; the follow team will be Alex and Roger. Todd and Gary will be your drivers."

"OK," Bill said, "got it."

"Once it's over," Mark continued, "Ross's guys will pick you up as soon as you get off the street directly in front of the gate. You can look the area over tomorrow and decide the exact spot for the pickup.

"We'll use station radios on channel four, repeat four, our secure frequency. Ross has seen to the radios; they're ready. Call signs—any suggestions?"

Ross and Bill looked at each other and smiled. "Entry team will be 'Sail-Cat', if that's OK with you, Ross," Bill said.

"Only if I can be 'Road-Hog'," Ross replied. "My two teams will be...'FUBAR' and 'SNAFU.'"

"Whoa!" Mark said. "I know this is a tiny op at the end of the world but it is important to me personally. Let's not jinx it."

For a moment Ross looked surprised, but then seemed to understand Mark's reluctance. "Of course," he said, "sorry, Mark. Sometimes us old whores forget ourselves. Any suggestions from you Bill?"

"How about...'Wide Load'?" he said.

"I like it," Ross said, "and maybe...'Necker's Knob.'"

Mark stared at them for a moment. "What's a 'Necker's Knob'?" he asked.

"The innocence of today's youth," Ross said. "A necker's knob was wonderful device fastened on the steering wheel. It really was a rotatable knob. A young man could keep his right arm around his sweetie's shoulder while driving entirely with his left hand...with the aid of the knob. My knob had a naked woman in it. What was in yours, Bill?"

"My mama didn't allow any naked women anywhere, anyway, anyhow. I had a Confederate flag in mine."

"Very sad," Ross said.

As total quiet settled on the assemblage. Ross and Bill stopped smiling at each other and looked at the rest of the young officers who were all staring incomprehensively at them. Kirby was staring even more owlishly than Bill remembered.

Finally Mark shook his head as if to clear it. "Perfect," he said in resignation.

"Alex and Roger will be 'Wide Load,'" Ross said, "and Todd and Gary will be 'Necker's Knob.' We'll need two more; I recommend 'Mr.

T' for Kwame and 'Tube Top' for Miranda."

"Miranda?" Bill said.

"Miranda and I will be at the Palm keeping tabs on 'Mr. T,'" Ross said, "while you guys bust your asses taking pictures in the house. If Kwame needs to be delayed Miranda can certainly do it and if he doesn't she'll finally get a fine night out at station expense. She deserves it; right, Mark?"

Bill assumed from Ross's comments that he and Mark had developed the camaraderie between tech and CO that was normally the product of many joint ops and many long hours spent in bars. He was very surprised that Mark, being so young, had had time to develop that kind of relationship with any tech. As he watched Mark's face, he was suddenly sure that had not yet happened and made a mental note to explain to Mark that Ross treated everyone, from the newest rookies to division chiefs, the same way.

Long ago, Ross had come from the Marines directly into the bang-and-burn group with excellent military skills and the rough, friendly manner of his peers. His men were devoted to him and he was an excellent officer, but he had never risen above team leader and had no desire to do so. As Nate had said after getting to know Ross, "He's the man you want when the shit hits the fan, but at embassy luncheons, you don't want to get him involved."

"Yes," Mark said a little hesitantly, "Miranda could use a night out at the best restaurant. I couldn't imagine a better secretary…"

Mark turned to Bill and Kirby. "Ross came up with a possible scenario to watch Kwame's movement in the restaurant and delay his departure if necessary," he said, "but I haven't had time to brief Miranda so I'm not sure she will…"

"No need for that." Ross said, "I'll take care of it. You have the rest of the op to worry about. I'll do it tomorrow—plenty of time."

"Right," Mark said, "yes…of course."

Mark took a few seconds to gather his thoughts again and then continued. "Just in case anyone is wondering, we can't involve liaison in this in any way. Bouaki's no fool and he knows Kwame's ambition, but he's old and tired and doesn't want to hear anything bad about any of his boys. There is no way he would ever approve this op and he will be highly pissed if he should find out about it, especially if we come up empty. Even if we're totally successful and we get something that nails Kwame, I'm going to claim I got the information from one of our agents in a neighboring country, or make up some other plausible scenario, depending on what turns up. So no mention of anything to liaison; the op is incompatible enough as it is. If we were doing this just about anywhere else we'd call in a complete new team to make the entry. Everybody understand?"

All in the room agreed they had the idea and were ready to proceed. "Any more questions at this point?" Mark asked.

"Is there any possibility the room where the safe is can be seen from the street?" Bill asked.

"The wall is too high to see over," Mark said. "Any more questions? OK let's break. Everybody show up bright and early tomorrow and let's plan it down to the last detail."

***

As usual Bill and Kirby stopped off at the hotel bar at the end of the day. As they settled down, Bill could tell Kirby had now had time to think over the situation he had just witnessed and was ready to ask questions. As if on cue, Kirby, said, "I have some questions about this thing we're about to do."

"I thought you might," Bill said. "Ask away."

"What if we get caught?" Kirby asked.

"Not a bad first question," Bill said, "but in this case it won't happen. This isn't Moscow or Paris or Hong Kong; the local police force is non-existent. And if Ross's men see we're in trouble, they'll get us out. The op might no longer be a secret, but we'll be OK. You notice how Nate up in NORTECH immediately approved it. If he thought it had a lot of blow-back potential he would have managed to get someone at HQ to put on the brakes until it got straightened out."

"How does Ross's locks expert know he'll be able to open the safe since he hasn't seen it?" Kirby next asked.

"That is a bit of swagger," Bill said, "but I know the fellow involved—name's Gene Cliffson. I've known him for many years and it can now be revealed he's just on loan to bang- and-burn from our Surreptitious Entry Unit at HQ. He's here to train some of the new special force in very simplified SEU techniques as part of the special training. To my knowledge, he has never failed at any lock so I'm sure he can take care of this one, even if it's fairly sophisticated."

"What then?" Kirby asked.

"Then," Bill said, "we go to work. We'll discuss this again tomorrow, but we can begin now. It will go this way: First we take a Polaroid of the room and the contents of the safe before we touch anything, so we can leave it exactly the same as we found it when we finish up. If there's a stack of docs, I want you to put them on the easel of the kit as fast as possible while I shoot. If they're bound, you'll have to hold down each page as I photograph it. You must put them back in exactly the same order. We'll do the docs first. If we find passports or something else, we'll get that next. If there's something unusual; some kind of object that isn't basically flat, or a large item, or one with unusual color, or one that just doesn't work for the kit, we'll photograph it with our hand-held cameras. They'll be loaded with Tri-X, not Pan-x, so we can hand-hold and still get a reasonable shutter speed in low light. I'll get Gene to operate the radio for us and help us in any way possible after he opens the safe.

"Tomorrow, we'll practice with the kit and try to imagine everything that could go wrong. Of course, our first mission will be to check the kit from A to Z."

"Did you say we'd practice with the kit?" Kirby asked. "What's to do except put the docs on the baseboard and take the pictures?"

"It does sound simple and it is," Bill said, "but I've seen enough Laurel and Hardy movies to know that simple things can get complicated—they were a famous comedy team, Kirby—don't worry about it. Anyway, if we can work perfectly together in moving the docs across the easel we might save a second per doc, and in a worst case situation, it might make all the difference."

"OK," Kirby said, "got it. One more thing; why doesn't Kwame have more security?"

"Another good question," Bill said, "and one Mark should rightly answer, but I think I can give you some idea. First off, Kwame is the son of the president of the country. No local teenager is going to throw a rock through his window and no jack-leg local thief is going to steal his chickens. Second off, he has no idea Mark is on to him. As far as he knows, his contacts outside the country are either unknown or accounted for in some innocuous way. Also he may have nothing to hide. We may not find evidence of anything beyond perfectly ordinary business records involving perfectly ordinary folks. Remember, Mark is so leery of saying anything to Bouaki that even if we find something, he's planning to say he got it somewhere else."

"Could Kwame notice Ross and Miranda at the restaurant and get suspicious?" Kirby asked.

"First, seeing anyone from the diplomatic community at the Palm is not unusual," Bill said. "Every high-roller of any kind dines there. Also I doubt if Kwame has ever seen Ross and I'm sure that tomorrow Miranda will not look like Miranda. Just because we techs almost never operate in disguise doesn't mean it isn't done a lot. Every station officer is fitted with at least one disguise before they leave HQ and some have several. Since Miranda is a pretty, perky brunette, my guess is that tomorrow she'll be a platinum blonde bombshell. When a woman gets a chance to be someone else she never chooses Eleanor Roosevelt over Marilyn Monroe, especially since Ross has it in mind that she may have to distract Kwame, although he didn't officially say that. I hope he handles the explanation well when he tells her what might be required."

Bill waited for more questions but Kirby fell silent, occasionally sipping at his beer and staring off into the future. Bill wondered if the untested young man might be having second thoughts. Finally he drained the beer, sat the mug down on the table with great authority, and said, "Thank God I signed on with this outfit instead becoming an architect like my parents wanted!"

Chapter 25

Ross and Miranda had gotten to the Palm early so that Ross could choose the perfect location: a booth at the back of the restaurant where he could see everything and where Miranda, facing him on the opposite side, would be completely hidden unless someone came all the way to the table. As soon as they sat down and ordered their drinks, he pressed the transmit button on the radio concealed in the loose, tunic-like shirt favored by the local men, and said into the tiny microphone concealed in his breast pocket, "Sail Cat, Sail Cat: Road-Hog here—radio check. How do you read?...Over."

Gene Cliffson, who was handling the radio for the entry team answered, " Sail-Cat here. We copy."

Ross adjusted the small, remote ear-piece and checked the reception for the rest of the teams involved, including Mark and his staff, listening to everything at the embassy. When all had confirmed they were in communication, Ross turned to Miranda. "Are you ready to dazzle if necessary in exchange for this excellent meal."

"Yes, Ross!" Miranda said, "of course, especially since I was committed to the thing before I was told. You know, it wouldn't be a bad idea for a station secretary to get a free meal at a fancy restaurant at station expense when it's not her birthday or Secretary's Day, or someone's promotion, or some operational event. Maybe she could even show up not in disguise."

"But you look spectacular," Ross said, "way better than usual."

"Thanks, Ross," Miranda said. "It's great to know you don't think I look good every day."

"Well," Ross said, "you always look terrific, but tonight we wanted you to be so spectacular that no one could resist you..."

"You mean blonde," Miranda said. "Men are so simple..."

"You do realize," Ross said. "that recognition by a spectacular woman in a public place is the absolute best thing that can happen to a man. The perfect situation is to be sitting at a bar when a spectacular woman comes through the door and stands there just long enough so everybody turns to look at her, then she walks directly over to you and gives you a little peck on the cheek in front of God and all concerned. It's worth a million dollars. And we have set it up just that way for Kwame, the lucky bastard. It will be a shame if you're not needed."

Miranda stared at Ross for a few seconds with a mixture of exasperation and gratitude. "OK," she said, "what if I'm needed?"

"We really don't think this will be anything but a free dinner," he began. "Alex and Roger, will trail Kwame to the restaurant and wait outside. If Kwame deviates from his usual habit and leaves early—say he gets a phone call or gets sick or picks up some woman immediately—the follow team will let everyone know. If the entry team can't get out in the eight minutes it takes to get back to Kwame's house, the follow team is prepared to cause an accident on the road. Of course, it's extremely unlikely that will happen."

"Let's throw caution to the winds," Miranda said, "and assume you're right. What happens next if everything starts out normally and Kwame follows his routine?"

"As soon as Kwame shows up in the restaurant," Ross continued, "I'll let everyone know. Then we wait. As soon as the entry team finishes, everyone goes home and we enjoy our dinner and I buy you a whole bunch of drinks in the bar."

"I think I'll call it an evening at the 'everyone-goes-home-stage,'" Miranda said. "What if the entry team gets hung up?"

"It will go like this," Ross continued. "If the entry team is still inside when Kwame finishes here in the restaurant, I'll let everyone know he's moving. If the follow team, doesn't see him outside almost immediately, Alex will come in to locate him and keep eyes on him—

we know he'll be in the bar if he's true to form. If/when he shows signs of moving again—and if the team is still inside—Alex will walk over to where I can establish visual contact. You only have to do something if the situation gets to that point.

"Then you head for the bar and mesmerize Kwame. I'll follow you after a couple of minutes and sit somewhere away from the bar but where I can see what's happening. Once the entry team is clear, I'll give you a signal and you can dump Kwame. If it looks like it's going to be hard to get rid of him, you let me know by putting on new lipstick. I'll have Roger come get you. You know Roger's as big as a house and is the only man I have ever met who looks like a Green Beret even when he's wearing a tuxedo. No matter how many ass-kissers and bodyguards Kwame has with him, they won't mess with Roger. Be prepared for him to treat you as a bored girlfriend who has sneaked out on him for a night of uncontrolled fun. All you have to do is argue with him for a minute and then get outta there …OK?"

"Uncontrolled fun?" Miranda said. "Well, that's no problem, Ross, except that I don't recall participating in 'uncontrolled fun' since Easter break in college. I may not remember it properly."

"You don't have to remember it," Ross said. "Roger will tell you what you've done."

"Do I get hazard pay or overtime for this?" Miranda asked.

"I would think," Ross said, "that being of service to your country and your chief would be compensation enough."

"To think I gave up a Mel Gibson movie on tape, where I can rewind and re-watch the best parts as much as I like, for this," Miranda said. "I must be crazy."

***

"Necker's Knob, Necker's Knob, Wide Load here. Do you read?" Alex said as they pulled out behind Kwame.

"Wide Load, Necker's Knob here. Go ahead," Gary said.

"Necker's Knob, be advised Mr. T. is moving," Alex said.

"Copy that," Gary said. "Necker's Knob will advise when we are in position." Turning to the other members of the team, he said, "OK, boys, let's load up."

Gary and Todd got into the front of the van while Gene, Bill, and Kirby got in the back. "Everybody ready?" Gary asked, "last chance to be sure."

When all agreed they were ready, Todd pulled out of the embassy parking lot and headed for Karga hill. When they arrived a few minutes later, he said into the radio, "All hands, be advised: Necker's Knob is in position."

All expected the next communication to be that the entry team was in, but as the hot, sweating group in the van stared hopefully at the front gate of Kwame's house, it was clear the guard was not nearly asleep. In fact he seemed to be in animated conversation with the house-boy. "What the hell is he doing?" Gary mumbled. "It looks like they're in an argument. Let me have the binoculars."

A moment later, he reported, "The house-boy's got the good booze out, but the guard is talking instead of drinking. They must be talking about women. If the house-boy would just change to religion or politics or something, maybe the guard would pass out. Sorry, guys," he said to his colleagues in the back of the van.

The next voice on the radio was Alex advising that Kwame had arrived at the Palm.

Ross spoke next: "Necker's Knob, Road Hog here, be advised Mr. T. has arrived my location. Is Sail-Cat in?"

"Road-Hog, negative, repeat, negative." Gary said. "Sail-Cat has not been able to move."

"Damn," Ross said to Miranda, "the entry team is still in the van and Kwame's already here."

"I knew it!" Miranda said in exasperation.

***

Bill could feel the tension beginning to build as the minutes dragged by. All in the van were completely drenched in sweat and he had already cautioned Gene and Kirby on a couple of occasions to keep drinking the bottled water they had brought along. Finally, Gary turned to them and said, "The house-boy's opening the gate; get ready."

Gary got out of the van to check the street and, once satisfied it was clear, nodded to Todd who turned to the trio and said, "Go!"

The three scrambled out, reached back to grab their equipment, and walked quickly across the street. They side-stepped past the snoring guard and moved quickly into the shadows as the house-boy re-locked the gate, then half-ran to the back of the house led by the house-boy. In a few more seconds they were safely in. As they sent the house-boy back out to watch the guard. Gene said into the radio, "All hands, be advised: Sail-Cat is in."

At the restaurant, Ross said to Miranda, "They're in."

"Put on your bandannas," Bill reminded Gene and Kirby, "no sweat drops on the docs."

As Bill began setting up the kit, he told Kirby to photograph the room and the desk top near the safe with the Polaroid. As soon as Kirby finished, Gene attacked the safe. "It's just a garden-variety wall safe" he mumbled to himself, "should be as easy as a Bangkok whore..."

Despite his prediction, Gene found himself toiling with the safe. The very fact that it had been in use for so long made his job harder as he could not feel distinctly the soft vibrations as the tumblers fell into place. Still, in less than five minutes, the safe was open. He pulled the door open very carefully looking for any traps Kwame might have set, but found none. As he stepped back, Kirby stepped forward to photograph the contents in place as best he could with the Polaroid. Bill then took his first look inside. "Damn!" he said, "we're going to have to be careful."

Inside was a sheaf of documents lying on top of a small lock-box.

Under the box was about a half inch of documents in folders. Behind this was a clutter of small boxes, loose slips of paper, and a pistol. "Kirby," Bill said, "feed me the docs on top first. Put everything back exactly as you find it. Gene, open the lock-box. We'll get to it if we can if there's anything interesting in it, but we must do the docs first. Once we get to the docs in the folders, Gene, you keep Kirby supplied from the safe and put every folder back in the same place with the same orientation. Ready? Let's go."

Kirby despaired as he saw the stack of documents amid the clutter, but he had no time to worry about it. Within a few seconds he was feeding the individual sheets of paper onto and off the easel of the kit as Bill photographed them.

Gene had the small lock box open in a minute or so. "It's money, Bill," he said, "what do you want to do about it?"

"I think just count it and note if there's any strange currency," Bill said without looking up from his task.

"Hello," Gene said a moment later, "there's stack of US dollars here. Looks like about...ten thousand."

"That could be interesting," Bill said again without looking up. "Liberia uses U.S. dollars—You don't think Kwame knows Taylor—let Mark figure it out if it means anything."

Gene finished the count and picked the lock closed again. He next began to move slowly through the rest of the items in the safe. There seemed to be nothing of interest until he came across an envelope containing photographs. "Photos, Bill," he said, "what do you think?"

"I recommend we copy any in which Kwame is shown with any other man," Bill said, "just to be safe. If there's any family-type photos or Kwame by himself, let's not worry with it. If you see anything that looks interesting, no matter what, shoot it. How do you see it, Gene?"

"Sounds fine to me," Gene said. "You want me to do the work or take Kirby's place and let him do it?"

"You go ahead, Gene," Bill said, "if you don't mind. Kirby and I have a good routine going now and I don't want to disturb it."

Kirby was feeling better about the task now that they were underway. The stack of docs was going down much faster than he would have imagined, but he knew they had started late and still had a lot to do.

***

"Uh-oh," Ross said as Kwame and his aides got up from their table and headed toward the bar. "Wide Load, Road Hog here. Mr. T. is moving."

"Road-Hog, copy that," Alex responded.

A couple of minutes later, Ross heard from Roger that Alex was inside. "Alex is in the bar," Ross said to Miranda.

For the next long interval there was no radio traffic at all. By now the entry team had been inside for more than an hour. Ross and Miranda engaged in brief conversations, but had gradually fallen almost silent as the long night wore on with no word from the team. Ross was thinking of checking in with Gene just be sure everything was all right when he saw Alex walk to the foyer of the restaurant just long enough to make sure Ross saw him. "You're needed," he said to Miranda.

She slid out of the booth and headed for the bar as Ross called for the check. As he waited, he advised the rest of the teams: "All hands, all hands: Tube Top has joined Mr. T. in the bar. Wide Load, be ready to intercept if necessary. Sail-Cat, how do you stand?"

For a moment there was no traffic and the wait seemed long. Finally Gene answered," Sail-Cat estimates thirty minutes, repeat: thirty minutes."

"Sail-Cat, understand," Ross said, "thirty minutes. I am now joining Tube-Top and Mr. T."

When Ross entered the bar, Kwame and Miranda were already in conversation and he could see Kwame was thoroughly charmed. He began to relax.

***

Finally the last document was photographed. While Bill closed up the kit, gathered all the film canisters, and began putting the equipment back into shoulder bags, Kirby and Gene carefully rearranged the contents of the safe exactly as they were in the Polaroid photograph. As Gene spun off the combination leaving the dial again on the same digit as he had found it, Kirby said, "Damn good job," and backed inadvertently into the desk. With a crash the items on the right edge fell on the floor. A few seconds later the house-boy appeared at the door with eyes wide in terror. He groaned as he saw the mess on the floor. "It's OK, it's OK!" Bill said, "go back and watch the guard. We'll fix it. Kirby, where's the Polaroid?"

For a moment, Kirby couldn't move, then he began a frantic search through his shoulder bag. "Here," he said as he handed it to Bill.

Bill began to meticulously replace the pens, pencils, photographs, desk set, and other items using the photograph. He even made an effort to put the same color pencils next to each other in the tray of the desk set. "Call Necker's Knob," he said to Gene," and let's get out of here."

In a few seconds, Gary had returned the summons with the assurance they were in position and waiting for the entry team. As they approached the gate once more, the house-boy was fumbling so loudly with the lock that they thought he might wake the guard. Finally he got the gate open again and stepped into the street. They stood in the shadows until the house-boy gave the 'all clear' and then eased past the comatose guard. "Thanks," Bill said quietly to the house-boy as they headed for the corner. Within a minute they were in the van once more.

***

In the bar, Ross heard the team was clear and when next Miranda glanced his way, he nodded slightly. As he watched, Miranda clearly began trying to get away from Kwame, but he wasn't having it. She

251

settled down once more and applied new lipstick. Ross moved toward the rest rooms and as soon as he was alone, he said, "Wide Load, Road-Hog here. Tube Top needs assistance." A second later, Alex responded: "Road-Hog, help is on the way."

Ross had barely sat back down when Roger showed up at the entrance of the bar. He hesitated as he looked around for a second, then stomped over to Miranda. "Where have you been, you bitch!" he began as he grabbed her by the arm. "I've been waiting for you for more than an hour! I didn't know what the hell to think!"

"I waited for *you*, you bastard!" she responded as she broke free of his grip. "I've been here for three days and all I got to do was sit at the hotel while you made your big deals. You didn't let me take a tour or shop or do anything and when you didn't show up on time tonight, I thought, 'screw you!' I'm having some fun whether you like it or not!"

"Your ass is on the next plane home!" he said. "This is the last trip you come with me—ever! Now get the hell out!" Here he grabbed her again and pulled her off the barstool. As he pulled at her she turned back to Kwame and stroked his face. "I hope to see you again," she said, "after I get rid of this bastard."

As Roger hustled her toward the door, everyone in the bar sat in stunned surprise at the loud outburst that had disturbed their evening. Just as she disappeared out the door, she threw Kwame a parting kiss. For another moment, no one spoke. Finally Kwame shook his head sadly and said, "White women...nothin' but trouble."

Chapter 26

Once the adrenaline had drained out of their systems the entry team felt completely exhausted, but Bill warned Kirby that Mark might want the film developed that night. Mercifully, all that was required was a situation debrief held for all hands in Mark's office. Once he was assured there had been no problem with security, he relaxed and congratulated them on a good effort. Bill and Kirby would develop the film starting early next morning with the roll containing the loose documents being developed first. After that would come the documents from the folders and finally the photographs Gene had copied. Mark announced there would be another all-hands on Monday, unless there was some reason to meet sooner, to assess the value of the operation and make sure no security problems had appeared in the interim. After that the meeting broke up in good-natured kidding. Miranda was half pleased and half incensed when she found she had been designated "Tube Top."

Kirby showed no interest in driving the short distance back to the hotel so Bill took the wheel. "I'm completely exhausted," Kirby said, "but I know I won't be sleeping tonight. Should we get a beer or two on the way up to the room?"

"Sure," Bill said, "but don't drink too much; tomorrow will be a very long day. Even with the Ektamatic processor, we'll be there for hours and hours, probably with Mark standing right at our elbow."

"How did it go?" Kirby asked. "Did we do any good?"

"Absolutely!" Bill said. "It went fine. You have to remember: we don't determine the intelligence value of the operation. Our only concern must be whether we did a good technical job or not. If techs had to grade their work according to the end result, we'd probably all be very discouraged. When Nate and I 'saved Mifuna' before, we had no idea anything had gone right. I would have bet the farm that we hadn't got anything.

"Many times you never find out the result of your work. If you trained the agent well, it may still be months before he does anything worthwhile. By then you might be reassigned and the original case officer might be in another assignment too. One of the most famous exploits in the history of OTS was a total operational failure, but the technical work was superb—that was an audio op; ask some audio tech to tell you about it. They'll all know what you mean when you ask. In this instance we'll know, probably by tomorrow, if we hit pay dirt, but our part will be officially perfect if we finish up by doing a good job developing and printing the docs."

"Sorry about knocking into the desk," Kirby said.

"Don't worry about it," Bill said. "There was absolutely no harm. Even if we hadn't had the Polaroid so we could reconstruct everything, it could have been blamed on the house-boy, and even that would have depended on whether Kwame would have ever noticed it. No mistake that can be corrected before damage is done is worth thinking about except that the exact same mistake shouldn't be made again. You're going to make mistakes all through your career; it's the nature of the work. Sometimes it will be absolutely unavoidable: you make your very best judgment and it turns out to be wrong. Other times it will be sheer carelessness—I know, you think that will never happen to you—but it will, probably after you become very accomplished and confident in your job. Sometimes you will be able to fix the mistake before it does any damage and nobody will ever find out. Sometimes someone else will catch it and fix it for you. But sometimes it will be obvious and ugly and everyone will know. Even that kind of error can be forgiven over time because everyone in ops knows they have either done something just as bad or they will one of these days. All you have to do is keep that kind of mistake down to a minimum and you'll always do just fine. What happened tonight isn't really even worth mentioning."

"You ever make any mistakes—big ones, I mean?" Kirby asked.

"This can't be a serious question," Bill said. "Not only have I made big ones but I have a way of making the kind of mistakes for which Murphy's Law was written: at the worst time, in the worst places, on the most important projects, in front of the most important people. Down home we call it the 'Turd-in-the-punch-bowl' kind of mistake; the kind no one can ignore even if they want to. Just stay away from that kind of thing and you'll be fine. There is one penalty that comes with even little mistakes, however."

"Let me guess," Kirby said, "buying the beer?"

"Why, thank you Kirby," Bill said. "That's a fine idea."

***

The next day was long, as Bill had predicted. He again handled the enlarger and exposed the paper. Kirby ran the prints through the Ektamatic processor and then fixed and washed the prints making them permanent as opposed to the stabilized condition in which they normally exited the machine. Mark had immediately retrieved the first stack of prints representing the sheaf of loose documents which had been on top of the pile in the safe. As they plowed through the other rolls of film with no further visits from Mark, Bill began to be hopeful. "I think there may have been something interesting in that first batch," he said, "at least enough to keep Mark busy for a while."

Since there was no word from Mark, they took a full hour for lunch and continued into the late afternoon. Finally, they printed the copies of the photos, which slowed them down somewhat. Unlike the docs, the photos needed individual adjustments on the enlarger to get the best combination of image size and sharpness for each face. By 7PM, they were finished. They put the prints from each roll of negatives into separate envelopes, identified them as to what folders they had come from, enclosed the developed negative strips, and headed for Mark's office. He was not there at the time but one of the other case officers took possession of their work and promised to pass it to Mark when he came back. Bill asked if the 'after action' meeting of station personnel had raised any concern, but was assured that Mark had been satisfied.

"Let's take the rest of Sunday off," Bill said as they drove back to the hotel.

On Monday, Mark called the "all hands" meeting for the conference room at 8AM. He announced there had been interesting information in the documents and that he had arranged a meeting with President Bouaki for later in the day. He was hopeful the president would find the information useful, but that remained to be seen. Apparently, there was no suspicion from Kwame that anything unusual had happened. Mark was satisfied they had done a secure and professional job. He thanked them all.

As they got up to leave, Bill said, "We're outta here, Kirby. Why don't you do your canvass today and get us a flight, tomorrow afternoon if possible, while I write up our training."

***

When they arrived back at NORTECH, Nate invited them into his office to welcome them home. He was very pleased with their TDY and especially with Kirby once Bill had told him all that Kirby had done and of his zeal for the work. After he thanked Kirby officially, the young man was excused, leaving the old friends alone once more.

"I've got a cable for you," Nate said, handing a sheet over to Bill. After Bill had read the cable over, he looked up at Nate and said, "Now I feel about as astounded as Kirby normally does. If I didn't know what had happened, I would think the real stud in our project was this OTS officer back at headquarters who talked Mr. Mark into ordering supplies for color photography, not the two grunts who busted their asses over a long weekend to get the color prints ready, especially since her psuedo is listed and we are described only as 'visiting technical officers.'"

"I reckon," Nate said, "that Mark, being a young man, was somehow entranced by the good judgment and operational savvy of the OTS tech who gave him the few days of technical familiarization at our office HQ before he hit the ground in Africa."

"No doubt," Bill said, "it was that tech who showed him the wisdom of, I quote: 'shipping color photo supplies to the station, supplies that enabled two visiting technical officers to do some color prints with which the COS subsequently impressed the president of the country, thereby enabling the formation of a closer relationship with the government over the last few weeks.'"

Bill placed the cable delicately back onto Nate's desk almost as if it were made of glass. "Please don't let anything happen to this; I may want to frame it later," he said. "As one of the two un-named visiting techs, I may want to bask forever in the glow of the one whose pseudo does appear on this epistle.

"I wonder if I did something to God so bad that he thinks I deserve Adele. It is truly remarkable that she could, by sheer chance, send color photo chemicals to the very station where Kirby and I would be assigned to use them, and that she would get most of the credit."

"It could be worse of course," Nate said, "the HQ desks could all want color supplies for their field stations, but so far, they have all stayed away from it in droves—more experienced officers, I presume. Anyway, I wanted to warn you and let you get this out of your system before you got back to the US of A."

"Hell," Bill said, "at this stage in my career something like this is laughable. All this means is that Mark is firmly on board the sensitivity train, probably has been since he was hired, probably doesn't realize the outfit was ever insensitive. I do hope however that if there is a God, maybe Adele will eventually find herself in the same position we were in a few weeks ago. Then she can do color photo in a third-world country. Of course, I won't know about it; I'll be retired."

"Are you still going next year no matter what?" Nate asked even though already knew the answer.

"Yep," Bill said, "the age of dinosaurs is almost over and I wouldn't want to prolong it. I could really get serious about computers and become an expert like our young officers but I'd need about a hundred years to match what they know when they get out of high school. And then, too, I think I want to retire before my memories of the old days get any more degraded by modern times and our faithful colleague Jim Beam. I want to remember words like 'now' instead of 'at this point in time', and 'short' instead of 'height-challenged', and 'capable' instead of 'empowered', and 'learned' instead of 'gained an appreciation for'; and I want to remember 'fireman', 'policeman', 'man-hole', and especially 'mankind' instead of 'fire-person', 'police-person', 'person-hole', and 'person-kind'. You know, Churchill wondered if the imprecision of the Japanese language didn't hurt them during the war; thank God we're not fighting them now.

"By the way, when are you coming back? I heard before I left they had named your replacement, but I couldn't get up with RC to confirm it."

"I'm finagling for a two and two but it will probably be next year," Nate said. "My replacement has been decided, but I will withhold the name until it's official. However, I'll be back TDY for a while in about six weeks."

"Your replacement is not some newly sensitive individual, is he?" Bill asked. "That's the worst; to find some old fart trying to be touchie-feelie. Being around that makes you feel like you're sucking on a perpetual lemon."

"It's a good thing our new supreme leaders will never hear this conversation," Nate laughed, "or you'd be given a dishonorable retirement."

"Yeah, you're right, of course," Bill said. "You know, maybe I'm more pissed about that cable than I thought."

Chapter 27

A little more than a month after Bill's return, he and Nate, now back on TDY, met again in the cafeteria where they visited the burrito bar as they had so many times before.

"I'll say one thing," Nate began, "the burrito bar clientele never changes. No matter how health-conscious we become, everybody backslides once in a while and has to have a burrito...not that either of us has ever worried about health."

"You got that right," Bill said. "If you look around this room, you see two types: the regulars immersed in the full burrito experience and the others who are looking uncomfortable and uneasy, afraid their wives or girlfriends or the local food police will somehow detect 'em.

"Did you ever reflect that mankind never advanced much until we stopped eating fruit and grains and roots and tubers and started to kill and eat nutritious animals. When we ate a lot of grains and grass, we didn't have time to do much except graze, but after a snack of wildebeest, we didn't have to eat again until supper. It gave us time to build cities, write books, go to the moon,...and finally invent the TV remote."

"I presume," Nate said, "that this is your own personal understanding of evolution."

"Yes," Bill said, "it was one of the many useful theories I evolved while on TDY in Africa."

"Funny you should mention Africa," Nate said, "that's actually why I called this meeting. I have news from deepest-darkest."

"The Mifuna City police finally sent Kirby a hundred speeding tickets?" Bill asked.

"No, no," Nate said, "something even more astounding. It looks like you saved Mifuna again. I thought you might not have heard about it, being exiled to the warehouse as you are and completely removed from all cable traffic."

"It could also be that whether someone saved Mifuna or not," Bill said, "makes no difference to any human being except Mark and President Bouaki. Probably not even most of the Mifunans care."

"Maybe you're right," Nate said, "but you better believe Mark's career will benefit. Mifuna may not be Milan, but one day Mark might have to save it; or Manila, or Macao, or Melbourne—and now he believes he can do it. One day he might get to write the 'We Won!' cable like Frank did after the Russians pulled out of Afghanistan."

"So what happened?" Bill said. "How do you know we saved Mifuna?"

"This is how," Nate said as he pulled a newspaper out of his valise. "About a week ago, we got this in the pouch from Mifuna. Miranda saved it for you and Kirby. Of course, I had heard about it from cable traffic, but I believe this is the best way to announce it."

Here Nate handed the paper over to Bill. Across the top of the first page was the headline: "Government Officials in Disastrous Boating Mishap." As Bill read on, he began to see what Nate meant. Nate remained silent until Bill had read the entire article and put the paper aside.

"Veeeery in-deresting, don't you think?" Nate said. "Kwame and five other high government officials drowned when their boat capsized on the way back from a local political festival across the river. Also, some lesser officials have simply disappeared and Lumumba hasn't been heard from in weeks. I haven't had a chance to talk face-to-face with anyone from Mifuna station, but it's obvious Mark and then Bouaki saw something in the docs you photographed that doomed Kwame. I'm sure the old man was just too tired and sick to try to persuade Kwame out of his evil ways or jerk him up by the scruff of the neck to straighten him out. My guess is he just said to Benjamin that he should handle the problem with delicacy—in Africa, I would consider this delicate.

"Were any of the folks in on it that you or Ross trained? Who knows. Kubo is now officially the successor to Bouaki and the old man will be stepping down very shortly in his favor. Kubo is on record that within two years, he will hold open and fair elections. Now whether it happens or not is another matter, but at least he means well."

For a few minutes the two sat in silence while they finished their food. "Well," Bill said finally, "I'm really glad the work we did was successful. How did Kirby take it?"

"At first," Nate said, "he walked on water and his head was so big he almost couldn't get through the doors but he soon cooled off. He's still very proud of the work and has enhanced your reputation as a living legend. Of course, he also tried to become a living legend himself until I counseled him that the 'living legend' title is better assumed after one has either risen to the ranks of management or is approaching the end of one's career. For a young man, there's just too many mistakes and set-backs ahead. I finally fell back on your parable of life: baseball. I explained to him that one of the reasons players aren't eligible for the Hall of Fame until they have been retired for at least five years is that it wouldn't do for a Hall of Fame member (or living legend) to strike out four times in a game or make three errors. He got the message."

Bill smiled but remained silent for a time. "You know," he said, "if any of our Mifunan trainees were involved in this, the media will eventually portray it as some dastardly Agency deed should Kubo fail or turn dictator. Even if he does well, some pompous, pious news anchor a few years from now, or some leftist author in the distant future, will point out that exile for the losers would have been a more humane way to handle it. Even when we do the right thing, there's always someone whose sensibilities are offended. The fact that the critics are so lacking in common sense you wouldn't trust 'em to put gas in your car won't matter; the network news shows will listen.

"I remember when Nixon opened China, and the usual liberal potentates were so astounded they couldn't recover quickly enough to be immediately critical, one network interviewed Shirley MacLaine. I remember Shirley said Nixon shouldn't have been the one to get off that plane in China. I guess she wanted it to be one of the Kennedys, or maybe a statesman from one of the other planets she had visited... Maybe it's a good thing nobody's ever heard of Mifuna.

"I think Kirby's going to be a fine officer. As idealistic as he is, he might even be a throwback—might look at it the way we did when we signed up."

"You might have signed up for patriotic reasons," Nate said, "but I was only fascinated by the adventure and romance."

"Right," Bill said. "You know full well you could quit right now and become an instant expert on intelligence policy, a consultant making as much per hour as a Washington lawyer, or a lobbyist for some weapons company—at triple your salary."

"You just proved my point," Nate said. "As soon as I get tired of adventure and romance, I'll be in a great position to start seeking money, the third side of the triangle of happiness."

"It's too late for me to start seeking money," Bill said, "so I'm still going to retire just about exactly as I first planned. After all, how much could it cost to get a used double-wide to stick on top of one of those hills down home. Then I'm gonna get myself one of those satellite TV antennas that would make NASA jealous, put some plastic pink flamingoes in the yard, get myself a really ugly old pickup, join the local Moose or Elks or Lions or some other animal, and complain about the government full time—except when I'm watchin' one of my 500 channels of TV."

"Sounds like a dream come true," Nate said.

Chapter 28

Although Mike had been almost despondent at the beginning of Nate's last story, realizing they had long ago passed into the next morning in the bar, he had found himself listening with genuine attention and interest. Nate was certainly a good story teller, he thought, or maybe he really was getting a crash course in useful information for his future career. He had even managed to continue to sip a little beer without losing his concentration. "So, did the work in Mifuna help Bill's career?" he asked.

"No," Nate said, "it was a very good op and it helped Kirby quite a bit; he was promoted early at the next cycle, but Bill was too late in his career, he had too many memorable mistakes behind him, he was ignorant of computers, and Mifuna was off everybody's radar. He went back to the warehouse and stayed there."

"Until now, you mean," Mike said.

"Yes," Nate said, "until his retirement."

"What about the problem with the exposed agents and all that?" Mike asked. "Was that ever resolved?"

"I was just coming to that," Nate said, "and about time too. It has been tomorrow now for a good while and it's about time to go home. Of course, this is excellent training for your future with the outfit. I can already see you've got the stamina of a journeyman tech officer—unusual in one so young.

"Now: what finally happened: Bill's personal exoneration began with a phone call I got from Plato Dinwiddie."

***

"Nate...," the voice said on the phone, "it's Plato. How're you

263

doing?"

"Fine, Plato," Nate said. "How about you?" He had not heard the Soviet technical referent's voice for so long he had not recognized it at first, and he could not imagine why Plato would be calling. They had not seen each other in person for years, basically ever since Plato had taken the SE referent job. Now Nate wondered why it had been so long and why they hadn't just run into each other at some function or other or at least at the cafeteria. "It's been a while," he said.

"Years," Plato said, "years...I guess you must be wondering why I would call you."

Nate certainly was wondering, but chose to pretend he was not so surprised. "I have no idea," he said, " but most of the time when I hear a voice from the past, it means someone's retiring and the party is tomorrow."

"Well," Plato said, "this does have to do with the past, but it's not a retirement. I promised Sam, before he retired out of counter-measures, that I'd keep you posted on anything new regarding the situation Bill got into with SE several years ago. Well, something has come up. Now keep in mind, Nate, that I'm still not privy to everything that goes on over here."

"OK," Nate said, "I understand you might not know everything. Now what's up?"

"A good while ago, Warner put Adele Spenlow in for a commendation," Plato said, "and she's getting it tomorrow."

Nate was too surprised to speak. Finally Plato said, "Nate?"

"Right, yes, Plato," Nate said. "I heard you. What's the commendation for? I'm now her ultimate boss and I didn't hear anything about it."

"That could be because this all got started while you were still at NORTECH," Plato suggested. "Then too, Warner Barret went back to his original job at Restoration Research well over a year ago so you wouldn't have heard anything from the D&E shop, and of course, maybe it's just the usual SE security. I don't even know if I'm supposed to pass this on, in fact. I should point out that the commendation is not for work done in your area; it was for an op Adele and Warner were involved in several years ago. As I understand it, that op is now officially over and at least one agent who was involved has been relocated to the US and debriefed. SE didn't want to acknowledge anything about it until everyone concerned had been accounted for one way or the other. That's why Adele is just now getting recognition."

"Recognition for what, exactly?" Nate asked.

"For preparing CYNOSURE messages," Plato answered.

"Plato, you know Sam and I thought the agent receiving those messages was compromised long ago," Nate said, "and that it was the way CYNOSURE was used that likely caused it in the first place."

"Look, Nate," Plato said, "it was a long time before I was even officially allowed to know about this thing and I have not yet seen the file on the agent you're talking about—may never see it."

"Plato," Nate said with exasperation, "I appreciate your calling me, but this isn't much help, especially not to Bill."

"I know that," Plato said, "and I'm sorry about it, but I thought you ought to be made aware at least—and there is one more thing: John Grun is now in charge of this section. The case falls under his control. I believe you two know each other. He always speaks very well of you and Bill. Seems you helped him out once a long time ago. Maybe he owes you one...?"

Nate hesitated a few seconds and then said, "Plato, Sam would be proud of you. Thank you. Now I owe you one."

"Don't mention it," Plato said, "just remember me when I finally come back home to OTS."

Chapter 29

As Nate entered John's office, he grabbed his hand in a firm, enthusiastic welcome. "It's good to see you again, Nate!" he said, "and congratulations on your new position. You've done very well for yourself."

"You haven't done so bad either, although you predicted it that night on the beach at Mifuna," Nate said. "In fact, as I recall, you also predicted Afghanistan and participated in it just as you said. That's really impressive."

"I have been a lucky bastard," John said, "but I did work my ass off too. Wasn't it Lincoln who said the harder he worked, the luckier he got?"

"I don't know," Nate said, "if I need a quote, I still call on Bill."

"How's he doing?" John said. "I swear I haven't heard a thing about him in years. He must be in management too by now."

"No," Nate said, "afraid not. In fact, his regular job has been testing supplies in our warehouse for more than the last five years although he does do liaison training now and then. He's still a thirteen and his going is imminent."

"You're shitting me," John said, "a thirteen—what the hell did he do, kick the Director in the nuts?"

"It's a long story," Nate said. "Maybe one night at Murphy's we can sit down and I'll tell you all about it, but Bill does happen to be the reason I'm here."

"OK," John said, clearly puzzled, "what's it about?"

Nate took a note card out of his pocket and pushed it across the desk to John. "Do you remember these five cases," he asked.

"No," John said.

"How about these?" Nate asked as he pushed another card across the desk.

"Yes," John said, "these I know of course—I think just about everyone in SE knows something about these, but I wasn't involved until after they were finished. Three of these were doubles, as I recall, and two were replaced. One of the two who were replaced was shot and one is still in prison in Russia although with the new regime, he might have a hope of release one of these days. FYI: These five weren't the only compromises we discovered."

"I'm only interested in these," Nate said. "We knew them first under the crypts I showed you a moment ago. Do you know how they were compromised?"

John hesitated, started to answer, and then leaned back in his chair. "We know their SW systems were detected; we reported that to OTS so your folks could put the systems on the compromised list and not use them again in Russia."

"We never believed the Russians or anyone else could detect our high-level chemical SW systems," Nate said, "no matter how sophisticated their counter-measures were. We thought the agents were detected through some tradecraft mistake, then made to reveal the SW systems, not the other way around.

"Do you know this asset?" Here Nate handed John another note card with SECLYDESDALE written on it.

John shifted in his chair. "OK," he said, "what about him?"

"This was the case where our CYNOSURE system was first used," Nate said, "and where Adele Spenlow prepared the messages. You gave her a commendation the other day for her work."

"Yes," John said, "that's right."

"Did you know that Bill was the only OTS tech who prepared at least one SW message for each of these compromised assets and that he was initially blamed for the disaster?"

"No," John said, "I didn't realize that; I wasn't involved in any of the cases. But I do know from the damage assessment that neither he, nor any other tech, was to blame."

"Can you tell me what really happened?" Nate asked. "I think I know, but I'd like to be sure."

John hesitated again, stared briefly at Nate, started to speak, then fell silent again.

"Suppose I tell *you*," Nate said, "and see what happens. I think CLYDESDALE was some sort of records keeper or maybe a personnel type or maybe someone who was of high rank but with low profile, who reported on Russian officers with some sort of weakness—maybe booze or money problems or women. Maybe he was asked to identify officers who might have information about various areas of special interest to us or who worked in sensitive areas we wanted to know about. I would guess, from his crypt, that he wasn't the sharpest knife in the drawer. We had been sending him microdots and, like ninety per-cent of all agents who received dots, I'll bet he hated them—didn't recover some of them. I'll also bet CYNOSURE's little bitty letters read out with a microscope was just what he wanted.

"But it would have been necessary to change the message carrier. CYNOSURE won't work on regular writing paper—too rough. It requires a different carrier, at least some sort of highly calendered, glossy paper to give a good smooth substrate so the laser can burn in letters with sharp edges, in dark areas to hide the messages. Adele probably chose a slick magazine or techpublication with a lot of black, printed areas; areas which always repeated since the message had to be in the same place each time—maybe a border around a table of contents or something. I'll bet the change in the carrier touched off a routine check by KGB counter-measures. Since a coated/calendered/printed sheet is totally unsuited for secret writing, they probably only looked for dots—in the repeating black areas—and found CYNOSURE. How am I doing so far?"

"Keep going," John said.

"I know that once SE found out the five agents were compromised, they immediately checked on Bill, the only link they had at the time, but very soon, they stopped looking at him. I think your CI people eventually figured out the real problem was that CLYDESDALE's mail was being read. The KGB probably detected our assets by working backward from requirements we levied on him—requirements they knew about from our incoming messages. I would guess they followed the requirements back to the areas where the information was available, watched the most likely of their people until they were certain which ones were working for us and then moved in. They turned those who would cooperate and took stronger measures with those who couldn't be persuaded. Also, knowing exactly what we wanted would have allowed them to put out some perfect dangles which we probably snapped up..."

"I'm not going to comment on that," John said. "Go on."

"I would guess that after SE figured out what had happened," Nate continued, "you began to use CLYDESDALE to pass false information, otherwise the cases would have been terminated right then. You turned at least some liabilities into assets."

"So who else thinks this way in OTS?" John asked.

"I don't think anyone else knows—or cares," Nate said. "This case was given completely to Adele and Warner Barret. In fact the ops chief in SW at the time absolutely refused to have anything to do with it after they, not his officers, were designated to handle message preparation.

"And since CYNOSURE was proprietary for an SE case—CLYDESDALE—we could never use it for anything else so we didn't list it in our operational battery of systems. Our young techs have never heard of the system, or the case, and now there's only a very few of our officers, all now in the highest management positions, who know about it. If Bill hadn't been implicated, they would likely not have heard about it at all. For most of them, their only involvement was when they were advised that Bill was in trouble, and when that inquiry was dropped, they were glad to stop thinking about it.

"Of course it affected Bill's career at the time, but all that is long ago and far away. The only reason I'm interested now is that Bill was never officially cleared. I'd just like to let him know for certain that he didn't compromise five agents and get at least one killed."

"I see," said John. "So what we say here will be restricted to us and Bill."

"Yes," Nate said, "absolutely."

"CLYDESDALE was a very good asset for a very long time," John began. "Maybe that's why we didn't connect him to the compromises until long after we discovered them. Of course, we didn't immediately terminate the five assets after we found out they were compromised because we didn't want the Russians to know we knew; and then we successfully used all of them to provide misinformation to the Russians—we should have known better.

"It was only by investigating Bill, and after a query from Plato Dinwiddie, that we finally settled on CLYDESDALE as the problem and realized we had an even bigger problem—and a bigger opportunity. We thought we were really confusing the Russians when we started sending bogus requirements to CLYDESDALE. That poor bastard was being buggered by both sides and never had a clue.

"Finally, after their whole empire collapsed, we managed to get CLYDESDALE out safely, or maybe the Russians just didn't care by then, but we considered it a coup at the time. However, just a couple of weeks ago, we got a high-level defector who knew about the case. It now looks like they weren't fooled. Someone tipped them off to what we were doing a long time ago. We're still looking for that bastard and we can't even pretend we suspect anything. Giving the woman the commendation for her past work on the case fits right into the 'everything's fine' scenario. Why does that matter now? Because we're looking for a mole right here at headquarters. We hope this little charade will convince him that the case is now finished and he has not been detected. Obviously, this is between you an me and only for old time's sake. You can't even tell Bill about the mole."

For a moment Nate sat completely still while staring at John. "A mole right here!" Nate said, "damn! Of course I won't say a thing. If our group can help in any way, John, please let us know. I guarantee our total cooperation."

"Thanks, Nate," John said. "If we need you, rest assured I will be calling."

"Anyway," John continued, "Bill was in the clear very early on. Sorry we didn't say that officially at the time. I wouldn't blame him if he were upset."

"It's OK, John," Nate said. "I'm not sure this actually hurt him except perhaps in depriving him of one more overseas tour and maybe not even that. I just wanted to know so that I can tell him he didn't get somebody shot. I really appreciate this, John. I owe you one."

"Nah, we're even," John said. "Maybe we'll do something good again one of these days. I'm really sorry we didn't think about Bill long before this, but with our usual SE security and the fact that we quickly found out he wasn't involved, I'm sure no one gave it a thought. And in our defense, we did tell Barret because CYNOSURE was compromised and we thought he ought to know."

"Warner knew about this?" Nate said.

"Yes," John said, "we told him as soon as we found out ourselves— not the whole thing, you understand—but as I said, we didn't want him pushing the system any more since it was officially compromised. We told him only about the compromise and that he should not divulge even that until we gave him the word. He never had any inkling his compromised system might affect any other assets—or Bill. Barret isn't operationally very savvy."

"Tell me about it," Nate said as he stood up. "Thanks again, John. This is a great favor."

Nate did not go directly back to his office, but took a walk completely around the campus as he thought about the conversation to come. That afternoon he called Bill.

**

"An office conversation as opposed to a burrito-bar conversation," Bill said as he sat down across from Nate in his friend's impressive office. "It must be important."

"Yes," Nate said, "and entirely and completely confidential."

"Oh, God," Bill said, "the sensitivity police are looking for me with orders to empower me with extra rights now that I've crossed into the special category of 'age challenged.'"

"Not this time," Nate said, "it's truly good news; you were never seriously considered as the cause of the five-agent compromise all those years ago. I found out from John Grun who is now the chief in SE. You remember John from our first adventure in Mifuna."

"Yes," Bill said, "I heard he had done very well after Afghanistan."

"Very, very well," Nate said, "but he still has fond memories of us. Here's what happened..."

Bill listened intently to Nate's explanation, then sat back in his chair without comment. Nate knew it was time for a break so that Bill could think it over. They went out to the coffee pot where they spent a few minutes talking over old times with some of Nate's staff. When Nate thought Bill had had time to mull over the information, they returned to the office.

"Now let me get this straight," Bill began, "CLYDESDALE was the unwitting gomer in all this, but he's now safe in the US—or somewhere. Adele and Warner unwittingly compromised CLYDESDALE but Warner knows only about the compromise and has been told not to say anything. He thinks only the one agent was blown. Adele doesn't even know that much and as far as she is concerned, she did an excellent job in a high-level case and has had it proved by getting a commendation from SE.

"All of OTS is in the clear because Mr. Willy refused to touch the case after it was given to Warner. And now nobody outside SE will know any of this because SE is still holding it close officially for reasons of their own which can't be divulged to me.

"The only folks who got truly shafted in all this were the good agents in Russia and yours truly. And what makes this so funny is that nobody actually intended to do any harm."

"Pretty much," Nate said.

Bill smiled in silent bemusement for a moment and then said to Nate, "I do appreciate your finding this out, Nate. I know it was a pain in the ass and you likely had to give John a marker for the information; I know how tight SE still is with 'need to know.' The information won't change my life or make me a .400 hitter, but I will sleep a little better on restless nights. Thanks."

"Don't mention it pardner," Nate said. "And don't worry about my owing John; he thought you ought to know too, and since we 'saved' him once, he figures we're all even."

"Nate, did I ever tell you the parable of Humberto Robinson?" Bill asked.

"No," Nate said, "either I've heard so many of your parables I've forgotten this one or I haven't heard it before."

"Humberto pitched for the Braves and Phillies at the end of the 50s," Bill began, "and in one game the manager called him in to pitch to a right-handed hitter. The other manager then substituted a left-handed hitter. Humberto's manager decided to have him issue an intentional walk to that batter and then took him out for another pitcher. Eventually the man Humberto walked, scored the winning run and Humberto got the loss.

"When I write my autobiography, I think I'll begin with: 'Call me Humberto.'"

Chapter 30

"So Bill knows he didn't compromise the agents," Mike said. "I'm glad it worked out."

"You'll get to know him tonight, or at least you'll meet him," Nate said. "The reason I haven't introduced you yet is that the retiree has to be the last to leave so there is still plenty of time, and then, too, I don't want to have to talk over a dozen others when we do join up.

"There is one final irony you should know about before we meet Bill: This week Adele made fourteen. She got an early promotion mainly due to her work with CYNOSURE. Just as he retires, Adele passes him on the ladder of success."

Mike stared for a moment, then said, "Does he know? Could he have missed hearing about it?"

"Mike…," Nate began, then hesitated, "You're too young to have any real idea what it was like for women a few decades ago, not just with the Agency, but just about everywhere. They really didn't get fair treatment. A very large proportion of us guys truly needed some sensitizing. Adele wasn't unique in any way, and she wasn't our first female tech; Betty was. She never intentionally did anything to cause any trouble for anybody. The reason I told you so much about her was simply because her career happened to intersect Bill's in so many Murphy's Law instances—and remember: the topic tonight is Bill's career.

"I will admit though that if anyone could fail to hear about the recent promotions it would be Bill, but the promotions are always sent out over our entire communications net all over the world. And if there is one thing sure to get everyone talking, it's who got promoted, and why someone else *didn't* get promoted. He knows."

"Damn!" Mike said.

"Don't worry, Mike," Nate said. "If there's one thing that has never bothered Bill, it's who did and didn't get promoted. And long ago we all got used to competing with women. In fact, Bill would have done much better in his career if he had paid a lot more attention to things like competition and why some moved up and some didn't.

"Actually, I hadn't thought about it, but this is working out almost as if I planned it: There is no way you could have met a man who has had more setbacks in his career—and you get to meet such a man on your first day. If you're ever going to get a reality check before you begin your career, this would be the perfect situation for it."

As Nate finished speaking, three of the five men sitting nearest to Dave got up to go. They shook hands all around and departed, leaving only Dave and Bill. "Looks like it's time for you to meet Bill," Nate said as he stood up.

When Nate and Mike neared their table, Dave and Bill stood up and Mike met Bill amid the usual insults and jokes. Finally, Mike was officially introduced and they sat back down. As they settled in Bill said, "May the brotherhood be reunited!" and all raised their glasses.

"Here's to the past, present, and future brotherhood," Bill said, "provided young Mike is a candidate for the future. What do you think, Nate, you know him best."

"Well," Nate said, "he's still here at last call and this is only his first day, so he has potential. He already knows how to identify a war story, although it will be years before he will be able to tell his own, and I told him enough about your career so he already has a good idea of what not to do. Also, I intend to take a personal interest in his career...Yes! I do believe he is a candidate for the brotherhood."

"Do you know how few people Nate has said that to?" Bill said to Mike. "I mean about the brotherhood; he says that foolishness about his interest in their careers to every young officer he hires."

"You should understand," Nate said to Mike, "that by the time I was in a position to help Bill in his career, it was in such a mess God himself would have been baffled. Therefore, you should consider his last remark as being uninformed."

"Boys!" Dave interrupted, "there's only two of us at this table who have careers and those of us who are finished don't care anymore. Let's talk about old times when the earth was young and the Agency controlled everyone's destiny."

"You mean we don't still do that?" Nate said. "Every time I look at the news I see us getting blamed for everything from assassination to crop failure."

"OK," Dave said, "I didn't want to say this but I've noticed that over the last few years—since you've been in high management—you have forgotten the basics. Being from the South you must remember that whenever any of our politicians got caught for graft or visiting prostitutes or trying to buy an election or anything else, they always claimed they were innocent victims of some Communist plot. And it worked; we always forgave them. Now, anywhere in the world, if some doofus dictator gets caught red-handed doing something nefarious or if his country is just simply going to hell for whatever reason, he can blame it on us so that the locals can find a way to forgive him. That does not, repeat not, mean we still have real control of the situation."

Just as Nate was getting ready to answer, the bartender announced "last call" in a very loud voice. "I think," Nate said, "that the barkeep knows we surely intended to participate in 'last call' but were just so involved in conversation that we missed his first announcement—another sign that we're losing our edge. Let's go."

Nate and Dave got up and headed to the bar, admonishing Bill and Mike to sit still; they would buy the last round for the rookie and the retiree. In a moment, they returned with four beers and turned again toward the bar. "These are just for us," Bill explained. "They're going back for their supply now."

Mike groaned, "I don't know about this..."

"Don't worry," Bill said, "they know us here. We can stay as long as we like."

"I wasn't thinking about that," Mike said, "I just don't know if I can handle two more beers..."

"It doesn't matter," Bill said, looking back to the bar where Dave and Nate had fallen into an animated conversation, "they just didn't want us to run out."

For a few moments the two sat silent as the veteran thought about the past and the rookie contemplated the future. Finally, Mike ventured, "Nate and I did talk a lot about your career tonight and it sounds like you two had some interesting times."

Bill smiled. "We did indeed," he said, "but every day is interesting in ops. I worked for years in industry and never got the least bit excited about a project—guess I just wasn't cut out for it. I know I wasn't a very good employee. But here, being a logistics officer in the Agency is more exciting that being a CEO in business—that's a personal opinion, you understand. But if you are cut out for ops, there is no better life.

"I remember the first time I saw the sunset from the Peak in Hong Kong I thought to myself: 'If the folks from my home town could see me now.' Actually, my very first thought was 'I wish the most popular girl in high school could see me now.'

"I saw places I could never have seen otherwise, or even imagined seeing. I met folks I couldn't have imagined either, and did things I still don't really believe. I once trained an agent in London where, before we started, the case officer opened a medium-sized briefcase he had brought along and passed it to the agent. The thing was absolutely full of money: dollars, Pounds, and Marks. The agent glanced at it, closed it up as if it was his laundry, and I started training. Before that, I had always assumed that kind of thing just happened in 007 movies. Don't get me started..."

"How about the down side?" Mike asked.

"The down side?" Bill repeated as if he had never thought about it before. "Well, I guess the one thing you might call a general problem is divorce; the outfit has a lot of divorces. I don't think it's so bad now, but when I came on, the management didn't really worry about wives—or women in general for that matter—and some of us didn't worry enough either. Now they make a real effort for those who have dual careers, and family services are a lot better than they were...Is that what you mean?"

"Yes, of course," Mike said, "but I was thinking about on-the-job things..."

Bill thought a moment before answering. "I guess every professional everywhere has to endure staff meetings," he said finally, "and some can't take the hard traveling conditions, and maybe some hate to write reports, but I don't think there really is any down side in tech ops if you're suited for it. Even a bad or unsuccessful day is still pretty good compared to ordinary jobs. Why are you asking questions like this on the first day? It must have something to do with Nate."

"Nate did say that if anyone had a reason to gripe," Mike said, "it would be you and that tonight would be a good time to hear what you had to say."

Bill shook his head and laughed out loud. "Yes," he said, "as usual Nate is exactly right on both counts. I have had some setbacks that I regret, and now that I'm officially retired there is no reason not to be brutally honest, especially this late at night in one of our favorite bars.

"First, every setback I had, with one exception which is still classified for some reason even I don't know about, was my fault. The only bad break I ever suffered was that I never got away with a single screw-up of any magnitude in my entire career. You have figure that aspect has to be sheer bad luck. But if I had a chance to re-write our Constitution, the first sentence would be: 'Life is not fair.' My career didn't approach Nate's, but if I had it to do over again, I would.

"The double-plays I hit into just reflect the way life really is and there's nothing to be done about it. If you look at the problems and difficulties and missed opportunities as if someone, even a higher power, has it in for you, you can easily be bitter about everything. You have to remember that life can short-hop you any time. You just have to take the error and move on—did you ever notice how God's Greatest Game so closely parallels life? The only serious regrets I have are all personal and have to do with people, not my career."

"Do you ever wonder about the morality of the work?" Mike asked.

"Jesus!" Bill said, "I thought you had had too much to drink. How can you ask me that heavy question in my condition? If I understand you, the question is how do I feel if we do something that turns out to be disastrous in the end. Right now, the best example I can think of is Afghanistan. I'm not sure about this, but it looks like the mujahedin may be as bad as the Russians.

"Well, in general, you have to remember that the armchair hand-wringers are all looking back while we had to live history forward. I'm sure the old lady who unleashed the water lilies in Florida's canals or the fellows who brought rabbits to Australia or pigs to Hawaii had no idea what was going to be the final result of those simple, well-meaning ideas either. It's the gun-control/NRA argument: is it people or guns that kill? Well, believe me, it's the people. When we train a liaison service, or even an individual agent, they are on their own afterward. We can't absolutely control them. Our bang-and-burn demolition experts train others in how to defuse bombs just as they train in how to use them.

"I admit that when I first came on board, I was uncritical about everything, but over the years there were plenty of things to worry about: Is the agent any good? Is he really a double? Why should we recruit this fellow anyway? What will be the end result of this training? Why should we spend so much on this proprietary communications system when the commercial version will be along in six months time? Sure we wonder; we're all smart in this outfit.

"But we are also much like soldiers. Every COS, division chief, branch chief, case officer, and tech are working against targets defined by our government. If a case officer doesn't get information on his target, he doesn't get promoted. The idea of the rogue Agency operative is bullshit. It's TV action-series stuff. I know of only two men who pitched an asset without authorization. One was successful and one failed but both were treated like pariahs for years because of it.

"I think our greatest worry overall is political will. We are directed by the Congress and sometimes directly by the President and all they have to do is change their minds and for them a project is over. They order us to cease and we do, but for those we've enlisted to help us, it's not that simple. Our case officers are constantly dogged by the fear they will have to abandon an asset, or maybe even an entire group, to their fate in a hostile situation. If you're asking about a genuine, never-resolved down side, that's it. For us techs, it isn't as tough since we don't usually spend a long time with an asset or group, but a single case officer could conceivably run a critical asset, or work with a given group, for years.

"I should mention, since you're certainly going to ask, that 'intelligence failures' are another thing that we sometimes get pissed about. There's two places for a failure: one on our end where we may misinterpret information we have or fail to get crucial information, but the most common failure is when politicians don't want to hear what we tell them. If they refuse to hear the truth or fail to take action when they do, they can still blame it on us because we won't respond. I don't know how many times I've seen some pompous congressman giving us hell on the five o'clock news when we knew full well he had good information in plenty of time to do the right thing. As Dave is famous for saying: 'If you want the truth, you'd do better watching roller derby that the network news.'"

As Bill neared the end of his monologue, Nate and Dave drifted back to the table. As he finished, they sat down. "Hey, pardner," Nate said, "hold on here. What's all this serious stuff tonight of all times. We've never been serious before, why start now?"

"All right, all right, Nate," Bill said, "you're right as usual. Mike, forget reality, it will only impede your progress."

"No, now wait," Dave said, "I've had enough beer so I think we could risk honesty for a moment. Besides, when in the course of human history has a young man on his first day, had around him veterans with such wide experience on the job and whose careers have turned out so differently. It would be a disservice if we didn't give him our advice..."

"Dave," Nate interrupted, "I recall the Arab proverb: 'He who would tell the truth should have one foot in the stirrup.'"

"I'm serious," Dave insisted. "Listen, do you remember the movie *2010* where the Russian and the American meet in the antenna field and one of them says, 'For one minute, we will tell the truth?'" We could invest one minute each...right?"

Nate sighed. "OK, OK, let's do it."

"Wait," Bill said, "Nate doesn't get even a minute. He's had a fantastic career and the day he retires, he triples his salary in some sort of high-level advisory position in government or as a consultant in some beltway-bandit scientific firm. Only Dave and I have useful comments: Dave because his career had a hard landing and me because my career never took off. You first, Dave."

"Jesus," Dave began, "I had twenty-seven years of fantastic and three years of very good at the end. I get $75,000 a year just to get up in the morning—and now every night is a potential Irish-bar night since I don't have to work next day. I'm afraid to even think about it because I might jinx it."

"Needless to say," Bill said, "Dave will have a few more bucks to spend than I will. I'll be in the $20,000 range, but that's still an awful lot for doing nothing. But that isn't the point. Can you think of anything you would rather have done and would you change something if you could. I wouldn't."

"Not me," Dave said.

"How about you, Nate?" Bill asked. "You may make a comment now."

Nate said nothing for several seconds, then slowly raised his glass toward the center of the table. The others followed suit. As the glasses touched, he said, "To the outfit."

"The old days," Bill said, "and the old-timers especially Sam."

"NORTECH," Dave said.

"OTS," Bill said.

As they fell silent and stayed that way, Mike felt compelled to say something. Finally he said, "May the brotherhood be reunited." The other three looked at him in surprise, then broke into a ragged chorus of agreement. Both Bill and Nate, sitting next to Mike, slapped him on the back. After that the veterans drained their glasses and Mike tried to do the same, falling just short in his efforts.

"We're gone," Dave said to the bartender.

"You boys drive slow," he admonished as they headed for the door.

Outside they shook hands once more and Bill and Dave headed for their cars in the almost empty parking lot while Nate and Mike stood in silence watching them go. As they drove away, Nate said, "The end of an era."

He let the quiet settle in again, then turned to Mike. Slapping him lightly on the back once more, he said. "And the beginning of a new one. Your adventure officially begins just a few hours from now."

"I'm ready!" Mike said.

Glossary

OTS-Office of Technical Service
Ops-operations
SW-Secret Writing, a branch of OTS
DO-Directorate of Operations
COS-Chief of Station
CO-case officer
PCS-Permanent change of Station
TDY-Temporary Duty for a Year, any temporary travel or assignment
CI-counter-intelligence
LP-listening post
OP-observation post
CMR-Consolidated Memorandum of Record, an inventory of accountable items
SE-Soviet Europe division
EA-East Asia division
NE-Near East division
AF-Africa division
EUR-European division
NDI-no deception indicated
Bluebird-dark blue buses with tinted windows, provided for use by agency personnel for routine travel around the Washington area
S&G locks-security rated, dial-combination locks
Simplex locks-push button combination security locks
Exfil-exfiltration
F&S-Flaps and Seals:-the art of surreptitiously opening letters, pouches and other such items
IG-Inspector General
South Building-former location of OTS

Microdot-1mm square piece of very thin film containing a secret message
Bullet lens-cheap magnifier, about the size of a rice grain, for reading microdots
Bubble-Agency auditorium
CYNOSURE-encrypted name for laser-prepared micro-text
EASB-East Asia stations and bases
CD-concealment device
DA-Directorate of Administration
NOC-non-official cover
Pseudo-computer generated name substituted for the true name of an officer in cable traffic
RH-restricted handling
SEU-surreptitious entry unit